BERLINERS

ALSO BY VESPER STAMPER

What the Night Sings

A Cloud of Outrageous Blue

The line separating good and evil passes not through
states, nor between classes, nor between political
parties either, but right through every human heart—
and through all human hearts.

Aleksandr Solzhenitsyn, *The Gulag Archipelago*

Vergangenheitsbewältigung:
confronting or reckoning with the past

Betriebsblindheit:
selective blindness

BERLINERS

VESPER STAMPER

ALFRED A. KNOPF
NEW YORK

The young, in every age, are the first to pay
for the folly of their elders.
To every student, around the globe, who has weathered
the recent seismic changes in our world:
I see you. I write for you. You are not alone.
It's time to reclaim your fire.

THIS IS A BORZOI BOOK PUBLISHED BY ALFRED A. KNOPF

This is a work of fiction. All incidents and dialogue, and all characters with the exception of some well-known historical and public figures, are products of the author's imagination and are not to be construed as real. Where real-life historical or public figures appear, the situations, incidents, and dialogues concerning those persons are fictional and are not intended to depict actual events or to change the fictional nature of the work. In all other respects, any resemblance to persons living or dead is entirely coincidental.

Copyright © 2022 by Vesper Stamper

All rights reserved. Published in the United States by Alfred A. Knopf, an imprint of Random House Children's Books, a division of Penguin Random House LLC, New York.

Knopf, Borzoi Books, and the colophon are registered trademarks of Penguin Random House LLC.

Visit us on the Web! GetUnderlined.com

Educators and librarians, for a variety of teaching tools, visit us at RHTeachersLibrarians.com

Library of Congress Cataloging-in-Publication Data is available upon request.
ISBN 978-0-593-42836-8 (trade) — ISBN 978-0-593-42837-5 (lib. bdg.) —
ISBN 978-0-593-42838-2 (ebook)

The text of this book is set in 11-point Gamma ITC Std.
The illustrations were created using acrylic ink and graphite.
Interior design by Cathy Bobak
Jacket lettering by John Hendrix

Printed in the United States of America
10 9 8 7 6 5 4 3 2 1
First Edition

Random House Children's Books supports the First Amendment and celebrates the right to read.

Penguin Random House LLC supports copyright. Copyright fuels creativity, encourages diverse voices, promotes free speech, and creates a vibrant culture. Thank you for buying an authorized edition of this book and for complying with copyright laws by not reproducing, scanning, or distributing any part in any form without permission. You are supporting writers and allowing Penguin Random House to publish books for every reader.

A NOTE ABOUT THE SETTING

The state of the world in 1961 combined postwar trauma with the new threat of mutually assured destruction. The nuclear bombs that annihilated Hiroshima and Nagasaki in 1945 demonstrated how high the stakes were in the game of our existence. Humanity had nearly lost control and was seeking to reset itself, in every sphere, from arts to governance, from economics to education.

While Marxist theory dated back to the early 1800s (emerging from philosophies of the previous century) and had been tried on smaller scales, Communism on a *national* scale in the Soviet Union, China, Cuba and elsewhere was an experiment that was less than fifty years old. It left a trail of bloodshed and suppression that would not be revealed for several more decades, vastly outnumbering the deaths in World War II.

This multinational march of totalitarianism was emerging at the same time as another new phenomenon: numerous civil rights movements worldwide, including in the United States. Black veterans of World War II returned to a country for which they had risked their lives but still denied them full freedom and equality. In the shadow of the Holocaust, many societies were beginning to recognize the necessity of enshrining equal rights under the law, acknowledging that the State exists to serve the *citizen*, not the other way around.

In 1945, Berlin, as the capital of the Nazi regime, was the final frontier for the Allied troops fighting in the European theater. Hitler's regime had all but collapsed as his hodgepodge army of old men and child soldiers—the *Volkssturm*—tried to hold out against Russia's Red Army and the British, American and French troops who were to follow.

In order to forestall the emergence of *any* government tainted by the Nazi order after the defeat of the German Reich, the Allies formed a power-sharing agreement that would diffuse governance and allow for Germany's reconstruction, both governmentally and ideologically. Thus, Germany as a whole—and Berlin as a capital—was split among the four victorious Allied powers. The "West" (the United States, Britain and France) and the "East" (the Soviet Union) represented two different approaches to rooting out Nazism from both the populace and the institutions.

Because the Soviet Union was already proceeding at full throttle with the Communist experiment, Joseph Stalin (and his German allies returning from exile) implemented a Socialist government in eastern Germany immediately, with a policy of totalizing conformity and suppression of the acknowledgment of former Nazis in their citizenry. In 1949, the eastern, Soviet-controlled sector of Germany proclaimed itself a new, separate country: the German Democratic Republic (GDR). It was neither German (as a puppet state of the USSR), democratic (as a one-party autocracy) nor a republic (as a centralized, top-down system), and the United States did not formally acknowledge it as a nation until 1975.

Meanwhile, in the western half of the country, the Allies initially began a process of denazification, but because National Socialism was deeply entrenched in every institution, they believed the best path toward a free democracy was a policy of reintegration and remembrance. They would accept the existence of former Nazis in their midst, openly acknowledge Germany's crimes, and aim to reconstruct the institutions along democratic principles, believing that cooperation with other democracies would make them welcome once again among the community of free nations.

Though Berlin was technically divided among the Allied sectors, it was an open city like any other. But by 1961, because of political repression and economic hardship, thousands of refugees were fleeing the Eastern bloc countries, including the GDR, every day, using the open city of Berlin as a gateway to the West. If someone could get to East Berlin, all that person would have to do was walk into a Western sector, claim refugee status, and continue on to another free, Western country. This resulted in a "brain drain" of professionals (such as doctors) and a shortage of skilled workers, which would be sure to crash the fragile economy if something was not done to stop it.

The GDR began to pass increasingly restrictive laws preventing East Berlin residents from working in and traveling to West Berlin, until the country's leader, Walter Ulbricht, took the ultimate action, erecting a barrier around the entire Western half of the city in the middle of the night on August 13, 1961. Even though it was West Berlin that was encircled by the Wall, it was East Berlin that would be truly captive for the next twenty-eight years.

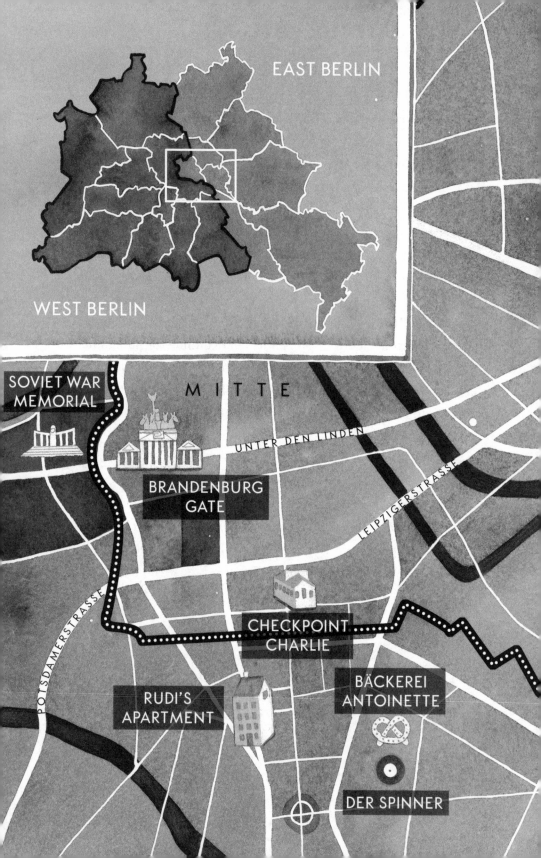

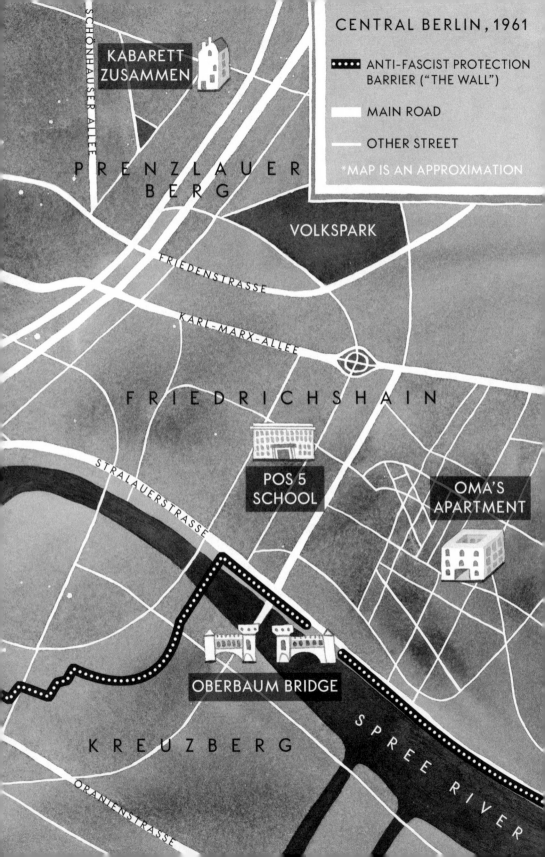

STUNDE NULL

When he thought about it years later, it was the book in the piano bench that had tipped him off.

Herr Richter was in the kitchen making a cup of tea while Rudolf waited in the parlor for his viola lesson, bored out of his skull. In the low golden light, the room so flowery, so pink, with its armchairs bedecked in cabbage roses, the ticking clock sent him into an afternoon drowse. Rudolf hated the viola. It had none of the panache of the violin, none of the glitter of the piano, which was his first instrument. He had only convinced his parents to let him take these lessons so he could get closer to Gerta.

Today she wasn't even home, out with Frau Büchner on some errand. So Rudolf, after chewing his nails to nubs, picking at the callus on his left index finger and rosining his bow a third time, lifted the hinged lid of the piano bench and rifled through to see if there was anything interesting.

And there it was. Under the Christmas carols and *Volkslieder*, a book written in those funny letters he knew only Jews could read, and underneath the title, the translation: *Yiddish Ballads*.

Rudolf chalked it up to the collection of an eccentric musical couple; people had already begun accumulating artifacts for the time when *those people* would be extinct. Even though he was given his *Hitler Jugend* uniform and told to be on the lookout for hidden Jews, it still did not click in Rudolf's mind.

But when, on another afternoon several weeks later, Herr Richter opened the cabinet to put more cigarettes into his brass pocket case, Rudolf spotted a small silver cup not much bigger than a schnapps glass and thought he made out the distinctive shape of a six-pointed star incised on its side. Then he knew.

It had to be true: Gerta Richter was Jewish. All this time, he had been fantasizing not about a *girl*, but about a *Jew*. It wouldn't have mattered before, in the days prior to the Nuremberg Laws. But it did now. The thought simultaneously repulsed him—mainly because he had been told it *should* repulse him—and excited him. He had something to report at the next HJ meeting. It pained him, too, because he knew he would have to renounce Gerta. Purge himself of her. He would have to harden his heart and train himself to hate her.

Because he knew he would have to turn Gerta in. It was the Right Thing to do.

That is how Rudolf found himself standing in the midnight dark, watching from the edge of the crowd, emotionless, as the girl he had been in love with since her first day in the children's choir was herded by guns and dogs onto a train with the rest of the filthy Jews of Würzburg.

That is how, the next day, he was able to march mechanically up the stairs of Gerta's flat with the throng of newly vested HJ and march Maria Büchner back down into the glaring sun of Residenz Square, to make her kneel on the cobblestones, and to personally shove the sign—which he had himself scrawled with the words *Jew Lover*—over the tangled bottle-blond hair of the famous operatic diva who had sheltered Gerta and her father.

That is how now, during the Battle of Berlin, he was able to grab a smoking Luger from the hands of a dying child soldier, younger than himself, just grab the gun from the bleeding-out boy who reached for Rudolf crying, *"Mutti . . . Ich will zu meiner Mama. . . ."*

Grab. Go. Do. Never feel.

Rudolf walked like an automaton through the crumbling city, ducking behind walls that stuck out of the dust like scraggly teeth. He shot anything that moved. Since his first decision to betray Gerta, his heart had become fossilized by thousands of minuscule choices. Years of convincing himself that down was up, east was west, wrong was right. Compassion was weakness. There was now no belief, no theory, no thought at all—only the animal will to survive.

So it was out of character for Rudolf Möser to save a girl's life that day.

He didn't know why he stopped for her. He'd passed dozens of dead compatriots and blubbering toddlers and old women with rubble falling around their shoulders. Buildings bulged and toppled in the non-light of war, dust obscuring all color and notion of time. Every landmark was blasted, the city formless, like a melted honeycomb.

But when Rudolf saw the girl hiding in that doorway, pointing a shaky pistol at whatever bastard would dare to mess with her, he knew he was going to help her. Not just help, but protect her. Not just protect, but marry her.

He saw it in her wild eyes. Standing out from the white war dust encrusting her face, her lips were deep red with lipstick precisely applied. There was something about that beautiful audacity that drew Rudolf to her like a supercharged magnet. For a moment, there was something else besides this war, besides buildings and bodies deconstructing themselves into hell and hate and noise. Those red lips drawn tight across her chalky face were more real than the shrapnel whizzing past his head.

He ducked into the doorway. She swiveled and pointed the pistol in his face. He put the rifle strap on his shoulder and lit a smoke. She didn't back down.

He could see that she was trembling, not from fear, but from muscle failure. She must have been holding that gun for hours. She could've shot him, and felt no regret, either. He analyzed her face as he smoked. For a second, a fleeting moment, he was aware of their youth. That as cockily as he stood staring down the barrel of a 9-millimeter *Volkspistole* while smoking a cigarette, as littered as his past was with atrocity, as sure as her aim was likely to be, they were only children. That red lipstick lay between two cheeks still round with baby fat, the dust not broken by one wrinkle. Rudolf stared at her.

He thought of Gerta. He wondered if she was still alive.

"How old are you?" he asked the girl.

"Fifteen," she said blankly.

"Next time, say eighteen," he said. "Come with me."

She blinked. She didn't move.

"Come with me," he repeated.

"I can't," she said.

"Why not?"

"I can't move my arms," she replied.

Rudolf advanced, took her pistol by its barrel, flipped on the safety and pried her numb fingers from the trigger. Instead of taking it away, he slipped the gun gently into the pocket of her trousers, took the girl by her khaki-clad shoulders and squeezed until the blood returned to her cold muscles. He puffed the cigarette as he massaged her arms, and the girl began to thaw, a tear carving through the concrete dust on her cheek. She put her head on the chest of this stranger and heaved a sigh of relief. And Rudolf held her as she broke down and sobbed.

Only then did they feel the first pangs of hunger in their bellies.

Ilse Fleischmann was dreaming about a faraway voice. Her father was calling her across a vast field, trying to tell her something important. She cupped her hands around her mouth and shouted, "Louder, Papa, I can't hear you!" But he would not come closer, would not step his foot on the sea of golden flowers between them. Instead, he picked up a bullhorn, and at his shout, the flowers all wilted into a sea of brown, decaying back into the ocean of rubble that was Berlin.

"We are your liberators," proclaimed the truck-mounted loudspeakers, in broken, Russian-accented German. *"People of Berlin, the army of the Union of Soviet Socialist Republics has arrived. We are here to bring you freedom and peace.* Freiheit und Frieden."

Ilse shook Rudolf awake. They were lying on a mattress in a corner of a ramshackle room in a shop, or what was left of it. The bombs were no longer falling. It was strange not to feel the world shake. Everything smelled of blood and rot and gasoline.

Water was scarce and oily. Now and then they managed to find a puddle in which to splash the grime off their skin. Today they planned to go to the Volkspark and try to bathe in the fountain there or, if that was dry, to walk all the way to Weissensee. It was the only thing on their agenda, besides, of course, finding food.

The loudspeakers passed again and again.

"We are coming door to door. . . . Announce your surrender by hanging a white cloth in your window. . . . You must hand over all food and weapons. . . ."

They had hoped to have a few days to collect themselves before facing anyone. They were scared of Allied justice. They were most afraid of Russian revenge.

Every time they crept out of some crevice to find their next hiding spot, Ilse passed another woman with those hollow eyes, the dead shuffle, and she knew: word was spreading about Russian rape gangs. *Komm, Fräulein* became the worst command a woman could hear. The bullhorns may have announced peace, but in the air was a gleeful vengeance: it was time for payback. Four years before, the Nazis had brutalized Russia, their old ally, in a surprise attack. Any remaining German Communists had been exiled or thrown in concentration camps with the Jews and Gypsies. Now the Soviet soldiers were drunk on booze and pillage and broken German women.

"I won't let them get you," Rudolf promised, several times each day. "Do you trust me?"

Maybe Ilse did trust Rudolf, and maybe she didn't; that was immaterial. He was *there.* So she stayed with him.

Ilse and Rudolf squatted in the shells of Berlin buildings, getting lucky every now and then and finding one with a roof, or a bed, or a cabinet of food. But they couldn't hide forever. The time of running was over.

They tore up the sheet from the mattress and tied the white fabric to their belt loops and backpacks as a sign of surrender. They shoved their few belongings into the packs and walked out into whatever street this was.

Berlin was totally devoid of geography. Tram cars lay on their sides; automobiles rested upside down in second-story stairwells. Women in the open air of their bombed-out apartments were donning aprons and sweeping away the dust, setting their tables and straightening the art on the remaining walls. The whole city was a theater of small stages.

As quickly as they could, Ilse and Rudolf morphed in and out of other groups. There was some safety in numbers, as long as the group didn't look big enough to riot. Whenever they saw Soviet soldiers ahead, asking for papers, Rudolf and Ilse ducked into an alley or courtyard. That's how they got caught.

Three Soviet soldiers stood at the end of the alley as though they had been waiting for a moment just like this, for two young Germans to fall into their hands and get their comeuppance.

"Du kommst, Schatzi," said the tallest one in terrible German, leering at Ilse.

Ilse's heart pounded. She looked in her periphery: maybe she and Rudolf could turn and run back onto the street. But there was another soldier coming up behind them. Her hands itched for her pistol, but it was in her backpack. She'd never get it in time.

One of the other soldiers pushed the tall one back and rebuked him in his own language. He approached Rudolf first, with his hands up as though *he* were surrendering to them.

"We mean you no harm, *deti*. You look hungry. *Da?*"

Rudolf and Ilse stoically refused to answer.

"You are scared of Russians. *Ich verstehe.* We are here to rebuild. See?" The soldier crouched down and picked up two broken bricks from the rubble. Rudolf grabbed Ilse's arm hard, ready to run or shield her with his body. Was this guy going to bash their heads in as a joke?

No, he went over to the wall and placed the bricks in a shell hole.

"We build," he said. "We are . . ." He muttered to his comrade.

"Good guys," said the other.

"We are good guys. Like in the movies. Now, we find you some rations. What are your names?"

Rudolf and Ilse registered with the Soviets and learned that they were in the neighborhood of Friedrichshain. Rudolf's grandmother lived just a few blocks from there. She couldn't have survived this destruction, but once he and Ilse filled their bellies with tinned fish and potatoes—a gift from Comrade Stalin—they attempted her address anyway.

Miraculously, there was one street sign standing in the rubble: *Mainzerstrasse.* Oma's street. And one building rose, almost unscathed except for the texture of shell holes. Oma's building.

They entered a corridor into the courtyard, winding a path through the debris, and climbed the stairs to Oma's flat. The elderly woman answered the door, looking leathered and tired, a cigarette hanging from her lips. But when she saw Rudolf, she pulled him in close and held him like a little child. And so Rudolf and Ilse moved into his grandmother's flat in the Soviet sector.

Oma had known privation—she had lived through two wars, four governments, a pandemic, widowhood—so her cooking was meager and formless and reliant on packets of powders. But it was regular, and she was happy to have mouths to feed. Something made her wary of Ilse, but Rudolf seemed happy, and as everyone came out of the postwar daze, people realized that family relations were of more worth than gold.

There wasn't anything like a real job to be had. Money was mostly worthless. Rudolf got a tip from another kid: cigarettes were the real currency, and not just new ones in packs, either. The spent butts could be torn up and recycled into new cigarettes to barter and eventually sell. He could get so many pfennigs per hundred butts, and even more if he rolled new ones himself.

Ilse was assigned to the *Trümmerfrauen,* the rubble women. For six marks a day and some ration tickets, she cleaned greasy soot off bricks, cleaned blood and flesh off pipes, cleaned shit off toilets. And so they rebuilt Berlin by hand. No one asked what they had been doing just a few months ago, when this was Hitler country. They all knew. They all silently agreed to forget.

Pretty soon, six marks a day wasn't enough to live on. Ilse foraged for coins in the rubble, or toys or trinkets to sell. Every now and again, she found a dress that could be mended and sold. One day, as she was hawking her wares on the Western side of the Brandenburg Gate, Ilse ran into her old Leipzig friend Henni, who'd just procured a fashion magazine from an American soldier, and the girls pored over the latest styles from the States.

"I know how to make a dress like that," Ilse said. "And I just found a lace tablecloth that I could cut up for trim."

Ilse and Henni made it their mission to re-create the magazine fashions. They sewed by hand late into the night. By day they sold their dresses out of a suitcase for ten marks apiece, guaranteed to make any war-worn girl who bought one look smart, modern and fresh. Ilse and Henni modeled their creations themselves. They curled their hair in rags and brushed it out full and fluffy. They put their lipstick on thick. They got the attention of their customers— but they also got the attention of the soldiers.

Soon they realized that they could make a lot more than ten marks if they'd go out with a soldier for the evening. Russian, British, American or French—it was all the same to Ilse and Henni. A little flirt, a little kiss, a little more. At least it kept them safe from worse. At least this way, they had a choice.

Ilse tried not to think too much of Rudolf waiting up for her in his Oma's flat. It wasn't as though they were *married*. As far as Rudolf knew, she was out with the girls. And as far as she knew or cared, so was he.

Maybe it was because she'd gotten so skinny in the last months of the war that Ilse's belly looked bigger, or maybe it was the nightly dinners the soldiers treated her to. Either way, the propositions slowed once a fellow would look down at her thickening waist.

By July, Ilse knew she was pregnant.

She had to tell Rudolf.

He was, at turns, overwhelmed, ecstatic, terrified, confused. But more than anything, he was stirred by a desire to undo all the death and destruction he'd been part of. To remake the world somehow, and to will it to be a *good* world, even in this heap of a city. Things had calmed down from the anarchy of a few months ago. There was order now, stability, clear streets with running trams and reliable food.

But Rudolf was uneasy. "Ilse, there's something I don't trust about the Soviets," he said as he sat with her on the sofa, rubbing her swollen feet. "Don't you want to move to the American sector? Or the British? The hospitals have a better reputation, and I heard they give more rations."

"Ugh, Rudolf, I'm so *tired*. I don't want to run all around town anymore," she replied. "A ration's a ration, as far as I'm concerned."

And so she stayed home, listening to the radio, reading magazines all day, quickly growing bigger than seemed proper. "Maybe you're having twins," Henni joked. That was the wake-up call. Ilse finally made Rudolf take her to a doctor.

It was true. Twins were in her belly. Before then, *the baby* had seemed like an abstraction, something that slightly annoyed her, that she could deal with later. But the look on Rudolf's face, as he tried to hold back from weeping with painful joy, made her grow up despite herself. Ilse was going to be a mother. Maybe Rudolf was these babies' father, and maybe not, but the children were going to need to be provided for, and he seemed to be staying put. So she stayed.

"Rudolf," she said after the doctor's appointment, "we have to get married."

"Really? You want to, Ilse?" He wiped his eyes with the heel of his palm and embraced her.

For Ilse, the question of *wanting to* was irrelevant. "Let's do it tomorrow. Find a chaplain or something. Your Oma can be your witness, and Henni will be mine."

And so it was.

Rudi and Peter came into the world on a snowy December morning, five weeks early, but ready for whatever would come next.

RUDI

"Rudi, hand me my damn cigarettes," said Oma Möser, shriveling into a coughing fit, emerging again to say, "No, not those, not those—the ones on top of the television. I know it's not a special occasion, but today feels different."

Rudi put down the empty pack of Karos he'd picked up from the side table and handed his great-grandmother her good West smokes.

"Where's your father?" she asked without thanks, patting the tattered sofa for Rudi to sit beside her. "He's late coming home."

Oma tapped the box against her palm, unwrapped it and drew out one cigarette with yellowed fingers. Then she did what she did all day long: lit the new cigarette with the one already glowing in her hand.

Rudi sat gingerly, trying to take shallow breaths. In his fifteen years of life, he'd never gotten used to the fetid smoke smell that permeated everything in their hole of a flat.

"I don't know, Omi," he said. "I think Peter had something after school."

"Well, *ja*, he always does, doesn't he?" Oma chuffed, looking at

15

the cuckoo clock near the television. "Oh, my program is on. Turn it up, will you? And fix the picture."

The black-and-white image crackled into a measure of clarity as Rudi adjusted the television antenna. He turned the volume dial up, higher and higher, as Oma demanded.

"That good?"

"Yes. What are they saying?"

"Yuri Gagarin became the first man in space today," the announcer said, betraying his own astonishment, *"as he orbited the earth for one hundred and eight minutes, descending back through the atmosphere and landing, to the surprise of an old grandmother, in a Russian potato field. . . ."*

"No way," gasped Rudi. "He actually went into *space?*" He sat next to Oma and leaned forward to see the tiny picture.

"He was up there"—Oma waved her hands around in the air wildly, shaking her cigarette ash everywhere—"flying above our heads, and we didn't even know it!"

"And it was a *cosmo*naut," Rudi said with dreamy pride. "Not an American. Serves them right."

"Back to earth, please." Oma patted Rudi's hand. "You have homework."

"I know, Omi. I'll be in my room," said Rudi, but before he could make his exit, the keys jangled in the apartment door and his father came in with Peter, who was carrying the mail.

Damn, thought Rudi.

"Here he is," his father, Rudolf, announced, "the big award winner!"

"What's this?" said Oma. "What's the award?"

"Oh, it's nothing." Peter smiled, tossing the mail on the table and planting a big kiss on his great-grandmother's papery cheek.

"An acting thing. Vati's just being dramatic. What's on the tube?" He plopped down next to Oma and put his arm around her shoulder. He grabbed the cigarette out of her hand and took a long drag.

"You brute," she said, slapping his arm and grabbing it back.

"Everyone's talking about it." Peter gestured toward the television. "A real-life spaceman."

"*Och,* I think I've lived too long," Oma groused.

"Peter was given a drama award at school, Oma," said Rudolf. "I'm taking us all out to celebrate."

"I'll get my coat," Oma said immediately. "Help me up, movie star." She hoisted her seventy-nine-year-old frame using Peter's arm and shuffled over to the coat tree.

Rudi turned off the television and watched the circle of adulation surrounding Peter. He rolled his eyes, made a quick escape to his room and closed the louvered double doors. He could have reminded the family that he had homework, but frankly, he didn't want to instigate a conversation about any of the following topics:

> *his lousy grades*
>
> *his bad attitude*
>
> *how he was never happy for Peter*
>
> *why he couldn't be a little more like his twin brother*

So Rudi sat hard on his bed and cast his eyes on the wall above Peter's trophy-clad wardrobe, its doors festooned with certificates and ribbons. His twin was the *Gruppenleiter* of their chapter of the *Freie Deutsche Jugend,* the Free German Youth, and Rudi was his co-chair, his glorified assistant.

He glanced over at his own bare bureau, with the black-and-white movie poster of *Die Mörder Sind Unter Uns* tacked to the wall above it. The only items on top were his secondhand Prakti camera, a bottle of cologne and the folded neckerchief from his FDJ uniform.

I like it this way, he told himself. *Minimalist. Clean. No expectations, no disappointment.*

Rudi opened the bottom drawer. He kept everything in the bureau in a vain attempt to preserve it from the smell of smoke. He took out his tan jacket, stood in front of the mirror on Peter's wardrobe door and smoothed his hair. He stared at his face, his patchy teenage afternoon whiskers, the hard expression under his dark eyebrows. He stared a few seconds longer, grimaced, then went back out into the living room just as his mother, Ilse, came in.

Ilse put a mesh bag of groceries down on the counter, and Oma filled her in on the dinner plans as Ilse unbuttoned her coat. She was not pleased. Rudi kissed her cheek, but Ilse didn't respond. He put his hands in his pockets.

"Peter, why didn't you tell me about the award?" Ilse huffed. "Why do I always find out about these things after the fact? People probably think I don't care about my own son."

Peter grabbed his mother into a hug, towering over her like a burst of sunshine. "No one would think that, Mutti," he said. "I didn't tell you because it wasn't a big deal."

"It *was* a big deal," said Rudolf. "That's why I'm taking us out to dinner."

Ilse looked at Rudolf and tightened her lips. "I hate when you spring these things on me. You knew I was going to make Spätzle tonight. We had a plan."

"Well, plans change," said Rudolf, his tone suddenly dropping.

"I suppose they do," said Ilse, staring at her husband. Peter and Rudi glanced at each other with raised brows.

"Oh, cut the crap," said Oma. "I want a beer. Let's go."

The Möser-Fleischmann boys were fraternal twins. Rudi was short, husky, dark-haired. Peter was thin, tall and blond. Peter was a bouncy, unrepentant optimist, but Rudi, dutiful and correct, was a bit of a brooder.

When they were three years old, Ilse threw her usual combined Christmas and birthday party. Peter climbed right up on top of Rudolf's piano as his father played—mind, it was a spinet, not a baby grand—and began dancing to Duke Ellington, really hamming it up, too, clicking his hips to the left and right, with jazz hands and everything. Who knows how he knew all the words to *It Don't Mean a Thing*, but he sang them all, like a male Shirley Temple.

That's how they knew Peter was going to be a performer.

Little Rudi stood in the corner with a plate of cubed cheese, staring at Peter as though he were an alien, or a god.

"Remember that twins share a mind and a heart," their mother had taught them. "There's no Rudi without Peter, no Peter without Rudi. Repeat after me: *twins against the world.*"

"*Twins against the world,*" they echoed. That phrase sounded in little Rudi's heart.

The boys each had their favorite parent—Rudi, his mother, and Peter, his father—but no one would have accused Ilse of favoritism.

Something changed once they started school. Ilse bought a used copy of Dr. Haarer's manual on parenting, *Die Deutsche Mutter und Ihr Erstes Kind*. It promoted a rigid approach for training tough

children, and she trusted Dr. Haarer. The fairy stories stopped, and the book of maps went back on the shelf.

From then on, she treated Rudi and Peter as a unit. Ilse dressed her boys in identical outfits until middle school. Differences in their behavior or personalities seemed to exhaust her now. It was as though she didn't want to tell them apart, didn't want them to have their own selves. So on went the little matching lederhosen, the white knee socks, the brown shoes laced exactly alike, bunny ears and all.

Rudi hated lederhosen. Had hated them, since the time he couldn't get them unfastened and wet himself in the kindergarten restroom. He had washed his legs the best he could, but he had to come back to class with his front all wet. The class twittered and sniggered, and Rudi looked to his twin to cover for him, to show him sympathy.

Twins against the world, right, Peter?

But Rudi thought he saw a smile slice across Peter's face as well.

PETER

Peter found his father unusually chipper as they hopped onto the tram car. In most families, a father's joviality would have been contagious. But contrasted with his typical reserve, Rudolf's mood was unsettling. Oma, Ilse and Rudi sat in terse silence as Rudolf chatted Peter up about his award and his post–high school options.

Rudolf didn't tell the family where he was taking them. They

never crossed the river to eat at a West Berlin restaurant, only to go to their favorite bakery, Bäckerei Antoinette, when they had a few pfennigs to spare. They disembarked at Kurfürstendamm, and Rudolf, walking briskly in the late-afternoon sunshine, led them to the door of The Jupiter. Ilse shot him an incredulous look. This was a restaurant for tourists and functionaries, not a working-class family like them—a piano tuner, a telephone operator and an elderly pensioner.

"I got paid in D-marks today," Rudolf said with a proud tilt of the head. "Worked on a piano at the American army base." He opened the door and looked Ilse dead in the eye. "*Bitte*, ladies first."

"*Danke*," said Oma, pushing past her granddaughter-in-law. "Don't mind if I do."

They barely knew how to act in a trendy place like this. Ilse nervously patted her hair and glanced down at her work dress. The walls were paneled in smooth wood, and the modernist kidney-shaped ceiling was illuminated by hidden lights. Most restaurants and shops in the Soviet sector were like either dusty attics or sterile warehouses. Rudolf sat across the table from Ilse, but they avoided looking at each other.

"I thought this would be your kind of place, darling," Rudolf said to his wife. "A bit of glamour."

"Don't you think we could have *saved* that Western money so we could get ahead a little bit?" she retorted, not looking up from the menu. "I was all ready to make that Spätzle."

"The doldrums, dear, the doldrums. We don't celebrate enough as a family. Besides, your Spätzle's rubbery."

Peter snickered and Rudi tried to suppress a smile. Their father wasn't wrong.

"Damn right," said Oma. "If you'd make them the Swabian way,

with eggs only, no water, like I told you . . ." They all knew Oma was a terrible cook. Still, she made two dishes that no one could beat: the most tender veal schnitzel and melt-in-your-mouth Spätzle.

"Thank you, Oma, but eggs are more expensive than water," said Ilse. "Well, if you're all in agreement, maybe you should try doing more of the cooking yourselves. You boys are almost grown."

Rudi could make the occasional omelet, but no one wanted to think of the disaster Peter might create if they let him anywhere near a pan. He faithfully fetched the mail, he could lead a meeting like a diplomat, but he never ventured beyond instant noodles.

"Here's the waiter again," Rudolf said, changing the subject. "Peter, what are you going to have?"

Peter looked at his father, unsure of exactly *how* much he intended to splurge.

"Please," said Rudolf. "Order what you like."

"All right, then, steak, medium-rare," Peter told the waiter, as though he did this all the time.

"Schnitzel Holstein," said Ilse, her manners suddenly faux bourgeois.

"*Solyanka*," said Rudi. He was painfully aware that they didn't belong in a place like this. Soup would do.

"Branch out a little, Rudi," said Rudolf, who ordered venison with pickled beets.

Rudi changed his order. "*Löffelerbsen*, then."

"Pease porridge, Rudi?" Peter teased his dutiful brother. "Ah, yes, to build the Socialist fatherland requires sacrifice. But you're in West Berlin today."

"You don't make your Spätzle with water, do you?" Oma asked the waiter. Peter chuckled. "Never mind—schnitzel, young man. And make the Spätzle *mit vielen Butter.*"

"But your blood pressure, Oma. Maybe you should take it easy on the butter," offered Ilse.

"Maybe you should sit on a—"

"So let's see that certificate, Peter," said Rudolf abruptly.

Peter handed him the little scroll.

"You know how I love you in those skits," said Oma, reaching across the table and patting his smooth cheek. "Like Rock Hudson."

"Rock Hudson," Rudi snickered. "More like Don Knotts!" The waiter brought water and laid a bread basket on the table. They all tore into the rolls with relief.

"So what does your teacher think you should do after you graduate?" Ilse asked Peter.

"She thinks I should take the Abitur and then go for mechanical engineering."

"Oh, really? I would have thought working for the Party," said his mother. "It wouldn't be hard, since you're the *Gruppenleiter*."

"Mechanical engineering could get you into the space program, though," said his father, eyes twinkling as he chewed.

"Why are we talking about this?" said Peter suddenly. "We all know I want to study acting."

The entire restaurant might as well have gone silent. Their table did, at least.

"Right," Rudi scoffed. "We'll all drop a pfennig in your hat when you're begging in front of the Soviet War Memorial."

"Really, Rudi?" Peter retorted. "What are *you* going to do? Sulk for a living?"

"Stop it, Peter," Rudolf reprimanded. "The award and your talent notwithstanding—"

"It doesn't make sense to take the Abitur and then throw it away," said Ilse practically.

"I know that. I don't want to take that route. I want to *study* acting. I want to *be* an actor."

"Sure, take classes at night for fun, do it on the side," said Rudolf. "But you have to earn a living. If I could have made a living as a musician, don't you think I'd be doing that instead of tuning pianos?"

"Maybe I'll go somewhere else, then, where I can make a go of it. Maybe I'll leave the GDR."

"You're not going to leave," said Ilse. "It's cutthroat out there. The capitalists will chew you up and spit you out."

"Capitalist *imperialists*," Oma chimed in, popping a bite of bread in her mouth.

"Your mother's right," Rudolf capitulated.

"I don't know," said Oma. "I think he should do what he wants."

"What he *wants*?" said Ilse. "Who gets to do what they *want*?"

The waiter arrived just in time. He lowered the heavy tray of food onto a stand. It was a far cry from the currywurst joint they usually frequented.

"If you'll excuse me," he said to Peter as he handed out the entrées, "I overheard you talking about studying acting. Do you know the Berliner Ensemble?"

"Of course," said Peter. "I love Brecht."

"They're holding auditions for the drama school."

"Are you kidding? Do you know when?"

"Saturdays, through June," said the waiter. "Go to the box office and ask for an application. I've already gotten a slot." He smiled with pride, then remembered that he was at work.

"Thank you," said Peter. "Thank you very much. And good luck!"

"Good luck to you," said the waiter.

The Möser-Fleischmanns unceremoniously dug into their food, not acknowledging Peter's stroke of serendipity. Opportunities like this *always* fell in his lap. More than anything, his family feared that he might actually do what he said.

Their fine dinner consumed, the family crossed the river back into East Berlin and passed the *Neues Deutschland* building, covered in three huge banners of Marx, Engels and Lenin.

"The Holy Trinity," Oma muttered, nudging Peter in the ribs.

Peter carried the rolled-up drama award in the pocket of his camel-colored jacket. He looked down at his feet, stomach rumbling with rare steak. This family was clumsily thrown together, like they'd each somehow stumbled onto a stage and had to improvise a part. Even his twin brother was like a stranger to him lately. All Rudi seemed to care about was the stupid FDJ.

Last year, after their *Jugendweihe,* Rudi and Peter thought it'd be fun to run for student leadership of their school chapter—go on some trips, get the attention of the girls, that kind of thing.

Peter won the election as student leader. Rudi came in second, but Peter made sure they reigned together—*twins against the world.* He couldn't have cared less about the cause or the Party. *For Peace and Socialism, Always Ready*—they all said it, but who really believed it? It was one thing to memorize the tenets of Marxism-Leninism to recite in class, but quite another to spend your free time becoming an acolyte or a proselyte. And Rudi was becoming a true believer.

Peter saw the grocery store coming up on the right. "I forgot," he told his family, "I have to grab something for school."

"Here," said his great-grandmother, handing him a bill. "Get some sauerkraut."

He ducked into the Konsum and looked around. In truth, he didn't need anything besides a minute to himself. He found the sauerkraut and a box of instant coffee packets and went to the front counter to pay. He glanced at a shelf above the cash register, where a framed picture of Chairman Walter Ulbricht was propped up in a shrine draped with red flags and a sign admonishing the workers of the world to unite.

There's no escape, he thought. *It's on the buildings. It's in the movies. It's even in the damn grocery store.*

Signs and slogans—the Western half of the city had them, too, but they were cigarette adverts and movie posters and sales flyers for fruits and veg, not portraits of Party men staring down at the populace like a pantheon of gods, monitoring the outsized ambition of a teenage actor.

As he left the Konsum with the sauerkraut and coffee and a last-minute pack of gum, he looked once more at the stone-faced leader of his half country. What was it that Marcellus said in *Hamlet*?

Something is rotten in the state of Denmark.

RUDI

The apartment was a rare prewar tenement—one of the better ones, but still the kind of functional box that manifested the mundane dullness of a country trying to forget its past. It wasn't more than a collection of right angles made of chipboard and scraps, just big enough to hold a postwar family: mother, a small child, perhaps the anomaly of a surviving father—not two teenagers and their great-grandmother to boot. It was a place in which to cook a packet pottage on the efficiency stove, and to eat from a tray by the sofa while watching a *Krimi* at night. A place to escape one's small life.

Rudi remembered learning in school about Paleolithic houses, stone-lined dugouts with nothing more than a hearth, some straw pallets and the household deities. This home was like that, with the same ethos: be happy you're not starving, and don't poke your head up above the soil line, or you'll be a prime target for wolves.

The walls were standard white, but so nicotined and twin boy–handprinted that the effect was, overall, beige. Nobody in the family was a decent housekeeper. Oma Möser was too old, and Ilse certainly couldn't be bothered unless there was a party. She set aside part of her meager paycheck to hire a cleaner once a month just to keep the place hygienic, more of a health necessity than a bourgeois indulgence. Everything *was* clean . . . enough.

The contents were all secondhand: the faded, mint-colored sofa, draped in an ancient afghan; the television that never could settle into a clear picture; the pair of rickety bookcases, one of which displayed Rudolf's carefully curated collection of used classics—Rilke, Proust, Aristotle—and, on the bottom shelf, photography books that Rudi picked up in thrift shops. The other case was stuffed with Ilse's pulp romances and back issues of beauty magazines, the dog-eared Dr. Haarer parenting book and Peter's scripts and comic books. Almost all of it was salvaged from someone else, from another time, a time of war. Even the back of the sofa had been clawed up by someone else's cat.

What could be expected on the salaries of a piano tuner and a telephone operator?

There was one thing they always bought new: good shoes. Ilse was fastidious about that, at least. Obsessive, even. "You could be wearing a three-piece suit," Ilse often said, "but if your shoes are trash, you'll look like you just crawled out of the war rubble." So although they could rarely afford a decent cut of meat, and despite the boys' constant growth spurts, their shoes were always leather, made to last and shined every Sunday evening.

After the dinner at The Jupiter, Ilse refused to cook. She didn't announce it to anyone—simply let it get later and later, until everyone was forced to scrounge. The small icebox was almost bare.

Friday afternoon was lazy and still. Rudi and Peter did their homework at the kitchen table. Oma poured her umpteenth cup of coffee and sat next to Rudolf on the sofa while the television blared a halting voice, translating into German from an unknown language.

It was a courtroom trial, but a real one, not a *Krimi* drama. Three judges presided from a modern-looking dais, shuffling papers while they listened to a robed prosecutor give his statements. Then the camera cut to a thin, balding man with thick glasses, sitting in a tiny clear box.

"Why is he in that thing?" asked Peter.

"It's bulletproof glass." Oma lifted her head from her coffee cup. "Assassins."

"It's . . . ah . . . yes," said Rudolf, "someone might understandably try to shoot him."

"Why?" asked Rudi. "Who is he?"

"That's Eichmann," said Rudolf. "Adolf Eichmann. He's a Nazi they found in Argentina."

"A lot of them fled to South America," Oma muttered. "Damn cowards."

"What language are they speaking?" asked Peter. "Are they in Germany?"

"Israel. Hebrew," said Oma.

"Damn," said Peter. "A Nazi on trial in Israel, of all places. You couldn't script that."

The boys came over and squeezed onto the sofa between their

father and great-grandmother. Rudolf squirmed and finally settled himself with his arms crossed over his chest.

The bespectacled attorney general, Gideon Hausner, recounted the epic crimes of the Third Reich against European Jewry. One after another, unceasing catastrophes piled up like successive punches in the gut.

Eichmann pulled a handkerchief from his breast pocket and started methodically wiping not his eyes, but a second pair of glasses besides the ones already on his face. He looked like a sniveling weasel, his eyes obscured by thick lenses, eyebrows perched on the frames like preening crows.

"What part did he play in all of it, Vati?" asked Peter.

Rudolf got up and wandered around the living room like a sleepwalker. He went to the dining table and began opening the mail.

He cleared his throat. "Everything, Peter. He did everything."

Unknown hours passed as they watched this opening testimony. No one had seen Ilse for hours. Or a couple of days, for that matter. All their bellies rumbled in unison from empty-stomached coffee and the last crackers in the cupboard. Someone had to buy some food.

Finally, Rudi got up. "This is ridiculous. I'm going to the Konsum," he announced.

"Good man," said Peter. "Can you get me some of those instant noodles?"

"*Jawohl,*" his brother replied.

Rudi pushed open his parents' bedroom door to look for money. The fetid cave smelled of stale sheets and rancid perfume, and it knocked him on his heels. The drapes were drawn. Ilse was in bed with the blue coverlet pulled up to her chin. She was awake, staring

across the room at a row of photographs on top of the small, cream-colored bureau. He knew which one she was looking at: a tarnished silver frame punched with sprigs of cherries, holding a portrait of her family.

Ilse's father had been a Leipziger of some stature, and there he was, in a tidy suit, with her mother, a Greta Garbo look-alike, hovering over grade school–aged Ilse, in a blouse and neckerchief, and her older brother, Martin, dressed like a miniature version of his father.

Ilse never spoke of her parents. All Rudi knew was that they died in the war, just before his parents had met here in Berlin. But he knew this photograph made her sad. Made her so sad, in fact, that plunging into darkness like this was becoming a fairly regular occurrence. He wondered why she kept the photograph out at all.

"Mutti," he whispered, "are you all right? Can I get you anything?"

"I'm fine, *Schatzi*. I just have a headache."

"Have you . . . had a headache all week?"

She didn't answer right away.

"I'm doing my best."

"I know." Rudi stuffed his hands into his pockets.

"Do you need something?" she managed.

"Only money for some groceries."

"That's my Rudi. Always helping. You know where to find it."

"Just . . . try to come out when you can, Mutti."

Ilse turned away, and Rudi knew the conversation was over. He slid her pocketbook off the doorknob, took out the billfold, grabbed some ostmarks and shut the door quietly behind him. He threw on his tan jacket and left without saying goodbye. The others didn't look up from the television in any case.

Rudi emerged from the building into the courtyard below and walked through the corridor onto the street. He put his hands in his pockets and fiddled with the folded money, flicking the corners of the bills with his thumbnail.

A sun-shower was retreating across the river at the other end of the Oberbaum Bridge, light glimmering behind the rain as through a sheet on a clothesline. The air was warm and cool at the same time, fresh and fragrant. Berlin after a rain always made Oma melancholy. *Rain washes the city,* she'd sigh. As though Berlin could never be scrubbed clean enough.

Rudi wandered over the invisible sector border, where two men were planting a tree in a gap in the sidewalk. They had already planted a line of them up the entire street, flowering trees, alternating pink and white. Rudi stopped and watched them, the warm afternoon light dancing on the flowers, glowing against the slate sky, life pushing up from the concrete, putting its roots down into the old earth of the city.

Mutti would love these trees, he thought. *Maybe I can get her to come out and see them.*

A plump woman in an overcoat passed by, her chestnut curls covered by a plastic hood. She looked old, like his friends' mothers. His mother wasn't like them. To Rudi, Ilse was the zenith of creation, elegant, like a green willow hanging above a still pond.

When they were children, Rudi and Peter loved to sit on the sofa on either side of her, looking together at the atlas that was so big, it spread across all three laps. Ilse pointed out rivers she had boated in and villages she had visited as a child, and ancient *Wälder,* the forests of fairy tales. With her words, she could make the boys see the rich soil, teeming with beetles and earthworms, make them smell the leaf mold. They felt the velvet pillows of moss under their feet, the dozen forms of moss that Ilse could name, the tiny white flowers that poked out of some and the soft rusty spikes that grew out of others. She spoke of towering pines and the wind sprinkling their tawny needles in fairy showers. Rudi and Peter sensed those woods in their skin, stirring in their bellies.

Oma would sit in the mustard-colored chair across from them and tell the old stories, like the one about the tinderbox and the dogs with eyes as big as saucers. The boys learned of the humble heroes who sought their fortunes in the caverns beneath those forest floors. Sometimes the soft cadences of their father's piano would hover over the stories on afternoons just like this, the light golden, their mother quiet and green.

But that mother had gone away years ago. She'd stopped gathering them on her lap, stopped telling them about the forests and caves. In her place, she'd left two Ilses.

The first Ilse fell into a new kind of quiet—today's quiet, closed in the cave, deep in the underworld with those big-eyed dogs. She was somewhere dark and silent, where Rudi couldn't find her. The underworld is, after all, a place to which one can only travel alone.

The second Ilse was a storm that bent the family diagonally, plucking their roots up from the ground so that by the time each tempest passed, they all leaned just a bit more, with just a little less footing. Her storms rushed in without warning, thrashing with energy as frenetic as a telephone switchboard.

Plug. Unplug. Patch the call through. Take the number. Sorry, no answer. Let me reconnect you. Push the wheeled chair back. Blow out through horse lips. Take off the headset. Fix your hair. Put the headset back on. Wheel the chair to the desk. Plug. Unplug. Patch the call through.

A whirlwind.

•••••

Rudi walked back into Friedrichshain and bought bread and jarred cheese spread at the Konsum. They were out of coffee, and there was only one green apple left in the bin. But the packets of Peter's favorite just-add-water noodles were available by the dozen. Rudi knew the others would have liked some sausage, but he didn't care much for meat, so he skipped it. They could come and buy it themselves if it meant that much to them—and besides, the ostmarks wouldn't stretch that far. They never did.

Rudi hoisted the mesh bag onto his shoulder and headed home through the soot-stained, rain-dampened Soviet sector. The gray-beige buildings of this half country towered over him as he walked the treeless streets of the German Democratic Republic, which was *not* the country behind him. The American sector, with its flowering trees, was the *Federal* Republic of Germany. Another country, across the street, where he bought his good chewing gum, where he and Peter went to the record shop and the bakery. *Federal* was another word for *bourgeois, privileged* and *aggressive*. And *Democratic* meant *peaceful* and *pro-worker* and *anti-fascist*.

Rudi believed in words, that they meant what people told him they *should* mean. He believed all the concepts on his school exams because he wanted peace, and knew it was worth fighting for. He trusted in a better era to come, so he believed in the *Deutsche De-mokratische Republik*. The Western sectors may have had better movies and pastries, sure. But that wasn't going to save the world.

Rudi ran his hand along the hip-high molding in his building's corridor and rang the bell of someone else's bicycle leaning against the wall. He tapped his toes through the puddles dotting the courtyard. He wasn't sure—if his mother had been here—if she would have scolded him for risking water stains on his shoes or jumped right in with him. It depended on the day.

When he unlocked the door at the top of the third flight of stairs, the apartment was as cacophonous as it had been tomb-like when he'd left. Oma was vacuuming the carpet, a cigarette dangling as she mumbled, "Well, after all, it is *my* house" under her breath. Rudolf's arms were full of bric-a-brac and papers. Peter was on his hands and knees scrubbing the kitchen floor. The radio was blaring the RIAS station with some old big band jazz.

"What's going on?" Rudi asked.

Peter looked up and, with the back of his hand, brushed a loose lock of hair from his forehead. "Mutti's got us cleaning," he replied.

"I can see that," said Rudi, "but thirty minutes ago she couldn't get out of bed."

As if on cue, Ilse swept into the kitchen, wrapped in her tattered pink satin robe, a towel piled on her head. Through the bedroom door, Rudi could see that her bed had been stripped and the drapes were pulled back, revealing the blue twilight.

"Rudi, you're making dinner tonight, I see?" She rubbed lotion into her face and swirled the rest on her hands.

"Sure, Mutti, but *was ist los?*"

"We're having a party tomorrow," she said, smiling, and with a cavalier toss of her head, she went back to her bedroom, humming a tune.

PETER

The occasion for the party was Lenin's birthday—a stupid holiday in Peter's estimation. Though he'd been schooled in the marriage of German Marxism and Russian Leninism, it had never made sense to him why they would venerate the long-dead leader of another nation, even if his own country orbited Russia the way Gagarin had orbited Earth just ten days before.

Peter leaned against the wall, reading a book about Russia he'd picked up at a shop in the British sector. Rudi spooned gherkins into a bowl for the buffet.

"Did you know Lenin's corpse is perfectly preserved, lying under glass over in Moscow?" Peter said. "They put Stalin next to him for a while, like some weird Romeo and Juliet. Until Stalin's body count was tallied. *Millions*, Rudi. Just like Hitler."

"Don't say that," Rudi countered. "Hitler destroyed Germany. Stalin saved it."

"If you say so." Peter shrugged. Rudi could be so naive sometimes. Peter grabbed a tiny sausage from a serving plate.

"Hey, don't touch that!" Rudi put a serving fork on the plate and glared at Peter to compel him to use it. Peter knew nothing horrified his brother more than touching food with one's fingers. That's exactly why he did it.

Stalin wasn't talked about much these days, ever since Khrushchev had exposed the former dictator's wanton killings and announced a new dawn in the East. Peter remembered the janitor taking down all the Stalin portraits at school one day, like he'd never existed. Marx and Lenin got to stay, though.

Peter went along at the youth meetings—he had to. He was the *Gruppenleiter*. But the slogans, the pomp and the whipped-up emotions made him suspicious. The twins didn't see eye to eye on it, but Peter, ever the life of the party, availed himself of the social opportunities and let Rudi make the speeches.

Their father got a pair of fresh hand towels out of the closet to put in the bathroom. "They'll be here any minute, boys," Rudolf said. "*And no political talk!* Remember, family words are not the same as friend words. Peter, don't let anyone catch you with that book. Put it in your room where no one can see it—how about in your pile of dirty clothes?" he teased, flicking the towel at Peter's legs.

The grown-up Möser-Fleischmanns weren't die-hard Party loyalists. They simply didn't kick against the goads. They had too much to lose to stand on principle. The occasional friend got harassed by the authorities, but life was simpler if one just went to the parades, carried the banners, brought kuchen to the trade union meetings . . . and kept one's mouth shut.

And besides, *any excuse for a party* was Ilse's philosophy. So today it was Lenin's birthday, and next week would be the First of May parade celebrating German workers. Rudi would bake something tasty in honor of the occasion, and Peter would consume the benefits.

Oma's old cuckoo clock struck six. The radio was blaring Ivo Robić as Ilse came out of the bedroom with her hair done up in a healthy bouffant. Green shift dress, white belt and white heels—she knew how to use frugal simplicity to great effect. She had Peter clasp her fake pearl bracelet onto her thin wrist and she praised Rudi on the spread.

"The lebkuchen smell wonderful, Rudi," she said. "You know"—she opened the front door and propped a huge dictionary against it as the first guests arrived—"you should work in a bakery!"

Everyone wanted to hear about the twins' plans for next year, whether they'd go on to university or an apprenticeship. Peter knew better than to tell anyone of his upcoming audition for acting school. Instead he said he'd *probably* try for Karl Marx University in Leipzig, and *probably* become an engineer. Everyone said he should *probably* become a politician.

Greased by a few shots of vodka, Ilse started telling her guests what a grumpy baby Rudi had been. She did this at every party in some form or another. Peter may have cried more but it was Rudi who was sullen and aggressive when they played together. You couldn't separate them, though, or both would cry as if they were being torn in half.

"They were so different, I always asked myself whether I was raising them unequally without realizing it," she said. "So I turned to Dr. Haarer. If that book was good enough for my mother's generation, it was good enough for me. And lo and behold, it worked! Look at them now," she all but shouted. "Look at my two handsome boys!"

Peter obliged her with a smile, but he wished he could disappear. He shot Rudi a look across the room, and Rudi shrugged.

Uncle Martin came in late, without a knock, and kissed his sister's cheeks right and left. A front-door handshake was the only greeting Martin gave to Peter. He waved to Rudolf, who sat in the corner talking to Oma, and made a beeline for Rudi, ignoring the other relations, with their canned canapés and cheap Riesling.

Peter had never really gotten along with his uncle Martin. At his *Jugendweihe* party, in front of everyone, Martin had offered to put in a good word for him at a friend's machine factory because kids like Peter needed to *tamp down the histrionics*. That was the day Peter lost all respect for his uncle. Martin always used words like *dramatic* to describe him. Peter was passionate, sure, but *dramatic?* No. There really could be no family warmth between Peter and someone who saw his fundamental personality as a flaw to be erased.

And so Peter went out of his way to avoid Martin. Rudi was Martin's favorite, anyway. The two of them never seemed to run out of tedium to talk about.

The guests and their questions about the future were grating on Peter's nerves. Performance was something Peter preferred to turn off when he was in his own home.

"Excuse me, *bitte*," he told the guests who were peppering him with inquiries about university. "I have something to ask my Omi." He sidled over to where his great-grandmother sat on the sofa, talking with Rudolf. Peter smushed beside her on the sofa and speared a pickle from the bowl on the side table with a toothpick.

"What are you talking about?" Peter intruded.

"This and that, *Junge*," Oma replied, lighting a smoke.

"We were just talking about my tuning job in West Berlin," said Rudolf cryptically.

"What about it?" asked Peter.

"It's a great opportunity. The exchange rate for D-marks is excellent. I'll work in the West and earn D-marks, but pay dirt cheap prices living in the East!"

"That steak dinner proved it," Peter chortled.

"Listen, Peter," Oma said abruptly. "Are you going to audition for that theater school or what?"

"Oma, don't encourage him," sighed his father.

"I mean to, *Schatzi*. I mean to encourage him."

"Peter," said Rudolf, "there's nothing wrong with acting as a hobby. But there's no guarantee of success. You can't support a family like that. Believe me, I know."

"Why, because you can't make a living as a piano player?" Peter chided carelessly. He knew it stung, and he immediately felt bad. "Sorry, Vati. I didn't mean it that way."

But his father rallied quickly. "In fact, yes."

Peter softened. "But have you ever really *tried*, Vati? I mean, everyone loves when you play. You could do it if you wanted to. I know you could."

"It wasn't possible for your father to start from zero," Oma said, "after the war."

"Well, *after the war* was a long time ago," said Peter. "And it's different for me. I'm still young. I can start on the ground floor. So I'm going for it."

Oma looked at Rudolf and shrugged. *He's right,* said her glance.

Rudolf looked into the distance and shook his head. "OK, Peter. I can't fight the inevitable." He got up and squeezed his son's shoulder. "And to tell you the truth, I don't really want to."

He left Peter and Oma and resumed his place at the piano, providing background music for Ilse's one-woman show.

"He wants what's best," Oma reassured Peter. "At least better for you than for himself."

"I know."

"He's . . . he's a man without many options. They were interrupted, that generation. Much as they did it to themselves . . . ," she muttered. She slid another cigarette into her mouth and lit it with the first, sucking in the smoke. "The Eichmann trial will be on later. You going to watch it with me?"

"Of course, Omi."

"It's interesting, no? Don't you think so?"

Peter nodded. "It's almost like a Brecht play."

"Really? How so?"

"Having him in that little glass box, you know? Of course, if Brecht were directing it, he would have hung a big placard above Eichmann's head explaining who he is. But the box is spot-on. It's like having a neon sign that says *This Man Is the Villain.*"

"That's a very smart device," she said, flicking ash into the marble ashtray beside her. "But it's not that simple, of course. You *do* know that, don't you, *Schatzi?*"

"What's not simple?"

"That villains are so easy to put in a box. Take Germany now.

There are still Nazis walking around free—in 1961! Closer than you think."

"Right," said Peter. "In the West."

Oma snickered. "Sure, Peter. In the West." She took a long drag. "You don't buy that line, huh?"

"No. But that's what your teachers say, isn't it?"

"That's what I have to put down on my exams, so . . . yes."

"So you want to talk about Brecht and his signs. There's nothing magic about a sign saying *You Are Now Entering the American Sector* or *Now Entering the Soviet Sector.* What, do the signs spray repellent to keep East Berlin *Nazirein?*"

Peter chuckled. "That's a good one, Omi," he said. "You should do stand-up."

"Well, here's me standing up." Oma patted Peter's knee and hoisted herself, snuffing out her cigarette in the ashtray. "I'm going to get something to eat."

The light was fading, and Peter reached over to turn on the lamp. He stretched his feet in front of him, crossed his arms and sighed. Ilse brought a few friends over to make a pit stop. They asked yet more questions about his post–high school intentions. He took a deep breath and obliged them with his cover story of studying engineering.

Peter's father rose from the piano and came to stand beside his wife just as she was telling her friends that Peter might also join the ranks of the Party. "There's been a change of plans," Rudolf said, and put his arm around her shoulder. "Peter's going to be an actor."

RUDI

The apartment and its hubbub receded into a murmur as Rudi stared out the window, ignoring the party din. He was meditating on the fading sunlight shifting on the wall across the courtyard, thinking about the new girl in his class. The sunlit stone glowed golden, transcending its concrete grayness. Rudi wanted to stay in this moment, to lose himself in the way the light moved like the girl's hair—

"Rudi, my boy!" A strong hand clapped his back. Uncle Martin put his arm around his nephew's shoulder and fixed his gaze on the view Rudi was taking in. The two of them stood together until the gold faded into blue.

"Beautiful light," he said. "This proves it. I am an expert gift giver." He drew a package from his jacket and tapped it to Rudi's chest.

"What's this for?" asked Rudi. "It's not my birthday."

"Open it," said Martin. "It's from my own collection."

Rudi unwrapped the brown paper and gasped. The camera was a Leica, an unreasonably extravagant gift. "Are you serious?"

"This should give you some better outcomes than that old Prakti you have now."

"Thank you, Uncle Martin!" Rudi beamed. It was true that the shutter of his Prakti was prone to jamming, and the focus was ever so slightly fuzzy.

"It's loaded with film," said Martin. "Go ahead, take a few photos. It'll make your mother happy."

Rudi roamed the party, looking for shots. He took a picture of

Oma, in a turtleneck and cat-eye glasses, smoking a cigarette and regaling Rudolf's co-workers with embarrassing stories of his childhood.

He took one of his mother, glass of schnapps in hand, dancing to the blaring music, her spark a foil to the fading glamour of her friend Henni.

He took one of Peter standing in the middle of the room, encircled by admirers, reciting the Goethe monologue that had won him the drama award.

And he took a photograph of his father, who glanced with hurt at the new camera that now replaced the Prakti he had given to Rudi for his *Jugendweihe*.

"It's fantastic, Uncle Martin," said Rudi. "I didn't realize how bad my old camera was until I looked through this lens."

"It's funny, isn't it?" replied Martin, swirling his drink. "How we get used to the most seemingly unworkable things?" He clapped his hands. "A toast!" he announced, raising his glass as the conversations hushed. "To Comrade Lenin, in the words of Dumas: *Das Leben ist bezaubernd; man muss es nur durch die richtige Brille sehen!* Life is lovely; you just have to see it through the right lens."

The guests toasted and drank. Martin lit a cigarette with the owl-shaped lighter Oma kept on the side table. "Humans are very adaptable, Rudi. Remember that."

PETER

At last everyone was gone. Peter and Rudi went around cleaning the apartment, discovering guests' cups and plates in the most creative spots—spinning on the turntable, in the corner of a doorway and . . .

"In the bathtub?!" Peter shook his head.

Rudi told him to wait to clear it and got his camera to snap a photo. "That's a new one. How . . . and why . . . ?"

"Do you really want to know?" The boys laughed. They grew quiet.

"How long has Mutti been in her room?" asked Peter.

"Since eight-thirty or so."

"Hmm." Peter scooped crumbs from the side table by the couch. He was glad that Rudi took it upon himself to check on their mother. Peter hated how she disappeared at the end of her own parties, leaving the mess for them to clean up, leaving their father sitting alone at the piano as they all recovered from the noise and the people and the reek of booze in the air. After the last drunk friend finally vacated and the apartment could be set to rights, silence rang in Peter's ears.

Oma made a simple soup for dinner, and Peter brought a bowl to his father. It was better that Ilse had vanished into her room to sleep it off. Peter was utterly exhausted. He simmered at the unfair burdens his mother put on the family. It was taking him longer than usual to shake off his anger. As he got ready for bed, he promised himself he'd go for a run the next morning to get it out of his system.

"Are you excited for tomorrow?" asked Rudi, sitting up in bed reading *Weltall Erde Mensch* like a good FDJ comrade.

"What's tomorrow again?" Peter asked, putting his running shoes by his bed.

"The dedication of the concentration camp memorial. Remember? Peter, you're *Gruppenleiter*! How could you forget?"

"Oh, right. Sure, Rudi, it'll be great." Peter didn't share Rudi's giddiness over ceremonies and banner waving. He plopped down on the bed and rubbed his face. There'd be no morning run tomorrow after all.

"I wonder how close we'll be to the front," said Rudi. "I'm going to make sure I get seen by *someone* in the Party—maybe even Comrade Ulbricht! Hey, Peter, make sure you're extra enthusiastic, OK? We have to make a good impression."

Peter slid under the covers and switched off his bedside lamp. He turned aside to the wall and curled up as tight as he could against the fury at his mother, the sorrow for his father, the annoyance at his brother.

A lump formed in his throat, but he managed a last word. "I won't let you down, Rudi."

"Thanks, Peter," said Rudi, turning off his lamp as a car rolled by on the cobblestones outside.

Peter woke up to the alarm before dawn, knowing that without a run, it would take him most of the morning to catch up to his own brain. He preferred to get the day into his bones so he could be equal to its challenges. When he was rushed, it was as if someone else were driving his body like a bulldozer through mud.

"Are you excited?" Rudi asked, springing out of bed.

Peter couldn't stop yawning long enough to answer. Frenzy didn't suit him.

He'd meant it when he said he wouldn't let his twin brother down. He and Rudi had been given a huge responsibility: their very own FDJ chapter had been chosen to lead the student delegation at the dedication of the new memorial at Sachsenhausen concentration camp. They'd spent a month making banners and practicing a song to sing in front of Chairman Walter Ulbricht himself. Peter found all of this stomach-turning, but for Rudi's sake, he was determined to fake it.

They walked to school in the dark. "If everything goes right, this could be a huge deal for me," Rudi said, an extra spring in his step. "For us. The chapter, I mean."

"So you've got things ready?"

"I made something like eight checklists."

"Of course you did." Peter may have had the charisma, but Rudi always had the clipboard. "What would I do without you?"

"We can't afford to drop the ball on this one. Unlike some brothers I know, I actually have to *try* to make the grade."

This was undeniably true. Peter was one of *those* kids, the ones who show up to class—saunter in, really—take a page of notes and that's that. The ones who never have to study, never break a sweat over a test, and ace it. Peter's memory wasn't exactly photographic, but he retained almost everything. It made memorizing monologues fairly effortless. Rudi, on the other hand, fretted and stayed up until all hours poring over his textbooks.

"All right, so what do we need to know about all this?" Peter asked.

"Be really focused—don't be sloppy about the pledge or the salute. You always rush, and it looks like your arm is made of jelly. Precision. We have to have precision." He stopped in front of Peter and adjusted his brother's neckerchief.

"Do you feel weird going to a place like this?" asked Peter.

"You mean a concentration camp?"

"Yes. Doesn't it creep you out? All those people who died there."

"No way. It's inspiring. Those people were heroes."

They turned the corner, and Peter looked up as the sunrise peeked over the school building.

They brought the flags and banners from the youth room and loaded them onto the waiting bus. Teachers brought out boxes of bagged lunches and slid them into the back of the bus while the other students filed on board. The twins found a seat together at the front, and they rumbled off to Sachsenhausen in a cloud of diesel.

The bus from Polytechnic Oberschule 5 pulled up to the whitewashed gatehouse of the camp, and the delegation spilled out. The students slid the banners out of the back of the bus, and a Party official showed them to their position in the parade. Peter did the glad-handing while Rudi gave commands, oblivious to the shuffles and moans of his classmates and the rolling of their eyes.

Peter had to admit, they all looked terribly smart in their blue uniform shirts in the brightening sunshine. Rudi handed him a rolled-up banner. Peter untied it, and the words *In the Spirit of Anti-Fascist Resistance Fighters* unfurled in the light breeze. Despite his cynicism, a pre-performance thrill swelled in his chest.

"Can you believe it?" Rudi mused. "Before we were born, the Nazis held thousands of Communists here as prisoners. And now here we are, the *next* generation of anti-fascists. Don't you feel like you could change the world, Peter? Don't you?"

Peter was distracted by a line of men marching solemnly past, wearing the blue-and-white-striped uniforms of their former captivity. Some of them had tears rolling down their cheeks, but they held their heads high as they walked through the iron gates welded with the words *ARBEIT MACHT FREI*.

Through two lines of helmeted People's Army soldiers standing at attention, the students processed toward a massive monolith emblazoned with red triangles. At the base of the monument stood a dais lined with flags of every Communist nation, united against the fascism of the past. Thousands were gathered under banners proclaiming:

Our Struggle Against War and Fascism Continues

Peace Will Always Come from East Germany

Down with the War Criminals in Bonn

Bulwark Against the Spirit of Nazism in West Germany

The West German delegation got the point. The East Germans constantly accused the West of carrying on the legacy of Nazism. The East German nation felt assured of its triumph, confident that in Communism it had been handed the key to defeating evil itself and that not one former Nazi remained within its borders.

Peter's flock of students arrived at the dais, close enough to see and hear Chairman Ulbricht, just as Rudi had hoped. But his earlier thrill had passed. Peter was bored. He fidgeted with the tassel on his banner, and Rudi corrected him with a sharp look as the crowd hushed and the chairman began to speak. His voice was unusually high and soft, echoing back in shrill waves.

Peter turned away and caught his brother staring at the new girl.

"I wish I had my Leica," Rudi whispered. "Why did I leave it on the bus?"

"You can always take her picture—I mean, you can always cut out newspaper clippings later," Peter teased.

"You know what? We should make a scrapbook. Between Gagarin and Sachsenhausen, it's turning out to be an eventful year."

The speeches were endless and intolerable. Every word of Ulbricht's high-pitched oratory rang with hubris. The language was so predictable that Peter could have pulled the words from a hat. He couldn't shake his jittery impatience with the buzzing crowd, the cold sun and the chill wind, the dissonance of triumphal language in this place of mass murder.

Peter wasn't used to death. He'd only ever been to one funeral before, at a church in West Berlin. That had felt proper somehow, with the bowed heads and mumbled prayer, the *ashes to ashes* and the *dust to dust.* But here at Sachsenhausen, the colorful banners, the speeches and the marching band made it feel more like a rally than a memorial. In the sunshine, the people around Peter transformed into apparitions, hollowed out and translucent. The former prisoners sat behind Ulbricht in their tattered striped camp uniforms, but Peter felt as though all the inhumanity and death had happened in another country. And according to the Party, it had: *that* country was *West* Germany, where the old Nazi guard continued, pushing forward their priorities to this day.

Peter's eyes drifted to the monolith, rising like a smokestack behind the dais. Ulbricht spoke of the heroes who'd died there:

". . . murdered only because they loved their people, because they loved freedom, peace and democracy more than their own lives, because they were Socialists . . ."

Is that why they were murdered? thought Peter. *Is that really why?*

The survivors on the platform shifted uncomfortably, chewing their lips, looking down at their hands in their laps. Ulbricht invoked heroes and martyrs and the war on *Antifaschismus,* but Peter waited for him to utter, for example, the word *Jews,* feeling the hollow of the word in his mouth, as though as soon as the leader said the word, it would fit into that waiting space like a puzzle piece. But that was one word the chairman did not utter. Apparently, in the horrors of the war in Germany, Jews didn't count.

After the students sang the *Weltjugendlied*, Chairman Ulbricht led the crowd in polite applause, and the marching band struck up a chord to end the ceremony. Peter gave a signal, and the student delegation parted to allow the dignitaries to descend the dais and pass through. Ulbricht paused as a marching band filed in front, close enough for Peter to smell an acrid odor coming off the chairman's suit, to see the close shave on his jawline coming right up to the Leninesque goatee on his chin.

Peter forgot all about Rudi's plea for him to focus. He stared directly at Ulbricht, his brow knit in confusion. The chairman reached out and shook Peter's hand. He was a surprisingly small man.

"*Für Frieden und Freiheit,*" said Walter Ulbricht. Rudi eagerly reached out his hand as well, but the chairman had moved on to the next person.

"*Frieden und Freiheit . . .*"

"*Frieden und Freiheit . . .*"

"*Frieden und Freiheit . . .*"

The procession seemed endless. Peter lost track of the minutes or maybe the hour it took for the camp to empty out. At last, thanks to a hard nudge from Rudi, he woke up. His knees were locked, and he shook his legs, earning a look of disdain from his twin brother. The FDJ delegation was the last to leave through the gate, through the avenue flanked by armed military personnel. As they crossed the threshold, Peter looked back at the monolith, embellished at the top with inverted red triangles memorializing the fallen Communist heroes.

It's not right, he thought as the bus pulled away. *I don't know why, but it isn't right.*

Dinner that night was an Oma special: not the typical dried soup but the kind from a can. Ilse was late getting home from work, as usual. They ate in silence. Peter stared blankly at a grimy painting hanging askew on the wall.

"How was the dedication?" asked Rudolf, breaking the silence.

"Great!" answered Rudi. "You should have seen it, Vati. What a crowd! All these leaders from all over the world . . . the banners, the music . . . and we were right up in front. It was amazing."

"I listened on the radio," Rudolf responded. "Were there really two hundred thousand people there?"

"*Ja,* and every single one of them had to leave before we could," Peter chortled.

"Peter," said Oma.

"Omi," Peter replied, slurping his soup.

"Don't slurp your soup."

"*Jawohl.*"

Rudolf and Oma chatted about the news, and Rudi leaned over and whispered to Peter, "Did you see her?"

"Who?" Peter picked up his bowl and drank.

"The new girl."

"Um . . . wide eyes, long curly hair?"

"Yes. We're supposed to introduce her at the assembly tomorrow. Do you . . . mind if I do it?"

Peter perked up. "Mmm, I see," he said. "Rudi has a love interest."

"Who has a love interest?" Oma interjected with her spoon in midair.

"This is really great soup, Omi," Rudi deflected. "Tell the truth— it's from scratch, isn't it?"

"That won't work on me, *Junge*," said Oma. "A teenage boy with a crush is visible from outer space."

RUDI

The auditorium at Polytechnic Oberschule 5 echoed with the flipping up of two hundred wooden folding seats. The dull room was brightened by the blue shirts of the older FDJ kids and the white shirts of the Young Pioneers. It was time for the monthly meeting of the *Freie Deutsche Jugend*. With thumb to forehead and hand straight like a shark's fin, everyone saluted the framed photograph of Chairman Ulbricht that hung above the stage. Peter led the pledge: *"Für Frieden und Sozialismus seid bereit!"*

And the entire auditorium responded: *"Immer bereit!"*

"We will now sing *The Song of the Party*," Rudi announced. A girl sat at the piano and played the opening measures, and the students sang, some lustily, some barely mouthing the words.

> *The Party, the Party, she is always right*
> *And, comrades, don't give up on her!*
> *If you fight for what's right, you are always right!*
> *Against lies and oppression we rise.*

The next part was only for the girls:

> *Whoever offends life is bad—and not too bright!*
> *To defend humankind is always right.*

The poetry wasn't exactly Pushkin, but at least the melody was rousing.

The opening festivities now concluded, Peter read a letter from the Volkskammer, thanking the Sachsenhausen delegation for bearing witness to the heroes and martyrs of the past and being the hope of the future of their Socialist state.

"And now," Peter announced, "my brother, Rudi, would like to introduce our new comrade."

The supervising teacher handed Rudi a paper as he came to the podium, feeling his cheeks flush. He was an easy blusher who never left anyone in doubt of his feelings. "This new comrade is from Leipzig," Rudi said. "She was a delegate to the World Festival of Youth and Students two years ago. Angelika Rosen, would you please stand and say hello?"

The new girl rose like Aphrodite being born from sea foam. *Angelika.* The name suited her. *Angelika of the cascading brown curls.* She wasn't just pretty—she hurt Rudi's eyes. Her brown eyes were wide as searchlights. She smiled—and what a dignified mouth. Rudi wanted to know that mouth intimately.

"Please give her a warm welcome," Rudi resumed, "and let's all help Comrade Rosen get acquainted." He yielded the podium to his brother and surreptitiously popped a mint.

Their official business concluded, Peter dismissed the Young Pioneers, and they filed out to their classroom to do crafts and learn kid songs. Rudi didn't waste any time. He pushed through the crowd as he ate a second mint, making sure it coated every surface in his mouth. He'd been looking for a reason to meet Angelika for days, and now was his chance. This FDJ chapter was his domain, and Rudi could show her the ropes. She would need a reliable guide to protect her from newbie mistakes.

Angelika stood among a growing group of girls, who instantly started chatting with her.

He tapped her on the shoulder. "Angelika?"

The other girls looked Rudi up and down derisively, but Angelika turned and gave him a friendly look.

"*Freundschaft,*" she greeted him.

"*Freundschaft,*" he managed. "I'm Rudi—I'm the one who introduced you up there. Since you're new, I can help you get comfortable . . . you know, show you around sometime."

"Thanks." She smiled. "That's nice of you, Rudi."

"Everyone at school belongs to the FDJ," he blurted. "Well, not everyone. The Christians and pacifists, they do their own thing. They say it's conscience, but I don't know what the big deal is. It's all right. No one's forcing them. Those kids don't want to go to university, anyway. They like the grunt jobs. Oh well, it's their choice, right . . . ?"

Rudi could tell he was talking too much. He did that when he got nervous. Angelika didn't get another word out before the other girls took her by the arm and whisked her away in a cloud of giggles. The kids receded until he was the last one in the assembly hall—but he thought he heard Angelika say, "I think he's sweet."

Peter strolled into the bedroom that afternoon and dropped his bag on the floor. "Well, that was easy," he said, beaming.

"What was?" Rudi inquired.

"I went by the theater and got an audition slot!"

"When did you do that?"

"You didn't see me duck out after the dismissal?" Peter took off his blue FDJ shirt and black shorts and tossed them on the end of his bed.

"Isn't the leader supposed to be the last to leave?" asked Rudi.

"You can't wait around for life to happen, Rudi," he said, pulling a clean shirt from the wardrobe. "You have to reach into the air and grab it before it's gone."

Rudi and Peter were six years old when they joined the Thälmann Young Pioneers at their grammar school, squirming in their seats at the new-student orientation as the leader, in full uniform, told the children all about the adventures, the songs, the *fun* they were going to have. They couldn't wait to start.

But Rudolf had not been as excited as his sons.

"Oh, don't be so rigid, Rudolf," Ilse had protested in a whisper. "Like they say, *Vorwärts für den Frieden!* You heard the young man; this is for peace! Besides, do you want your children to be the only ones who aren't in the club? They'll feel so left out."

"There's just something about kids and politics that doesn't mix, Ilse. Don't you remember when we did it? It's too similar. I don't want to see my sons in government uniforms, making salutes. No matter what it stands for."

"Why would you ruin it for your children over something abstract? They'll get bullied, Rudolf. Especially Rudi. He's sensitive, you know. It's the rest of us who would pay for your so-called conscience. You don't want that for us, do you?"

"No, of course not," he'd sighed, and reluctantly signed the permission forms.

That week Ilse had tried to scrape together the money to buy the boys' uniforms, but they were just shy of the full amount. They had to buy *two* of everything, after all. The boys would have to start with merely the red triangular neckerchiefs. Rudi and Peter competed to see who could tie theirs faster—knotted properly, Rudi made sure.

Their teacher had sent a discreet letter home, offering them his kids' Pioneer hand-me-downs, but in this one instance, Ilse's pride wouldn't let her accept secondhand goods. She bought one piece of paraphernalia at a time, and Rudi and Peter were excited when they could show up with a new cap or belt or camp mess kit.

There was *always* an event for the Pioneers. Monthly meetings, service projects, recitations, enrichments, field trips, camping weekends—Rudolf usually found an excuse not to go, but every time the boys put on their uniforms, Ilse gleefully snapped their photo.

"Say *twins against the world*!" she prompted them.

"*Twins against the world,*" they parroted, and another photograph went into the scrapbook.

Now that he'd breached the wall of awkwardness, Rudi started seeing Angelika everywhere. In the hallways. In morning assembly. He worked up the nerve to speak to Angelika again a couple of days later between classes.

"Angelika!" he called. "Uh . . . *Freundschaft!* Do you remember me? Rudi. Möser-Fleischmann. Would you like a mint? I mean, not that you need one . . . uh . . ."

"Oh, hello, Rudi . . . sure," she replied, taking one from the tin. She looked nervously at the horsey girl next to her, who was somehow capable of smiling and frowning at the same time.

"How are you getting on?" Rudi asked. "You know, with the new school and everything?"

"It's been fine. A little different from my old school, but the kids are nice."

"I'm nice," he blurted. "I mean, you're nice. I mean, I'll be nice to you."

Angelika and the other girl laughed. "I'm sure you will, Rudi. Is there something you . . . want?"

He braced himself. "I want . . . yes . . . I want to ask you to have a milkshake. With me."

"All right," she said.

"Bitte?"

"I said yes, Rudi. I'll go out for a milkshake with you. Today?"

"Today. Yes! How about at the Eisberg Milchbar? The one by the bridge?"

"Sure. I'll see you after school."

Rudi's every muscle was alive and twitching. He floated down the hall, like a tram connected to an overhead wire. He shook himself out of it. Rudi was a walking smile.

Angelika said yes. Milkshakes with Angelika. That is a very, very good development. Today is a very good day.

He wasn't sure how he'd be able to wait through the rest of the school day, but somehow he did, though he retained nothing of his lessons. Every minute lasted an hour.

Rudi, unlike his twin brother, had only ever kissed one girl, back at a rally when he was thirteen. He didn't even know her name until afterward—*Julia.* She and Rudi had stared at one another all day long, across the spring fields, the dining hall, the classrooms. Later that night at the bonfire, he'd sat next to Julia on a log and was bold enough to kiss her without even saying hello. He did it like he had seen Cary Grant do to Ingrid Bergman in *Notorious,* fast and unapologetic. But as soon as their lips made contact, she pulled away, shot up and excused herself to rejoin her girlfriends.

And immediately they were all looking at him and laughing.

Rudi realized with horror that he had bratwurst breath, and there was no recovering from that. He had never tried again, not with any girl. But hoping against hope, he started to carry a tin of mints, just in case he stumbled into a lucky moment. He studied movie kisses like calculus because he never knew when he might have a chance to redeem himself.

Finally school ended, and Rudi practically skipped to the Eisberg Milchbar. He got a table outside, with an umbrella to shade against the late-spring sun. He asked the waiter to wipe down the table and chairs, and then Rudi wiped them down again with a napkin.

He chain-popped mints while he waited. The horror of his mishap with Julia could *never* repeat itself. He vowed that he would never again suffer that fate on such a preventable premise.

"Hi, Rudi," said a voice like wind chimes.

He looked up and saw Angelika. Her eyes were the deep brown of a forest pool in one of his mother's stories. *You are so damn pretty,* he almost said out loud.

"Hi," he said, barely. "Have a seat."

Rudi got up and pulled the chair out for her, trying to channel every electron of masculinity he possessed into this moment. He handed Angelika a paper menu printed with penguins and icebergs and other Arctic icons.

"My treat," he offered. "Anything you want."

"Thank you, Rudi, that's very nice," she said, and looked down at the menu with a subtle smile.

A small, meek waitress came and took their order. They recognized her as another student from school, and the three of them shared the awkwardness of it. Rudi and Angelika both ordered the same thing: vanilla milkshakes with strawberry syrup and chocolate cookie crumbs.

"So, how do you like POS 5?" asked Rudi.

"It's fine." She smiled. "It's school. I guess I'd rather be doing anything else."

"Well, what do you like to do—for fun, I mean?"

"Back in Leipzig I played football, went out with my friends, the usual. How about you? I guess you like photography?"

Rudi lifted the camera he wore around his neck and put it in his book bag. "Forgot to take this off!"

"Maybe you could show me your pictures sometime."

"Oh, I'm just an amateur." Rudi's hands began to sweat.

"I'm sure they're beautiful."

"What else do you like to do?" Rudi deflected.

"I like going to movies."

"I do, too. . . . Oh, and baking!"

"You bake?" Angelika giggled. "I don't know any boys who bake."

"A lot of famous bakers are men, you know."

"OK, Rudi. What do you like to make?"

"I'm best at butter cookies, but I'm always trying to perfect my strudel." The waitress returned with their milkshakes.

"Oh, I *love* walnut strudel," said Angelika, wide-eyed. She sipped her shake.

"Walnut. Duly noted. Maybe I'll make it for you sometime." Rudi swirled his straw, wondering if that was too forward. "So . . . you went to the World Youth Festival?"

"Yes, in Vienna. It was amazing. People came from all over the world. Do you like to travel?"

"I've never been very far outside Berlin," he said. "Oh, well, we went camping near the Black Sea once. That was fun."

"Where would you go, if you could?"

"Maybe to Russia, I guess."

"Of course you'd say that," Angelika chuckled. "All the good Party boys want to go to Moscow."

"Why, where would you go?"

Angelika didn't miss a beat. "Israel."

Rudi didn't let his disapproval show. "Israel? Why would you want to go there? It's a settler colonial—"

"Let's say it's an ancient dream."

"Are you—you're not—"

"I'm Jewish. Are you surprised?"

"I've . . . never met anyone who's Jewish before." The realization confused him. In school they talked a lot about defeating *Antisemitismus*, but in a big city like Berlin, it seemed strange that this was his first Jewish acquaintance. "Why did you leave Leipzig?"

"We had to move," she said. "My father changed jobs."

"Oh? What does he do?"

"He . . . manages a building," she said. "What about yours?"

"Piano tuner. My mother's a telephone operator. What about your mother?"

"Dead. Cancer. In Moscow, actually."

"Oh."

They stirred their milkshakes with their straws. This was going south quickly. Rudi sank a little in his chair.

Suddenly Angelika leaned in and looked him right in the eye. "Rudi, look, you're cute, and awkward, and I like that. So we can just go out sometimes, OK? It doesn't have to be a big deal. Just ask me out again." She took a long last sip, kissed him on the cheek and waved goodbye.

"Sure," said Rudi, waving back, the feeling of her lips lingering on his cheek. "No big deal." And then he died and melted into his milkshake.

Berlin stood open and creased into four awkward sectors, like a map that can't be folded back up into a neat package. The city was a scale model of the world's empires: British, American, Soviet, with a French footnote, coalescing like cardinal points around a new magnetic pole.

The British and French empires were waning, and the American and Soviet ones ascending as the only two that mattered. Sixteen years before, they had cooperated in defeating Hitler's manic project of domination through slaughter. Now they competed for dominance by amassing troves of nuclear weapons, putting Hitler's darkest ambitions to shame.

Both empires—Soviet and American—were founded, for the first time in human history, not on groups of people but on ideas. It was 1961, and Berlin was the gateway between these two opposing worlds.

School let out on Friday, and Rudi and Peter saw their father waiting out front. Rudi smiled and waved goodbye to Angelika while Peter cheerfully strolled over to Rudolf.

"Hey, Vati," Peter greeted him. "Off work already?"

"My afternoon tuning was canceled," said Rudolf. "I thought we could go to Der Spinner. I'm meeting a friend there."

"Great! I've been wanting to look at some Elvis records."

"I wish I could," said Rudi. "I have a math test tomorrow."

"So?" Peter shrugged. "Study later."

"You know that doesn't work for me, Peter."

"Come on, Rudi. I'll quiz you on the way."

"Fine, fine, I'll go."

"Do you have money with you?" asked their father.

"A little," said Rudi sheepishly. "I might save it for the bakery, though."

"I like the sound of that!" said Peter.

The afternoon was still warming up when Rudolf, Peter and Rudi crossed the river on Oberbaum Bridge into the neighborhood of Kreuzberg. They walked in the dim cool of the covered bridge's brick-arched corridor, trading short, sharp hoots to hear their voices bounce around. Passing bicyclists rang their handlebar bells to hear the echoes as well.

They turned up Skalitzerstrasse and walked along the elevated road until they came to a redbrick church. Across the street was their favorite record shop. Der Spinner. It took up the whole block and drew kids like a magnet from all over Berlin. The front window gleamed with metallic decorations, new releases and posters of famous bands.

"Peter! Rudi!" shouted the owner as they pushed into the crowded shop. How Tobias managed to remember the name of everyone who walked into his shop was a marvel. "Go over to the American section—I just got more Motown albums in. You've got to check them out. And, Herr Möser—"

"Rudolf, *bitte!*"

"Rudolf, there's a new recording of Chopin nocturnes, over there on the wall display."

"*Danke,* Tobias." Rudolf excused himself and went straight to the classical section.

Listening stations with headphones were dotted throughout the store, and one had an enclosed booth for a total audiophile experience. In the after-school hours, the demand for a spot at a listening station was intense. Etiquette required that a customer play no more than half a song, then yield to the next person, but one couple was hogging the booth, less for the music than the excuse to squeeze together.

The boys passed the displays of new turntables in glossy wooden cabinets and joined the horde of other teens thumbing through the stacks of vinyl records. Of course, everyone was crowded around the Elvis collection, chattering and checking each other out. Rudi knew the girls would look right past him to his brother, so he escaped the crowd, went over to *Jazz* and put his head down into the rack of John Coltrane singles.

"Coltrane, huh?" said a voice beside Rudi, in English. "Good taste."

"Natürlich," Rudi said with a nod. He noticed the green military uniform, but the first thing he'd noticed was that the man was Black. In all his fifteen years, Rudi had never seen a Black person up close.

"American?" he asked, trying not to stare.

"As apple pie."

Rudi didn't know what apple pie had to do with America. He must have misheard—after all, his Russian was better than his English.

"Why aren't you over there with your pals," said the soldier, "in the rock 'n' roll stacks?"

"I am sorry, sir, my English is not very good. Can you repeat?"

"I meant I'm surprised to see a kid your age browsing jazz."

"Ah! Jazz is my favorite!"

"No kidding? Who do you like?"

"John Coltrane, Miles Davis . . . and old musicians, like Duke Ellington," said Rudi.

"Old!" The soldier laughed indignantly. "That's what I listened to when I was your age. Wouldn't call it *old*."

"I am . . . sorry," said Rudi.

The soldier smiled. "Don't worry about it," he said. "This music keeps you young. Do you know this album?" He pulled out a record with a brightly painted cover: *Mingus Ah Um.*

"No, I don't," said Rudi.

"Well, let's give it a listen," he said. There happened to be a listening station next to them that the rock 'n' roll kids hadn't commandeered. The soldier cued up the needle and handed Rudi the headphones.

The band built from bass to piano to trombone, and before he knew it, Rudi was in the groove, looking at the soldier and smiling. The energy made him think of riding the S-Bahn through the city, watching buildings shimmering in the sun as they went by. He slid a headphone off one ear. "I like it!" he said.

"Excellent," said the soldier. "My name's Charles."

"I am Rudi," he returned.

"Nice to meet you, Rudi." They shook hands as Rudolf approached.

"Ah! I see you already met my friend!" said Rudi's father.

"Rudolf!" said Charles. "This is your boy?"

"Yes, and here comes my other one."

Peter joined them, the girls' eyes still trailing him. "I got what I came for," he told Rudi, holding up a brown paper bag. He slid out the Elvis single, then saw that he'd interrupted a conversation. *"Entschuldigung,"* he said. "Excuse me."

Rudolf introduced them. *"Peter, Rudi, das ist Charles, mein amerikanischer Freund."*

"I speak English, Vati," Peter chided. "Hi, Charles, I'm Peter."

"Pleasure."

"We're going to the bakery," said Peter. "Do you want to come?"

"Sure!" said Charles. "Can't beat recommendations from the locals. Let me settle up first, though." Charles paid for his records, and they filed through the swarm of kids out of Der Spinner.

"Herr Charles, with you, we can practice speaking English?" Rudi bumbled.

"Sure, if I can practice *sprech*ing my *Deutsch*!" Charles laughed, and the others did, too.

Around the corner, Rudi, Peter, Rudolf and Charles pushed into Bäckerei Antoinette, jingling the bells on the front door as a baker carried a tray of sweet cheese balls from the kitchen and slid it into the display behind the counter. Hundreds of warm golden spheres were nestled close enough together that they wouldn't roll around but not so close that they'd be crushed. One by one—or dozen by dozen—they'd be gone by evening.

Laborers and businessmen came in for afternoon coffee pick-me-ups. Kindergartners swung their legs on the chairs, waiting for their grandmothers to dole out treats. Clusters of loud teenagers packed tightly into a corner table, the girls sneaking looks at Peter while Rudi tried with all his might to maintain his composure.

"I will get that table over there," said Rudolf. He went to put his valise down on a chair, then rejoined Charles and the boys at the counter.

"I'll take four of"—Charles turned to Rudi, pointing to the tray the baker had just shelved—"what do you call those? They look good."

"Oh, they are *Quarkbällchen*," Rudi replied.

"*Kwak-bale* . . . ," Charles managed, laughing. "What you said. What's inside? I don't like those jelly ones, the . . . Berliners." He laughed again. "I mean, I like *you* all, *you* Berliners. Just not the *jelly doughnut* Berliners."

"It is made with . . . *Käse*?" Rudi turned to Peter for help with the translation.

"Cheese," said Peter. "Quark . . . it's bumpy, you know? Soft?"

"Oh, like cottage cheese," said Charles. "But it's sweet, right?"

"Yes. They are very good." Rudi beamed. "Delicious."

"How do you say *delicious*?" Charles asked.

"*Lecker,*" said Rudolf.

The boys and Charles pulled out their billfolds, but Rudolf paid the cashier for all four of their orders. Charles thanked him and popped a whole quark ball in his mouth. "*Leckah,*" said the soldier, reaching over the pastry case to thank the baker, who wiped the pastry residue on his apron, then eagerly shook Charles's hand.

They sat at the table, savoring the fresh, warm pastries. There was something about Charles that drew Rudi in, like he'd known him his whole life, though there was an ocean between their worlds.

"So . . . Charles . . . ," Rudi attempted in English, "you are in the army?"

"I fought in the war," said Charles. "Now I work over at the sector border. Not much to do, to be honest."

"You've been here in Germany since the war?" Peter asked with astonishment.

"Oh, no. I reenlisted after my wife died. Something pulled me back into the service," said Charles. "I'm in the Military Police now, in the 385th. But back then I was in the 183rd. Helped with Buchenwald after they liberated the camp. Brutal." He dispassionately popped the last quark ball into his mouth, held up his hands and pointed to the napkin dispenser on the table. "But I'm sure your parents taught you all about that."

Rudi handed him some napkins and smiled nervously. He didn't know how to reply. One didn't mention these things in public. German history was spoken of in very precise terms, in very specific places.

"*Leckah. Danke,*" said Charles, pensively wiping his hands and mouth and mustache. "Mmm. It's like a beignet. Ever have a beignet?"

The boys shook their heads.

"They're from Louisiana. By way of France, I suppose. But a doughnut's a doughnut in the end, isn't that right?"

"Yes, I think so," said Rudi. He hoped he was understanding English, but he had to translate every word in his spinning head first.

"Kwak-bales," Charles attempted, "beignets, zeppoles, churros, sopaipillas—any kind of fried dough, I've tried them all over the world, courtesy of the United States Army. And I know how to make them all pretty well, too."

"Really? You bake?" Rudi was excited to meet someone who shared his appreciation for baking.

"Sure! Learned from my dad. The best baker in the South. We always talked about opening a shop together, like this one. I still might go to culinary school. On the GI Bill, you know."

"Rudi bakes all the time," said Rudolf. "You should try his stollen! He bakes like an Oma!"

"*Ja,* you should see him in an apron!" laughed Peter.

Rudi's face flushed.

"That's a good idea, actually," said Rudolf. He tore a piece of brown paper from Peter's Der Spinner bag and wrote the address. "We live right over in Friedrichshain. Can you come for dinner . . . next Sunday?"

"That's awfully nice of you. Your wife won't mind?"

"Of course not," said Rudolf. "You're new to Berlin. We'll help you feel at home."

"Tell you what," said Charles, rising to resume his shift at the sector border, "I'll bring dessert. Beignets? No, on second thought, can't fry much in my little kitchen—makes the place stink." He pondered, then snapped his fingers. "Profiteroles, yeah. I'll make profiteroles. You can tell me what you think, Rudi."

"All right, I will make something good also," said Rudi.

"*Auf Wiedersehen,*" said Peter. "Nice meeting you, Charles."

"*Auf Wiedersehen* yourself," said Charles, shaking hands with them all. "See you next Sunday—*mit* doughnuts."

MAY

PETER

Rudolf came into the kitchen, hands in the pockets of his sport coat, and smiled over his sons. Rudi was busy putting the finishing touches on his Sunday afternoon stollen, and Peter was gathering the dishes. Oma was bustling about, trying to get the rest of dinner together for their guest, and Peter had to precisely choreograph his movements to keep out of her way. He got out the forks just in time to hear a knock at the door.

Rudolf answered it and welcomed his friend inside. Charles held a bakery box in one hand and a small bouquet of flowers in the other. A military-issue canvas satchel was slung over his shoulder. It was different seeing Charles in civilian clothes—a black leather jacket, black slacks and a pale green button-down. Without his army cap, a touch of gray showed in his hair.

"Hey, kid." Charles greeted Peter as Oma joined her great-grandson by the door. "And who is this beautiful young lady?" Charles handed her the flowers.

"Your friend has good taste in women," Oma said to Rudolf in thickly accented English. "He can stay."

"Charles," said Rudolf, "this is my grandmother—"

"Call me Oma," she said. "I'm everybody's grandma."

"Danke, Oma." Charles gave the matriarch a most charming smile and bow. "Your English is very good!"

"I watch a lot of television," she replied. She took Charles's jacket and hung it on the coat tree, drew the Karo cigarettes from her pocket and held them out to him. "Do you smoke?"

"No, ma'am. I quit after the war."

"Good for you. I'm too old to quit." She beckoned him into the living room, lit up with the owl lighter and clicked on the radio. The sound of RIAS and its English-speaking emcee rushed in. Something about a ticker-tape parade for an American named Alan Shepard and a space flight.

"Ha!" Charles exclaimed. "Did you hear about that? I guess we're not sleeping under Gagarin's Soviet moon after all."

Rudi smirked. "The Soviets will always be first," he said.

"Well, we'll see." Charles winked.

Just then Ilse emerged from the bedroom. She had barely made an appearance in days, but here she was, hair up and makeup done, looking as fresh and sunny in her flowered dress as though she'd been integral to the preparations all along. She halted almost imperceptibly when she saw Charles.

"My wife, Ilse," said Rudolf. "This is Charles, my friend from the army base." She smiled at Charles and took the bakery box from him.

"A pleasure, ma'am," said Charles. Ilse smiled curtly and turned to put the box in the kitchen.

Rudi emerged, wiping his hands on a dish towel. "Rudi!" Charles greeted him, pulling a record out of his satchel. "Thought you might like this."

"The Mingus record! *Vielen Dank*—thank you!" Rudi invited

Charles to look at their vinyl collection, and they put the Mingus on for dinner music.

"Meine Damen und Herren"—Oma beckoned, blowing a long plume of smoke—"dinner is served."

They all packed around the dining room table. The Möser-Fleischmanns never had people over for dinner. Ilse's parties, with their music and booze, could put an illusory gloss over their lives, but a gathering this intimate couldn't mask a thing.

Oma passed around boiled sausages, boiled sauerkraut, boiled carrots and mustard.

"It's been months since I've had a home-cooked meal," Charles gushed. "This is real grandma cooking, that's for sure."

Everyone tried to hide their smiles. Oma's food was not fine cuisine—almost everything was reconstituted from a packet or spooned from a jar. But Oma took the compliment.

"Very kind of you, Charles," she said, spreading mustard on a bite of sausage. "How did you and Rudolf meet?"

"Rudolf came to the army base to tune our piano, and we hit it off. Then I met the boys at the record shop. Are you a music aficionado, too, Oma?"

"I have always enjoyed my grandson's playing," said Oma.

Ilse barely spoke. She watched the conversation go on, eating slowly, observing but not contributing.

"Do any of you play instruments?" They all shook their heads. "Ah, the shoemaker's children have no shoes." Charles pointed at Rudolf with his fork. "What do you like to play, Rudolf? I only heard that bit you played at the base."

"Klassische Musik," Rudolf replied, *"und auch Jazz."*

Charles looked at Rudi. "That must be where you get it from."

"Und Sie?" Rudi asked. "Do you play an instrument, Charles?"

"Ha, no, but I play the radio pretty well," said Charles. "And the record player, too!"

Ilse smiled politely as Rudi translated for her. She cleared the table, went to the kitchen and returned with the box of Charles's pastries and Rudi's stollen.

"Now, before we open that, I do have to apologize," said Charles. "I was going to do my baking, but I was called on duty, so I had to pick it up at the bakery instead. But it should be pretty good."

Ilse poured the coffee as the family passed around the desserts. Charles praised Rudi's stollen, and everyone agreed that the store-bought pastries were fine, but they couldn't wait to try Charles's homemade ones next time.

"Have any of you ever heard of Mahalia Jackson?" asked Charles, tucking into his second piece of cake.

"No, I . . . I don't think so," said Peter.

"Gospel music?" Charles sipped his coffee.

"Gospel . . . in a church?" Rudi looked at Peter and shrugged. "I've never been to church—only on school trips."

"They probably don't sing this kind in churches around— Wait, did I just hear you say you've never *been* to church? Didn't you ever take them, Oma? Help me out. . . ."

"Here in paradise," said Oma, "we don't need religion, so they tell us."

"Well, kids, we've got to remedy that. Mahalia's doing a European tour. You're all going to have to come. This Saturday!"

"But we have school . . . ," Rudi demurred.

"School on Saturday? What kind of country is this? Call in sick! Rudolf, get someone to cover for you. We'll get the train to Hamburg, make a day of it."

Ilse spoke for the first time. "Hamburg! You are not taking my children to *Hamburg*," she huffed in English. "We don't even know you!"

"Ilse, I'll be with them," said Rudolf, switching their conversation to German.

"It doesn't matter. *Hamburg?* It's a town of whores!"

Peter could almost *hear* Oma biting her tongue.

"Ilse, you're embarrassing our guest. Let's talk about this later!"

A volley of quippy German ensued between Rudolf and Ilse, including some pointed words referring to Charles that he must have recognized. He looked down at his coffee cup and swirled it around.

Peter was mortified by his mother's words. He tried to speak to Charles underneath his parents' sufficiently loud conversation. "I'm sorry," Peter told Charles, sotto voce.

"I understand, Peter. People are who they are."

The argument ended abruptly, and Ilse rose from the table. "Do what you want. No one cares what I think anyway." She cleared her place without further comment and retreated to her room once again.

There was an uncomfortable quiet in the apartment. A dog barked outside, and a siren came and went.

"Please excuse my wife," Rudolf said at last.

"Well," said Charles. "I'm not everyone's favorite flavor. I hoped it would be different. At least I know up front where I stand."

"I really want to go with you," Peter apologized. "But I'm getting ready for a big audition."

"Break a leg, young man," he said. "What about you, Oma?"

"These old bones are not getting on a Hamburg train, *Liebschen*, I'm sorry," said Oma.

Rudi spoke at last. "Vati . . . can we go? You and me?"

Rudolf mulled it over and glanced at the bedroom door. "Why not?"

"I don't want to put a wedge in your family, Rudolf."

Oma slurped her coffee. "We have other wedges, don't worry."

"All right, then. If you're sure. I'll look for you two Saturday morning at seven, bright and early, at the main station," he said. "I'll get the tickets. And, Rudi?"

"Yes?"

He winked and leaned back in his chair. "I'll bring *homemade* snacks this time."

RUDI

"*Guten Morgen!*" said Rudolf as he and Rudi met Charles in front of the Hauptbahnhof.

"Good morning, kind sirs," said Charles, and they all shook hands.

Rudi hoped no one from school would pass by and turn him in for Saturday truancy. He'd brought little with him but the camera around his neck and his tan jacket.

"Smart that you brought one, too." Charles pointed to Rudi's jacket. "It's warming up now, but it gets cold up north at night." He held out a bakery box to Rudi. "Look, I brought breakfast, as promised."

Rudi opened the lid, and a tantalizing smell arose. A grid of perfect golden profiteroles lay tucked together like sleeping babies. He looked up and smiled. "Homemade?"

"My specialty. Well, one of many! Let's save them for the train. We'll get coffee on board."

They went straight to their gate. Charles had already bought their tickets.

"*Bitte*, Charles, let me pay you," said Rudolf.

"Oh, no you don't," Charles replied. "You don't pay for church. The glory is free."

They boarded the train and chose seats with a table between them. The announcer called, *"This is the train to Hamburg, making all stops . . . with connections to Hannover. . . ."*

"You know your way around better than I do," said Rudolf.

"Well, I got around a lot during the war," said Charles. "It's different now, obviously. I didn't expect to like Germany so much. I'm thinking about staying once my service is done, maybe doing pastry school. It's ironic, but there might be less trouble here for someone like me than there is back home."

"Someone like you?" asked Rudi. "What trouble do you mean?"

"Well, in case you haven't noticed, Rudi, *I'm Black.*" He gave a stifled laugh and tipped his head back against his seat. The train pulled away from the platform.

"I noticed," said Rudi.

"I'll bet you did. Bet your mother did, too, the other night."

Rudi didn't know what to say as his mind glitched between English and German. His mother wasn't a bad person. He'd never seen her interact with a Black person before, but that wasn't unusual for Berlin, where the only non-Germans tended to be soldiers, and her generation kept their distance. Rudi shrugged off his discomfort and held up his camera.

"I am a photographer," he said. "I notice everything."

"Fair enough." Charles smiled and looked out the window. "Isn't it funny? Only sixteen years ago, this country of yours was exterminating anyone 'non-Aryan.' And now—most of the time, at least—I feel more at ease here than in my own country. Tell me, Rudolf, where'd all those Nazis go, anyway? They still around?"

"Oh, no, not where we live," Rudi interjected. "They're all in the West."

"Well, how about that." Charles looked thoughtfully at him for a moment, smiled, then excused himself. "I'll go get us some coffee."

Charles came back clutching three cups and placed them on the table, then took a pile of napkins out of his pocket. He opened the pastry box and gestured to his companions. *"Bitte."*

Rudi obliged and took a big bite, powdered sugar poofing onto his shirt. He chuckled at himself, embarrassed, but his eyes went wide at the taste. He made faces of delight at Charles as he chewed.

Rudolf helped himself, too. "Charles, damn, these are good!"

"I'm glad you like them. So, Rudi, who's older, you or Peter?"

"My brother and I are twins."

"You're kidding! Me too!"

"You are also a twin?" Rudolf asked.

"My sister. She's a school principal in Boston. Man, you stumped me, though! I can usually tell twins right away, identical or fraternal. You're pretty different. Tell me more about Peter."

"Hmm." Rudi took another bite. "He is perfect."

"That's not something brothers usually say."

"Well, he's smart and funny—very funny, actually—and talented. He's an actor. Talented with girls, also."

"He's got it all, huh?"

"Ja." Rudi shrugged.

"It's all right," Charles sympathized. "My sister's pretty perfect, too. Now that we're older, I *mostly* love her." He laughed, and Rudi relaxed in the ease of being understood.

The train pulled into the grand old station in Hamburg. They disembarked and strolled along the Lombard Bridge, dodging bicycles and dogs and children. Across the lake, stately, block-long buildings with verdigris roofs reflected in the water.

"You should see this lit up at night," said Charles. "It looks like a fairy tale."

"Yes, it does," said Rudolf. "I have been here many times."

"Oh?" said Charles.

"Yes, I came during the war myself. Maybe our paths—" He stopped himself. "Then again . . . I was so young."

They stopped by a *Brauhaus,* where Rudolf bought a picnic lunch of pretzels and wurst. They sat on a bench along the tree-lined street, shaded from the sun. After eating, they talked the rest of the way to the *Musikhalle,* taking in the sights. Rudolf and Charles remarked on what buildings remained or were newly built. At last it was time to go in and find their seats.

The concert hall was packed. Many Americans filled the hall. The atmosphere was expectant—everyone seemed to know they were in for something special. Charles struck up a conversation with a trio in army uniforms, and Rudi and his father made halting small talk while they browsed their programs.

The lights went down, and a formidable woman came onstage in a long satin gown with a fluffy corsage pinned to her chest. She took her place with poise and smiled as the piano began to roll. She started to sing—in a soft, matronly way—a song about smiling even when you're sad.

But all of a sudden, she burst:

> *Oh, be forgiving if someone abuse you*
> *For the good Lord looks for such . . .*

She reined her voice back in, and never stopped smiling. Her hair had come undone from its tight coif. Rudi saw a fire in this woman that reminded him of Oma when her wild love peeked out. It was a fierce kindness. Mahalia's voice, like Oma's wit, was a sword that she knew when to keep sheathed and when to draw for a fight.

Without pause, the pianist launched right into the next song, and Mahalia's voice exploded once again. It wasn't like the shrill, incendiary explosion of an Ulbricht speech, but the joyful exuberance of someone truly occupying herself, singing only what she knew.

Then sings my soul, my Savior God, to Thee . . .

Her soul really did sing, and it really did lift the entire music hall like a rocket. Rudi closed his eyes and saw the earth disappear from beneath his feet as stars came into view, and he could swear he saw Sputnik rotating past him as he rose and rose on the voice.

My SOUL!

Rudi didn't want to look at his father or Charles. He was afraid they would be able to see the chasm in his being. What good was singing about a soul when there was a shadow crouching at Rudi's feet, right there underneath the folding theater seat, waiting to snatch him and pull him into itself?

But he had to look, and he did look. Rudolf was leaning forward, his elbows on his knees, transfixed. Sneaking a glance in the half dark, Rudi saw a shimmer on Charles's cheek. He sat back with his legs crossed, and Rudi knew that this music, this joy, this pain, must have felt like a letter from home. For an hour they orbited Mahalia, and Rudi felt his spine grow straighter.

The lights went back up and they finally moved. "What *was* that?" Rudi asked.

"That, my young friend, was gospel music. You've had an audience with the queen."

Rudi couldn't speak. Neither could his father. They left the *Musikhalle* and wandered outside, breathing deeply.

"You're welcome," said Charles. "Next time we're at the record shop, we'll start your collection."

They made their way back to the train station, crossing the Lombard Bridge.

"It really does look like a fairy tale," said Rudi.

"Speaking of fairy tales," Charles prodded, "any girls on your horizon?"

"There's one."

"Special?"

"What can I say? She is an angel."

"Well, be good to her. That's all I can tell you. Time is not a thing to be wasted."

They caught their train and collapsed into their seats, exhausted and happy.

"Have you made good friends at the base, Charles?" Rudolf asked.

"Aww, I'm older than most of those kids. They're eighteen, twenty. Haven't even started life yet. I'm thirty-four, widowed. I can relate to them—it seems like just yesterday I was a private—but I can tell they don't want an old head like me around when they go out dancing. They're still fresh and vibrant. They haven't seen what I've seen. But it's all right. I have my own options. It's simply good to breathe the free air."

Rudi brought the negatives from the Lenin party and the concert to school on Monday and set up in the darkroom. He printed a contact sheet and looked at it through the loupe. The Leica from Uncle Martin truly was a superior camera to Rudi's old Prakti. These shots were really good—for one thing, they were in *focus,* and the camera's sensitivity made his photographs look better than they ever had.

He chose three images to enlarge and print full-sized: Oma by the window, the light across her face giving her the air of an ancient queen. Rudolf and Charles in front of the *Musikhalle,* toasting each other with bottles of sparkling *Apfelsaft.* The third image emerged from the chemical bath, coming through its gauzy veil to reveal a rare moment—his father and mother standing together. That was remarkable enough. They were having a conversation with their neighbor, Dr. Meier. He'd been telling a funny story about a patient, and Rudi's parents' eyes twinkled with laughter. True, they weren't happy together, but they were *together,* and they were *happy.*

Rudi stared at the photograph for a long time. He reflected on the dinner the week before, the argument between his parents and how awful and awkward it felt to see his mother through Charles's eyes.

He made a second copy of the picture, dodged and burned here and there to bring out the lights and darks, and pinned both prints on the line to drip-dry.

The next day he stopped by the darkroom after school, rolled up the dry prints, tied them with string and put them in his backpack. Just as he was coming out of the darkroom, he saw Angelika in the hallway. He instantly got warm all over. He was glad they were alone.

"Hi, Angelika!" He grinned.

"Rudi! Hi!" She kissed him on the cheek. "Were you in the darkroom?"

"I was just picking up some prints."

"Oh! Can I see?"

"Well . . . I don't usually show—"

"Come on, there's no one around. I won't be *too* judgmental!" Angelika winked at him.

"Really, maybe next time. I was heading home, though. Do you want to walk together?"

"All right."

Talking to her, being with her, lightened Rudi's heart with a cautious hope. Maybe his parents had felt like this once, young and fluttering, the world fading into the background. Maybe there were moments he didn't see, like the one in the photograph, of laying down their verbal weapons and even making truces. After all, they had gotten married in the first place. They must have loved each other at some point.

At the S-Bahn stop, Angelika squeezed his arm and kissed his cheek again to say goodbye. Rudi couldn't imagine anyone being deeper in love than he was.

He came home in a daze, put his book bag on the table and wandered around the apartment. He noticed a framed photo on the bookshelf, one he'd passed unnoticed for years: Rudolf and Ilse's wedding. It was in a dark-paneled room in some city building. Ilse looked much the same as she did now. Only the fashions were different, her flowered dress belted and flaring out like petals from the top of her pregnant waist. Her blond hair was long and curled under, forties-style. A justice of the peace stood before them, and on either side, a less gray but just as snarky-looking Oma and a younger and thinner Henni. Rudolf was putting the ring on her finger.

Of everyone in the photo, Rudolf had changed the most. He was war-toughened but thin, a teenager who didn't quite fill out an adult suit. Rudi recognized himself in his father, the shape of the chin, the eyebrows, the short stature.

The young Rudolf beamed at Ilse, in love to his core, the way

Rudi looked at Angelika. He imagined what it would feel like to hold her hand. Ilse's head bent down toward her newly ringed hand resting in Rudolf's. Her lips were only slightly upturned. Her eyes were closed.

Rudolf came out of his study, and Rudi turned around suddenly.

"*Abend,* Rudi," said his father. "What are you looking at?"

"Nothing—your wedding picture," said Rudi.

"Find anything interesting?" he said with a sardonic chuckle, tapping a cigarette out of a pack.

Rudi waved his father over to the table. "Vati, I have something for you."

"Oh? *Vas ist das?*" Rudolf kept the unlit cigarette between his lips.

Rudi untied the string and let the photographs fall open. They wanted to curl back up again, and Rudi was embarrassed that he hadn't packed the prints flat instead. He spread out one of the prints, and he and his father held it down.

Rudolf gazed at the scene of himself and Ilse, as a *couple,* engaging in a moment, with the kind of self-forgetting required for even the smallest fleeting joy.

"Hold this, will you?" he asked his son as he let go of his side of the photograph to light his cigarette. He stared down at it and smoked. "Interesting," he muttered. "Look at that."

"Do you like it, Vati?"

His father didn't answer right away. Then he rolled up the top print and patted Rudi's shoulder with it. "Thanks, Rudi," he said. "Keep tweaking the contrast. You'll get it right eventually." He retreated back to his study and shut the door.

Rudi was motionless for a whole minute. He felt the back of his neck tingle and his palms begin to sweat.

He knew it. His father hated the photograph.

Before he was aware of what he was doing, Rudi picked up the second copy and tore into it, like a lion in rage, his fingernails scraping against the glossy coating of the paper. He crumpled the remains into a wad and shoved it in the rubbish bin. His face was inflamed now, and a drop of spit landed on his shirt.

At that moment, Peter came home.

"Hallo, Rudi," he said. "You all right?"

Rudi stared at his brother—his bright eyes, his confident shoulders—and his face fell. Rudi had no words for the Crown Prince. He grabbed his bag and slammed into Peter's shoulder as he walked out the door, into a world of futility, where one son's offering smelled like roses and the other's like dreck.

Rudi ran down Mainzerstrasse to Frankfurter Allee, against the heat rising in his blood, the spring wind doing nothing to cool his face. No matter what he did, how hard he tried, he could not get at that intangible something that Peter seemed to have by nature, by virtue of *not being Rudi.* Rudi wanted to be a student leader? Peter won the election. Rudi dreamed of going to space? It was Peter who had the chops to be an engineer. Rudi wanted to do something creative? Peter won the awards for artistic excellence.

But the one thing that mattered most, that Peter possessed and Rudi lacked, was the love of his father.

Rudi shoved people aside as he ran. He wanted out of this family. They had no regard for him or the growing chasm between himself and his brother. His mother was even more of a stranger. He wanted to get as far away as possible from all of them.

He heard footsteps gaining on him. Maybe it was one of the Volkspolizei. Running down the street like this, maybe they'd suspect him of shoplifting. So he'd be taken down to the precinct, and his father would come pick him up, pay the fine and take him home. More shame, more disapproval. Rudi ran faster. The more he kept running, the more he could put that off.

But it wasn't the police.

"Hey, *Dummkopf,* slow down a little," Peter panted, grabbing Rudi by the arm.

Rudi shrugged him off and stopped.

"What's wrong with you?" asked Peter.

"Get out of my face."

"What did I do?"

Rudi looked at Peter with lips clenched white. He didn't answer.

Peter shoved Rudi's shoulder hard. "All right, then. That's payback for pushing me at home. Now tell me what's wrong!"

Rudi pushed back, and Peter reciprocated. They grabbed on to each other and locked in, brother on brother, pulling and pushing with no place to go but the ground. A crowd of cheering kids formed around them, encircling them like a coliseum.

They buckled to the pavement before they knew it was coming, and Peter found himself on his back, Rudi's arms still intertwined with his. Rudi freed an arm and tried to take a swing, but Peter kept his elbows locked. Rudi looked down at his brother but didn't see him at all.

Fifteen years of coming in second, of stymied dreams, of frustration at his own shortcomings, turned the person beneath Rudi into nothing more than a lump of flesh, scrawled with the word *failure.* Despite the adrenaline and rage fueling Rudi's muscles, Peter was clearly stronger.

Two brutish hands grabbed Rudi and pulled him back to his feet, clutching his arms behind his back. The Vopos had, in fact, arrived to break up the fight.

"Listen, *Junge*, public fighting can get you time in prison. That what you want?"

Rudi clenched and huffed and refused to answer. But the Vopo holding him demanded it.

Peter interjected. "Leave him alone—he's my brother!"

"I don't care who he is. The two of you are breaking the law."

"Please, we fight like this all the time," Peter lied, turning on the charm for the police officers. "We're twins."

Rudi felt the Vopo's grip slacken. The officer shoved Rudi toward his brother and began to disperse the crowd. "Next time, keep your family squabbles behind your front door, and let your parents deal with you hoodlums. Don't waste my time. *Verstehen?*"

"Yes, sir," said Peter, putting his arm around Rudi, who squirmed under it, panting and red-cheeked. The boys walked back home in silence.

Peter smacked Rudi's arm, ran his fingers through his hair and straightened his clothes. "What was that about?" he asked.

"I don't want to talk about it," Rudi responded through clenched teeth, shoving his hands deep into his pockets.

"Well, you came at *me*, Rudi, so if I did something to deserve that, either give me a chance to make it right or keep your damn hands to yourself. Aww, look at this—you broke my jacket zipper!"

They passed the telephone company building, where their mother worked. Rudi pictured her down in the basement with the other switchboard operators, connecting phone calls from everywhere—between Mitte and Charlottenburg, between Berlin and Bonn, between Germany and France.

"Do you remember when Mutti told us that she made a mistake on the switchboard numbers and ended up connecting two long-lost lovers?" Peter mused.

"Or that time she put the Soviet ambassador on with the American ambassador by accident?"

"She could've started another war!" Peter laughed. "For someone who spends all day patching lines of communication, it'd be nice if she could do it in her own family!"

Their laughter cleared the last bit of hostility and Peter put his arm around Rudi's shoulder again. This time, Rudi didn't shrink away.

"What does Mutti always say?" Peter nudged him.

"Twins against the world," Rudi replied. "Except it's not like that anymore, is it?"

Peter shrugged away the question. "Whatever's bugging you, Rudi, you can tell me. I know when you're upset, anyway. Something happen with Vati?"

"Forget it," said Rudi.

"Suit yourself."

Peter pointed at a poster on the column across from the telephone building. *"Yuri Gagarin,"* he read. *"First Man in Space."* The cosmonaut grinned from within his bulbous helmet, the rich colors of the background already fading, the wheat paste peeling after bouts of spring rain.

"I wish I could do that," Rudi daydreamed.

"What, go to space?"

"Mm-hmm. Take photos of what's up there."

"Maybe there's some kind of path through the FDJ, some summer program."

"My grades aren't good enough," Rudi lamented. "I'm sure yours are, though."

"Ja, but I have other . . . other stars to shoot for," he chuckled as they walked through the corridor into their building.

Rudi clenched his teeth. Peter had all the options he could wish for. But Rudi pictured his own face in that helmet, the space capsule shooting up through the clouds in a burst of smoke and flame, away from all of this shell-pocked concrete and gray sameness, out of Peter's shadow and into the unfiltered light of the sun.

A surprise torrent of rain pounded the roof of the assembly hall as the kids joined the monthly meeting of the *Freie Deutsche Jugend*. They performed their ceremonies, made their announcements and filed into the warm, stuffy youth room. Rudi and Angelika were filling in the last strokes of paint on yet another banner for the upcoming parade.

Nie Wieder Krieg, Nie Wieder Faschismus

Peter was talking, of course, to a group of girls by the window. Rudi put down his brush and went over, clapped Peter on the back and congenially reminded them all to stop chatting and get back to their activities. The girls reluctantly dispersed.

Rudi finished the banner, and he and Angelika cleaned up the paints. They went out to the hallway and rinsed the paintbrushes in the janitor's sink. Their hands touched in the warm running water. They linked their fingers. Leaned into each other. Angelika put her head on Rudi's shoulder.

The brushes had been clean for a while when they heard Peter call everyone together.

"Comrades, it's time to sign up for summer service!" Peter announced to raucous cheers. "Volunteers are hanging the sign-up sheets. Make sure you act fast—the best assignments fill up quickly! It's going to be a great summer, as always, building a better German Democratic Republic for the kids coming after us!"

The kids cheered and talked until he called again for quiet.

The FDJ youth room buzzed. Rudi got his Leica and began snapping pictures for the chapter newsletter. The school year was coming to an end; the excitement of summer plans was beginning. He tried not to be obvious about it, but he included Angelika in more than a few of the photos.

There was definitely a hierarchy among the summer service jobs. Most kids wanted to go somewhere international, like Moscow or Kiev or a town on the Baltic coast. No one wanted to be in Berlin at the height of summer. Farmwork was high on the list because there was the most fun to be had after hours. Digging trenches or working in a mine was obviously not as desirable—though there were those die-hards desperate to prove themselves devoted Socialists by taking the jobs no one else would. Peter immediately put his name on the list for a farm in Potsdam, right on the outskirts of the city.

Rudi, of course, wanted to work with Peter, but he was so busy taking photos that he didn't get to the lists in time. Every slot on every list was filled—except one.

He felt his will turn to sludge as he signed his name in tiny letters on the sheet for the sauerkraut-canning factory. Could it be that his summer was already sunk so quickly? He tried not to think too hard about it. He fumbled with his camera and took some more photographs for the newsletter, hiding his disappointment behind a dutiful attitude and telling himself it was all part of serving the Workers' and Peasants' State.

The volume swelled with chatter. Peter stood at the front of the room and clapped his hands for silence.

"Thanks, everyone! I hope you all were able to get the assignment you wanted. See you next month!"

They lined up and saluted, pledged *"Seid bereit! Immer bereit!"* once more and said goodbye until the next meeting.

The rain had eased to a light but steady drizzle by the time Rudi and Peter got home. Without an umbrella, they were drenched to the skin. The brothers got out of their soaked FDJ clothes, and Peter took out a dress shirt from the wardrobe.

"What are you dressing up for?" asked Rudi. "You going somewhere?"

"I'm going out with that girl Gisela," Peter responded, buttoning his shirt.

"But we have homework."

"Finished already." He pulled a sweater on over his head and put on a pair of dark gray slacks.

"How do you *do* it?" Rudi marveled, drawing his knees to his chin. He had a pile of homework. After grammar, he still had astronomy, Russian and civics. He threw his pencil down on the bed, leaned his head against the wall and rubbed his eyes in frustration. "I'm going to be up all night!"

"Don't know what to tell you," Peter said, combing his hair. "Maybe you need to stop daydreaming about going to outer space." He snatched Rudi's textbook off his bed and looked at the cover. "Have fun with civics, *Bruder Ruder*!"

The key finally turned in the lock after midnight. Rudi sat in bed with his lamp on, reading his dog-eared copy of *Weltall Erde Mensch*, the book every East German teen got for their *Jugendweihe*. He heard Peter doff his shoes by the front door, put the keys on the hook and hang his jacket on the coat tree, its pocket jangling with pfennigs. Rudi had left their bedroom door open so that no one would hear the squeaky hinge that no oil could fix.

Peter entered the room softly, sat on his bed and began unbuttoning his shirt. His hair was a bit damp from drizzle. He hung his shirt over the wardrobe door and pointed at Rudi's book. "I can't believe you actually read that."

"Never mind," whispered Rudi, closing the book and sliding it under the bed. "How did it go?"

"That was the worst date I've had in my entire life," Peter said, emphasizing each word. But Rudi could make out the twist of a smile on his brother's lips.

"How can that be?" Rudi asked, propping himself up on one elbow. "Gisela's so pretty! If it was that bad, you wouldn't be home so late."

"A nice body's nothing if you don't know how to use it," said Peter piggishly. He slipped off his pants and got under the covers.

So many questions ran through Rudi's mind. He couldn't believe his twin capable of a bad date.

Rudi hated him for it.

Rudi wanted to study under him like a disciple.

"Well, now you have to tell me everything," he whispered. "How did Peter the Great end up in the gutter?"

"Let's make one thing clear: *I* am not in the gutter."

"My mistake."

"It didn't start off so bad," Peter began. "We met up at the *Bahnhof,* and we were going to see that comedy—*The Liar.* She kept snapping her bubble gum. I was a little annoyed but I got over it. I have to give her one thing, though—she was actually really funny. Laughed at my jokes—"

"Of course."

"And even gave a few back to me. I was kind of impressed. And I thought, *OK, maybe I should look past her quirks and start over.* Anyway, we found our seats in the Kino and started watching. Then she put her hand on my knee. But . . ."

"What do you mean, *but?*"

"She just plopped it there like a limp fish. I held it anyway, and leaned in to kiss her, because why not? I felt bad. I could tell she hadn't done this before. I guess you don't imagine that pretty girls will be bad kissers. I tried to help her, I really did . . ."

"Go on."

"But then she put her arms around me. And, Rudi, I kid you not, this phrase came into my head: *ham-handed*. Ham-handed—like when someone makes an awkward attempt at something? I mean, you should know how that is."

Rudi brushed off his brother's teasing. "Right. Right."

"Only, this was literal. It really felt like she had two hams, honest to God, attached to her arms and she was just thumping me on the back with them."

Rudi hated this part, when Peter was setting up a funny bit. Especially because he knew it was kind of mean, and Rudi didn't want to be mean. He tried to resist giving in, but he couldn't stop the smile from coming. He pressed his lips tight.

"So I'm kissing her, and I'm thinking of these big, raw hams hanging in a butcher's window, and I start to think, *I believe it would be more pleasurable if someone had actually tied a couple of hams to a broomstick and beat me with them.*"

Rudi tried to stifle a laugh and made a sound in his throat. Peter was winning.

"So then she starts to move her fingers down my arms, and I swear to you, they felt like . . ."

"What?"

"Knockwurst."

That was it. Rudi lost it. God, he hated falling for this.

"No, I mean, it felt like she was wiping my arm with a bouquet of sausages. Cold ones. Plucked right from the sausage water."

Rudi sniggered and put his pillow over his head to keep from waking Oma. It didn't work.

"*Ey! Jungs! Haltet die Klappe!*" Oma shouted from her tiny room.

"Sorry, Omi," they said.

"*Ssscheisse . . . ,*" Oma cursed slowly. Then they heard the flick of the owl lighter and the pucker of her first drag.

Rudi and Peter laughed into their pillows until quietness came over them.

Rudi meditated on Angelika, on their hands touching, the smell of her hair when she'd leaned on his shoulder. "So, do you think you'll ask her out again?" Rudi inquired, but his brother was already snoring.

"You can't win them all, brother," Rudi whispered with a sigh as he turned off the lamp. "Even you."

PETER

Sometimes the theater was a rural town hall affair, a bunch of countryfolk deciding to put on a Christmas pageant. Sometimes it was a major national production, with a cast and crew of hundreds.

But the dream always began with Peter backstage, holding a clipboard, ushering the cast members on or off to their cues. Suddenly the director would run up to Peter, frantic, and tell him that the lead actor had taken ill. Or gotten into a motorcycle accident.

Or . . . or . . . or . . .

And they needed *him* to take the leading role.

Peter, scrambling, would try to explain to them that he didn't know any of the lines or the songs (it was *always* a musical in these dreams) and that, furthermore, he was a lousy singer—his three-year-old Shirley Temple routine notwithstanding.

There was nothing for it. The costumers would stuff Peter into clothes that were either too tight or falling off, smear some makeup on him and send him onstage just as the lights came up on his terrified face. The overture would swell into the bars of the first song: Peter's solo.

And somehow, even though he was making it up as he went along, the other cast members and even the orchestra would begin to follow *his* cues, as though he had been the playwright all along. But as soon as he was getting the hang of it, and his memory was kicking in, and the audience was on board—

Peter would wake up.

He awoke in the middle of the night and looked over at Rudi sleeping, the streetlight falling across his face. He thought of the way he'd regaled Rudi with the story of his date with Gisela. Even if it was all true, her awkwardness, her clumsy touch, it *was* mean, even crude. He had a way of doing that, of collecting faults to deflect attention from his own awkwardness. Peter made a good show of his prowess, but the truth was, he was embarrassed at what a bad kiss would say about him. Maybe it had been Gisela's first, who knows? And all Peter could find to do was make fun of her for it.

The rush that came from making people laugh? There was nothing like it. But after a bit like that, he'd crash.

He picked up his notebook from the nightstand.

Is it right to make people laugh at someone else's expense? he wrote.

What if the person isn't there? What if they're in on the joke—does that make it all right?

Things felt different at fifteen and change than they did at thirteen, and certainly at nine. Getting older came with a new, unwritten script he was supposed to follow. He looked at little kids now and felt so bad for them, their silliness, their embarrassing antics. He wished he could help the poor saps to know what he knew, but of course they'd have to find out about life for themselves, too.

Peter looked at his brother again in the almost dark, wishing they could be kids again, knowing the veil was torn and that the only thing to do was learn their lines. He felt worse for Rudi. His brother was so hopelessly naive, so trusting of what he was told. The edge of Rudi's copy of *Weltall Erde Mensch* peeked out from under the bed, dog-eared like an old lady's Bible. The theories and solutions the Party offered were a kind of script. Every problem in the world had a tidy explanation: capitalist imperialism. Western colonialism. Bonn fascism. The whole thing could be wrapped up in about fifteen phrases that were repeated and recombined on every page of every textbook, on every test, in every television program, whether the evening news or even *Sandmann,* the show they loved as kids. Even the food packaging at the Konsum was done with Socialist ideals in mind. They couldn't just be pickles. They had to be *Socialist* pickles.

Peter lay in the dark, wondering what he would do when he graduated. *I'll save whatever money I make from this summer job, and then I'm going to leave this place. Go West. Maybe I can convince Rudi to come with me. Maybe making your own rules is more important than scrambling to find your lines in someone else's script.*

RUDI

In the twins' earliest memories, Rudi and Peter's mother was always smiling, even when she was angry. *Especially* when she was angry. She was always impeccably made up, either going out with friends after work or throwing parties at the flat. Except for the dark times, when she disappeared into her room. This was life with Ilse, and they all had their strategies to make the best of it.

She had only gotten home five minutes before, but already Ilse was in the bathroom putting on her makeup. Her purse hung on the doorknob, and she stood at the mirror in her stocking feet.

"You're going out again?" Rudolf pressed, leaning in the bathroom doorway, hands in his pockets.

"I told you, I'm going dancing with Henni," Ilse replied, pulling her eyelid down to apply eyeliner. "I've had a long week, Rudolf. My job is stressful. I don't get to sit alone at a piano all day"—she mimicked the repetitive actions of the piano tuner—"plinking notes."

"*Plinking notes?* Hmm. I imagine plugging wires into a switchboard must take a certain genius." He tapped his forehead, mocking her.

"Shut up."

"You think you're the only one with a stressful job? I have to make up the shortfall from your paycheck after you spend it all on lipstick and cocktails."

Ilse looked her husband in the eye. "Are you accusing me of stealing from this family?"

"If you want to put it that way."

"You have no idea how *I* cover for your pathetic income," she said, ice-cold. "You don't even notice the things I do. I pay for the boys' clothes, I pay for—"

"It's not enough for you to throw a party every other weekend? You have to find one every other night?"

She turned back to the mirror and blotted her lipstick on a tissue. "I'm a thirty-year-old woman, darling. I have to live young while I have the looks to go with it."

"Don't you care what *I* think? Not once have you ever dressed up for *me,* Ilse. Everyone else, but never me."

"You want me to dress up for you, Rudolf?"

"No, I want you to *show* up for me."

Rudi and Peter sat at the dining room table staring down at their homework, but their pencils hadn't moved since the fight began. Oma came over and nudged them, and they followed her into the kitchen.

"It wasn't always like this," she said, frying up finger-sized sausages in a pan. "When you boys were babies, we were a nice little family."

"Why do they fight like that?" asked Peter.

"*Ach,* who knows. It's probably the war."

"Omi, the war ended sixteen years ago," said Rudi.

"The war brought people together for all sorts of reasons. In other times they might not have given each other a second look. Memories and emotions, they're only beginning to come out now. For all of us."

"If they hate each other that much, they should get divorced already," said Rudi.

Oma shot him a look of such disgust, it made Rudi shrivel and Peter flinch. "People endure much more than this and survive," she said. She slid the sausages onto plates and put a spoonful of mustard on each. "But look," she sighed, "if they hadn't gotten together, you two wouldn't be here. And then what would I do with my life?" She gave them each a smoky peck on the cheek. The three of them ate quietly, standing in the kitchen, then crept into the hallway to wait out the rest of the storm.

"I only stayed with you because I was pregnant," Ilse seethed. "I gave you my best years. I wanted to have fun, go to parties, travel!"

"The war took your best years, not me. The fact is, Ilse, *I* wanted that kind of life more than *you* did," Rudolf shouted. "And I could have had it. At least I had a skill. All you had were the cheap tricks of a cheap woman."

Ilse slapped Rudolf so hard, her wedding ring split his lip with a sound like a water drop. At that exact moment, there was a knock at the front door.

Ilse shoved her husband out of her way and grabbed her purse, snatched up her shoes and stormed out of the apartment barefoot, past two men in hats and overcoats. One of the men had thick, dark-rimmed glasses and a pouty mouth. The other made Rudolf wonder for a moment how it was *possible* to get that clean-shaven.

Rudolf came to the door, dabbing his bloody lip with his handkerchief. "Can I help you?" he asked.

"Herr Rudolf Möser?" said the man with the glasses, eyeing Rudolf's laceration.

"Yes. That's me."

The other man, with the smooth baby face, handed him an envelope. "You have been working in West Berlin," he said. "You are to cease working across the border immediately. By order of the Ministry of State Security."

Rudolf looked at the envelope and calculated his words. A visit from State Security wasn't like a visit from the telephone repairman. He decided to make light of it, despite the mess on his face. "Come on, everyone works in West Berlin, don't they? I mean, my employer *is* here in the GDR, but I just take side jobs when they come up."

"Yes, we know," said Glasses. "But if you persist in robbing the State of its labor force, your employer may be forced to cease operations, and *you* will be under threat of eviction from this flat. *Verstehen?*"

"Yes, I see."

"One more thing: please be careful of the company you keep. Having American soldiers over for dinner may . . . confuse your loyalties."

"Well, after all, it is my house."

"Oh, no, actually your . . . grandmother's, I believe?" said Baby Face condescendingly. "Right. Thank you, Herr Möser. Have a good day." The men turned sharply and went down the stairs.

Rudolf retreated to his study. A minute later his piano erupted with loud fugues.

Oma and the boys sat in the living room in silence. No one knew which edge of this frayed fabric to pick up. It was obvious things couldn't go on like this, but what could be done about it?

Peter grew agitated, rubbing his hands on the knobby fabric of the sofa. "I have to get out of here," he said. He grabbed his jacket. "I have an audition to prepare for."

PETER

Peter's audition for the drama school wasn't to be held on the main stage of the Theater am Schiffbauerdamm, or even in the small black box theater, but in a side room, and he was a bit deflated at the thought. He was used to being made much of. But as he eavesdropped on the other applicants listing off their bona fides, he became acutely aware that his own résumé consisted of little more than school productions, FDJ icebreakers and readings in friends' bedrooms.

The girl signing him in was beyond pretty, her hair pulled back into a dark ponytail, with long, lush bangs half covering her eyes. She wore all black—a boatneck top tucked into slim pants—and it all fit her like a dream. She asked Peter the necessary questions, didn't smile, didn't give away any emotion. She did, however, keep stealing glances at him from underneath her bangs. *This* he was used to—yet his mind tussled over whether this girl's glances were of interest or disdain.

At last she took his application, clipped it to a board and ushered him through the lobby, through great double doors into the magnificent baroque theater. Peter thrilled at the upward thrust of the ceiling, surrounded on three sides by ivory balconies, like tiers of a great wedding cake. He could almost hear the invisible audience, the murmur of anticipation before a show begins, the sound that always swelled his heart.

A little rise in the floor made the plush red carpet shift under Peter's feet, and he stumbled. He was glad to be behind this girl so he wouldn't lose face. He was glad to be behind her, too, so he could gather her body in with his eyes and distract himself from the stage fright he never admitted to.

Through the stage-right door, the carpet changed abruptly from red to tan, and from the painted plaster curlicues of the proscenium gave way to the utilitarian beige of a back hallway. After guiding them through a maze of corridors, the girl opened a plain door with a little window in it and led Peter into a small rehearsal room. It was clad in blond wood and had a mirrored wall crossed by a ballet barre. There was no theatrical lighting, just a nondescript modern chandelier on the ceiling and a brass lamp on the desk where the director sat. An old red Persian rug in the middle of the room made it feel a little warmer and more homey than the non-space it really was.

The girl handed the clipboard to the director, announced Peter's name and leaned against the wall by the door, where he thought she could size him up properly.

There was another person stationed at the door. Peter knew from his gray suit and the small notepad in his hand that he was from State Security. The Stasi. The presence of the gray bureaucrats was noticeably increasing—now there was always a security representative present at any school function, political rally and sporting event.

Peter tried to ignore him and took his place in the dead center of the rug.

"Peter Möser-Fleischmann," said the director, looking out at him above her glasses. "Interesting combination of surnames. What will you be offering us this morning?"

"Comrade Director," Peter responded, "this morning I will be reciting for you from *Mother Courage and Her Children.*"

"Oh *Gott,* you and everyone else," the director muttered.

Peter quickly did his subtle pre-audition routine to set himself in the mental space of the scene:

Take a deep breath.

Count to ten.

Tap each finger on the leg.

Two deep breaths, get the first line ready.

And he began.

More than a week of afternoons passed. Peter came home from school each day nervous as a rabbit. On Thursday, he almost crashed into the mail carrier. He bumbled, trying to conceal his eagerness, asked for the mail, and ran up the three flights of stairs in a flash, almost dropping the whole pile. He could hardly get through the door fast enough.

"*Ey!* Peter! Where's the fire?" said Oma, glancing up from her program.

"It's nothing, Oma." Peter dumped the mail on the table and sorted through it, looking for that one letter. Among the bills and notices and reminders of Party meetings, there it was—a pale blue envelope:

Das Berliner Ensemble, Theater am Schiffbauerdamm, Berlin

This was it. His answer. But he found, now that it was in his hands, that he couldn't bear to open the envelope.

Rudolf had taken Peter to see the revival of Brecht's *Threepenny Opera* two years ago. That show was a revelation. It did away with all convention, with its skeletal scenery, naked lighting and hand-scrawled signs spoiling any secrets. Different from the skits at his FDJ meetings, different from the campy, semiannual school plays, different from the bonfire acts at the youth summers, the Berliner

Ensemble was real and raw and intentional. Bertolt Brecht had given the stage a new purpose: to change the world through theater. It wasn't about emotion or escape—it was about truth. And Peter saved his money to be able to see new plays as soon as they premiered.

There was no escape during one of Brecht's plays. Even though he'd died a few years before, his presence in the productions was still palpable. You couldn't rest comfortably in the illusion of simulated reality. Brecht's work called for alertness, for identification. The problems in his plays were *your* problems. The solutions lay in *your* hands. When Peter watched these plays, read them, recited them, he felt like he really *could* change the world.

That was when Peter knew—*really* knew—that he had to be an actor. Now he was about to find out whether he would be accepted into that very company's exclusive drama school.

Peter rifled through the silverware drawer for a knife. He leaned against the counter, took a deep breath and sliced open the top of the envelope. He read:

> *Dear Comrade Möser-Fleischmann,*
>
> *Thank you for your interest in the Berliner Ensemble.*
> *We regret to inform you that we do not have a place for you*
> *in the drama school at this time. However, we encourage*
> *you to audition again in the future.*
>
> > *Best wishes,*
> > *Helene Wiegel*
> > *Director of the Berliner Ensemble*

A ripple of disbelief washed up his spine. That was it, then. He hadn't made it. He hadn't measured up, to the company . . . to himself. He hadn't proven his family wrong. Peter folded his arms across his chest and stared.

Oma came in to refill her coffee cup. She poured from the carafe and added a spoonful of sugar. She opened the green cabinet, took out the package of biscuits and put two on a plate. She stood across from Peter and dipped a biscuit in her coffee.

"What's wrong with you?" she asked, munching.

Peter held up the letter and frowned. "I didn't get in."

"What, to the theater school?"

"Yes."

"That's surprising."

"I know, I thought after I got that award . . ."

"You're not used to hearing the word *no*, are you?" she chuckled. "Well, after all, you're not even sixteen yet. They would've given you baby roles."

"That's true. I guess it was a long shot. But there was so much I wanted to do."

Oma did that thing everyone hates: she grabbed Peter's chin and gave it a squeeze and a shake. "Forget it. If it's not this school, it'll be another." She got out a third biscuit and carried her coffee and plate back to the living room. Peter heard the flick of the lighter and smelled the first puff of smoke, the only one that's sweet before the bitterness.

He opened the envelope to put the letter back in and noticed that there was another slip of paper inside, just a small note, the kind you'd pass to a friend in class. He unfolded it.

KOLLWITZSTRASSE 105, PRENZLAUER BERG. CELLAR. SATURDAY, 6 PM. TELL NO ONE.

Peter read it again, again. Who was the note from? Should he go? What was going to happen at that place, on that day, at that time?

Had he done something wrong in front of the security agent? Or was it from the girl?

He knew some kids who had been arrested by the Stasi for things like graffiti or making jokes about the regime. But *he* hadn't done anything like that. He'd simply read a monologue. And apparently, not very well. His head began to ache. *Kollwitzstrasse 105. Saturday at 6.* He memorized it, then flushed the note down the toilet.

RUDI

The ticking of the nightstand clock ricocheted in Rudi's brain. He had read the same sentence in his science textbook twenty times, and his legs began to get restless. Just as he hurled the book across the room, Peter came in through the louvered doors.

"First you jump me in the street, and now you try to throw a textbook at my head?" he joked. "I thought we made up!"

Rudi attempted an awkward apology.

"I'm just kidding," said Peter, but he wasn't himself. He flopped onto his bed, rubbed his face with both hands and sighed.

"Wie gehts?" said Rudi.

"I got the letter," said Peter.

"And?"

Peter rolled his head to the side and looked at his twin. "I didn't get in."

"What? Are you sure? Did they get the wrong Peter?"

"No, it was me," said Peter. "But it's nice that you assumed they made a mistake."

"Did they give you a reason?"

"No. Hey, Rudi, I don't really want to talk about it. My head hurts. I need to lie down." Peter turned toward the wall.

"OK." Rudi watched the afternoon light play on the wall above his brother's form. It took a lot to get his twin to submit to an afternoon nap, but if Peter said his head hurt, everyone knew to shut things down. Peter's breathing became slow and even, and a light snore proceeded from his mouth.

It scared Rudi when Peter was laid low, though he didn't recognize the fear as fear. It reminded him of his mother going dark. Rudi was used to his stomach tightening like this, his breath coming almost to a complete halt. If he'd known how to name such things, he'd have been able to admit how utterly he depended on his twin's energy. It was Rudi's gasoline. Jealousy made him want Peter to fail, or at least to not be great. But Rudi was tied so tightly to his brother, that even if he was always a step behind Peter, at least it meant he was moving forward.

Rudi heard the front door close softly and his father murmur something to Oma. The bedroom door opened, and Rudolf peered in with a grin. He was about to say something when he saw Peter sleeping.

"Come with me up to the roof," he whispered. "Peter'll come later."

Rudi left his homework on the bed. He and his father walked into the hall and climbed the stairs two stories to the roof. Hardly anyone came up here. In the stairwell corner, a broom and dustpan had fallen over long ago. Water had pooled at the threshold to the exit door and mildewed at the edges, making the air musty and acrid. A dim light from under the door shimmered on the surface of the puddle. Rudolf held the door open for his son, and they went out to the roof.

The night was warm, and Rudi breathed deeply of the fresh air that was *not* tinged with cigarette smoke. He still harbored a seed of anger toward his father over the photograph, but his grudge subsided in favor of curiosity.

"Remember when we used to have picnics up here?" Rudolf mused. He and Rudi leaned on the half-wall and looked up at the stars. "You were so little—we were always afraid you'd get too close to the edge. Berlin looked different then. So did you. We all did," he chuckled.

"The last time we had a picnic, I think I was . . . nine?"

"That's about how old I was when I last looked through one of these." He beckoned Rudi to the corner of the roof, facing east, where a cream-colored telescope with brass fittings stood proudly on a tripod, pointing at the heavens.

"Wow, Vati," said Rudi. "It's beautiful. Mutti let you buy this?"

"Well, Mutti doesn't know. No one does. Only you."

"Really?"

His father peered through the lens and adjusted various knobs and dials. "I'll show Peter later, but I'm glad it wound up being just the two of us."

Rudi couldn't help reaching out to touch the smooth enamel along the length of the telescope. The brass was old-fashioned, with Art Deco–style accents. It pivoted effortlessly on its oak tripod. On top it was engraved with something familiar but seldom seen in Germany anymore: an eagle holding a laurel wreath, a swastika at the center. Rudi shuddered.

His father must have sensed his discomfort and made an excuse. "It was secondhand, of course, at the flea market. I got a great deal. All the new ones are sold out because of Gagarin's flight. This is the same one I had as a boy. Same exact—I couldn't believe my eyes. The color, the tripod, everything. I used to take mine to a field by my house and stay out until I heard my mother calling me—sometimes ten or eleven at night. I couldn't bear to come in, and I'd cry all the way home. Here, take a look."

Rudi hesitated. He found it hard to be excited in the presence of such a tainted relic. But he put his eye to the scope nonetheless. "I don't see anything," he said. "It's just gray and black. How do you find what you're looking for?"

"Here, let me adjust it," said Rudolf. "You know, I memorized every constellation in the Northern Hemisphere. Half of the Southern, too. I thought I'd get to travel once the war was over, playing concerts, seeing the world. I wanted to know the skies before I got there so I could stargaze from anywhere. But things change. All right, look now."

Rudi looked again, but it was dark to him. All he could make out was a blurry shape of light. He looked at his father and shook his head.

"First you have to find the moon," said Rudolf. "That's easy because you can see it clearly with the naked eye. And because it's a crescent tonight, you can distinguish it from the other objects, and you know you're looking at the moon. Look again, and aim it there."

Rudi pressed his eye to the viewfinder, swiveled the telescope on the tripod. "Still blurry."

"Look again," his father repeated, turning the focus. The shape changed but was unclear. "Anything?"

"No, Vati."

"Maybe it's the city lights, eh? Interfering with the night sky?"

"Maybe," said Rudi, standing straight and shoving his hands in his pockets. *Or maybe it's me.*

"I'm going to make this work for you," said Rudolf. "Don't worry."

The roof door creaked open, and Peter came out, his hair tousled and his shirt half-untucked.

"I thought you had a headache," said Rudi.

"It's getting better. I heard Vati say something about the roof. I didn't know if I was dreaming."

"Here, Peter, take a look," said Rudolf.

"What is that?" Peter asked, peering into the scope. "One of the satellites?" Rudi couldn't believe his brother could see something right away.

"Must be," said Rudolf, taking a look for himself. "Yes, it is. Rudi, you have to see this."

Rudi looked, and this time he could see something moving across the lens. Yes, it was a satellite. It almost took his breath away, it looked so close. Could it see them, at that exact moment?

"Hey, will you look at that," said Peter. Rudi looked up from the telescope; his brother was pointing at the sky.

"What?" All Rudi saw was the faint field of distant stars obscured by the city lights.

"Shooting star," said Peter. "But it's gone now."

PETER

What do you wear to a secret meeting, with an unknown person, when you don't know what's going to happen? thought Peter. *Should I wear my suit? My school clothes? Is it a date? Is it prison? How do you dress for prison?*

Peter opted to look clean and responsible but not fussy: navy button-down shirt, dark brown pants. He wore his good shoes, the black ones with the pointy toes, and walked to the U-Bahn station. The subway rattled along the tracks, and he wondered if anyone could tell that he was doing something clandestine.

He jogged up the station steps, went four blocks east and turned onto Kollwitzstrasse. He found the address but passed it on purpose, crossed the street and went once around the block so he could see if anyone was watching him or the building. No one, as far as he could tell. The door was unlocked. He went in.

The hallway had once been a bourgeois foyer, with ornate Art Deco wallpaper and a milk glass light fixture overhead. But since the war, everything had faded to a colorless pattern scrimmed over plaster. He had been in a hundred prewar buildings just like this, so finding the basement door was easy. Peter heard voices. His heart beat faster.

When he opened the door, a wave of smoke and booze hit him in the face. He descended the stairs and stopped on the bottom step. Thirty or so people were crammed into the cellar. They were of all ages, but mostly young, sitting around café tables smoking and drinking beer or schnapps or soda. A record player piped out tinny jazz. And on the wall against the stairs, there was a small stage.

Peter looked around, wondering if whoever sent the note would make themselves known so he didn't have to stand here looking so awkward.

"Peter," said a female voice, just loudly enough to be heard above the crowd. It was the girl who had checked him in at the audition. "You made it."

"Oh, it's you!" said Peter, pleased but nervous.

"I'm Renate," she said, taking a sip from a brown bottle. As at the audition, she never smiled.

"Pleasure," said Peter, and he meant it.

"Let's sit," she replied. She led him to a table to the right of the stage. "Do you want something to drink?"

"Sure. Orangeade?" he said.

"Not beer? Schnapps?"

"No, thanks." He blushed. The truth was, he wanted all his wits about him right now. And alcohol reminded him too much of his mother.

"Suit yourself, *Junge,*" she said, and went to get the drinks. Under the staircase was a bar, lit with a salvaged neon sign. While the bartender poured their drinks, the girl chose another record and put it on the turntable.

"Bill Haley," she said, sliding the orange drink to Peter. "Do you like him?"

"I love rock 'n' roll," he said. Peter still had no idea what this place was or why he was here—but he played it as mature as he could.

"So, student summer's starting, right? What are you going to do?"

"I got a farm placement." Peter was proud of himself for that one.

"Oh, you moved fast!"

"Well, I'm the student leader. It wouldn't really do for me to work in a sauerkraut factory or something. How about you?"

"I graduated last year. I got to go to Prague for leadership training," said Renate.

"Lucky," said Peter.

She was suddenly serious. "Listen, Peter, can I trust you? You're not a dummy, are you?"

"I don't think so," Peter laughed. Renate did not laugh.

"You can't tell anyone about this place, or that we met here. Do you understand?"

"Yes."

"I assume you didn't leave my note lying around, right?"

"Absolutely not. I ripped it up and flushed it."

"Good man. This is Kabarett Zusammen. We're a club of artists, musicians, actors like you and me. We don't go along with the Party. In fact, we go against the regime."

"That's dangerous."

"You're right. We could all be arrested, tonight. But it's not as dangerous as giving them the deed to your soul."

Something jumped in Peter's heart. He'd had his suspicions that there was something wrong with the way things were. Oma made the occasional quip, nothing that could get her in trouble, but she and Peter shared a telepathic link about it. Never, though, had he heard anyone say it so forthrightly.

"Down here we do what we like, say what we like," Renate continued. "Up there you get off at the wrong U-Bahn station and you end up in questioning. Not here. Here, we're free."

"So why did you bring me here?"

"There was something about your audition . . . I liked the look of you. You're obviously young and naive, but you're confident, passionate. You're all wrong for Brecht, of course. I could tell you weren't going to get what you wanted there."

"Thanks?" Peter was still disappointed about the audition, but she was right.

"Peter, do you know how many people I watched audition for the drama school?" Renate asked. "Guess how many of them are here? *Zero.* But I could see you wanted to do more than act; you wanted to *create.* So I took a chance on you. You won't let me down, right?"

"I'll try not to. . . ." Peter suddenly felt on the younger end of his age. Renate may only have been a year or so older than him, but she seemed wise, experienced, and he wanted to stay by her side. He'd never felt this way about another girl.

"We meet here every Saturday. It's an open stage—just bring something to share, hop up there and do it. We hang out a bit first, loosen up, and then the fun begins. But we shut down by ten so we don't attract the authorities. Besides, people have to go to work, you know. And school." She winked.

A stocky, redheaded guy wearing a white shirt tucked into jeans got up onstage, and everyone applauded. "That's Arno," said Renate. "This is his place."

"*Willkommen im Kabarett Zusammen!* Before I read the list of tonight's performers, I want to direct your attention to the art on the wall. This month's paintings are by our very own Günter! Stand up and take a little bow!" The painter rose awkwardly and nodded to his friends, and Arno began to read the lineup. He told a couple of jokes, then introduced the first act.

A juggler carried up a basket of items and told the bartender to start a certain song on the turntable, but he couldn't get the cue right. Twice, the juggler dropped the little rubber balls. It was a rough start, but eventually he relaxed and finished the routine. It turned out he was pretty good when he didn't overthink it.

As the next act was setting up, Peter leaned toward Renate. "Why don't you just go to the Distel, or a cabaret in West Berlin?" he asked. "Then you wouldn't have to hide out."

"Are you kidding?"

"What? You could just move this whole thing across the river to Kreuzberg. Or you could register with the Ministry of Culture."

"So all the artists should have to get their acts approved by the Party, or relocate? I don't think so. State Security would clamp down on us, registered or not. And those official clubs are for tourists and old folks. Besides, I like living on the edge a little bit."

The next performers came on and sang two English folk songs, and for hours, Peter reveled in the freedom of the cabaret. Some of the acts were awful. A couple were brilliant. But everyone got applause. Everyone belonged. And most of all, *she* was here.

There wasn't a chance he would miss next week.

RUDI

Rudi folded his hands on top of the desk and looked straight ahead, but underneath it he bounced his leg to keep himself awake. Civics and politics class should have been the most interesting for someone as devoted to the Party as he was, but the stuffy classroom and the heady concepts weren't conducive to paying attention, especially this close to the end of the day. Frau Weiss was a humorless teacher who smelled of cheese and made the world seem like a lost cause.

"Settler colonialism," she began, "is a natural outgrowth of Western imperialism based on capitalist greed and exploitation of resources and peoples. Can anyone give me an example of this?"

"America," said a boy in the front row who always answered first.

"Great Britain," said another girl.

"Israel," said Rudi.

"Very good, Comrade," Frau Weiss commended him. "Yes. The Zionist expansion may be said to be the epitome of this in our own time."

Angelika raised her hand.

"Yes, Comrade?"

"But . . . it's a country of Jews. Isn't that—"

"Antisemitic? Of course not," Frau Weiss dismissed her. "That's what the Zionists say to garner sympathy." She went on with her lesson.

Rudi glanced at Angelika. Her lips were drawn tight and tears filled her eyes. She rose slowly, took the hall pass and left the classroom, careful not to let the door slam.

The bell sounded for the end of class, and Rudi oozed out of his seat along with twenty other bodies, pushing their hormone-laden scent into the stale summer air. Depending on the season, the hallways could either be a cool relief or the next circle of hell.

Rudi braced himself, hoping his sweatiness wouldn't repel Angelika if he ran into her.

And then he saw her alone by the bathroom door. He'd never seen her in school without being flanked by at least two friends.

"Hi, Angelika," he called behind her—loud enough to be heard but not loud enough to embarrass her. He came closer, and they walked side by side.

"Hi, Rudi," she said, lifting her head. She didn't look like herself. Even in the heat, her lips were pale and her eyes were circled with dark, as though she hadn't slept in days.

"Are you all right? Is everything— Wait, where are your friends?"

"You tell me," she replied. "I think they're taking an Angelika vacation."

"That's stupid," said Rudi. "Why would they do that?"

"I have my suspicions."

"What, do you have the plague?" he teased, playfully bumping her shoulder.

Angelika turned abruptly toward Rudi. "Look, you don't have to hang around me. You and your brother are FDJ leaders. Protect your reputation. It's all you've got."

"Don't be so upset," said Rudi. "Let's talk after school, all right?"

Her warm brown eyes scorched him, and her color started to return. Rudi wondered what he could have said to make her angry.

"You'd better mean what you say, Rudi." She hiked up her book bag and walked away toward her last class.

After school, Rudi saw Angelika by the bike rack, alone again. She was trying to yank her bike free, but the front reflector was stuck. The girls she usually hung out with were sitting on the stone wall, looking at the two of them. Rudi was familiar with being looked at askance, scrutinized, maybe even quietly mocked. This time, though, it wasn't aimed at him, but at this amazing girl who made his insides feel like a war of the Titans. Whatever was happening, he resolved to stick up for her.

Rudi helped free her bike and set it right. Angelika got on, looking ashamed at needing the help.

"If you're really serious about talking to me," she said in a low voice, "come to my house for dinner. And then we'll see. We eat at six." She slipped him a piece of folded notebook paper with her address on it and rode away. The girls turned their gazes to Rudi and released their pent-up laughter.

Rudi did his homework with surprising speed and accuracy. He shaved, washed his armpits twice and tried to twist the front of his hair like he'd seen on a poster of James Dean. It didn't work with his short crop, and he kept twisting and twisting it as he got ready. He hadn't dressed up in a while, and the shirt he'd pictured wearing was now too tight.

"You going somewhere?" asked Peter, plopping down on his bed.

"Out." Rudi twisted his hair.

"With a . . . what's that called . . . a *girl*?"

"Angelika invited me over to dinner. At her house."

"You're going to meet her *parents*?"

"Just her father," Rudi said with faux coolness. "Her mother . . . died. Can I borrow your gray shirt?"

Peter chuckled. "Go ahead. But first let me fix this." He got the pomade out of his wardrobe and smushed some into Rudi's hair, fixing the twist into a tolerable shape. "Wow." He whistled. "Rudi on a date."

"Shut up." Rudi punched his brother's arm, but with a smile.

Rudi thought he knew every corner of Berlin, but this was a neighborhood he'd never been to before. Neither the S-Bahn nor U-Bahn got close, and he had the feeling it wasn't the safest place to be. There were no stores and few cars, and bombed-out buildings from the war outnumbered the functional ones. The only sounds were of barking dogs, crying babies and shouting mothers. East Berlin was gray, all right, but this block was grayer.

At last he came to Angelika's building, a courtyard-style quad like his. The door paint was bubbling, like it had an allergic reaction. He opened the door into the vestibule and stepped into the central courtyard. It smelled like stale urine and spilled liquor. He felt immediately that the Workers' and Peasants' State was purposely ignoring this corner of its capital.

He didn't have to ring or knock. Angelika was leaning out the top-floor window, waiting for him. "Rudi, I'll be right down," she called.

She didn't say a word as she led him up four flights of stairs. They entered the apartment, and Angelika closed the door behind him. She stood beside him, but Rudi was frozen to the floor. He was looking at an apartment that was, for all intents and purposes, empty. It would not have been fit for one person, let alone a family. He could take in the whole place in one glance—a small main room with a bare window overlooking the courtyard, and a single tiny bedroom off to the right. This was one of those prewar buildings with a single shared bathroom out on the landing to service the entire floor of apartments. He was glad he'd gone at home before he left.

The peeling wallpaper faded into a monochrome of washed-out beiges. The wood floor was splintered with worn patches; in some places, metal sheeting had been nailed to it to cover holes. A tall glazed ceramic heater occupied a third of the wall next to him, and two rolled-up bed mats stood propped in the corner. Three folding chairs were clustered around a small card table, and beside the sink, a tiny spot of counter held an electric kettle and a hot plate, upon which rested a small steaming pot. It smelled of a generic soup.

But had Rudi turned slightly to the left when he'd come in, he would have noticed that the entire wall was filled, floor to ceiling, with books. They were not on proper shelves or in bookcases but resting on planks of wood and salvaged bricks, the whole structure supporting itself like a living organism.

The bedroom door was open slightly, revealing another bedroll and the only other piece of furniture in the apartment: a worn chair with torn armrests, which barely contained the tall man sitting in it.

"Papa, my friend is here," Angelika called, and the man rose slowly and came into the main room.

"*Guten Abend,* you must be Rudi," said her father with a tired but earnest smile. He was an impeccably groomed and clean-shaven man, with a thick head of graying hair, and he wore a brown three-piece suit that was pilling with age. He shook Rudi's hand. "I am so pleased to meet you. But I must apologize that you find us in much reduced circumstances."

Rudi didn't know how to respond. "My great-grandmother told

me not to come empty-handed," he said, and gave Angelika's father a plastic-wrapped *Marzipanstollen.*

"*Danke, mein Herr,*" said Herr Rosen with a playful deference, and gave the cake to his daughter. "Put this on a platter, will you, dear?"

Angelika's older sister came in carrying a bag of groceries. She was tall like her father, with the same forehead and high cheekbones. She wore the practical dress of a nurse's uniform, and her hair was slicked back into a ponytail. "Oh, *hallo,*" she said to Rudi.

"Sasha, this is Rudi," said Angelika. "We go to school together."

"Nice," said Sasha dismissively. "Papa, I brought the Apfelsaft you wanted and the other things. . . ."

"Set them out, *Schatzi.* Rudi, come. Do you like books? *Bitte,* look at my collection." He led Rudi over to the wall of books.

"Well, I . . . I'm kind of a slow reader," said Rudi.

"I am, too. I like to savor," said Herr Rosen. "But regardless, there are some books everyone ought to read. The Russian novelists, for instance. You must be taking Russian in school?"

"Yes, sir," Rudi said with pride. "It's actually my best subject."

"Well, Dostoevsky must be read in Russian. And of course Tolstoy, Pushkin . . . but these are perhaps too heady for a boy your age. I used to read *The Brothers Karamazov* to the girls every night! It took two years, but we did it, didn't we, Angelika?"

"We did, Papa," Angelika sighed.

"I learned to read Russian in Moscow during the war. I was a loyal Communist. Loyal!" he crescendoed, but quickly resumed his etiquette. "My parents hated it, of course, that I joined the Party. . . . If only they had . . . Well, it saved me. During the war, I went to Moscow, and I alone survived."

"Did you come back to Berlin with Comrade Ulbricht?" Rudi asked.

"I waited a while in Russia first. I had met my wife there, and the girls were so little, you understand. So we came when there was something solid to come to, because, of course, piles of rubble are no place to raise children. And yet, regardless, I am reduced. . . ." He gestured to the close walls of the flat. "But come, Rudi, you are my guest. I am sorry I couldn't have entertained you in our other flat. It was well appointed, and their mother would have fed you until you burst. But she died. And not long after, so did my reputation. So here we are. But you like *solyanka*, don't you?"

"Herr Rosen, you may think I'm joking, but *solyanka* is my favorite," said Rudi.

"Spoken like a true comrade. Well, let's be seated around my little table. A table is a table, but with family and friends it becomes a banquet—a feast! Here, let me get the chair for you. You are the guest of honor." He brought the armchair from the bedroom and beckoned Rudi to sit in it. Herr Rosen sat in one of the folding chairs, looking like a bear on a toadstool.

"Please, sir, I don't need it," said Rudi.

"I insist," said Herr Rosen, seriously enough that Rudi obeyed immediately.

Angelika and Sasha set out bowls and laid a loaf of bread on the table. Herr Rosen began to ladle soup into their bowls.

"Since I was expelled from the Party, I have been on a search to recover the faith of my fathers. So we will wash our hands before the meal. All right, Rudi? You'll follow."

Angelika brought over a small plastic pitcher and bowl. Her father took a skullcap out of his pants pocket and placed it awkwardly on his head. He poured water over his hands into the bowl, then passed it to Angelika, and she and Sasha did the same.

Rudi was obliged to copy them, but his discomfort grew. What did he mean, *expelled from the Party*? And why the ritual?

Herr Rosen picked up the loaf of bread and said a short blessing, and each of them tore off a piece and ate it. "My wife did these things in her own quiet ways, Rudi, quiet ways. It wasn't to be seen in our circles and isn't to be tolerated now, all of this superstitious nonsense. One must be ideologically consistent in all things. But that is no longer required of me, because I am a worm, and no man. *Die Partei ist immer recht,* right, Rudi? You know that song, don't you?"

"Papa, let's eat, all right?" Angelika pleaded. Herr Rosen calmed and lifted the spoon to his mouth, and everyone followed. Rudi burned his tongue, and winced at the saltiness of the soup.

"So, Rudi," Herr Rosen began, "what do you like to do with your time? Besides studying Russian, of course."

"Well, I'm a student leader for the FDJ," he responded. Herr Rosen sat up straighter. "Actually, my twin brother is student leader, but I'm his co-chair—"

"Rudi's a photographer," Angelika interrupted. "You should see his photographs in the FDJ newsletter. They look professional."

"No, not professional," said Rudi with feigned humility.

"What do you like to take pictures of?" asked Herr Rosen.

"The city, mostly. And portraits."

Herr Rosen slurped his soup. "Would you take mine?"

"I . . . I suppose . . ."

"You're putting him on the spot, Papa," said Sasha.

"No," said Rudi, "he's not. Herr Rosen, I'd be honored to take your portrait."

"With my books, of course."

"Sure. All right."

"Come one of these days, after school. The light through this window is nice in the afternoon."

They finished the soup, and Sasha cleared the dishes. Angelika put the *Marzipanstollen* on the table and sliced it.

"I'm sorry it's from a package," Rudi confessed. "Normally I'd have made one myself but there wasn't time."

"Yourself!" Herr Rosen exclaimed, turning to his daughter. "He bakes, too?"

"Yes, sir."

Herr Rosen patted his knees with resolve. "Next time, then, something homemade, please. It's been a long time since I had a homemade cake."

They finished the cake, which Herr Rosen pronounced "tolerable," and Angelika walked with Rudi down to the courtyard.

"Do you think the girls should still hang around me now?" said Angelika. "They found out about my family. You see how it is. I live in a hovel. I have nothing. My father doesn't manage a building. I lied. He was in the Volkskammer, but he exposed how they were purging Jews from the Party, and now he works as a janitor in an old-age home. And you—you're an FDJ leader. It wouldn't do to be seen with the daughter of someone who got kicked out of the Party, now, would it?"

Rudi looked at her, and all he could see was how her passionate words shaped her mouth.

He kissed her. She kissed him back. Her lips tasted like almond cake.

And he hadn't even thought to pop a mint.

PETER

Peter pulled on his dark blue trousers and tucked in a short-sleeved button-down with a pattern of little light blue dolphins leaping back and forth. He wished he had some more mature clothes. He wished it weren't so hot outside. Maybe if it were cooler, he could at least put a sweater on over his shirt. He could borrow a shirt from his father, but Rudolf didn't have anything better. Was it really this hot, or was it the stage fright? Peter scrutinized himself in the wardrobe mirror. He pulled off the dolphin shirt and stood in his white undershirt. He fixed a stray hair, slipped his billfold in his back pocket, put on his shoes and headed out to Kabarett Zusammen.

The only thing Peter carried with him was his paperback of *Faust*. He was going to recite the passage that had won him the drama award. He guessed that the best strategy to recover his confidence was to go back to the point of his greatest success and start again. If Brecht wasn't the right direction for his life, maybe tonight, by returning to *Faust,* he'd get a better sense of what was next.

He took the S-Bahn to Husemannstrasse, did the routine roundabout walk, assessing whether it was safe to go into the building. He decided to walk one more time around the block to be safe, and finally he went in.

Peter restrained himself from making a beeline across the room to Renate. First he signed up with Arno for a slot on tonight's list. He would go on fifth. He was glad that his stupid stage fright would have time to settle.

Peter wasn't the type who just wanted to get things over with. He liked the struggle, the feeling of pushing through something hard.

It wasn't the kind of catharsis found in Greek dramas. To Peter, catharsis was indulgent—there was nothing special about the simple release of tension. No, there was something about the tension itself that Peter thrived on. Like a caterpillar emerging from a cocoon, the struggle gave him the strength to *become*.

When it whispers its name to me in the dark, he thought, *then I'll know what the next step is. I'll know.*

"Renate!" He waved her over. And then something surprising happened.

Renate smiled at him.

Peter felt a new strength in his caterpillary muscles. He bought her a drink, and they sat down at the same table as the week before.

Arno got up, loosened the crowd with a couple of jokes and introduced the first act, the English folk duo with decent harmonies. In Renate's presence, the next few performers went by in a blur. Suddenly Peter heard his name being called. He took the stage and looked out at this new audience, hiding in a cellar for the sake of a bit of art.

Count to ten.

Tap each finger on the leg.

Take two deep breaths . . . and begin.

> *You can't lead, if you can't feel it, if it never*
> *Rises from the soul, and sways*
> *The heart of every single hearer,*
> *With deepest power, in simple ways.*
> *You'll sit forever, gluing things together,*
> *Cooking up a stew from others' scraps,*
> *Blowing on a miserable fire,*
> *Made from your heap of dying ash.*

Let apes and children praise your art,
If their admiration's to your taste,
But you'll never speak from heart to heart,
Unless it rises up from your heart's space.

He was oblivious at first to the silence that followed; every bit of him was in the character of Faust. But then he began to wonder, for a moment's moment, if he had failed again. Doubt slid into his collar and was just about to bite when—

The first clap. The second. And the room was suddenly filled with applause. Not the slow kind from an embarrassed audience, but the kind that comes from being truly moved, from the experience of something singular. Peter didn't want to spoil the moment, even by breathing. He had done it. *The magic.*

Peter took a bow and came down from the stage—into Renate's waiting arms.

The next several performers went by, long enough for Peter's high to subside so he could focus on his surroundings. A lanky guy with horn-rimmed glasses and an old tie took the stage. He was so morose and awkward, no one knew what to make of him.

"When I was a little boy," he began wistfully, "my Mutti used to tell me fairy tales. My favorite was *The Brave Tin Soldier.* 'Once upon a time, darling, there was . . . ,' she'd begin, this magical world surrounding us as though we all remembered what it was like in that faraway past, until it would resolve, beautifully, with *The end.*" He gave a nostalgic wave in the air.

"That was in the capitalist past," he said, suddenly serious and pounding his fist in his palm. "Now we're in a new world. We're waking up to the new dream of Marxism-Leninism! In *this* world, all the fairy tales begin with *The end,* and end with *The beginning's just around the corner, comrade! The last Five-Year Plan was only prepara-*

tion for this Five-Year Plan. Meanwhile, shut up and meet your damn quota, or we'll throw you, your opa and your little dog in the clink!"

Everyone fell apart. No one was expecting this guy to be a *comedian*. He never broke character or cracked a smile, but kept eye contact with the audience and went right on to the next bit.

Peter's mind caught fire with the possibilities. He suddenly recalled his mother's parties, the effortless jokes that came from his lips—the ones timed just right to pull his family back from the brink of a fight. The elation he felt when he could get Rudi out of a funk with a bit of razzing. Of course he'd seen comedians on television, heard them on the radio. But he'd never considered doing his own bits onstage. Was this still acting? Did it matter?

He felt Renate's eyes on him. She must have known that something was churning in his mind. He looked at her, and got a bit choked up.

"Thank you." He nodded. "Thank you for bringing me."

"Well, well, who do we have here?" Peter waved a brochure as he entered the apartment with the mail the next morning. "Brigitte Bardot!" He pointed to Oma, who smiled faux bashfully. To his bespectacled father: "Billy Wilder!" To his mother, who was pinning her hair: "Jayne Mansfield!" To Rudi, looking up from his astronomy homework: "And Peter Ustinov, everybody! The gang's all here! In town for the eleventh annual Berlin International Film Festival!"

"Is that—" Rudi pointed.

"Yes, my good man, these are the movie listings for the Berlinale! We've got *La Notte, No Love for Johnnie, Zone of Danger*— Oooh, this one looks good!" He chuckled. "*Romanoff and Juliet.* Wonder what that's about?"

"Let me see," said Rudi, reaching for the brochure. He scanned the list of films for the names of famous directors. "Antonioni . . . Kurosawa . . . Godard . . ."

"Well, this is where I exit the scene," said Rudolf. "I've got a bass bridge repair over in Treptow. Have fun, boys."

"And I have the night shift," said Ilse.

"Oh, Ilse," said Oma, "get that tinned herring for me on your way to work so I can have it for the morning."

"I will."

The boys said goodbye to their parents and got back to the brochure. "How about *Romanoff and Juliet,* Rudi?" asked Peter. "It's playing tonight. I'm in the mood for a comedy."

"Homework can wait," said Rudi. "Let's go."

Peter stirred in the middle of the night when Ilse came home from work. It was so quiet, he could hear her unbutton her overcoat, kick off her work shoes and slide her stocking feet into awaiting slippers. She sighed heavily.

"Abend," he heard Oma greet Ilse. She never slept all the way through the night. "Did you get the fish?"

"They only had two tins left. Did the boys like the movie?"

"They were out at the movie until eleven. It seemed like they had fun. Do you want some of this with cheese and bread?"

"Nein, danke. I'm going to bed."

Not two minutes later, the voices in the bedroom rose in clipped extracts. Peter and Rudi sat up in bed.

"I don't want to do this anymore," came Ilse's voice.

"When *did* you want to, Ilse? Ever?"

"No. Don't do that, Rudolf. I've done this by the book for fifteen years."

"By what book? The one by Dr. Haarer? You know she's the

reason people our age are walking around without hearts in their chests, don't you?"

"My mother raised me by that book."

"I rest my case."

"My job here is done, Rudolf. I'm finished. They're almost sixteen, about to graduate. They don't need me."

Peter and Rudi looked at each other. Peter's heart pounded and he gripped the blanket until his knuckles turned white.

"They'll *always* need you. You're their *mother.*"

"The die is cast early. They're fine. They'll be fine."

"But what about you and me?"

"We're over. In fact, I want you out."

"You want *me* out?"

"Yes. Now."

"Now? At four in the morning?"

"Ugh, sleep on the sofa, then. I don't care. But make a plan."

"You're kicking me out. Hmm. That's funny, because this is *my* grandmother's house."

"Then we'll both leave. We'll apply for new apartments. Or—I'll live with my brother."

"Your brother's apartment is a laboratory, and he sleeps on a cot. This is nonsense. Ilse, you're speaking *nonsense.*"

There was silence. Rudi and Peter sat stock-still, staring at the closed bedroom door. Then, as one, the twins got up and went to the living room. Oma sat in the dark. Peter and Rudi sat on the sofa, and the three of them listened to the fight.

Rudolf spoke softly from the other room. "Don't you think we should find a way to try? I worry about you, Ilse, when you get low, you know? It's been happening a lot. I want to help."

"I don't need your help," she spat.

"Why would you do this, then?"

"Because I *want* to. I just don't want to be married anymore."

"Maybe it's not just about what you want."

"What if it *is*? I'm not cut out for this—marriage, children, keeping house. I want my life back!"

"God, Ilse, you make me so tired. You really still think like a child. Like I interrupted your fun and games, and you're going to pick right back up at sixteen."

"Thirty-four and you're nothing but a stodgy old man," she began to yell again. "You always were, even at seventeen."

"No, Ilse, this is what it actually looks like to be an adult!"

"Get out. Get out get out get *OUT!*"

There was a thumping like pounding on flesh, and Rudolf came out of the bedroom, Ilse slamming the door behind him. He saw Oma and the boys, ran his fingers through his hair, picked up his copy of Rilke's *Letters to a Young Poet* from the side table and hurled it at Oma's cuckoo clock. The wood shattered, and the springs fell out, bouncing up and down like something out of a cartoon.

"Rudolf," said Oma, rising slowly, "go take a walk. Boys, come have some herring and bread. Morning's early today."

When Peter was eight years old, the city was in turmoil: the East German workers refused to kill themselves to meet the unreasonable new quotas set by the government, so they took to the streets. Rudolf had to walk the boys to school, and that made Peter feel like a big baby. So he'd gotten up onto a knee-high wall in front of the Good Samaritan church, yelled to Rudi and Rudolf, "Watch me!" He did a backflip, only he rotated just shy of his goal and connected his head to the corner of said wall.

And now the migraines came weekly, starting with a familiar feathery darkness like a vignette at the edges of his sight. He knew the nausea would be next, and then the darkness would close in as the pain took over his entire being. The only remedy was sleep, and if he said the word *headache* or even pointed to his head, everyone knew not to get in the way of his retreat to the dark bedroom.

He felt one coming on just as he heard his mother come home. He wondered which version of his mother had just walked through the door.

"Rudi, shut the light, please," Peter groaned. He hoped Ilse would just go to bed, not veer in there to say hello or anything like that. As it was, there was a bang—a slam of the bathroom door. A glass breaking in the kitchen.

"Headache?"

"*Ja.*"

"OK, I'll finish my homework in the other room. Sorry, Peter." Even the shuffling of papers was intolerable, like paper cuts to Peter's brain.

As Rudi opened the bedroom door, Ilse stood there, drunk, bobbing her head awkwardly like a lizard, trying to keep her balance with her head since her feet were clearly failing her.

"Hi, Mutti," said Rudi, squeezing past her.

Peter peered through one open eye and saw his mother.

"Peter, get up," she slurred.

"I can't," said Peter.

"Sit up and face me."

With a will outside of himself, he rolled over and hoisted his body up. The pain plunged through the whole column of his being.

"Your school called me," said his mother. "They are not happy with you."

"Must have been the wrong Peter," he said weakly.

"They told me you're skipping some of the FDJ events. They're wondering if you're still loyal to the Party."

"Mutti, please. Not now. Please."

"Don't you know what that can cost me? If my kid doesn't make the Party happy?"

Ilse advanced.

She slapped Peter on the side of the head.

Pain seared through him like a glowing hot sword, and he crumpled to the bed and whimpered. Oma rushed in.

"What the hell is going on here?" she shouted at Ilse. "Did you just hit a child in my house?"

"I'm sorry, oh God, I'm sorry, Peter! I didn't mean to!" His mother seemed to sober as she fell on the bed and tried to wrap her arms around her boy. But Peter shoved his mother away and ran to the bathroom to vomit.

Peter's headaches could range from inconvenient to existential. This was hell. Never had his mother laid a hand on him.

He emptied himself and let his head throb until he could stand and rinse his mouth. Oma's yelling only stopped when his mother retreated to her bedroom, still making loud cries of remorse. Peter passed Rudi on the couch with his school books piled beside him. Peter collapsed on the bed. Oma came in with a cool, wet washcloth and put it on his forehead. She sat up with him until he began to drift at last, to the sound of his mother sobbing in her bedroom. She just couldn't control herself enough to be quiet when he needed it most. She couldn't be the one in here with the wet washcloth.

"Something about the FDJ," he muttered as he fell asleep. "They're not happy. The Party isn't happy."

"Never mind," said Oma. "You can think about that in the morning."

That is, if he ever woke up from this nightmare.

RUDI

"You have a date, I presume?" Rudi asked. He came into the bedroom with his homework, as usual.

"Don't know if I'd call it that," said Peter, buttoning his shirt, still not himself. Rudi had tiptoed around his brother that morning. But Peter had seemed functional in class later that day and now he was getting dressed up. "She's not my girlfriend."

"What's her name again . . . Renate?"

"Mm-hmm." He played it cool, but the sound of her name made a smile flicker on Peter's lips.

That was the ticket. Rudi notched up the teasing.

"Fine, she's not your girlfriend. But you haven't gone out with anyone else since you met her." He mocked his brother in a singsong voice: "Wow, Peter, are you going to marry her?"

"Am I being interrogated?" Peter laughed. "I'm lucky she lets me breathe the same air as her."

"All right, all right. So where are you going?" Rudi bit his nails.

Peter paused, deliberating on how to respond. "Can you keep a secret?"

"You can't keep a secret from me. I can read your twin mind."

"I'm serious, Rudi. You can't tell a living soul."

"What is it? Is she having your baby or something?"

Peter punched Rudi in the arm. "Gross. Look, I'm dead serious. *Swear* you won't tell."

"Fine, I swear!"

Peter sighed. "I've been doing shows on Saturdays. At a cabaret."

"Where? Did you get a job at the Distel? Let me guess, you got the role of Dumb Teenager Number One!" Rudi threw himself backward on his bed in laughter.

"No. This one's underground. Nobody can know, do you understand?"

"A secret cabaret! Does anyone else know—do you know anyone there?"

"A couple of kids from school. Mostly university students. It's in Prenzlauer Berg."

"What do you do there?"

"A bit of everything—skits, monologues. A couple of people there write short plays. Singers, poets, slapstick acts. But my favorite thing is stand-up."

"Comedy?"

"Yes."

Rudi waved his hands in the air. "Like Jerry Lewis?"

Peter laughed. "Sure, you goof, like Jerry Lewis."

"But what's to hide, Peter? There are other places to do it that aren't so risky."

"We say what we want there. We don't have to lie. Let's just say Glasses and Baby Face wouldn't like it."

"Yeah, those Stasi guys . . . Wait a minute, Peter. You could get in serious trouble. You'd have to step down as FDJ president, or . . . you could even get kicked out of school for this. Our whole family could get caught up—"

"Not if you don't say anything."

Rudi bit his thumbnail. "Is this why you've been skipping events?"

Peter glared at Rudi in silence.

"I understand," said Rudi.

"Good." Peter ran pomade through his hair and combed it.

"So you see? You can't say a word." He grabbed Rudi suddenly by the shoulders, his face steely. "Not a word."

"Jawohl!" said Rudi, his heart suddenly beating like a rabbit's. He shook Peter away and straightened his clothes. "So . . . can I come?"

RUDI

"I can't believe I'm doing this," said Peter in a hush as they walked to the tram stop. "Remember: don't speak to me, OK? Not on the train, or on the street. Actually, stay a few meters back. And whatever you do, don't mess things up for me with Renate."

"Fine," said Rudi.

Rudi and Peter walked with their hands in their pockets. They'd learned as kids to walk at a pace that didn't attract looks from other people. They took the train in complete silence, did the precautionary circuit around the block and entered the building once they were sure there was no one looking.

The wall of cigarette smoke in the vestibule hit them instantly. Peter looked at Rudi again and stuck a warning finger in his face. Rudi put up his hands in surrender.

The cellar glowed hazy red from candlelight and the salvaged neon sign above the bar. Paintings and posters hung everywhere. Rudi's head buzzed with the smoke and heat and crowd. Peter waved Renate over.

"Who the hell is this?" She glowered at Rudi from beneath her bangs.

"Don't worry, he's safe!" Peter assured her.

"You're too new to judge that, Peter. Who *is* he?"

"He's my twin brother."

Renate's shoulders softened. She twisted her mouth. "Twin?"

Peter and Rudi nodded. "Fraternal," said Rudi.

"All right. But, Peter! Never, ever again. *Niemals.*"

Rudi saw Peter shrink two inches. He felt bad for getting Peter in trouble—but he didn't mind seeing the Crown Prince taken down a peg, either.

Rudi followed Peter to a table, and just as they were about to sit, Rudi saw *her.* Angelika.

What was *she* doing down here? Wasn't she new to Berlin? How could she have found out about this place so fast? Rudi made his way over to her, past thirty cigarettes at eye level.

"Angelika?"

"Rudi! What are you—"

"I was going to ask—"

"My sister." Angelika pointed to Sasha, out of uniform now and wearing a blue blouse and checkered pants and drinking a beer. "Top-secret, right?"

"We won't let on," said Rudi. "Do you want to sit with us?"

"Who's *us?*"

Rudi led her to the table. "This is my brother, Peter, and his . . . friend Renate." They gave each other tentative handshakes.

"Is this *her?*" Peter smiled at Rudi, who could've socked him.

"This is Angelika. Remember, the new girl in our FDJ chapter?"

"Oh, sure," said Peter, pretending to recall.

"You're Sasha's sister, right?" asked Renate. "What is this, bring-a-sibling night? Please, be careful, or you'll get us all locked up. And I'm not going to jail for a couple of kids. Of course I don't mean you, Peter. You're not a kid to me." She brushed his arm.

Peter blushed redder than the neon light. "*Kids,* she says. She only graduated last year." He gave Renate a teasing nudge.

They sat down, and the emcee hopped up onto the stage.

"Willkommen im Kabarett Zusammen!" he announced to raucous applause. "I'm your host, Arno, and so, anyway, enough about me— we have a full list tonight, so to keep us in clockwork German timeliness, I will give each act a one-minute warning at the three-minute mark. Right! First, we have . . . a newcomer! Angelika will be bringing us a song. *Bitte, Fräulein.*" He made a magnanimous gesture and cleared the stage.

Rudi was astounded. Angelika smiled at him and took her place on the tiny stage. Sasha handed her a guitar, and she began to sing. It was a folk song in a minor key. The language was almost like German, but different. Rudi didn't catch every word, but he understood the ache behind the melody, like the dark river in his mother's woodland tales. He got lost in the song, and so did the entire room.

Angelika struck her last chord, smiled at Rudi and came down from the platform. This girl was unafraid to stand out. If Rudi had to sing in front of people, it would have been sheer terror.

They pulled their chairs right next to each other. He put his arm around her shoulder and she leaned against him. Rudi was intoxicated by Angelika's performance and the feeling of her so close. Act after act went by, and he was hardly aware of them. But when Peter's turn came, second to last, the room took on a new energy. The audience knew him now, and they whooped and called out as he launched right into a monologue by Fulda. There was no doubt that his brother was a singular talent. Peter had the whole room in a trance. Even Rudi forgot for a moment that this was someone with whom he'd shared a womb. Peter descended to wild applause and slaps on the back.

After the last act, people milled about, talking to the performers.

The tables were pushed and stacked against the walls, and Arno put dance music on the record player.

"A reminder that we have to clear out, quietly and intelligently, friends, at ten o'clock!" Arno announced. "Two songs, and then we close."

Rudi stood speechless by Angelika. He remembered what it was like to kiss her. "Hi" was all he could manage.

Angelika turned toward him and smiled. "Hi," she said. "What'd you think of my song?" she asked. Even now, the sound of her voice shimmered through his skin.

"It was . . . it was . . . ," he stammered, and shook his head.

"That bad? Negative ten, right?"

"No. The complete opposite," he said, surprised at her self-deprecation.

"Thanks," she said.

"What language were you singing in?"

"Yiddish," she said. "There aren't many people left who know it. So my parents made sure we spoke it at home."

"Your father's a good person," said Rudi.

"Wish you could have met my mother." She reached out her hand and squeezed Rudi's. Her skin was soft, but her grip was like iron.

Rudi was surprised at how easy it was to talk to her. Away from the drama with the petty girls from school, they could relax and talk about books and film, especially the Berlin Film Festival.

Peter finally peeled away from his adoring fans to come say hello to his brother.

"We're going to catch a late movie at the festival," said Rudi. "You should ask that girl—the one you say isn't your girlfriend."

"Renate? Oh, no, I don't think she'd go with me—"

"Don't," Rudi laughed. "Don't think! Just ask her! Besides, I put in a good word for you."

"What?"

"*Ja,* she likes you," Angelika concurred. "Sasha told me."

"*Ask her.*"

"OK," Peter reluctantly agreed, hardly daring to believe it. "I'll meet you outside."

Rudi reached into his pocket and held out his tin of mints. Peter popped one into his mouth and willed his legs to move on the adrenaline from his brother's words.

PETER

Renate stood in the middle of the room holding a bottle of lemonade, talking to Sasha. Why couldn't she be in a dark corner somewhere? At least then, if he failed, he wouldn't feel like an anchorless dinghy in the middle of the ocean.

"Renate, *hallo,*" he said. "Sorry again about my brother."

"So, you're a twin, huh? I thought he was definitely your *little* brother," she teased.

"Rudi? He's actually older, by six minutes." Peter chuckled and swallowed. "Uh, we're going to see a movie at the film festival and . . . would you . . . like to come?"

Renate's smile grew wider. "Peter, I would really love to."

"You would?"

"But I have to get up early in the morning for work. Second job."

"Oh. Never mind. Sorry."

"But I could go out next week before the cabaret. I get off at three."

"Really?" He was shocked. Did she actually say yes to a real date?

"Yes. I'm glad you asked, Peter."

"I'm glad, too," he bumbled. "I mean, glad you said yes. *Tschüss.*"

Peter turned around so fast, he didn't know if she said goodbye back.

RUDI

The next Saturday brought the end of school for summer, and Rudi packed up his desk, and Peter's, too, since he'd stayed out with Renate extra late the night before. He'd brought his camera with an extra roll of film, and a small box of his homemade butter cookies to give to Angelika's father. But as he tucked in his notebook, Rudi found a note slipped into his desk.

BE CAREFUL WHO YOUR FRIENDS ARE

The note was decorated around the border with blue and yellow triangles, the unmistakable colors of the FDJ. On the corners, the triangles overlapped into six-pointed stars. Some blue. Some yellow.

He'd been getting little hints like this for the last couple of weeks. Angelika's popularity had been short-lived once her father's disloyalty had become clear. But Rudi walked with her anyway. They didn't talk; the air was charged with hostility directed at Angelika, and by extension, at Rudi. But he knew he couldn't let her walk alone.

Angelika spoke in a barely perceptible voice as they wrangled her bike from the rack. "You shouldn't hold my hand or anything," she said. "Not in public."

"I don't care what anyone thinks," he said defiantly.

"*I* do. I don't need any more trouble than I've already got."

"Who's *they*? Those girls?"

"Wow, Rudi, are you serious? No, not those girls. The people running your show. The *Party*."

Rudi scoffed. "Why would the Party care about a couple of kids having fun?"

"You know why. Of course you do."

"They have more important things to think about. Listen, don't worry. I'll set the tone for our comrades. I won't let anyone make you feel uncomfortable."

"Ever since we were little kids, what did they tell us? That we are the future of Germany, and that we can't let any fascist element cloud our judgment."

"Right."

"*You're either with us or against us,* right? Well, my father's made himself an enemy of the Party, Rudi, so everyone's made up their mind about me. I'm now a fascist element, and that has consequences. Even for someone who's co-leading the FDJ."

For a moment, Rudi considered the implications of this for himself. "Are you always this much of a pessimist?" he asked.

Angelika huffed in frustration.

They took the inconvenient trip back to her tiny flat in silence. When they opened the door, they found Angelika's father sitting in his one chair, reading by the window. He was dressed down today, in an undershirt and slacks. He looked surprised to see them.

"Ah, Rudi! You remembered us!" he said, rising immediately.

Rudi brought the box of cookies out of his book bag. "Of course, Herr Rosen! I didn't forget to bring your—"

Herr Rosen held up a finger. "Let me get into some better

clothes," he muttered as he went into the bedroom and shut the door. "I still have my suits, after all," he called. "Suits and books."

Rudi and Angelika waited by the bookshelf. Rudi read the titles aloud in German, Russian, English. He noticed some Hebrew spines among them. A little knob of unease began to press in his belly, and he didn't know why. He heard Angelika's breath. Felt her near him. Leaned over to her. She leaned toward him and turned her face. "I'm sorry I lashed out," she said quietly.

The bedroom doorknob rattled.

"I'll make some tea," said Angelika, and she abruptly went and filled the electric kettle with tap water.

Herr Rosen emerged, buttoned up in his brown three-piece suit. He put on his skullcap again and fastened a small pin onto his lapel: a blue-and-white flag with a six-pointed star.

"I'm ready for my close-up, Mr. DeMille," he said in English, laughing, his eyes twinkling as he carried the chair over to the wall of books. Rudi took out his camera, loaded it with film and took a reading with his light meter.

"All right, Herr Rosen, would you turn your body toward the window, yes, and your head—that's it, slightly more." He took another reading and closed down his aperture a stop and a half. "You're right—this window does get nice light."

"So it does, Rudi. And are you glad that school is out?"

"Yes, sir!"

"You have your student summer assignment?"

"Yes, I am . . . ah . . . working in a factory." Rudi blankly mimed checking the light. "A canned goods factory."

"Good, good. Joining the ranks of working men," said Angelika's father. "So"—he straightened his tie—"I hear you and my Angelika have grown fond of each other."

Rudi looked at Angelika for a cue. Was it all right to say it openly—to her father?

"Yes, Herr Rosen."

"And I understand you went to Sachsenhausen."

"Yes, sir." He had to take a photograph, for goodness' sake. He snapped the shutter. "I led our FDJ chapter—or my brother and I did—at the dedication of the memorial. There were flags from all the Socialist nations—they said there were a hundred thousand people there, maybe two hundred thousand!"

"That is a big number. A large number of Jews also died there. Did you know that?"

"Yes, we paid homage to all the heroes and fighters against fascism."

"The *heroes and fighters,* ah. The *martyrs.* And the victims?"

"Yes, of course."

"And what about the Jews? Did Ulbricht mention us in his speech?"

Rudi wasn't sure how to answer. "Well, I saw people in uniforms. . . ."

"He did not mention us, Rudi. This I know because I read the speech." Herr Rosen leaned his elbows on his knees and looked straight at Rudi. "Do you know there are fewer than a thousand Jews left in the entire GDR? Here, in the capital of the first country to claim to have officially stamped out antisemitism?"

Rudi released the shutter. "No, sir, I didn't know that."

"Now, why would Jews feel the need to flee once again, after such a promising start?

"I don't kn—"

"Religion is the drug of the masses, that's what Marx said. So all you have to do to wipe out *hatred* of Jews is to wipe out the *religion* of the Jews altogether. Logical, yes? Hitler tried to wipe out our bodies, but Marx, Lenin, Stalin—they tried to erase our souls."

Rudi didn't know what to do, so he kept shooting. He figured the man was trying to be candid, to get a more natural portrait. "Uh, this is looking very good, sir. You'll have a very nice portrait when we're done." He tried to change the subject.

"Do you think this is about my ego, son? That a disgraced man of fifty is eager to have his photograph taken by a teenager in his closet of a flat? No, Rudi. I want to give you an opportunity to capture on film a rare, exotic creature—an open Jew in the *Deutsche Demokratische Republik*!"

"Papa, stop, please," Angelika said calmly, as though she knew this was going to happen.

"Why? Rudi here is the future of the Workers' and Peasants' State, *Schatzi*, the first anti-fascist state in the history of the world." Herr Rosen's neck was turning red. "A *Gruppenleiter* in the Free German Youth. He might want to remember through his camera the time he was in the presence of a real, live Jew, not just one in his textbook lesson on that spectral theme called *Antisemitismus*. A *Jew*, Rudi—and a Jew who still prays!"

Angelika ran to her father and put her arms around him, whispering to him in Yiddish. Rudi felt himself exit his brain. Inside he was paralyzed—he knew he should put down his camera, but he was so disoriented, he lifted it to his eye and caught Angelika in his lens, the light on her too lush to miss. He knew, his rational brain knew, that taking photographs in a moment like this was the height of insensitivity. But the mixture of shame and passion and love for her father threw strange, triangular shadows all over her face. She looked straight into the lens.

Rudi pressed the shutter.

"Rudi, put the camera down and go home," said Angelika's father, his voice suddenly soft and calm. "Maybe it's best you don't show these to anyone after all."

149

PETER

A migraine had taken hold the night before, and Peter had barely gotten home and shut himself down in time to avoid being sick. Oma was asleep on the couch, his father dozing in the chair with his book of Rilke poems across his chest. Peter would have to contend with the sound of the television and the blue light filtering in through the louvered doors.

There was, in Peter's half-awake mind, a seed of terror that his mother would come home and hit him again. But he needn't have worried. Since that awful night, Ilse had come home from work even later than usual, after everyone was in bed. She didn't talk to anyone, didn't interact at all. She simply went into her room and shut the door. Rudolf had taken to sleeping on the sofa. Peter didn't know what to say about any of it.

Eventually he fell into a dreamless sleep. Thank God.

He was surprised when the remains of Oma's cuckoo clock struck one in the afternoon. The day was already hot and lazy. He was supposed to have gone to school to clean out his desk. He hoped Rudi would do it for him. Otherwise he'd have to charm the secretaries into letting him in over the summer. Peter dragged himself out of bed to get some juice. He was in a T-shirt and undershorts, and he felt like he'd been through a war.

Oma was back at the television, as usual, watching the Eichmann trial, as usual. Peter carried his glass of juice to the sofa.

"*Guten Morgen, Omi.*"

"*Morgen, Schatz.* Sorry we didn't wake you—you were a mess. I told Rudi to bring your things home from school for you."

"Thanks, Omi. Speaking of—where's Rudi? He should have been back by now," he asked.

"Went to his girlfriend's house."

"Where's Vati?"

"Tuning a piano at . . . ah . . . somewhere."

"Where's Mutti? In her room?"

"What else?" Oma shrugged.

"Oh," said Peter, and drank some juice. He watched a few more minutes, but finally decided to put on real clothes, make himself some lunch and attempt to eke a day out of the next few hours until it was time to leave for his date with Renate. He got his notebook and decided to write down some of his jokes.

Are the Russians our friends or our brothers?

Clearly, our brothers. You can choose your friends.

"Oma, what's that joke you always tell . . . about the apple machine or something?"

She clicked off the trial and came to the table. "You mean, *What is huge, makes a lot of noise, guzzles twenty liters of gas per hour and cuts apples into three pieces?*"

"Yes, that one!"

"An East German machine made to cut apples into four *pieces."*

Peter laughed. "That one always gets me." Had anyone else been home, he'd be ticking them off with his one-sided snickering. He wrote down every joke he could remember. Pretty soon he'd have a collection big enough to fill a slot at next week's cabaret.

There was a knock at the door. It was Charles.

"Guten Morgen!" he said. "Where is everyone?"

"Scattered to the four winds," said Peter.

"My favorite American!" Oma waved Charles inside. "Where

have you been? Why haven't you visited? *Komme, komme,* I'll make us some coffee."

Charles took a tentative step over the threshold and headed for the kitchen. "Is . . . ah . . . Frau Fleischmann . . . ?"

"Sleeping," said Peter.

"Don't worry about her. This is my house." Oma spooned instant coffee into three mugs while the kettle heated up.

"All right," said Charles. "I smell cookies. Rudi's been baking?"

"I think he made some cookies for his girlfriend," Peter said. "But look! He left some here for us." He opened the tin on the counter and offered a cookie to Charles.

"I'll meet you in the living room," said Oma, taking one for herself.

"I stopped by to see if anyone wanted to come with me to the record shop."

"I wish I could!" said Peter. "But I have plans today."

Charles looked at Peter's bare feet and pajamas and laughed. "I see that," he teased.

Peter smiled, pouring boiling water into the cups. "I'm heading out soon—I have a date."

"Now that's how you spend a Saturday! Well, let the guys know I stopped by, will you? And tell Rudi I want to meet his girl before I conclude she's a figment of his imagination!"

"If I hadn't seen her with my own eyes, I wouldn't believe it, either!" Peter munched on a cookie. "You know, if you give me five minutes, we can leave together."

"Sounds great," said Charles, sipping his coffee. "I'll go commiserate with your grandmother on the state of the world."

He walked toward the living room just as the bedroom door opened, and Ilse came out, looking dour and disheveled. She and Charles stood face to face in the hallway.

"Ma'am," said Charles.

"*Was ist los?*" said Ilse, turning red.

"We were just leaving," said Peter.

"Please, Peter," Ilse responded in German, looking directly at Charles, "tell your father to ask my opinion now and then about who comes into my house." She pushed past Charles to the bathroom and shut the door.

Peter and Charles walked together to the S-Bahn stop. Peter felt sick over his mother's behavior, but he didn't have language to address it.

"You seem a little glum," Charles said.

"Me? Oh, I woke up late. I was getting over a headache."

"Do you get them often?"

"Once a week or so. It was a bad one."

"I used to get those a lot after the war. The bombs probably rattled me around too much. Always made my wife fret. But she knew how to take care of me." Charles smiled. "I don't get migraines anymore. Maybe you'll grow out of them."

"Maybe," said Peter.

They walked a block in silence.

"Charles? I . . . am sorry about my mother."

"Yeah. About that. Let's just say I'm disappointed but not surprised. It's only been sixteen years since . . . Well, usually, I take people as I find them. But I have to tell you, this is a tough one."

"I hope you won't let her stop you from coming—"

"Listen, Peter." Charles sighed. "I appreciate the friendship. It's nice for an older fella, an expat like me, to be friends with the locals. But I just left this kind of thing behind in my own country. I'm not going to fight this war on foreign soil, too. Not if I don't have to."

"What are you saying?"

"I think I need to back away, Peter. I've got to choose where to put my energy. What I'm saying is, this is goodbye, all right? Tell your Oma and your father I wish them the best. Rudi, too. Guess I'll never get to meet those girlfriends of yours."

Peter's heart sank. "I understand. I would probably do the same. If you change your mind . . ." They shook hands and parted. "Goodbye, Charles," he called.

"*Tschüss,*" said Charles. "See you around, kid."

Peter got on the tram and watched the city pass by, wishing there was a way for him to walk away so it didn't make Charles seem cavalier, too.

RUDI

Rudi came home that afternoon as Ilse stepped out of the bathroom, looking wrinkled and tired. She disappeared back into her room, to the surprise of neither Rudi nor his great-grandmother.

Twenty minutes passed, and there was a knock at the front door. "*Ach,* it's like a revolving door here today. Can you get that, Rudi?" Oma hollered. "My knee is giving me trouble." She began a coughing fit that provided the soundtrack for the next five minutes.

Rudi got up and answered. Who should be standing there but Glasses and Baby Face.

"Is your mother home?" asked Baby Face.

"I'll get her," said Rudi. He managed to rouse Ilse by stressing the importance of answering the State Security when they came calling. She wrapped her robe around her pajamas and came out. Her hair was unkempt, and her mascara had left black half-moons under her eyes.

"Frau Ilse Möser-Fleischmann?" Glasses read from an envelope.

"Yes. That's me."

Glasses handed her the envelope. "Your television antenna is facing the West," he said. "You are to turn it back east. By order of the Ministry of State Security."

"What does it matter . . . ?"

"If you persist in receiving Western imperialist propaganda—"

"*Capitalist* imperialist," Oma interjected from the sofa, in between coughs.

"Ahem, yes, propaganda against the State . . . if you persist, you will face the confiscation of your television."

"Confiscation of my television?" Ilse protested. "But everyone watches these programs."

"You don't want to set a bad example for your children, though, do you?" Baby Face nudged his chin toward Rudi. "Allow misleading information into your home? Think of what that would mean to their future. And their future is our future."

Ilse looked at the envelope and nodded. "Thank you, comrades. I'll make sure my husband turns it back around."

"You can be sure of that," Oma called. "My television's not going anywhere."

"Thank you, gentlemen," said Ilse, starting to close the door on them.

Baby Face put his hand on the door. "Also, Frau Möser-Fleischmann . . . ," said Glasses, looking at his notepad.

"Mmm?" said Ilse, annoyed.

"I have here that you have missed several days of work this month. May I inquire as to your health? Do you need to see a doctor? We can help you arrange an appointment."

"I'm fine. Just a little under the weather."

"We have quotas to fill, *gnädige Frau*," said Baby Face. "Our Workers' and Peasants' State needs all hands on deck."

"We'll pay you another visit to see how you're feeling," said Glasses with a smile, "if you miss another day at the telephone company. All right?"

"Thank you for your attention to this matter," said Baby Face.

"Feel better!" said Glasses.

Ilse shut the door, stared at the envelope again and shuffled back to bed.

Rudolf came home that evening with a bag of takeout. He tried to get Ilse to come out of the bedroom and have a little dinner with the family, but it was an instant argument.

"I don't want to come out. I never know who you're going to bring home. I don't like the company you keep."

"Well, Ilse, I don't even *know* the company *you* keep. Except for that bottle next to the bed."

There was nothing for it but to move dinner down to Boxhagener Platz and eat on the grass. Rudolf spread out their picnic, and Oma filled him in on the tender concern that State Security had shown to their little family.

"I'll turn the antenna around when we go back in," Rudolf promised.

"Just long enough to get them off our backs," said Oma. "I can call my friend to ask what happens on my program, at least for a couple of weeks." She took a bite of a meat pastry. "But, Rudolf, you have to get Ilse to get out of this funk. She can't play games like this with her job, not with those weasels on her trail."

"It's not a game, Oma," he replied, lowering his voice. "I don't know how to get her out of it. Don't you think I would if I could? I've always just ridden it out. She snaps out of it eventually, and then she's back to her after-work drinks and her friends and her parties."

"We both know it's getting worse, *Schatz*. Every time, it lasts longer. She's going to lose her job. She needs to go to a doctor." She tapped on her forehead. "This kind."

Rudolf looked over at their building, then gathered his currywurst and soda. "I'm going back up to practice that Bartók *Mikrokosmos* piece," he said, circling his hand around his face. "Clears the mind."

PETER

"I'm working on a stand-up routine," Peter told Renate. He sipped his milkshake and leaned back, watching people pass their sidewalk table at the Eisberg Milchbar.

"Really? You're a dramatic actor. You think you can be funny?"

"*Ja*. I mean, how hard can it be? I make people laugh all the time. I've been doing it since I was little."

"Do you have any jokes?"

"A whole collection! Mostly Communist jokes."

"Peter, everyone knows those old jokes."

"Not like I'm going to tell them."

"Suit yourself." She smirked.

"Wow, Renate, thanks for the vote of confidence." Peter chuckled and sipped again.

"Don't misunderstand me, Peter. You should try it. I'll laugh, I promise."

"With me or at me?"

Renate gave him a sly smile and sipped her shake. This girl made Peter's chest ache so hard, he thought he might be sick.

At that moment, Angelika's sister, Sasha, came walking toward the Milchbar. She was dressed in a nurse's uniform, and a small mesh bag with her nurse's cap was tied to her purse strap.

"Sasha! Hey!" Renate called to her. "Come sit with us!"

Sasha quickened her pace and pulled up a chair, looking nervous. "I'm glad I found you," she said, her lips barely moving. "There's no cabaret tonight. We had a scare."

"Oh Gott," said Renate. "Who did they get?"

Sasha took a mirror out of her purse and pretended to check her makeup. "Günter. They busted into his place and grabbed him and interrogated him for eight hours. They slashed some of his paintings, Nata. I'm reeling."

"Did he tell them anything?"

"He said he didn't crack."

"Well, he must have said *something* to make us cancel the show."

"They tried to get him to admit there was a gathering. He told them he just gets together with friends in Friedrichshain to play cards and talk about art. Hopefully that threw them off. Maybe they'll look there and not in Prenzlauer Berg."

"That was close, Sasha, *mein Gott.* We'll get word to the others. Do you want an ice cream or something?"

"No, thanks. I volunteered to work a night shift so they wouldn't suspect me. They just moved me to the psychiatric building and there's a lot to learn. I'd better get going. Nice to see you, Peter. Tell your brother Angelika says hi." Sasha winked and put her mirror away, snapped her purse and left them.

"That's not good," whispered Renate.

"Has this happened before?"

"No, we're really careful. I don't know how they suspected Günter. But we can't let our guard down." They sat pensively for a while, finishing their drinks. "Peter, do you have time to go somewhere with me?" she asked.

"Sure," said Peter. "I guess our night is free now."

"Good." She got up abruptly and started walking away, and Peter had to jog to catch up with her. They got the S-Bahn north into Pankow, but Peter didn't ask where they were going. Sometimes it was better not to know a thing until you were already in it.

They arrived at a prewar building so badly pocked with shell scars it seemed like it was made of crumbs, like a bomb had incinerated the top layer and sent it into a decade-and-a-half-long undoing. Renate pressed the buzzer by a nameless tag. Twenty seconds later, they were let in, and Peter and Renate climbed two flights to a landing with one heavy wooden door. Renate pushed it open. No words were spoken, no *Hello, is anyone home?* or *Come in.* She beckoned Peter in and shut the door behind him, locking it. The layout of the flat looked very much like his, typical of Berlin apartments that had been patched together after the war. Unlike Peter's dingy place, though, it was empty. There was no furniture, but it had incredibly fine woodwork—the honey-colored doors were carved with Palladian motifs, and there were built-in bookcases with turned molding completely bare.

They walked through the flat to a back room next to the kitchen. Only this one room was occupied. A woman stood to greet them, dressed in tea-colored corduroy slacks and a light blue short-sleeved blouse. A cigarette smoked itself in the ashtray next to her chair.

"Hello, Renate," she said.

"Hello, Mutti. This is Peter."

"*Freut mich,* Peter," said Renate's mother. "I am Vera Schenning. Please, sit down." She gestured toward a single bed in the corner by the window. Peter felt funny about sitting with Renate on a bed in front of her mother, but its tight military folds made it feel more like a stone table than a bed.

"How are you feeling, Mutti? How's your heart?"

"Ticking like a cuckoo clock," she chuckled.

"I heard about Günter," said Renate.

"Yes, he came to see me."

"Is he all right?"

Vera opened a small icebox beside her chair and drew out two bottles of sparkling water, popped the caps and handed them to Renate and Peter. "He'll be fine. Just a bit shaken. How about you? Did it scare you when you heard?"

Renate drank half the bottle before she answered. "A little."

"Remember what I told you, Nata. Those who inflict terror do it because they themselves are terrorized. Look in their eyes. You will always be able to see the fear in their eyes."

"I know."

"Günter told me that he looked in their eyes, and he saw the fear. And that helped him to stay strong. He'll be all right."

"Mutti, I brought Peter to meet you because he's getting serious with the cabaret, and he needs to know what to expect, just in case. He should know your story."

"Are you sure, Nata?"

"I'm sure."

"Peter, has my daughter told you anything about my past?"

Peter had taken a swig from his bottle and almost choked. "No, Frau Schenning."

"In a normal world, my actions would not be controversial, nor their consequences so severe. But this is not a normal world."

"OK." Peter leaned forward and prepared himself.

"I was a researcher at the university. Around—what was it?—eight years ago now, a gentleman used to come to see me, a committed Socialist. A good man. He had suspicions that the Party was purging Jews."

"But the Party—"

"Officially stands against this, yes? When you take your pledge at your FDJ meetings—*always ready*, always ready to fight *Antisemitismus*—do they talk about 1953? The purges of Jews in high positions?"

"No," said Peter.

"The Party called Jews imperialists, said that all their talk about Jewish survival was distracting from the class struggle. The leaders riled up the Party with conspiracies about Jewish control over money, Jewish domination of Palestine. Did you know this?"

"No."

"Well, this man I helped, he survived those purges. He kept quiet and played the game, but as time went on, he couldn't live with himself. So what did I do? I helped him dig up information on what he saw. It turns out that the Party here and in other Communist countries had a problem with Jews who actually wanted to be Jewish. They saw that as a conflict with a religionless society. And forget about anyone who supported a Jewish state.

"So they fired them all, decimated their options. There were show trials. Executions. This gentleman and I managed to get a report to the Western press last year. The Party didn't suspect us until about six months ago. But vultures begin to circle when your movements slow, when they think you're weakening.

"And so they gave us a choice: confess our treason and go to prison—in which case, our entire families would have suffered—or become recluses. I had to separate from Nata's father. For their sake."

"They made you break up your family?"

"What else could I do? Now I'm a squatter here, confined to one room of what used to be a life in progress. They made Nata and her father move out, so I'd have to stay in this constant reminder of what I lost. I can only afford to heat one room of my own flat. But this is a safe place, at least, and Nata doesn't have to pay for my so-called crimes."

"Why don't you move to West Berlin, or try to leave the country?"

"Because the consequences of any action I take will be visited on my family. I can't leave my daughter to the Party's predations. There are others who need a place to come and be strengthened. And now you know where you can come if you should need that."

Peter's mouth was so dry, he knew he wouldn't be able to quench his thirst, but he took a sip of sparkling water.

The sound of the buzzer startled Peter, and he spilled water on his shirt.

"Excuse me, let me see who that is," said Vera. "Nata, would you get Peter a towel?" She went out into the main room, pressed against the wall and looked sideways out of the window.

"Ah," Vera sighed, returning from the other room. "It's a friend. I have to be careful about how people come and go, Peter. Eyes every-where. Will you see yourselves out and let him in?"

"Of course, Mutti," said Renate. "Thank you. I love you."

Vera embraced her daughter, and Peter thought Renate looked so small, so like a little girl in the arms of her mother.

"Nata, since the cabaret isn't meeting tonight, let's be extra cautious. Have everyone gather here next Saturday. Peter, you'll come, won't you?"

"Of course."

"Good. You're cute. Renate should keep you around." She shook

Peter's hand and looked at him closely. "There's only one thing to remember, *verstehen?*"

"Yes?"

"If you live in truth, they cannot affect you with their lies."

Renate and Peter left the building. "Let's go to a different S-Bahn station," she suggested. "Change up the route."

The lowering sun flung their long shadows against the buildings, and Peter thought it must be nice to be a shadow, ringed with gold, without substance that could be hauled into a police station and pressed for information. *How would I do?* he wondered. *Would I be strong, like Günter? Would I crack?*

"You all right?" asked Renate. "I know what she said is intense. I just thought you should know what you're really getting yourself into."

"I suspected."

"There's one more piece she didn't tell you. The man she kept speaking of? It was Sasha and Angelika's father."

"You're kidding. . . ."

"No. They destroyed his life. Anyone who questions them, they label a danger to the country unto a thousand generations. Peace? Freedom? Friendship? Only if you keep your mouth shut."

Peter thought about his brother. What would happen if the authorities knew who Rudi was going out with? For that matter, if they knew about Renate and himself? These were children of dissidents. The stakes suddenly seemed very real indeed.

But what business was it of the Party apparatus? Their comings and goings, their thoughts, their beliefs, their jokes and books and music? The families they were part of?

"I'm glad we went," he said. "I have a lot to think about."

Renate stopped in front of Peter. She looked so deeply into his eyes, it scared him. He'd never looked this closely at a girl. He saw beyond her prettiness, her wide eyes and full mouth. He saw into her fear and, even further, to her resolve. He couldn't believe he'd ever looked at another girl before Renate.

And then she pulled him in and kissed him. And Peter became, in a moment, fully alive.

"Monday! First day of student summer!" Peter said, stretching the sleep kinks out of his muscles. He was still riding high on Renate's kiss. Whether he turned to the right or the left, he felt a surge of her presence in his chest.

"You excited?" he asked Rudi as he bounded out of bed and started getting dressed.

"To work at a sauerkraut factory?" Rudi lay motionless, staring at the dawn light on the ceiling. "Thrilled beyond belief."

"Look on the bright side, though. Free kraut for the whole family."

"Sure, and the smell of fermented cabbage coming out of my pores."

"Well, I'm going to be working on a sheep farm," Peter laughed. "Which is worse?"

Peter put on work clothes, but Rudi told him to wait. "Don't you think for the first day that we should represent well?"

"What, wear our FDJ shirts?" he teased.

"Just for the first day."

"Oh, you're serious? Fine, but I'm bringing a change of clothes."

"I guess you're right," said Rudi. They brushed their teeth and walked to the tram stop.

"So, I think I'm going to ask Angelika to make it official," said Rudi. "You know, to be my girlfriend."

"Like, a human girlfriend?"

Rudi punched Peter in the arm.

"OK, what's she like? Offstage, I mean."

"She's kind of . . . I don't know . . . amazing. We've gone out a few times, and I think she likes me."

"Well done, Rudolf Jr.! You didn't scare her off."

Peter remembered what Renate had told him about Angelika's father being kicked out of the Party. He couldn't risk revealing what he knew about their family, but he wanted to know more about them. He spun his question into a jab. "Is she a die-hard Socialist like you?"

"Mmm . . . I wouldn't say so."

"Trouble in paradise already?"

"I don't know. Maybe she'll get on board. There's time."

"Well, I may have someone kind of amazing, too. This weekend."

"A new girl?" Rudi laughed. "We'll see if you're still talking about her by next week."

"We'll see if your girl's still talking about *you* by next week!" Peter retorted. His tram arrived, and he hopped on. "Good luck at the factory!" he called, leaning out the door.

"Have fun with your animal friends!" Rudi mocked.

"Bring home a big jar of cabbage, stinker!"

Peter plopped into a seat beside an elderly man in an old hat. Thankfully the morning wasn't hot yet, or the tram would have been devoid of oxygen. He took the paperback of *Faust* out of his bag and opened to a dog-eared page. He began to read, but after turning two pages, he realized he hadn't absorbed a single word.

Renate filled his thoughts instead, this beautiful girl who took a chance on him after a botched audition, bringing him into this new life he'd landed in at Kabarett Zusammen. Was he really this lucky?

In spite of the risks, the freedom and creative energy he felt at the cabaret made all of his school plays and drama competitions feel somehow manufactured, dictated. Oh, he loved Brecht and Goethe, he always would. But in that smoky cellar, Peter felt more authentically human than he had in his entire life. *On that stage,* he thought, *people will get what I do and why I do it. There's no ceiling. I can try anything I want.*

He almost missed his transfer to the U-Bahn at the Hauptbahnhof, but finally he arrived in Potsdam, just outside the city limits. Four other kids were there, two girls and two boys from other schools. A truck came, and they piled into the hay-strewn truck bed and rode off to the farm. The farmer came out of the house to meet them, a wizened old man in dusty dungarees and a hand-knit red sweater.

"This farm was in my family for two hundred years before the Party seized—I mean, *collectivized* it," said the farmer, his voice tinged with bitterness. "They say it belongs to you *Jugendliche* now, to the Workers' and Peasants' State. But in my eyes, you're on my land, and I want things done my way. As long as we understand each other, it should be a good summer. *Ja?*"

"Jawohl," the five of them answered.

"All right, let me show you around. If you don't have rubber boots, I have extra pairs. You"—he pointed at Peter—"you'd better wear some work clothes tomorrow. Wouldn't want you to dirty that nice shirt."

Peter reached into his bag and pulled out his old denim work shirt and held it up.

"Good man," said the farmer. "Figured your mother made you dress up. But you planned ahead. Good man."

Peter changed his shirt as they walked. The farmer led them to each outbuilding and showed them where to find tools, feed and drinking water. He gave Peter and one of the girls pairs of work boots.

There was a mouse hiding in hers, which offered a bit of comic re-lief, and even the choleric farmer laughed. Peter felt it would be a good summer, indeed.

When they finally came to the pasture where the sheep and lambs were, something in Peter quieted. The gentle eyes of the crea-tures were so endearing, he couldn't wait to be with them. He and the girl with the mouse boots would be in charge of the sheep, while the others were given jobs like minding the crops and the machinery. But the two of them were to care for this flock, watch for harm and tend their wounds. They were each given a whistle and taught to command the farm's three sheepdogs. As soon as the farmer called the dogs over, one of them, a fluffy red dog with honey-colored eyes, came right up to Peter, tongue and tail wagging, begging him for a pet. Peter obliged.

"That's Fox," said the farmer. "She doesn't usually like people. You must have a way about you."

Peter patted Fox's soft fur and bent down to look in her eyes. "We'll take good care of those sheep, won't we? Yes, we have a pact," he announced.

Fox did not leave his side the entire day. Peter practiced his stand-up routine for the dog. He told her about Renate, and about his dream of leaving Germany altogether and starting a new life.

The sun began to fall as they piled into the back of the truck and headed for the station. A spider's web fluttered from the hay like a golden thread. Peter was exhausted and satisfied, ready to go home, ready to return. His mind was clear, and he loved the world.

The air was stale in Vera's flat when Renate and Peter arrived early for the meeting the following week. Renate found an electric fan in a closet and pointed it out the window to blow the hot air away.

"It should cool down by the time everyone gets here, and then I can turn it around and bring the evening air in," she said.

"Good plan," said Vera, fanning herself with an old pamphlet.

"I brought strawberries from the farm," said Peter, holding up a paper bag.

"Strawberries!" Vera exclaimed. "What a luxury!"

"The farmer likes me. He's not supposed to give food away, but I'm good with his sheep, so he gives me perks."

"The thought of you with a shepherd's crook, like some biblical patriarch!" Renate laughed as she rinsed the berries and put them in a bowl.

"My aunt used to put up buckets of preserves," said Vera. "Ah, those carefree summers, when your strawberries actually belonged to you."

The small clock in Vera's room chimed the hour.

"I'll man the door, Mutti," said Renate.

"No, Nata, let's have Peter do it. No one will suspect him. Peter, take this book and sit on the bench outside the building." Vera handed him a key and a hardbound copy of Camus's *The Plague*. "Our people will come to you and give the password. Unlock the door and let them up. One at a time, though. Each person must give you the password individually. Do you understand?"

"What is the password?" asked Peter.

"*What use to the herds, the gift of freedom?*" Vera answered.

"Pushkin," said Peter. "Makes sense."

Peter stationed himself outside the apartment building and began to read the Camus book. The blazing sun was soon shrouded by gray clouds, and Peter could smell rain coming. One by one, over the course of an hour, familiar faces from Kabarett Zusammen appeared and gave him the password. Sasha and Angelika came; even Arno showed up. Günter was the last to arrive. Eventually Renate came down and gave a quick whistle to signal Peter to join her up-stairs. The book was too good to stop reading, but he closed it just as a steady shower began.

The barren living room was full of cabaret folks, but it wasn't the same bustling atmosphere he was used to in Arno's cellar. Their hushed voices faded upward into the high, carved-plaster ceiling. A small circle formed around Günter, his friends putting soothing hands on his back, wishing him well, hugging him, thanking him for his courage. Renate turned the electric fan around, and the coolness of the rain blew in.

"Let's gather now," said Vera, barely needing to raise her voice. "Günter, I want to say right away that we are all incredibly proud of you, your strength and resolve."

Everyone nodded as they sat in a circle on the parquet floor. Renate sat between Peter and Günter and passed the bowl of straw-berries around. The others had brought things to share as well.

Vera poured everyone glasses of sparkling water, and then she sat in the one chair brought out from her room. "We'll begin with a discussion question. Nata, would you please?"

"Brecht said, *Art is not a mirror held up to reality, but a hammer with which to shape it.*"

A skinny man with thinning blond hair interjected. "Actually, that was Trotsky, not Brecht."

"My mistake, Thomas," Renate responded with a hint of snark. "Well, what does everyone think of that? Is art a mirror or a hammer?"

"I don't know," Sasha pondered. "I never think about it. I just know the art I like when I see it."

"It's a mirror," Günter countered. "Art says more about the viewer than it does about the artist."

"But what about the posters hanging in the hallways at school?" suggested Peter.

"That's not art, though. That's propaganda," said Günter. "Big difference."

"But how can you tell?" asked Peter. "At first, nice to look at, they're aesthetic; but every time I see that stuff, I feel like I *am* being hit with a hammer that's trying to shape me. *Do Your Part in the Five-Year Plan! Everyone into the Battle for Peace!* No, art *should* be like a mirror. A good *actor* doesn't become the character—the *audience* does."

"Peter has a few opinions." Renate laughed, and so did everyone else.

"Peter," said Thomas, "it's one thing to have you come to the cabaret, but coming here is on another level. Groups like ours have been infiltrated by informers. Before any of us say another word, how do we know we can trust you?"

"I guess . . . you don't," Peter acquiesced. "How do I know I can trust you?"

"You don't," Arno piped up. "That's the risk we all take. It's why we all showed up here."

"Arno's right," Günter interjected. "I'm not sure why they brought me in for questioning, but I don't blame any of you."

"What happened?" asked Peter. "When you were arrested?"

"Günter?" asked Vera. "Can you . . . ?"

"Yes, Frau Schenning. I'm all right." Renate put her hand on Günter's back, and he began to tell his story. "I'm coming back from the art store, just bought a couple canvases, a couple tubes of paint. And all of a sudden, I feel two people on either side of me grabbing my arms. Just holding on to me, like we're three friends taking a walk. *Gunter,* one says, *we'd like to ask you some questions. Come with us.* And they put me in a car and tell me to keep my head down. If I look up, they yell at me. I try to see where I am, but I lose my sense of direction.

"They interrogate me for hours. I never go to a cell or anything. I just have to sit on this little chair. My legs fall asleep, and I fall asleep, and I can't feel my body anymore. They keep asking me if I know about any secret cabaret, and I say, *What cabaret? I'm a painter, not a performer.* I just keep saying that I want to get back to my painting.

"And I meant it! And I remembered what you said, Frau Schenning, and I looked in their eyes. And I knew I would make it. Because they were just people. They kind of . . . lost their power over me. I wasn't afraid."

"Well said," said Vera, "and well done."

"The only hard part was when I came home and saw what they'd done to my paintings."

Sasha moved next to Günter and put her arm around his shoulder. "The art you make from this is going to be even better," she consoled him.

"But that's nothing compared to what Arno and his family went through," said Thomas.

"Arno doesn't have to rehash that, Thomas," said Vera.

"No, no, our new friend should know," said Arno. "Everyone should know what the Party is capable of. Why should we have to live in fear of our own countrymen again? Who are the real fascists, if not the ones going house to house, looking for hideouts, slashing paintings?"

Arno proceeded to tell his story. It went far back, to before the Nazis took over, to the point when the country first lost its sanity, to the point when neighbors measured their virtue—or at least their safety—by their tenuous relationship with the truth. His family had a rock-solid commitment to living in truth. Arno's two cousins were part of the White Rose resistance group, the students that secretly distributed anti-Hitler pamphlets. Both of them were executed.

"No one can predict when they'll run afoul of the folks in charge. Meantime," Arno concluded, "I say we make some art."

Peter broke the silence. "Can I ask a question?"

"Anything," said Vera.

"There's that line in Hamlet: *The funeral baked meats did coldly furnish forth the marriage tables.* It's always confused me. How did we permit a second dictatorship on the heels of the first? How did we not learn that lesson—we went from the Nazis to the Communists overnight. It's like we *want* to be controlled."

Thomas spoke up. "They said we *needed* their dictatorship, because we Germans were so tainted that we couldn't be trusted to change. They said we needed *them* to educate us, to let them stamp out the past. And people were in such shock that they rolled right over and went with it. We served it to ourselves."

"It's the swastika, or it's the hammer and compass," said Arno. "It doesn't matter what logo you put on it when you're forcing people into a cage. They call anyone who disagrees with them *fascists*. But that's a trick. Fascism isn't a system in itself. It's how the system's carried *out.*"

"So how do we stand in the face of untruths?" Vera asked the gathering.

"Don't agree to anything you know isn't right," said Thomas.

"Don't put anything in your art that isn't true," said Günter.

"Don't take the bait," said Sasha.

"That last one is everything," said Vera. "They want to unsettle you, disturb your equilibrium. Don't take the bait."

"All right, everyone," said Arno, rising. "We'll be back at my place next Saturday. Frau Schenning, thank you for your hospitality. Everyone feel OK?"

Morale had sufficiently lifted, as had the rain. Person by person, the gathering dispersed with warm embraces.

Peter and Renate were the last to leave, after they cleaned up and said goodbye to Vera. They took out the trash and dumped it in a wastebasket in the park. The mist from the rain shower rose into the trees. At last, they came to a covered colonnade and went inside.

"I took a big risk, bringing you to my mother's place," said Renate. "You heard what they can do to you if you're caught. So do you want to be part of this, Peter? This is your chance to back out. But if you do, you can never come back. And we can never see each other again. Your choice can't be about you and me, though. It has to be about the truth."

"No, this is right. I suspected that things weren't what they seemed. Now that I know, I can never unknow. I can't be part of anything that would crush other people like that."

"That's what I was hoping you'd say." Renate came closer and slipped her arms around Peter's waist. He pulled her toward a stone column and gathered her in. He kissed her. He drew in her honesty, and their kiss grew so intense that they were pouring themselves into each other. It began to rain again, so they stayed in the shelter of the colonnade, promising each other to always live in truth.

RUDI

The Sunday after the first grueling week at their summer jobs was hotter than hell. Peter and Rudi had slept fitfully, sweating through the sheets and waking up every hour with unquenchable thirst.

They lay spread-eagle on their beds, and Peter told Rudi of his odd dreams, of running through buildings, in and out of shadows, of Renate reaching to him from heights he could not climb, of wild animals wandering around the apartment, eating through the walls.

"I'm dying to get out of here," said Peter. "Do you want to go to Teufelsberg? We can swim in the lake after."

"Yes," said Rudi. "Shady woods sound really good right now."

The twins packed their backpacks lightly—a change of shorts, towels, billfolds, canteens. They raided the cupboards for snacks, kissed Oma on the cheek and set off for the mountain on the far west side of Berlin.

The train car wasn't any cooler, despite the open windows. When they arrived at Grunewald station, they thought of jumping in the lake first, but as they entered the forest canopy, the feverish heat gave way to a refreshing breeze. Memories of Ilse and her maps scrolled through Rudi's mind, the fresh, springy moss under his feet. He longed for the mother of his childhood.

"Do you remember what Vati told us about the forests after the war?" asked Peter. "That the Allies cut them down for reparations?"

"It figures," Rudi grumbled. "Greedy capitalists ruin everything they touch."

Peter shrugged and pointed to the self-seeded saplings dotted around. "Good thing they're growing back here pretty quickly."

They climbed the base of Devil's Mountain, up through scrub brush and broken bottles. Higher, higher they climbed, the grass nicking their legs, their sweating and panting making them wish they'd taken that dip first.

"We're here," said Rudi at last, taking a swig of water from his canteen.

They stood with their hands on their hips, looking out at the vast cerulean sky on all sides. Up on this mountain, sector borders were invisible. It was only sky and gold grass on the pile beneath their feet.

Rudi took out his camera and began to shoot photographs of the panorama, the forest below, the bulldozers and his brother, strong and proud against the sky, like a Soviet poster. He half expected to see a red banner with Lenin's face materialize behind him.

"Let's have lunch," Peter said.

They sat on their towels in the shadow of a huge bulldozer and opened their packs. They ate bread and cheese and an entire jar of pickles as they looked out over the city.

Exoskeletons of bombed-out buildings still dotted every neighborhood in Berlin. As many as the workers pulled down, there were always more to reckon with. This very mountain was man-made, a mound of the debris the *Trümmerfrauen* couldn't salvage, piled right on top of an unfinished Nazi college. The bucket brigades were long gone. Now, week by week, dump trucks deposited loads of war rubble on Teufelsberg to make room for the new *Plattenbau* buildings, prefab cement cubes that builders assembled into lifeless apartment blocks. Still, among the dust and sterile stone piled on the mountain, grass and trees took hold almost overnight, growing tenaciously on the discards of past darkness.

"Look at this city." Peter gestured over Berlin. "What a mess."

"I don't know, it's not so bad," said Rudi. "Look at all those new apartment buildings. They're making a lot of progress. They've got to be a lot nicer than our cramped flat."

"True enough."

The boys lay on their backs, gazing across the skyline for a long time, listening to the earthmovers pushing the mountain together below them. They watched a pair of birds circling so high above them, they couldn't tell whether they were hawks or vultures.

Finally, they descended to seek shade below the tree line. They leaned against a towering alder, looking up at the dancing light and shadows.

"Peter, hey," said Rudi, "I never really asked you about the audition."

"Yes, you did. What about it?"

"No, I mean, since you didn't get into the drama school . . . what do you think you're going to do after graduation?"

"Do the extra two years of school, take the Abitur, I guess. Keep auditioning for things." He got fidgety. "I think I might step down as student leader, too."

A surge went through Rudi's chest. "What? Why?"

"I'm not sure I believe any of it. All they do is churn out carbon copies of distant, hypocritical adults who don't believe it, either. They're just too scared to get on the bad side of the Party."

"That's really cynical, Peter. Some people really do believe."

"Do you? Believe in building Socialism and all that?"

"I do," said Rudi, turning to face his brother. "I think there's a better future ahead of us. In fact, I want to work for the Party after we graduate."

Peter glanced over at his brother and met his earnest look. "Then maybe you should take over if I resign."

Rudi thrilled to the suggestion, but he didn't let it show.

"I feel like I'm made to do something, something big and important," said Peter. "I don't want to give up my soul just to fit into the machine, to be some invisible gear in a tangle of other gears."

"But you have to be part of *something*, Peter. Everyone does. And people worship the ground you walk on. Why would you give that up?"

One of the birds soared overhead through a break in the canopy. "Remember that model airplane contest?" Rudi continued. "How old were we, eight? You and I worked as a team, and our plane was the first one to crash. But we worked together and figured out what was wrong. We had to scrape away the dried glue, reset the wing and reglue it. We didn't win, but we figured out the problem."

"I think you hadn't fully pushed the wing into the slot, so it was crooked," said Peter.

"Of course it was my fault," Rudi huffed. "That wasn't my point."

"What *was* your point?"

"That it's . . . not about who made mistakes or anything, but what got the plane in the air. It's not only about what's good for you, Peter. It's about the *common* good."

"You're right, Rudi. We do have to be part of something. But I'm not looking to be a model airplane. I want to be a living, soaring, clear-eyed hawk named Peter."

"Whatever," Rudi chortled. "Sometimes I don't understand anything you say."

Peter was quiet for a long time. "I was with the people from the cabaret last night," he told Rudi. "Some of them have been hauled off to interrogation or even prison. They're just artists, students, professors, journalists, trying to live their lives. Why do people think they can treat others that way? Is that part of building the future?"

"Maybe you don't see the whole situation, Peter. You just met these people. You don't know what they're really about. There are consequences for breaking the law, you know."

"But what if the law is wrong? And what if the law is always changing? Aren't I allowed to stand against that?"

"If they're trying to tear down the Party, I mean, they have to be held accountable."

"Accountable? For speaking their mind?"

"Come on, you can speak your mind. Who's stopping you?"

"Do you think it's normal for guys to knock on your door and tell you which way to point your antenna?"

"It's fine if you have nothing to hide."

Peter studied Rudi. "You know, there are two kinds of people in this world. One kind will point a gun at you from two hundred feet away and say they're shooting in self-defense. The other kind is happy to walk right up to you, look you in the eye and tear off your face with their bare hands."

Rudi started to feel unsettled. His brother kept staring at him. "Which one are you?" asked Rudi.

Peter paused. "I don't know yet. Sometimes it scares me that I think, under the right circumstances, I could do something terrible—and enjoy it. Which one are you?"

"I could never be that cruel," Rudi protested. "I'd only ever shoot in self-defense. Even if it was from far away."

"I guess we're different, then. Really fraternal. Because killing someone from afar is chickenshit." Peter got up and stretched. He did a handstand and walked on his hands for a minute. "God, it's hot. Want to go swim, *Bruder Ruder*?"

"Sure," said Rudi. Maybe it would cool his heating blood.

They headed down to Teufelssee, full of sweat and dust. Peter ran to the lake, grinning and tearing off his shirt. He threw his bag down at the shore and hurled himself in, splashing and making a ruckus like a kid. "It's *cold*! Rudi, come in!"

Rudi watched his brother, paddling and floating, spitting water from his mouth like a fountain.

He walked into the lake as Peter sloshed water at him with a flat hand. Rudi got closer, looking Peter in the eye. He put out both hands, wrapped them around Peter's throat and slowly, mechanically, pushed him down under the surface. Peter flailed, his arms and legs looking for something to grab on to, to leverage himself away from the murder. Rudi could feel the fight go out of Peter as frenzied bubbles came to the surface. It was interesting. It didn't feel like he thought it would.

It was a relief.

"Aren't you going to swim?" Peter called, shaking Rudi out of his reverie. Rudi was still standing by the edge of the lake. He walked into the water, frightened by what had just played out in his mind. He was scared—of himself. Even if it was only in his imagination, he'd risen up to kill his brother. It was wrong. He knew it was. So why didn't it feel that way?

"Rudi? You all right? *Was stimmt nicht?*"

"Nothing, I . . ."

"Well, snap out of it!" Peter pushed his brother in the head playfully and shoved him into the water. Rudi launched himself out to the middle of the lake, far from Peter, floating under the scrutiny of the bright sun.

Rudi's fantasy dissolved, and the two of them swam for the rest of the afternoon, exhausted, skin pruned, and hungry.

"Hey, let's get a milkshake," Peter suggested as they gathered their things and started for home.

They stopped at the Milchbar closest to the tram stop. Peter had chocolate with caramel, Rudi strawberry.

So much was changing. They had always lived the parallel lives of twins, but time was only revealing their differences. Rudi wondered if they'd even stay in touch after graduation. The boys chatted all the way home, where they bumped into Oma, coming out of the apartment with her purse and a scarf tied over her hair.

"Where are you going, Omi?" asked Peter.

"Out for a breath of fresh air," she quipped. "There's none left in there."

Rudi and Peter hung up their bags and kicked off their shoes.

Even full from their milkshakes, they reflexively headed toward the kitchen to make a snack before settling in, but they stopped short in the doorway. Their parents were sitting at the table, hands folded, between them only a small bud vase with the fake daisy sticking out of it.

This was immediately suspicious: it looked like Ilse and Rudolf had been . . . talking. They never did that, not on purpose, not without screaming.

"Sit down, boys," said Ilse.

"We have plans—" said Rudi and Peter together.

"Plans can wait," said Rudolf. *"Bitte."*

"Mutti and I have decided on the arrangements," said Rudolf the next day. He came into the kitchen as the boys were drying the day's dishes and put his hands on his hips. "Peter, you're going to stay here with her. Rudi, you and I are going to get an apartment nearby."

"What? Why?" Peter took the dish towel off his shoulder and threw it on the counter. "Were you going to ask us?"

"Frankly, I don't have to consult you," Rudolf quipped. "Rudi, start packing. I'm aiming to move in the next two weeks, as soon as I can find a place."

"Where's Omi going to live?" Peter protested.

"She'll stay here, obviously," said Rudolf. "It's her flat."

"Shouldn't you be the one to stay?" Peter challenged his father. "She's *your* grandmother!"

"Your mother says she doesn't have the energy to move right now. We agreed that I'll move out if she gets help."

"Vati, they'll kill each other," said Peter. "Without you here between them—"

"They'll stay out of each other's way, don't worry. They've been doing it for years."

Rudi knew Oma could hold her own. The truth, he could see, was that Peter was scared for himself. Ilse was drinking more, in and out at unpredictable times, her mood wildly mercurial.

"I don't understand why Rudi doesn't stay with Mutti and I go with you," Peter protested. "We all know Rudi's her favorite."

Rudi didn't understand the arrangement, either. Peter didn't have the same relationship with their mother as he did. He wouldn't be able to take care of her like Rudi could. This all seemed so pointless, so stupid. Why now, when he and Peter had so much to do before they entered their last year of school? There were the exams, ceremonies, competitions—it had always been hard enough to pull off when the family was together. Now there was packing, papers to sign, finding an apartment. Rudi left the last dish for Peter to dry and pushed past his father.

"I'll be in my room."

"Rudi, wait," said Rudolf. "You can't just hole up in there. I know you didn't go to the factory today. Why don't you go out with your friends, or with that girl . . ."

"What am I supposed to do, Vati, throw a party? My parents are splitting up! Do you know how embarrassing that is? For student leaders? Couldn't you wait until we graduated?"

"You don't even *know* the pressure that's on me, *Junge!*" Rudolf exploded. His own raised voice seemed to startle him, and he instantly softened. "I wish it were different, Rudi. Believe me. I'm only saying that you should get out of the house and take a break from all this. Take your camera and go to the park. *Something.*"

Rudi huffed and rolled his eyes. "Fine." He went to his room and grabbed the Leica. He slipped on his shoes and slammed the door behind him.

He was in no mood to put the lens to this horrible world. Instead he took the tram as close as he could to Angelika's neighborhood and called her number from a pay phone. Her father answered.

"*Hallo*, Herr Rosen," he said. "May I speak with Angelika?"

Her father didn't answer right away.

"Herr Rosen?"

"Yes, ah, the butter cookies were delicious," he said, and hung up the phone.

PETER

When the boys came home on Tuesday, Rudolf told the family he had signed the papers on an apartment in Prenzlauer Berg and had a move-in date of the fifteenth of July, that coming Saturday. He'd decided to leave his piano for now because he didn't have the time or money to move it. The suddenness shocked the boys, and Oma could barely suppress her vexation.

Ilse, on the other hand, was unbearably chipper. She was getting the freedom she wanted without any of the work. She didn't have to pack her things or file any of the paperwork; someone else would clean up the mess. She readied herself to go out, whistling as the door closed behind her.

Oma joined the twins and her grandson at the table. She was not smoking. Except for the hum of the icebox, it was quiet in the apartment; from outside came the soundscape of keys pulled from pockets, children playing in the courtyard, and the click of Ilse's shoes going down the stairs.

Peter picked at the stray threads on the blue tablecloth. The evening was intensely lonely, the light turning from gold to blue. Other people were putting their feet up and telling each other about their perfectly average days as they recovered from the summer heat. Peter, though, had never felt more alone.

Ilse didn't come home until morning as Peter was getting ready for the farm. She kicked off her shoes and went right for the bathroom to splash her face. She came out, dabbing her face with a towel, and saw Peter standing in the hallway. She kept rubbing her face with the towel, her makeup smearing. There was so much makeup. They stared at each other. His mother felt like a stranger.

"Is there something you want to say to me?" Ilse asked.

"Not really."

"Are you sure? You look upset."

"Do I?"

"I think you have something to say," she said, going to the dining room and taking a seat at the table. "You should say it."

"Only that I knew this was coming," said Peter, following her. He sat and looked her in the eye. "I've always known that you and Vati would get divorced."

"Did you." The makeup was almost off, except for a broken line of eyeliner along her bottom lids and the stain of her magenta lipstick ghosted around her mouth.

"I made my peace with it months ago. And here's how I feel: if you want to screw up your own life, that's fine, but I have things to do."

"What things, Peter?" she sneered. "What do you have to do?"

"I have to live my life. And I'm going to. But—"

Ilse scoffed and began to check her nails.

"But I feel bad for you, Mutti. I don't know what happened to you."

"Nothing happened to me, Peter," she sighed. "You're being so dramatic. Sometimes married people fall out of love. It happens."

"I'm not talking about you and Vati. Just you. You're . . . a different person." Peter felt a lump growing in his throat. He didn't want to cry in front of his mother. He swallowed three times to hold it back. "You never hit me before."

"Are you still upset about that? I had a little too much to drink. Are you going to forgive me or what?"

"I've never experienced pain like that in my life," he said, the tears coming all at once. "I felt like I was going to die. It felt like you were killing me."

Ilse lowered her head. "I said I was sorry."

"Mutti, I heard what you said to Vati. That you were done, that you didn't want to raise us anymore. Is that true?"

Ilse looked up at Peter, her face suddenly stony. "I never wanted to be a mother, do this conventional family thing. Do you even know how exhausting you are, the two of you? *All* of you? Of course I'm done. You're old enough to look after yourselves. I deserve a life, don't I? When is it *my* turn?" She got up and shoved the chair toward the table, turning on her heel back to her bedroom.

Peter stared after her, stunned, as though she'd slapped him in the head again. He pressed his fist against his lips, his mouth full of salt. It wasn't worth trying to hold the tears back; they filled up and spilled down his neck. He heard muttering and shuffling from the bedroom, and his mother came out with a bundle of laundry. She'd changed and wrapped a scarf around her head, and she left for the coin laundry, leaving her son at the table, dependent on his own resilience.

All day at the farm he clung to Fox, and the dog somehow knew not to leave Peter's side. Peter was drowning in an ache for the mother he once had. At the same time, he felt like he was hammering together a raft to buoy him up, resolved to get on top and ride this out, and not to let Ilse define his life.

The only person he wanted to see that evening was Renate. He pulled himself together, washed up and went to see her at the theater. She'd be working at the box office, and if he got there soon, he'd beat the customers.

He passed Rudi in the courtyard, and boy, did he stink from work. But Peter wasn't in the mood to tease him about it. He gave his twin a weak smile and told him he'd be back later.

The S-Bahn rumbled on toward Friedrichstrasse station. Peter was utterly numb. He had no thoughts or plans, no theories about how his mother had become this person Peter didn't recognize. There were only images of her, snapshots of defining moments: Ilse clapping when he danced on the piano as a three-year-old, tying his first Young Pioneers scarf around his neck, sitting on the couch with the atlas and her stories. What now? The wide, red-ringed eyes as she told him, to his face, that she was done being his mother. It was too bizarre to make him cry again. It was the most outrageous thing a kid could hear. It was absurd. Even darkly funny.

When he got to the theater, he tapped on the glass of the box office, and Renate let him in.

"Peter," she said. "This is a nice surprise. But you don't look good."

"Could I just sit here with you?" he asked. "You can put me to work."

"All right . . . here, you can put these tickets in envelopes and write the last names on the outside."

"Sounds easy enough."

"Do you want to talk about it?" She put her hand on Peter's shoulder, his neck, his cheek.

"Not really."

"I get off at nine. We can get something to eat then. All right?"

"Thanks," said Peter. He began stuffing the envelopes, and slowly the wave of customers built up until Renate was completely occupied. It was just as well. He didn't need her attention, only her presence. As long as he didn't have to be alone.

RUDI

The next couple of days were unbearable—not because things happened, but because nothing did. The hours were entirely mundane. Rudi went to the factory, Peter to the farm. Rudolf to his tuning, Ilse to her switchboard. And Oma to her card games with the neighbors, though she was less spry lately and slept on the sofa a lot. After the shock of the separation, ironing out the details was like watching the family die in slow motion.

Friday evening rolled around again, and the boys ran up the stairs together like children. This was the night Rudi and his father would be leaving the apartment. They weren't going far, just a few blocks north, but it had the finality of a death.

"Hurry up, Rudi," Peter urged. "Can't you unlock that door?"

"What are you in such a hurry to get in there for?" Rudi huffed. "What is it, paradise?"

"I have to make a phone call. And you have to take a shower."

"I'm not the only one, farm boy. A phone call to who?"

Peter didn't answer the question.

"Renate. Got it."

Finally Rudi pushed the apartment door open, wrangling the key out of the lock. Peter shoved past his brother and grabbed the black phone, knocking the receiver off the base, and pulled the cord as far as it would reach. The louvered doors of their own bedroom offered no privacy, so he tumbled into Vati's study, empty but for the abandoned piano, and shut the door.

Rudi let the front door close behind him, unburdened himself of his book bag and kicked off his loafers. But he didn't go inside. Instead he leaned his back against the door and stared in, as though it were the home of a stranger. Everything was about to change. He was surprised that even after the packing up, it didn't look all that different. Maybe his minimalism had paid off.

Rudi had lived here his whole life but never *looked* at the place, and something in him wanted to preserve things as they were, before it all changed, tonight. Rudolf would be here soon with the moving truck.

What is this place? Rudi asked himself as he surveyed the room. *Is this what home is supposed to feel like?*

The apartment was quiet, but the kettle was still steaming on the stove. Rudolf must have just made his coffee and left to get the truck. Rudi walked slowly through the room, running his fingers along the threadbare blue tablecloth covering the tiny "family table."

He went to the icebox and poured himself a glass of milk. He almost gagged. *Powdered,* he thought. *When Vati and I are in the new place, the first thing I'm going to do is get real milk.* He stirred in a little malt powder and gulped it down, enjoying the relative quiet in the house, Peter's soft chattering on the phone, the shush of tires on the wet street outside.

The carpet was patchworked with ghosts of the few small pieces of furniture that Rudolf had taken to go to the new flat. Each spot only showed how dirty their situation had become, the nicotine-yellow-brown mask over a fresh Wedgwood blue.

Oma sat, as usual, on the sofa, watching a program. Eichmann again. Rudi sat next to her, and Peter came out of the study and sat on her other side. And for once, Rudi didn't mind the smoke.

The July sky was already dark when Rudolf came home. "I've got the keys to the truck," he said. "We should get going."

Peter rose and shook his father's hand. "Goodbye, Vati."

"I'll see you soon, son," said Rudolf. It looked like there was more he wanted to say, but he hugged Peter instead. "I'm leaving the telescope here for now. Maybe we'll look for some satellites again soon."

He embraced Oma. "I'll check in on you, Frau Möser," he said. "You'll be all right."

"Of course I will. Now get out of here." She smacked Rudolf on the rear end with her newspaper.

Ilse came out of her room and put up her hand in a little wave. That was it, for fifteen years of marriage, two children—for surviving a world war together. Barely a wave to end all things.

"Goodbye, Ilse," said her husband. He paused and looked at her, but she was examining her nail polish. "Right," he said to Rudi, picking up his bag. "Time to go."

Rudi hugged his mother and great-grandmother. "I'll be back later to get some things from our room," he told Peter.

"Take care of yourself, *Bruder Ruder*," said Peter. And Rudolf Sr. and Jr. left the apartment.

Rudolf had only his valise and the keys. Rudi carried a suitcase of clothes and his book bag. "Where are the boxes?" he asked.

"Follow me," said Rudolf.

The truck was parked outside their building. It was as small as the sum of their two lives. Rudolf got into the cab.

"Shouldn't I put the bags in the back?" Rudi asked.

"Not yet."

They drove to a dark, empty parking lot in an industrial area, and Rudolf opened the back of the truck. None of the small pieces of furniture he'd moved from the apartment were inside. No boxes, either. There was merely a piano wrapped in moving blankets. Rudi heaved his suitcase inside. His father unstrapped the piano from its restraints, rolled it aside and lifted a hatch in the floor where it had been. In the space beneath were their boxes. Rudolf took Rudi's suitcase and book bag and fit them in the space, rolled the piano back and strapped it down again.

"What's going on, Vati?" Rudi whispered. His father did not answer.

They drove for a few blocks up Karl-Marx-Allee, but then Rudolf turned abruptly south.

"Vati, you're going the wrong way. Prenzlauer Berg is to the right."

Rudolf did not respond.

As they approached Schilling Bridge, two border guards stepped into the road and motioned for the truck to halt.

"*Scheiss,*" Rudolf muttered under his breath as he rolled down the window. "Rudi, not a word. Act natural."

"Papers," the guard demanded. Rudolf handed him two booklets. "Reason for exit?" said the guard.

"Delivering a piano," said Rudolf.

"At night?"

"It took a long time to get it down the stairs," Rudolf lied.

"You couldn't deliver it in the morning?"

"What, leave a piano in a truck on the street? If it got stolen, it'd be my head on a spike."

The guards made Rudolf get out and open the liftgate. They shined a flashlight inside and saw nothing but the lone piano, strapped to the wall.

"Do you have the bill of sale?" Rudolf produced a pile of paperwork, complete with clipboard and pen.

After waiting long enough to make Rudolf sweat, they waved the truck through, and father and son crossed Schilling Bridge into the American sector.

Everything was heightened by the silence—the click of the turn signal, the atmosphere of the night streets, the questions shouting in Rudi's brain.

"I lied to you, Rudi," said Rudolf as they drove into the bright lights of West Berlin. "There's no apartment in Prenzlauer Berg. There's a church basement in Friedenau. That's where we're going. We are no longer citizens of the *Deutsche Demokratische Republik*."

PETER

The alarm clock rang without mercy the next morning, and Peter silenced it before it could do much damage. His parents had always hated being woken earlier than necessary, so he'd developed quick reflexes. But he suddenly came to when he realized that he didn't need to protect the household in the same way. His great-grandmother was already awake, his mother was sure to be asleep and his brother and father . . . no longer lived there.

A loneliness settled on Peter's chest like a little gray imp. He had to get up and go to the farm, but he wished he didn't have to walk to the S-Bahn stop by himself. Peter managed to pull himself together and make it to work, but that heaviness didn't leave him the whole day. Fox seemed to sense it. She sidled up to Peter whenever he wasn't herding the sheep, and Peter was glad for the company.

A week passed, and each day, he was sure Rudi or his father would come back to get some more of their things. He was surprised at how little they'd taken. Rudi even forgot his toothbrush, that *Dummkopf.*

Sunday, Peter decided to kill time at the record shop with Renate. He felt his shoulders slumping the whole way to Der Spinner, until he saw her from down the street, leaning against the big window.

"What! You cut your hair!" said Peter, touching the ends of Renate's new pixie cut. Her bangs were still long over her eyes. It made her neck look even more graceful. "You look like a cute little mouse."

"And your hair's getting longer," Renate observed, leaning in and straightening a stray lock. "You should give it a twist in front, like Elvis."

"I will, *Maus.* Yes, that's what I'm going to call you." He kissed her soft cheek and brushed her lips. It was so easy to kiss her, like she put breath back into his body.

"Only if I can call you *Katze,*" she said, putting her arms around his waist. "Have you heard from Rudi?"

"No. My father didn't leave an address or a phone number or anything. I wouldn't even know where to look."

"They're probably busy getting things set up. Two bachelors—you know. Probably don't have a fork or plate between them."

"You're right. I'm sure they'll come back soon. Let's go in—I want to see if they have anything new from France."

"You don't want *Itsy Bitsy Teenie Weenie Yellow Polkadot Bikini?*" Renate poked him.

"On you, maybe!" He laughed and pulled her close, and they walked into the shop like one person.

Der Spinner was in a Sunday morning calm, nothing like the after-school hours. The pop stacks were mostly empty, but the classical stacks were attended by older, graying folks. Musicians browsed the sheet music. But Peter recognized a familiar face by the counter, talking with Tobias.

"Charles!" said Peter.

"Peter!" Charles came over and hugged Peter. "Look at your hair, man! You going beatnik on me? And who's *this,* may I ask?" Peter could sense Charles holding back his razzing.

"I'm Renate," she said, shaking hands with Charles.

"Pleasure." He gestured toward the turntable on the counter. "You two out for a spin?" They laughed at the pun. Tobias groaned.

"That's a good one," Peter teased him for the dad joke. "I'll use it in my routine."

"Routine? What's this?"

Renate shot Peter a look of caution.

"Oh . . . just some friends. We tell some jokes, drink soda, you know. . . ." Peter thought Charles would like Kabarett Zusammen, but he had to remember to keep his big mouth shut.

"Know any good ones?"

"Only in German—my English isn't *that* good."

"Well, have fun, then, and work on some jokes in English for me. Hey, Peter, how's . . . how's your dad? There's a concert at the base coming up, and I was thinking . . ."

"I was going to ask you the same thing. I haven't seen him in a week."

"You haven't seen him? Why? Doesn't he live with you?" Charles chuckled.

"Well . . . not anymore. My parents . . ." He looked at the ceiling for the English words.

"You're not telling me . . . Peter, did your parents split up?'"

Tears welled in Peter's eyes, and he tried to laugh them away. *"Ja."*

"Oh, no, no, no." Charles put his hand on Peter's shoulder. "I'm sorry, young man."

"I'm sorry, I never cry."

"That's all right, you have every reason to," said Charles. "Go on."

"Rudi and my father got a new place, but they haven't told us where. No address, no phone number. Just drove away, and that was that."

"I'm sure he'll turn up. Maybe he'll come by my border crossing when I'm on duty. I'll keep my eye out, all right? He's not going to leave you high and dry."

"Thank you, Charles."

"Listen, Peter, if you need anything, you know where to find me. This isn't the end of the story, right?"

"It never is," said Renate.

"That's right, young lady. Especially when you think it's all over."

RUDI

The owner of Berlin Piano Tuning and Repair was a deacon in the Kirche Zum Guten Hirten, the Good Shepherd Church, in Friedenau. Herr König, therefore, had a talent for organizing aid of various kinds. Publicly, it was feeding the poor, visiting the sick and looking in on pensioners. But privately, his specialty was forging identification papers.

He'd done that years ago, smuggling people out of the country, especially Jewish musicians. After the war, there'd been a lull in demand for his services in a city that, in theory at least, was now open to the world. But in the last several years, as Ulbricht clamped down on things like factory quotas, immigration visas and crossing the sector border to work, that had changed, and Herr König had a familiar suspicion that he'd be getting even busier soon.

He liked Rudolf Möser. After a tuning job, his eager employee would demonstrate how good the instrument sounded by showing off with a piece, which gave the company a reputation for refinement. The job at the US Army base had gone so well, he offered Rudolf a full-time position. After the visit from Glasses and Baby Face, Rudolf asked him to get his family out of East Berlin, and Herr König was more than willing to keep Rudolf's job open for him while they hatched a plan.

And now a client had moved out of the city, leaving a piano behind in her flat, and Herr König saw his chance. He had a friend pull up the floor in one of his company trucks to build a secret compartment and told Rudolf to use it. As for the decoy piano, he said Rudolf could keep it. Herr König had the new identification papers made, but only for Rudolf and Rudi—staggering their escape would be less suspicious. Peter and Oma would have to come across later. And Ilse . . . if she wanted to.

It was in the basement fellowship hall of Good Shepherd that Rudolf and Rudi, along with five other refugees, spent their first night in the West.

Rudi and his father went down to be processed at Marienfelde in the morning, and that evening, after waiting in an interminably long line, they were given official immigration papers and a starter allowance. The fact that Rudolf already had a job in West Berlin was to his advantage; everyone else was getting sent to the interior of West Germany. That distance would have been too much to bear. At least here, Rudolf was in the same airspace as both of his sons.

There were no apartments to be had, and Rudolf prepared Rudi to stay in the church basement that night as well. But Herr König gave them the good news that a parishioner's apartment had just come available in Kreuzberg, and Rudolf could have it before it went on the market. It was an incredible stroke of luck. It happened to be right by Bäckerei Antoinette, within walking distance of their old place in Friedrichshain. When the time came to bring the rest of the family over, they could simply cross on foot.

So here they were, in three rooms and a kitchen. The place smelled of plaster and cooking gas, but it had its own bathroom, which could be a luxury in these prewar buildings. It had been broom-swept but needed a good deep clean. Luckily, Ilse's spontaneous parties had taught Rudolf and his son how to scrub a place down.

As Herr König came in carrying a couple of bedrolls, he apologized that, due to the increase in refugees, furniture was in short supply, and he counseled them to buy it themselves secondhand when they could. But he had the piano brought and set up by the window.

Their few smuggled boxes were stacked in the corner, and they unrolled the sleeping mats in the bedroom. Herr König put two newly cut keys on a single ring on the kitchen counter and, with a wink, wished them good luck in their new country.

"Since we're so close to the border here," he advised them, "I wouldn't tell anyone where you are just yet. Especially not the rest of your family." Then he left father and son alone in this new place, with its bad lighting and torn wallpaper.

"Let's go get something to eat," said Rudolf. Rudi followed him out into the night, and they collected a hodgepodge of foods from street vendors and brought it up to the flat.

They ate sitting on the floor, backs against the wall, feet outstretched, watching the lights beam in through the window. Rudi took furious bites of his street wurst and swigs of bottled Apfelsaft. They didn't speak. They hadn't spoken, in fact, since they crossed the border.

Rudi knew his father's eyes were on him. He turned his head aside as he ate and stared at the new piano. The one at home in East Berlin was chestnut brown and had water rings from Rudolf's endless cups of coffee and tea. This one was black and glossy and from a reputable maker. A foreign piano in a foreign land.

Rudolf held out the paper bag to collect Rudi's wrapper and napkin. He rustled through one of the boxes and found his small tool bag, with a hammer, a box each of nails and screws, a screwdriver and a wrench. He tacked bedsheets up over the windows and made up the bedrolls, and father and son fell asleep in their new place.

The morning sun streamed in through the bedsheet curtains. Rudi was surprised at the good sleep he had, agitated as he'd been the night before. He got up to look through his suitcase. His father was already up, opening boxes, and soon came the sound of the piano top creaking open, the familiar clank of wrenches in his kit and the piano being tuned. They had nothing of substance but that *stupid* piano—the ruse for their escape, the only language his father knew how to speak.

There's a belief, maybe a myth, that the best piano tuners in the world are blind. When one sense is impaired—the wisdom goes—the others are more finely attuned, and the technician can hear the nuances of tone that might be lost from the distraction of the visible world. Why this didn't make Beethoven switch to sculpture instead of composing when he lost his hearing, no one can say. But perhaps Rudolf's silence was a kind of muteness. Perhaps words would have cluttered his ability to hear the finer frequencies.

As Rudi dressed, the twang of the piano strings made his neck impossibly tense, as though his father's wrench were twisting his spine. He came out from the bedroom and stood, watching Rudolf tune.

"Is there something you need?"

"Why did Herr König say not to tell anyone we were here?"

"Because we did something the Party wouldn't approve of."

"We can't even tell Oma? Mutti? Peter? What about my girlfriend?"

"I'm going to get in touch with them, Rudi, of course. We just have to be smart about it, OK? I'm going to bring everyone over eventually. That's the plan." He finished tuning the upper strings and began again from the lower.

"Where will they fit?" Rudi folded his arms and scoffed.

"This place is only temporary. You'll see."

"Why did you do this to me? Why did you bring me here? You know Mutti needs help. She needs us. Why did you take me instead of Peter, anyway? He wants to be in the West. Are you so selfish that you couldn't wait until Peter and I were grown? Until we could decide for ourselves?"

Rudolf did not answer. He kept on tuning. The warping notes swelled Rudi's eyes in their sockets. He reflexively grabbed his camera and an extra roll of film, took his key off the key ring and shoved it in his pocket. He rushed out and let the door slam behind him.

The man in the first-floor flat stood in his doorway, his shirt unbuttoned halfway down his chest, playing a saxophone, with a smoking cigarette stuck in the strap. When Rudi came down the stairs, the man stopped, took a drag, placed it back in the strap and blared the music again. Rudi couldn't bear the noise. He thrust himself out onto the street and turned left.

His head pounded, not from the noise now but from the tension he could not release. His legs felt robotic, like he was half-human, half-machine, propelling his mushy human upper half through the streets of this city. He knew where he was; Kreuzberg wasn't a foreign country, except that it was. But having an address on this side of the border made the landscape feel alien and unreal. Everything seemed to close in on Rudi. Even the sky felt compressed.

I had a life. I had my comrades. I had the FDJ. My things. My future. I had a girlfriend.

He passed store after store, photographing the excesses of West Berlin. He thought of all the money changing hands, money that would go to line the owners' walls with expensive art, to line their stomachs with fat, to perpetuate fascism. Did his father care so little about his own family that he was willing to tear them apart just for some . . . goodies?

If everyone would just stay together. If everyone would just stop being so damn selfish.

Through the afternoon, Rudi shot and shot until the last roll of film was spent. He walked home, hungry, his emotions wrung out. When he got back to the flat, Rudolf was playing the piano softly from the second floor, the mellow saxophone riffing off him from the first floor, the two neighbors making music through the barrier between them.

"Where did you go?" Rudolf demanded as soon as Rudi walked in the door.

"Why do you care?"

Rudolf lit a cigarette and lowered his tone. "I care because I risked a lot to get us here. And because you have to register for your new school tomorrow."

"Why can't I just go to my own school? I could just take the S-Bahn. It's, like, a kilometer away! They don't have to know I live here. I could still give them the old address."

"Rudi, you can't tell *anyone* you're here. No one at your other school. Not Peter or Mutti or Omi or Angelika. Do you understand?"

Rudi stared at his father with such contempt, his mouth began to quiver. He peeled off his sweaty clothes, threw himself down on the mat and cried his frustration until he passed out.

PETER

"*O*ch," said Oma. "My knee is giving me such trouble." She winced and held on to the edge of the kitchen sink.

"You've been going out a lot lately, Omi," said Peter, spreading margarine on a piece of bread. "Maybe you should stay off your feet for a bit."

"Don't slow me down, *Junge*." She wagged her finger at her great-grandson. "You're the one who still needs someone to take care of you."

Peter laughed. "Come on, I'm a big boy now. I'm a workingman!" He tugged at his dirty work clothes.

"The thought of my Rock Hudson tending sheep!" Oma broke into her raspy smoker's laugh, which became a cough, which made the pain shoot down her knee again. "Help me to the couch, will you?"

Peter felt his great-grandmother's frailness as he supported her. He could have carried her, but in a million years, she wouldn't have let him. Her pride was well earned. She'd been on her own for decades after losing her husband in the First World War, and she wasn't about to depend on anyone now. Except for a hobble over to the sofa.

"Peter, *setz dich zu mir.*" She beckoned, patting the seat. "I want to talk to you."

"What is it, Omi? The birds and the bees?"

"No, I'm not joking right now. This is serious. It's about your mother."

"All right."

"Peter, we have to face some facts. She may not know how to show it, but your mother loves you and Rudi. She was always . . . troubled. Things with your father were never good. She wanted you to be taken care of, though. I'll be honest, I always thought she would run out on this family, but she didn't."

"Until now."

"Well, notice, for all her bluster, she's still here."

"In name only."

"Yes, that may be. She may be making a slow exit. But she won't leave until she knows you're all right. And neither will I."

Peter looked into Oma's face. This was a woman with a steel will.

"This is painful," Oma continued. "I know. It's not ideal. When you're a kid, and you're not feeling well, you want someone by your side to put a cool cloth on your forehead. But childhood has to end. For some, it's a natural transition, and that's what we all want, of course. For others, like your parents, it's taken from them too soon, and it can be difficult to learn how to be an adult. You're lucky, though. You're almost grown. And you can thank your mother for staying as long as she tolerably could."

"*Thank* her? Are you serious—"

"No, Peter, you can't blame her. She is not you, and you are more than a mere extension of her. What you must do is find compassion for her. Not only as your mother, but as a woman who is sick and doing the best with the little she has. That is what grown-ups do: forgive, learn and move into their own future."

Peter reached for Oma's hand and squeezed it. They sat like that for a while.

"Now, Peter?"

"Yes, Omi?"

"Go take a bath. *Du stinkst.*"

Peter lay in the tub until his fingers pruned up. He looked at his body, a man's body, hairy and thick. He wasn't a boy, he knew that, but part of him had been of two minds. He could be a man when he wanted to be independent, to traipse around the city, kiss girls, sneak around at illegal cabarets. But when he came home, he wanted to be a child, fawned over by his parents, palling around with his twin brother.

He sat up in the bath. The water had grown cold before he noticed, and now it felt gross. He got out and dried off, looking at himself in the mirror. His hair was growing out, and his mother wasn't going to tell him to cut it anymore. His broad shoulders would have to bear the weight of his own decisions. He was almost sixteen, and in a year, he'd be out of school. No teacher would impose exams on him. Only God knew where his mother would be. He and Rudi might have to help take care of Oma when she got too weak to keep up her social life.

Where is Vati? Did he forget about me?

As Peter pulled his clothes on, he looked over at his brother's empty bed. In all of these changes, he missed his twin most of all. He had shared almost every experience with Rudi, and just like that, overnight, they'd been cut apart. He didn't know where his brother was, or how he was. The not knowing swirled in his head. He took a deep breath. *I won't give myself a headache over this,* he thought. *I'll just keep trying to find him.*

The telephone rang, and Peter answered it. It was one of Oma's friends, calling to check in on her. She peppered Peter with questions about his future. Peter managed to worm his way out of the conversation to hand the phone to Oma. He pulled it over on its long cord and propped Oma's knee on the sofa, then set her up with her smokes and lighter. She yammered away, and Peter left with a smile.

It had rained all day and was cooler now. The summer sun wouldn't go down for hours. Hair still wet from the bath, Peter wandered down the street and along the river, feeling his height, his long legs under him, carrying him where they would. He crossed into the center of the city and through a parking lot, below which, sixteen years before, Adolf Hitler had blown his brains out alongside his mistress and his dog. Above Peter now, a dozen satellites crisscrossed silently through the last particles of the earth's atmosphere.

The light turned gold, then pink, then lilac as Peter walked through the Brandenburg Gate and toward the Soviet War Memorial.

It had been a while since he'd been here on a field trip. He was embarrassed at the memory, at the thought of goofing around with Rudi on the tanks as their teacher tried to instill some reverence in the class of squirrelly middle schoolers. Now it seemed to him a memorial to questions he wasn't sure had answers.

"Peter?" a girl's voice called.

"Oh, Angelika," he replied. "What are you doing here?"

"I thought that was you. I was taking a walk."

"Me too," he chuckled.

"I'm glad I bumped into you. I've been calling all week, trying to find Rudi."

"Why didn't you come to our house if you couldn't get through?"

"I shouldn't have to hunt him down. Anyway, every time I call, your grandmother tells me he's out. Is he avoiding me?"

"Wait, didn't you know he moved last weekend?"

"Moved? What do you mean? Why did he move, and you didn't?"

"My brother, the Great Communicator," Peter sighed. "Our parents are getting divorced. Rudi and my father moved to someplace in Prenzlauer Berg. But it's been a week, and they haven't left an address or a phone number. They haven't even been back to get the rest of their things."

"What?" Angelika was flabbergasted.

"Believe me, I'm as confused as you are. I've gone to the record shop, the bakery, the Milchbar, all our hangouts, but nothing."

Angelika and Peter stared up at the statue of the trench-coated Soviet soldier atop the colonnade as the first star appeared in the darkening sky. Finally she took a small notebook out of her pocketbook and tore out a page.

"Here's my number," she said. "Will you give me a call if you hear from him?"

"Of course."

She walked through the gate onto Unter den Linden back into East Berlin. Peter watched her go, happy for his brother's luck with a girl so pretty, and mad that Rudi hadn't told either of them where he was.

That idiot, he thought. *She's only going to look for you so long before she moves on.*

RUDI

Monday morning dawned dim and rainy. Rudi opened the window above his bedroll to relieve the humidity. His pajamas clung to his skin, and he disgusted himself. At least at home he had a fan on the nightstand, but there were no creature comforts here.

They had been in West Berlin for a week, and every morning promised the same dissonant beginning: waking up in a strange apartment, in an ersatz bed, trying to remember where he was, and then the anger welling up, until he couldn't stand to lie there anymore. It was the anger that fueled him.

I don't want to be here. This isn't normal. This isn't home.

Rudi squeezed through the tiny hallway into the kitchen and opened the icebox. There was half a bottle of Apfelsaft and some deconstructed leftovers from dinner, but he would rather go hungry than eat that first thing in the morning. He found a sleeve of crackers in the cupboard and ate two before they sucked all the moisture out of his mouth. He stuck his head in the sink and drank right from the faucet, dried his mouth on his sleeve, went back into the bedroom and rifled through his suitcase for clean underwear. Thankfully, he had one pair left.

He got dressed and grabbed his book bag. The books from his old school were still in there, as useless here in the West as his old notebooks from primary school, full of clumsy handwriting and early math.

I had one year left to graduate. One damn year.

One at a time, Rudi took out the books. White knuckled, he barely avoided throwing them at the wall.

I finally made it to my last year in school. And now I have to go backward. Who knows what classes will transfer over?

Rudolf came into the bedroom, rubbing his bleary eyes. He put on his glasses and ran his hand through his hair. "I met the neighbor downstairs yesterday," he told Rudi. "The one who plays saxophone. Oh, good morning, sorry."

"Mm-hmm." Rudi left a pencil and half-filled notebook in the bag and put in his camera.

"His name is Willi. We walked to a lounge for a drink. It turns out they were looking for a pianist. Easy drink-and-conversation tunes for tourists, that kind of thing."

"Uh-huh."

"The pay is . . . hmm . . . modest, and the scene is pretty lowbrow, but— Rudi, are you listening?"

"Go ahead."

"Do you understand? I'm finally going to earn money as a musician! It'll be Saturdays and Wednesdays. The downside is that I'll get home around four in the morning. I'll have to sleep in on Sundays and Thursdays. But I'll leave you some of my tips. You can get a nice breakfast once in a while. Now, how does that sound?"

I guess a couple of marks is the least he can do for kidnapping me, Rudi thought.

Willi started playing his saxophone downstairs. A violinist who lived above the tobacco shop got an early start on practice, too. The music was like sandpaper under Rudi's skin.

"Why are there so many musicians?" he asked. "It's so noisy here."

His father ruffled Rudi's hair as if he were a little boy and opened his newspaper. "A lot of clubs in this neighborhood, it turns out," he replied. "And a conservatory, too. I feel at home already."

"I'm going to Antoinette's to find something to eat," Rudi said.

"Bring back something for me?" Rudolf asked, handing him some pfennigs. "Coffee and, um . . . something sweet. You choose."

Rudi took the money and added it to his allowance, stuffed it all in his pocket and left.

There was no question that his father lost money in this move to the West. He was now earning his pay entirely in D-marks—but being a refugee in West Berlin meant no more Eastern discounts. An ostmark was valued at only a fifth of a D-mark, a worthless exchange. Rudi still had a paycheck waiting for him from the sauerkraut factory, and now he would never see that money. He'd had to give his father his entire stash to change over on the black market, and now all their worldly wealth was kept on the kitchen counter in a coffee canister. Rudi was allowed to take one D-mark per day, no more.

Their family had never had much, but the shortage of money was demoralizing. Right now Rudi would have been working at the factory, hanging out with his friends, making his *own* money, spending time with Angelika. He'd be getting ready for his apprenticeship and have a sure-thing job waiting for him at the end of it. Now there was nothing for it but to try to finish his education in a new school in September, in a new system. He'd be going to school with the class enemy, the worst people on earth. How was this better?

The rain had stopped, and humidity rose off the sidewalk. As he stepped out onto the street, Rudi pined for the courtyard of his old building, that middle space between the apartment and the street that helped him set his mind straight in the early mornings before he had to face the world. He turned left toward the bakery.

There was one stroke of luck about this whole thing. He'd ended up in the very neighborhood that he and Peter liked best. The record shop was two blocks away, and their favorite bakery, Bäckerei Antoinette, was down the street. Since he'd last been there, the owner had put up a poster of Marie Antoinette in the window proclaiming *Let Them Eat Cake!*, holding a platter of their excellent Berliners, the pillowy jam-filled doughnuts named after this city of contradictions. Rudi went into the tiny shop, pressing through a crowd of locals, and demanded his usual: *"Zwei Kaffee. Schwarz mit ein Zuckerwürfel. Und ein Berliner. Ah—nein—zwei Berliner."*

Rudi left a handful of pfennigs on the counter and breathed deeply the aroma of just-out-of-the-oven pastries. He barely made it out the door before digging into his Berliner, and it was gone in three bites. He wished he could eat the one he'd bought for his father, too, but a smell was all he could allow himself.

He passed by the sector border, sipping coffee from his paper cup. He had crossed this imaginary line between nations many times, but this time it meant something different. He slowed down and looked. Some of the soldiers were not much older than him, having enlisted right after high school. That could have *been* him. The morning shift ended, and fresh soldiers changed places with the ones who had stood guard through the night. Now that he was off duty, one of the tired guards pulled out a harmonica and began to play.

•••••

Rudi sat at the kitchen table that evening with his Russian textbook, taking notes. What did it matter if he wouldn't be studying it anymore? He liked the language, and he never knew when it would come in handy.

Rudolf came home with a bag of groceries. "Look what I got—*actual* milk!" Rudolf said, taking the bottle out of the bag and waving it in the air. "No more powdered for us. Oh, and I picked up the paperwork for your new *Hauptschule*. It's a really nice place. I think you'll get a much better education there than at your polytechnic school."

He slid the papers toward Rudi, but Rudi refused to answer. He kept taking his notes, pressing the pencil harder into the paper.

"What's the problem?"

"Nothing. Thanks for the milk. That's great—we can have real milk. Hooray for us."

"Oh, come on, Rudi."

"Everything was fine back home. *I was fine.*"

"Yes, Rudi. But you weren't *free.*"

"Am I so free here, having to start my life from scratch?"

"You think it's over, Rudi, but it's just different."

"It's all your fault," Rudi hissed. "You stole my future."

"What future?" Rudolf shouted. "You think the future was *yours?*"

A brutal moment of silence passed between them. Rudolf took a sip of his coffee, and Rudi felt his father's eyes on him. Even if it was an argument, it was strange to have his attention, to have no one else in the house competing for his energy. This might have been the most they'd talked in months.

"Listen, son," Rudolf said, all business, "I'm sorry to bring this up, but you're going to need to get a job as soon as possible. I can support us, but there's no extra, not yet. If you need clothes or books or money for the movies or anything, that's on you. I'm sorry."

Rudolf put the rest of the food away, took an apple to the living room and played a slow piece from Bach's *Goldberg Variations*. Rudi took a deep breath. As his father played, in spite of his anger, the tight-corded rope in Rudi's throat slackened. He picked up the school paperwork and began to fill it out.

The next morning was already warm at seven o'clock when Rudi headed to the new school to drop off his forms. He found the office and asked the secretary what he should know about his schedule. She explained the room-numbering system, the way his classes broke down by day, the tests he could expect. But his bigger questions were out of her expertise. She picked up the phone and asked for assistance.

A tall, gray-haired and blue-suited man came out of a room off the main office. He introduced himself as the Direktor of the school. Rudi told him that he had come from East Berlin and was worried that his classes would not transfer, especially since his old school didn't even know he was here. The Direktor took him into his office and compared Rudi's previous credits with the *Hauptschule*'s graduation requirements. There were some problems, he said, most notably the emphasis on Socialist theory that did not apply here. Rudi might find he needed to relearn certain frameworks. But he should be able to graduate on time, as long as he kept up his grades.

The Direktor then took him on a tour of the school building. Something inside of Rudi was skeptical of the man's intentions. Rudi wasn't cold to his friendliness but didn't entrust himself openly to the Direktor, either. There was one question that needed an immediate answer, though. Did he know where Rudi could find a job? The man didn't have any helpful advice. He conferred with the office staff. *Go door to door* was the consensus. Didn't the school offer any job training? Apprenticeships? Not this school, they answered. Most graduates went directly on to take the Abitur and then university. That would have been at a *vocational* school.

And so Rudi had to screw up the courage to look for his first real job. Before the factory, any money he'd earned back home was through word of mouth—odd jobs, selling things to friends, pocket money from his few relatives and their friends. Thankfully, he had always been frugal.

The thing about West Berlin was, there were *so* many stores and businesses. So many. And there were multiples of each kind of store. Book shops. Grocery stores. Tobacconists. Pharmacies. How many ladies' shoe stores did one city need? Rudi had lived his whole life in Berlin, but now that he saw things as a resident of the West, the difference was suddenly stark.

He went into each and every store, but none of them were hiring. He went home, defeated and exhausted, and settled into an easy dinner: a can of soup, a slice of bread. And some real damn milk.

The next morning Rudi was surprised to find that despite yesterday's talk of austerity, his father had left him some breakfast money. He went to the bakery and ordered his usual.

Why hadn't it dawned on him before? He asked the cashier if the bakery was hiring, and the kid told him to wait a minute. Rudi took a seat and ate his Berliner nervously. He burned his tongue on the coffee.

The burly owner came out from the kitchen and sat down with Rudi. He introduced himself as Herr Otto.

"So, *Junge,* you're looking for a job, are you?" He eyed Rudi like he was a kindergartner. "Do you have any experience?"

"I already know how to bake lebkuchen, dinner rolls, butter cookies . . . and stollen . . . walnut, apple—"

"I see you've memorized the entire menu," Herr Otto laughed, his belly bouncing. "It's going to be on an entirely different scale, you know. We sell a hundred stollen a day, five hundred dinner rolls."

"You'll train me, right?"

"Well, I'll tell you, maybe it's fate—I just lost one of my people yesterday. Can you do a four a.m. shift?" He crossed his arms and lifted an eyebrow.

"Um . . . school starts in September."

Herr Otto thought about it, giving Rudi a skeptical looking-over. "Closing, then? Sweeping up, getting things ready for the morning bakers?"

"*Ja*, I can do that."

"All right, son, you're hired. I'll see you Monday. Four in the afternoon. Don't be late!"

PETER

Arno obviously wasn't expecting anyone when Peter walked in the door of the building. He was carrying a tray of beer glasses from upstairs and very nearly lost them when he saw the boy's silhouette.

"Peter! What are you doing here so early?" He began descending the stairs with the tray.

"I . . . ah . . . I wanted to get here before the crowd," Peter said as he followed him into the cellar.

"Why?"

"I thought it'd be quiet. . . ."

"Calm before the storm?"

Peter laughed. "I guess so. Arno, can you put me, maybe, fifth on the lineup tonight?"

"Sure. Nervous?"

"A little."

"Why? You always do well with your monologues."

"I'm not doing a monologue tonight. I'm . . . I'm going to do some jokes."

Arno laughed as he put the tray of glasses on the bar and began to put them away. "Stand-up! From the dramatic actor!"

"What? Can't a guy try something new?"

"*Natürlich.* Listen, Lenny Bruce, make yourself useful and light the candles, *ja?*" He kept chuckling to himself.

Peter felt his confidence melt a little at the edges. Well, he'd show Arno and everyone else. He knew he could make people laugh. He did it all the time at school.

The cabaret filled up with the usual folks. The familiar faces put him at ease. He knew they'd be encouraging. He had a good collection of jokes memorized, but had a keyword from each one scrawled on his hand just in case.

Renate showed up during the first act, and Peter chided her for being so late when she knew it was so important to him. She apologized and said the S-Bahn had had an electrical problem, but Peter was starting to get on edge as his time got closer.

The folk duo sang a lullaby, and then Angelika did her usual, beautiful songs. Peter psyched himself up to be as funny as possible.

Finally it was his turn. He jumped onstage and launched right into his act.

"*Hallo, hallo, hallOOO!*" he hooted, moving skittishly around. "How is everyone doing tonight?" There was a murmur and a few stray claps led by Renate. Peter brushed it off. "So tonight, I'm going to do something different for you—GDR *Witze!*"

He cracked his knuckles and began.

"What is huge, makes a lot of noise, guzzles twenty liters of gas per hour and cuts apples into three pieces?" Peter waited for someone to shout something out, but it was quiet. So he continued: "An East German machine made to cut apples into four pieces!"

An audible groan erupted where he'd expected a laugh. *More energy, more energy,* thought Peter. He began to bounce on his feet.

"You know, I've always wondered something: Are the Russians our friends or our brothers?" He waited again. "Clearly, our brothers. You can choose your friends." This time no one even groaned. The silence made his head swim.

"One more. You guys want one more?"

"No!" someone shouted.

Peter had to look down at the notes on his hand. "What's the difference between Communism and capitalism? Capitalism is man's exploitation of man, but Communism is the exact opposite!"

What happened next had never happened to Peter in his entire life.

The audience began to boo.

Peter looked at Renate with dread. She sat, unmoving, biting her lip. He began to sweat. In a panic, he swung his head over toward Arno, who stood with a bar towel in a glass, in mid-wipe. Arno put the glass down on the bar and jumped up onto the stage.

"Thank you, Peter Möser-Fleischmann! Let's give him a round of applause. Next up . . ."

The five seconds it took to descend the stage amid the chaotic mix of laughter, mocking applause and residual booing was as endless as the recessional through Sachsenhausen on dedication day.

Peter sat next to Renate. She quietly put her hand on his knee and kept staring forward as the juggler took the stage.

He didn't have the wherewithal to ask how he'd gone so wrong. He had never *not* done well at something—school, acting, even the farm. The other performers, the audience, bottles clinking—the sounds were simultaneously as thick and vaporous as the cloud of cigarette smoke.

The last act finished, and Peter leaned over to Renate. "Can we get out of here?" he said.

"Sure." She squeezed his knee, and they rose to leave. But one by one, the same people who had heckled him came over, patted his shoulder and wished him well.

"All right, so you bombed," said Arno. "What are you going to do about it?"

"I mean . . . I didn't *bomb* exactly. . . ."

"They booed you off after three jokes. I call that bombing."

"One bad night doesn't mean anything," said Renate. "The point is getting right back up there next week."

"Besides," said Arno, "those weren't even your jokes. And if they're not *your* jokes, then they're not true."

"He's right," said Renate. "A comedian's job is to tell the truth."

He and Renate stepped out into the warm night and strolled beneath the streetlamps with few words.

"What did you mean, *a comedian's job is to tell the truth?*" asked Peter.

"It's what an artist does. Any artist." Renate fished a stick of gum out of her pocketbook.

"What about expressing yourself?"

"What about it? My mother says you can't draw water from a dry well. Expression that comes from lies will eventually leave you to die in the desert."

"You're only a year older than me," Peter laughed. "How are you so wise?"

"I've lived a little, that's all."

They stopped for a bite to eat, said goodbye and parted ways at the tram stop. Peter climbed aboard the S-Bahn and let it carry him across to Friedrichshain, to the gritty mirage that was home. Oma sat at the dining room table in her housecoat and slippers.

"You're home early for a Saturday," she said sarcastically.

"Really, Omi? It's midnight!"

"Oh, my mistake, *Junge*. I'm going to sleep. Lock the door, will you?" She went into her room and lit a late-night cigarette.

Peter lay in his bed, mulling over the routine, dissecting it to find out where he'd gone wrong.

Tell the truth, he admonished himself. *Whatever you do, tell the truth.* But what did that mean, exactly?

AUGUST

RUDI

The first three days at the bakery were hell. It was as though Rudi had never held a pastry before. He screwed up time after time, and Herr Otto yelled at him in front of everyone. He even jammed the cash register and had to do the math in his head while a line built up out the door. He wished he'd never asked for this job. No amount of money could atone for his embarrassment.

On the fourth afternoon, though, something clicked, and he found a flow. He was able to smile while he packed boxes with stollen, kuchen and tortes. His tongs were full of *Quarkbällchen* when Charles walked in. Thankfully, he was holding a paper bag underneath them, because he almost reverted to his clumsy self.

"Charles! *Wie gehts?*"

"Why, Rudi Möser-Fleischmann," the soldier replied, reaching over the counter to pat Rudi's shoulder. "I could ask you the same thing. There's some people looking for you."

"Looking for me? What do you mean?"

"Don't be nervous, kid. You're not wanted by the police," he chuckled. "I'm talking about your brother."

"You saw Peter?"

"Yeah, at the record shop, with his girl. He told me about your parents, man. I'm really sorry." He leaned over the display case, deliberating. "Let me have four of those quark balls when you get a chance."

Rudi knew he didn't have to be afraid. The American wasn't going to turn him and his father in to the GDR authorities. Still, his hands trembled as he collected Charles's order.

"I figured I'd run into you at some point," the soldier said. "Peter said you didn't leave your address. You want me to give it to him if I see him? Just write it down for me."

"That's all right, Charles. I'll call him. We have been unpacking. Very busy," Rudi lied.

"All right." Charles paid him and took a bite of one of the still-warm doughnuts. "Good to see you, son. Tell your pops I said hello."

"I will."

Rudi watched Charles walk out, but his conscience brewed. He told his boss he was taking his break, untied his apron and ran after Charles.

"Wait." He came up alongside the soldier, breathless. "I didn't tell you everything."

"All right, Rudi, what's up?"

"You have to keep this a secret."

"You're a spy," Charles chuckled. "That's it, isn't it?"

"My father and I crossed over. I didn't want to. But we are refugees now."

"Yeah, I thought it was strange seeing you work at the bakery, since they banned *Ossis* from working in the West."

"He told me not to tell anyone, but he would want you to know."

"Well, OK. Your secret's safe with me. Why don't you give me your info? I'll keep it confidential." Charles pulled a small notebook out of his breast pocket and tore out a blank page.

Rudi hesitated, but he took the piece of paper and gave Charles his address and phone number. Charles folded the note and paused before putting it in his pocket.

"Listen, Rudi, that whole thing with your mother . . . there was no sense stirring up a hornet's nest. But your dad might need a friend right now. Let him know I'm . . . I'm at the record shop every Thursday. And you come, too. Music's a language everyone can speak. We'll call it music school."

"Music school. All right."

Closing time came. Rudi wiped down the stainless steel counter in the kitchen and tidied up for the early-morning bakers who would arrive at four a.m. He washed his hands and wiped them on the towel hanging from his apron, grabbed the keys from the hook under the register and got ready to close up.

"*Hallo*, Rudi."

He almost jumped. It was Uncle Martin, sitting in the back corner of the bakery, tan suit, dark tie, hat on the table in front of him. He leaned back casually in the chair with his legs crossed, hands clasped in his lap. He smiled at his nephew.

Rudi startled. "Uncle Martin! I didn't hear the bell."

"Oh, you must have been too busy to hear. It's good to see you again, nephew. Been some months, hasn't it?"

"Yes . . . um . . . is there something I can get you? Nothing's as fresh in the evening, but if you don't mind . . ."

Rudi didn't know why he was nervous. This was his favorite . . . well, his only uncle. But no one was supposed to know where he and his father had gone. In this moment he realized that he had seen the sector border as some kind of gateway into a different reality, when really it was as porous as it had ever been.

"I just came to say hello." Martin smiled. "We miss you back at home. Shame about your father."

"What do you mean?"

"Leaving your mother like that, without a word, taking you away, out of your own country."

"He didn't leave her. They split up."

"That's what he told you?"

"Well, yes. They sat us down and told us they were separating. They were fighting all the time."

"Oh. That's not what she told *me*. Dear."

"And he didn't take me *away*. I'm not a child. I'm practically grown."

"Yes, you are, Rudi. Almost grown." Martin shook his head softly. He took a brown paper bag out of his valise and handed it to Rudi. "I brought you something. Here, take it! You can never have too much."

Rudi opened the bag and looked inside. "Film! Thank you, Uncle Martin."

Martin clapped Rudi on the arm. "You're welcome."

"The Leica is *so* much better than the Prakti," Rudi said, putting the bag down. He told his uncle to wait a minute while he locked the door and pulled down the shade. He poured them each a cup, shut off the coffee machine and pulled up a chair next to Martin.

"Listen," said Martin, "I hate that you and Peter are apart. Your *twin*. I can't imagine—you've never been apart, have you?"

"It's OK." Rudi shrugged.

"Do you ever think about going back? Just a year left, and the last one with you and Peter as student leaders! What a shame to miss it."

"All the time. It's different here."

"Do you like the West?"

Rudi shrugged. "Getting paid to spend time with pastry's been nice. Beats sauerkraut. Movies are better here, honestly," he chuckled. "But people here don't believe in anything."

Martin ignored him. "Where are you developing your pictures?"

"Well, I haven't been. The darkroom at my new school is closed for the summer. I have a lot of undeveloped rolls. I guess I'll print them someday. . . ."

"I have a darkroom you can use. In my apartment."

"You do? I've never seen it before."

"With all my cameras, don't you think I take pictures?" He laughed. "It's a little side room. You wouldn't have had any reason to go in there before. Last time you were over, I don't think you were really shooting yet."

Rudi took one of the boxes of film out of the bag and turned it over in his hand. "I miss Mutti."

"I know you do."

"Do you know . . . if she's been all right since we left?"

"She's been sad. It's hard to see my sister like that. But she'll be all right. I'm sure she misses you, too."

"I wish I could see her."

"It's funny you say that. I've been thinking—what if you could come and go? Cross the border whenever you like? I'm sure your girlfriend would love to hear from you."

Rudi laughed. "I'm sure Angelika's moved on. Vati won't let me tell anyone we're here, let alone go back. Those days are over."

"Well, not for everyone. I have an old school friend—I'll bet I can pull some strings, get you a special pass so you can go back and forth across the border like before."

"Really? Wow, Uncle Martin, Vati will be so happy! We can see Omi, and he can—"

"I'm sorry, Rudi, but it's got to be only you. Your father can't come back. It's amazing they haven't lured him back to face justice."

"What do you mean?"

"Well, right now your father is—I hate to say this, but I'm sure you understand—he's a criminal. You both are, actually."

"Criminals?"

"Fleeing the Republic gets you fifteen years' hard labor. Didn't you know that? Besides, since you're not yet an adult, they could add kidnapping to that charge."

Now Rudi was scared. "I didn't want to leave. . . . Vati tricked me." He didn't know why he said that. He scrambled to correct his words. "Besides, we have papers now. We're citizens here."

Martin laughed and held up Rudi's new West Germany identity card. "You mean this?"

"Where did you get that?"

"You shouldn't leave your wallet just anywhere." He pushed the card across the table to Rudi and took Rudi's wallet out of his pocket. "You don't understand how any of this works, Rudi. You're guilty of betraying your country. *Republikflucht.* Fleeing the Workers' and Peasants' State, stealing labor from your comrades. It's practically *treason.*"

Rudi's head was all in a muddle. "I thought maybe that . . . once you had your papers here, they just sort of . . . let you go."

Martin laughed. Laughed and took a long sip of coffee. "If only it were so simple. Just think of your mother, and your brother. You wouldn't want them to come under suspicion, would you? For helping you flee? And think how much you want to protect your father from the consequences of his crimes. Oh, and your Omi, of course." He got up and collected his things. "I'll come see you again soon, and you'll let me know what you want to do. All right, Rudi?" He turned the dead bolt and let himself out while he put on his hat.

•••••

Rudi brought home a box of leftover Berliners on the brink of staleness. His father was elated and put on water for tea. They took advantage of being two bachelors without stupid rules like a well-rounded dinner.

Rudolf leaned back, chewing a doughnut, and unfolded his newspaper. "It's so good to read something other than *Neues Deutschland*," he sighed.

"It's time for the trial," said Rudi, getting up and flicking on the new-to-them television. "May I?"

"Go ahead," said Rudolf.

Rudi didn't tell his father about his uncle's visit. Why would Martin offer to get Rudi a border pass, but not Rudolf? And how did Martin have the ability to make that offer? He was an optometrist with a hobby of tinkering with old machines, not some diplomat.

In the bulletproof box, Eichmann nervously arranged items on the small ledge in front of him: the microphone stand, the stack of papers, the second pair of glasses, his notepad, his pen. It was understandable that the Nazi was getting more nervous with each new witness. The worse the crime he was accused of, the more he protested that he was *just following orders* or *merely a little cog in the works.*

"Have you noticed that he's got a twitch in his right eye now?" Rudolf mentioned.

"Every time we watch this, the corner of his mouth hikes up another centimeter," said Rudi.

"But he doesn't *react*, exactly. When they talk about some really shocking thing he did, he doesn't say anything. Like a machine."

"A machine whose face is just changing in slow motion." Rudi imitated the gradual morphing of Eichmann's face, and they laughed freely together until they remembered the seriousness of the testimonies they were watching.

One man told the story of a day when all the teen boys his age were sent out to a football field. A board was set up that the kids had to pass under. If they were shorter than the board, they got gassed. That was that. Kids his age eliminated by arbitrary games. Were those SS guards *just following orders,* too?

He felt a righteous indignation grow in his belly. There was something about watching the trial with his father, in all its raw revelation, that made it feel like they were on the same team—that they were of a different fabric than this Nazi in the bulletproof box, different than all those monsters. His whole life, his father had felt like a stranger, but once in a while, Rudi saw a light in him, as though someone had turned up a flame in the middle of his chest. This was one of those times.

"Deep down, I did not consider myself responsible and I felt free of guilt," Eichmann said with a cold stare. *"I was greatly relieved that I had nothing to do with the actual physical extermination. The part I was ordered to deal with was quite enough for me."*

"Bastard," said Rudolf.

"In your police interrogation," said the prosecutor, *"you said that if the Reichsführer had told you that your father was a traitor, you would have shot him with your own hands. Is this right?"*

"If he had been a traitor, probably."

"No! If the Reichsführer had told you so. Would you have shot him—your own father?"

"If he had proven it, I would have been duty-bound, according to my oath of loyalty. Yes."

Rudi looked sideways at his father. He wanted to tell him everything—that he'd told their secret to Charles, about the offer of papers from Martin—but something checked him. He wanted this closeness between himself and his father to remain, to grow, and to do that, he would have to show Rudolf that he was happy to be here.

Martin came back to the bakery the next day. He walked up to Rudi at the counter and ordered a Berliner to go.

"Have you thought about my question?" he asked, looking down and counting out his change.

"Yes . . . I'm not sure, though. I don't want Vati to get in trouble."

"I'll make sure that doesn't happen."

Rudi turned back to the rack of pastries and began shuffling them into order.

"Look," Martin said softly, "just come over, bring your film to the darkroom and see the rest of your family. I won't tell anyone. Only one thing: under no circumstances can you tell any of them that you went over the border. Understand?"

He slipped Rudi a booklet underneath a five-D-mark bill.

A moment hung between them, and Rudi put out his hand and took the passport.

Martin was a collector of mechanical things of all kinds—not only cameras but typewriters, radios, telescopes. He lived alone in a one-room flat with a picture window overlooking the crunchy brown grass of a neglected *Platz*. It was a large room—unlike the tiny hive of rooms that was Rudi's old apartment—with a single bed and a wardrobe, an icebox and a hot plate. The walls were painted bright white, lined uniformly with shelves containing his collection, neatly displayed and meticulously dusted. Against the wall was a table at which he both ate his meals and worked on his machines, taking them apart and reassembling them, cleaning each part with a soft cloth. The flat always smelled of rubbing alcohol and strong coffee.

This was how Rudi had remembered it, though it had been a while since he'd last been there. He knocked on Uncle Martin's door at ten in the morning the next day. Martin answered, dressed in a brown short-sleeved shirt with a tan zigzag across the chest, quite casual compared to the natty suit he'd worn to the bakery, yet not a hair on his head was out of place.

"Rudi!" Martin embraced his nephew. "You came. I'm so glad. Come in!"

Sure enough, Martin was working on his machines, the table covered with bits and bobs. His bed was tightly made. The beige drapes were closed. Light came in through the sides of the curtains.

"Let me fix us some coffee," said Martin. "I only have Presto, I'm sorry. I'm a simple bachelor."

"That's fine," said Rudi, wandering over to the worktable, where Martin had disassembled a typewriter. The body lay on the floor, and the key mechanism was exposed like a skeleton. As Rudi looked closer, he noticed that each type of tiny gear and screw was in its own pile. There was a can of machine oil and a cloth, a loupe and a set of screwdrivers of various sizes in a zip-up case. Rudi wanted so badly to mess around with all of this stuff. It got the better of the little boy in him.

Martin handed Rudi the cup of Presto and gestured for him to sit on the bed while he covered the table with a white sheet. Maybe he could tell that if he let Rudi sit at the table, order would be lost.

"So!" said Martin. "How did it go at the border? Did they give you any trouble?"

"One of them looked at me a little too long. It was pretty nerve-racking. But I decided to just hand him the visa and not say a word."

"Smart man. Let the papers speak for you."

"Thanks for getting them for me. I'll go see my mother after this."

"She'll be so glad to see you! Did you bring your film? Shall I show you the darkroom?"

"Definitely!" He held up the bag of film rolls.

"Ambitious!" he laughed. "Let's start with one. I can develop the others later, if you like."

The darkroom was, sure enough, a little side room off the main one. If he'd been conscious of the door in the past, Rudi would have assumed it was a closet. It had a double entrance to avoid light pollution, a counter around the perimeter of the room, a sink and a work surface in the middle. Negatives and prints were clipped on drying lines. It was spick-and-span, not a fleck of dust in sight.

"Have you developed negatives before?" asked Martin.

"No, I only had one semester in the darkroom, and the teacher always did it for us," said Rudi. "She only let us print. I think she didn't trust us not to screw up the negatives in the dark."

"Oh, I thought you'd been doing this longer! All right, I'll walk you through it. We'll practice in the light first, and then I'll shut them off, and you'll know exactly what to do."

So they did. With the lights on, Martin showed him how to mix up the developer, stop bath and fixer and have them all ready for each step in the process. He then set up each piece of equipment so that Rudi could find them, in order, in the pitch-black, when the tiniest photon of light would ruin the film completely. Rudi practiced pulling the film out, cutting the leader, spooling the film onto the spiral holder, cutting it off from the canister, putting it in the developer can, assembling the lid. Finally he mimicked flipping on the light. By the fifth time going through the motions, it was like breathing.

"You're ready!" Martin exclaimed. "Here we go." He flipped off the light, and they were in unearthly darkness. Rudi did so well,

Martin let him process four rolls of negatives this way. Rudi squee-geed them dry and hung them on the line. Martin turned on the overhead light, and the two of them washed up.

"I'm proud of you, Rudi! You got that right away. Very adaptable, we humans, aren't we?"

They went back into the main room, and Martin made them each another cup of coffee. Rudi was riding high on getting this right and having Martin's vote of confidence, of being in his real country, on *this* side of the city, where he belonged and even the instant coffee was familiar.

"You know what, why don't we pay your mother a visit together?" Martin suggested. "She should just be getting off her shift about now."

Rudi and his uncle took the S-Bahn to the apartment. It felt good to walk through the corridor into the quiet of his old courtyard for the first time in weeks, with the benches where his old neighbors gathered for chats and smokes. He wondered if his mother would be there yet, or Oma or Peter.

When they got upstairs, Martin knocked at the door. Rudi had never waited at his own door before. Had the hallway always been this dingy?

"Who's there?" came Ilse's voice.

"It's Marti, and I brought a surprise," said Martin, putting a finger to his lips so Rudi wouldn't give it away.

"Come in, it's open," she replied.

Ilse was at the table, dressed in her work clothes and looking through the mail. She didn't look up at her brother. "What did you bring me, Marti?"

"Mutti?"

"Rudi!" Ilse stood up, and mail scattered everywhere. Rudi ran to his mother like a little boy and started to cry. Almost sixteen years old, and crying in his mother's arms. He couldn't remember the last time he'd hugged her. He was taller than his mother by three inches now, but all he wanted to do was shrink and curl up in her lap. She smelled like rosewater lotion and a slight touch of alcohol.

"Where have you been? Why didn't you come by after you moved? You didn't have to stay away just because you moved a few blocks!"

Rudi looked at Martin over his mother's shoulder. His uncle gave him a serious look.

"I'm sorry, Mutti," he said, wiping an embarrassing tear with his sleeve. "There was just a lot to do."

"Well, make sure you leave your address and phone number this time!" Ilse sat Rudi down and fixed him some tea and toast. He watched her slice an apple with a paring knife, in that swift motion that made the fruit seem to come apart on its own. This was the mother he'd wanted back for so long but knew he could never really have. He soaked it in anyway. She was having a good day.

Someone at the door both knocked and rang the bell. Martin answered it.

"Martin! What are you doing here?" the visitor asked. The voice sounded familiar. It was Baby Face. Glasses wasn't with him this time. Rudi's mind scrambled. He slipped his hand in his pocket and touched the visa from Martin.

"Dieter, you idiot!" Martin laughed and slapped him on the arm. "Ilse, Rudi, this is my old friend Dieter. This is my sister and my nephew. What are you doing here?"

"I'm just delivering a message to Herr Möser. Is he here?"

"No. . . ." Martin stalled. "He's out. I'll give it to him, though."

"Fine, fine," said Baby Face, handing Martin an envelope. Rudi wasn't sure, but it looked like Martin passed something else to him at the same time. "Look me up sometime, will you?"

"I will! Take care of yourself! *Tschüss!*"

Just as Baby Face was leaving, Peter came home. Rudi sprang up to meet him, and they hugged, pulled away and punched each other in the shoulders.

"Ugh, you smell like a barn!" said Rudi.

"*Hallo?* I'm a shepherd."

"Where's your staff and halo?"

"Shut up! I like it! The animals love me."

"You said it, not me!" Rudi could barely speak through his merciless laughter. Martin and Ilse tried to contain themselves and failed. Martin politely excused himself to leave as he wiped away a tear of laughter.

"Oh *Gott*," said Rudi. "Please go take a shower!"

"OK, I'm going!" Peter said, ambling toward the bathroom. "But then you and I are going out!"

PETER

That night, after the movie, Peter decided to skip the cabaret to spend time with his long-lost brother. With a lump in his throat, he made up Rudi's old bed for him, tucking in the sheets and Rudi's favorite bedspread.

"You don't have to do that," said Rudi, opening his old dresser drawers to see if he'd left the smallest thing behind.

"No, I want to," said Peter. "I really . . ."

"You missed me? Is that what you want to say?"

"Pfft. No."

"You're on the verge of tears, Peter. Admit it—you missed me!"

"A little. Especially when I bombed last week."

Rudi sat on the bed and took off his socks. "Bombed? How could Peter the Great possibly bomb?"

"I tried to tell some jokes at the cabaret. I don't know what I was thinking. And before you try to make me feel better and say stuff like *I'm sure it wasn't that bad,* trust me, it went worse than you think."

"Worse than *I* think? Must've been pretty bad, then."

"Well."

"You're going to try again, though. You always do."

"Maybe. But this time I know what I have to do—first of all, I have to write my own bit. And second . . . I can't pull my punches anymore. I have to say what I really think about life, about the Party; they're not what we thought they were. They do really bad things to people."

"Oh, come on, Peter."

"You don't know the stories I've heard. They pick people right up off the street and throw them in jail. They come into your apartment when you're not around."

"They wouldn't do that if people didn't have something to hide."

"That's not true. Sometimes it's just for having a different opinion, or having the wrong friend."

"There's no point in getting in trouble for nothing. I mean, you *could* write under a pen name or something."

"I don't think so." Peter pondered the possibility. "At least not yet. But look, I want to hear about you. What have you been doing this whole time?"

"There's not much to tell. Vati moved us into a hovel. My circumstances are much diminished."

"Well, they could get better, you know. I saw your girl, Angelika. I bumped into her at the war memorial. She was asking about you. She said you didn't tell her you moved. Why not?"

"I can't. . . . It's complicated."

"Rudi, don't mess this up. She's fantastic, and for some strange reason, she likes you."

"I'll get in touch with her soon. I will."

The brothers talked into the night and only turned in as dawn filtered through the blinds. They managed a brief sleep, and parted ways after breakfast. Seeing his twin made him feel repaired, like a little frayed patch had been darned back together. But he'd forgotten to ask Rudi for his address and phone number. He'd have to wait until Rudi stopped by again. He supposed he could go to the kraut factory to look for him. But then he supposed he'd rather smell like sheep than cabbage.

At the farm the next day, he settled under a tree with Fox and watched the sheep graze. He took his notebook out of his pocket and began to write notes for a new bit. The visit from Rudi had energized him, even if his twin hadn't understood his newfound drive. The ideas came faster than he could write.

Later that evening, as he sat on his bed practicing the new jokes, he heard his mother come home, speaking low to someone whose voice he didn't recognize. It was a man's voice. Peter's ears perked up. Was it Baby Face or Glasses giving her a hard time again? No, it didn't sound like them, or any of their neighbors. Could it be that his mother had another man in the house?

Suddenly there was a crash from the kitchen and a shout from the man's voice. Then Oma joined the fray.

"Get out of my house!" she hollered. *"Raus! Raus, du . . . du Hurensohn!* How do you dare to bring another man into my grandson's home?"

Peter bolted up, ready to confront whoever it was in the house. But then the front door slammed and Oma knocked on his bedroom door.

"Don't worry," she said, peeking her head in. "They're gone."

"Who was that, Omi?" asked Peter.

"No one of consequence. I'm going to sleep by the phone. Don't answer it, and don't call anyone."

Sure enough, the phone rang in the middle of the night. Oma picked it up at half a ring and muttered something, and then Peter heard her get ready and shuffle out somewhere.

In the morning, he found a note from Oma on the table.

PETER,

    YOUR MOTHER HAS BEEN TAKEN TO THE HOSPITAL, AND I HAVE GONE TO SEE HER. THE ADDRESS IS BELOW. PLEASE COME WHEN YOU ARE ABLE.

                    OMI

Peter rang the farmer and told him he had a family emergency. He made his way to the hospital, all the way up in Lichtenberg. It was a vast campus, and he had to ask for help three times before he found the right building.

The lobby was bustling. Peter now realized how terrified he was. *Who was that man? What did he do to Mutti?* Peter thought with horror that he might see his mother pushed in on a gurney, with tubes sticking out of her, on the way to an operating room. But it didn't seem to be that kind of place.

"I'm here to see Ilse Möser-Fleischmann?" he told the receptionist.

"And you are?"

"I'm her son Peter."

The receptionist had him sign a book and showed him the way to the room. Oma was in the hallway, standing by the door. She looked positively ashen. When she saw Peter, she sniffed and raised her chin.

"You called out of work?"

"*Ja, Omi. Was ist los?* What is all of this? Why is Mutti here?"

"This isn't pretty, Peter, I want to warn you. But it's good that you came. Let's go in."

Oma took him into the room. There was a partition just past the door. It was dark, with the lights out and the shade drawn, and a television cast a bluish light. And in the corner, a pile of blankets on a narrow bed was pulled back just enough to reveal the face of Peter's mother.

"Mutti?" Peter barely got the word out.

Ilse looked like a child lying there on her side, staring at the television. At his voice, she lifted her eyes, puffy with tears, and smiled at her son. "Peter," she whispered. And then she lowered her eyes. One tear rolled out, and she stared once more at the television.

Peter approached her and crouched down by the bed. He put his hand on her arm; he smoothed her hair. He thought of every time he had scorned her, dismissed her, turned her over to Rudi so he could get on with his life. And he was ashamed.

"Mutti, what happened to you?"

"*Komme,* Peter," Oma coaxed, her voice barely audible. She squeezed his shoulder. "Let's let your mother rest now."

Peter rose, patted his mother and tucked the blanket around her just a bit more. "I'm here, Mutti. I'll be right outside." Ilse responded with a faint, hollow smile.

Oma led Peter to a room filled with tables and chairs but few visitors. Pale yellow curtains hung over the windows. It was brighter than his mother's bedroom at home, to be sure, but it still had a dimness to it. To the side there was a coffeepot and a basket of cookies. Oma poured coffee for two, Peter got their snacks, and they sat at a table by the window.

"This is a psychiatric hospital, Peter," said Oma, dunking her cookie. "Your mother, she's . . . unwell."

"Why? Was it that man? Did he hurt her?"

"He was just the catalyst for something that's been coming for a while."

He thought of his mother, shrunken in the bed. "Why is she so quiet?"

"They gave her something to calm her. She was, ah, she had . . . mmm . . . how do I say this—"

"Say it."

"It's hard to understand . . . hard to explain. . . . She had a delusion, Peter, that she was in a movie at the big film festival. And apparently she believed this boyfriend of hers was also in the film. Things got out of control, and he got scared and pushed her and ran away. And so they found her running through Alexanderplatz, um, naked. So they brought her here and sedated her. She's not hurt. But she's going to be here awhile."

Peter stared into his cup. He couldn't believe this was happening.

From the corner of his eye, he saw a nurse in a white uniform come in. It was Sasha, Angelika's sister, from the cabaret. Peter knew she was a nurse—at a psychiatric hospital, even—but he couldn't have imagined how that would intersect with his own life. He was about to say something to her—here was someone he knew, someone who might understand. But she glared at him, her lips drawn tight into a thin white line, and Peter understood he must not let on that they knew each other.

"Comrade, may I get you anything?"

"No, thank you, young lady," Oma replied.

"No, thank you," Peter echoed, "comrade."

"I believe another visitor has just arrived," said Sasha. "So you're aware, visiting hours are almost over."

Peter heard his name being called and turned to see his uncle Martin coming toward him. Martin held out his hand, and Peter shook it, weakly.

"Good," said Oma brusquely. "You're here. I'm going to take Peter home. The nurse will fill you in."

"That's fine, Frau Möser," said Martin. "Are you all right, Peter?"

"Yes," he said, "but I feel a headache coming on."

"Then we'd better get into the fresh air," Oma said, helping Peter out of his chair. "Here, Peter, finish the coffee, and we'll take the biscuit. It will help."

"Feel better, Peter," said his uncle. "I'll stop by to check on you."

It was the most his uncle had said to him in years. Peter didn't want Martin to stop by or show concern or anything. He just wanted to go home. To be alone. No, that wasn't true. He wanted his father and his brother, more than anything. And he didn't know where to find them or how to tell Rudi that their mother was lying in a bed far away, lost in her mind, far away.

The house was stuffy and silent when they got home. There were no words for what they had just seen. Peter was trying to make himself believe this was even real—his mother in a psychiatric ward, his mother like a tiny rag doll beneath that mound of blankets. The question of what was to happen next was the furthest thing from his mind. He sat on the sofa, staring at the blank television screen.

Oma attempted some nourishment for the two of them and put it on the side table.

"Peter," she called, "come and sit. I want to talk to you about something."

Peter poked at his plate and listened to his great-grandmother as though she were the radio.

"I think the time has come for me to leave," said Oma.

Peter lifted his head and barely whispered, "What?"

"It's only you and me here, *Schatzi*, and we don't need all this space."

"I wouldn't call it *space*, exactly, Omi."

"Still. Fine. It's more that this place is . . . too full of history. I'm old and tired. I feel my heart slowing down, and I don't want to end my life in this grayness. I want you to move to the West with me. We can go through the refugee center."

"But what about Mutti? She lives here, too!"

Oma put her hand on Peter's arm. "She's not leaving the hospital, Peter."

"What do you mean?"

"Don't worry, Peter. She'll be safe and looked after. Besides, we'll only be a few more stops away on the train."

"I don't know."

"Peter, you've been talking about getting out of here for months now."

"I know—"

"You may not have the chance much longer. I've been hearing Ulbricht say some things on television that don't give me confidence in his intentions."

Peter sat back and looked out the window. Of course he wanted to go. His heart thrilled at the thought of walking across that sector line for good and never looking back, of being able to say what he liked, go where he wanted without always looking over his shoulder.

But Renate. And Kabarett Zusammen. And his fellow artists, trying to hold it down for each other. He was part of them now.

"When are you planning to leave?" he asked.

"Soon. I'm not packing anything. There's nothing here I want, anyway. Nothing but my *Peterling.*" She patted his cheek with her old hand.

"I have to think about it, Omi. I want to talk to my girlfriend."

"Peter, if you choose not to come with me, I will still go. But I will make sure you have what you need. And if you change your mind, you can come whenever you choose."

Peter went for a long run on Wednesday morning.

"Omi?" he called, slipping off his sneakers and putting the mail on the table, but there was no answer. He thumbed through the mail. He tore open an envelope from POS 5 and saw that it was next semester's class schedule, about which he could not have cared less. There was a letter from the asylum, which he would leave for Oma or Uncle Martin to handle. And beneath it all, a small blue envelope, written with just his name in Oma's handwriting. He'd read it later. He and Renate were going for a walk in the park before she went to work.

The silence was thick when Peter got out of the shower and dressed. Renate would be here any moment. In fact, she knocked just as he slipped on his second shoe. He didn't invite her in. They left right away.

Peter had to walk pretty slowly to avoid getting ahead of Renate. They walked through the Volkspark in the morning sun, drinking bottles of lemonade. The glare of the sun felt unduly harsh on Peter's face. Even Renate's presence felt oppressive, and he hated thinking that. She tried to regale him with the latest gossip at the theater, but he barely heard her.

Renate finally pressed Peter. She took his hand firmly and asked, "Are you going to tell me what happened?"

"What? Oh. Maybe later."

"Are you going to sign up for a slot on Saturday?"

"My bit's not ready."

"Why not?"

"Family stuff."

"Your brother? You said he came back?"

"It's not really important, *Maus*. Hey—there's going to be a bonfire at the farm on Friday. It's a campout. Can you get off work?"

Renate looked a little taken aback at the sudden change of subject, but she let it go for the moment. "Definitely!" She beamed. "That sounds fun."

"Good," said Peter. They strolled up the path to the Märchenbrunnen fountain.

"Aren't you glad it's almost over?" Renate asked. "You won't have to take that long train ride every day."

"Honestly . . . not really. It's been nice to be out of town. I like the animals, especially the dog. Fox, you know, the one I told you about? Wish I could bring her home with me."

"I had a dog when I was little, when we lived with my father." Renate smiled at the memory, and Peter noticed how pretty she was when she let down her guard. "His name was Monti."

"What happened to him?"

"My father had to find him a new home when we moved. I miss that dog. A house feels a lot less empty with a dog in it."

"I'm getting to know a lot about empty houses lately," said Peter.

"You mean since Rudi and your father left?"

"Not just them." He stopped walking and crossed his arms. "My mother, ah, my mother's gone."

"Where did she go?"

They walked to a bench beside the fountain. Families were picnicking in the shade, and little kids hung on the sculptures of fairy-tale characters. "Hmm." Peter nodded, as if remembering how recently that kind of innocent life had been his. "She's in the hospital, Renate."

"Is she all right? Did she have an accident?"

"Ah, no . . . she . . . she's in a sanatorium. The one where Sasha works, actually. She's my mother's nurse, if you can believe it. What a small world. . . ."

Renate took Peter's hand and forced him to look at her. "Peter, you need to tell me what happened to your mother."

Peter's eyes flitted every which way. He was suddenly having trouble catching his breath. "I don't really know. I . . . I don't think I ever knew her at all."

"Peter, breathe. Try to tell me."

He focused on Renate's face, but once his eyes stopped moving, they filled with tears. "She's been drinking a lot. I barely see her—she's either out or passed out. She . . . she hit me."

"What?"

"But she felt bad about it. She didn't mean to do it. And I guess she's been going out. With other men. You know, not my father. And the other night, one of them was there, but my great-grandmother kicked them both out. Next thing I know, she's in an asylum, lying in a bed, sedated. She's not coming home, apparently."

"Mein Gott."

"Please don't tell anyone."

"I won't."

"I don't understand. Why did my father take *Rudi*? Rudi's always looked after Mutti. I don't know why they had to split us up at all, but *I* was closer to Vati. It's not fair."

"*Ja,* when they decide things like this, they can't fathom how it's going to affect us."

"We always pay for the stupidity of adults," Peter huffed.

"Truth," Renate said with a sardonic chuckle. "Now listen to me. You're going to be all right, *Katze.* Do you hear me?" She rose and slung her pocketbook over her shoulder. "I have to go to work. See you Friday, for the bonfire?"

Peter wrapped his arms around her waist and kissed her. He held on to her as long as he could. "Come to my place at six."

"I'll be there."

Renate and Peter got to the collective farm as the sun was setting. They hadn't said much on the train, so he'd had time to think about his situation, and he was surprised at how clear he felt.

The farm was aglow with the fading light and the friends he'd made, the girl he was falling for, good food and the approaching end of a bizarre summer. All night they danced and talked and sang. Peter tried out some of his new jokes in casual conversation, and people genuinely laughed. *That's good,* he thought, *I'll try these tomorrow night.* Everyone rolled out blankets, and Peter and Renate held each other and kissed like mad, with Fox curled up at their feet. The bonfire died out, and as the stars revealed themselves and the satellites orbited above them, they lay down and slept in the yard until a new morning arose.

●●●●●

243

Peter arrived back home and shuffled through the mail. There in the pile was the blue envelope Oma had left for him. Maybe it was a thoughtful note about how sorry she was that he had to see his mother in that condition. But it wasn't that.

Schatzi,

I am sorry to handle such things in a letter, but the situation is what it is. So what shall we do about it?

For a long while now, I've been planning to go away. I did not see events playing out this way. I hoped the family could stay intact until you and Rudi had graduated, but that was not to be. I am old and tired, and my heart is not in the best shape. I need someone to take care of me, and that cannot be you.

If you receive this in time and want to join me, meet me at the S-Bahn at two p.m. Friday. If not, I will be in touch soon with an address. When the time is right, I want you to join me.

Peter, I tried to instill in you a straight spine and two strong legs to stand on, and I see it. You are young, but you are capable. Your uncle Martin will care for your mother, my friends will care for me, and you will need to care for yourself. Visit your mother, be kind to her, but do not take on her burdens.

I have left you some money in a cookie tin. There is a loose tile in the wall behind the toilet. Please find a new hiding place for it, and spend it carefully. The rent is paid through your school year. If there is anything in the apartment to sell or throw away, do it ruthlessly.

I know we do not say it often in our family, but I love

you, and everything I have done for our family is out of love
and, somehow, hope. Live your life.

Your Omi

He read the letter four times before he understood that Oma Möser had really gone. All of her things were still here, it seemed. But then, there was very little that was truly hers. He wondered what it must have taken for her to detach herself from this place, where she had lived for over forty years. Her bed had been made up, clothes hung neatly in her closet, but she was gone. With a hollowness he didn't think possible, Peter knew that she would not return.

This is it, he thought. *I'm truly on my own.*

Peter's heart was rimmed with sadness, but he knew he would be fine. It wasn't as though he was truly alone. He had Renate. The gang at Kabarett Zusammen was becoming a little family. There were places he could go if he needed to.

The money was where Oma had said it was, and he couldn't believe he'd lived here all this time and not noticed the missing grout around that tile. Inside the tin was a manila envelope with five hundred D-marks. He decided to tape it to the underside of Rudi's old dresser while he planned a better hiding spot.

RUDI

The sound of the piano poured from the apartment window, but Rudi didn't recognize the song. Something new his father was trying for the lounge gig, he supposed. He must be home early.

Maybe one of his tuning jobs had been canceled. Maybe he wasn't feeling well.

Rudi pushed the front door open and headed for the stairs. The smell of paint pinched his nose; someone was renovating in the back flat. Willi the saxophonist was leaning in his doorway in his robe, smoking and staring down the hallway, listening to the piano.

"*Guten Tag*," said Rudi. The man nodded halfway and kept staring and puffing.

Rudi went up, unlocked the apartment door and slung his bag onto the kitchen chair. The piano piece was slow, meditative, right for a summer afternoon. His father must be in a reflective mood.

Rudi turned toward the living room. He didn't want to disturb his father, only to say hello. But it wasn't his father playing the piano.

It was his great-grandmother.

In Rudi's whole life, he'd never seen Oma go *near* a piano. She was the smoker, the storyteller, the ballbuster. But the musician? He stood in the doorway and watched.

"*Hallo,* Rudi," she said, neither stopping nor turning around.

"I didn't want to disturb you."

"I saw your reflection in the window."

"I didn't know you played, Omi," he said, entering the room. He sat next to her on the piano bench.

She continued playing. Finally she spoke. "Satie's *Gymnopédies*. I haven't played this in, oh, twenty years."

He wanted to ask her where she'd learned to play. If she'd taught his father. Why she'd never played at home. But something else had to be answered first.

"Omi? Can I ask you a question?"

"Yes."

"What are you . . . what are you *doing* here?"

Oma ended the piece, looked at Rudi and sighed. "Taking my first deep breath in a thousand years." She kept her foot on the damper pedal and let the last chord waft into the summer air.

Rudi was antsy for concrete answers. "Can I, ah, get you something? I think we have some instant coffee. Are you hungry?"

"Coffee—yes, that would be good." Oma picked up her purse from the piano bench and walked slowly into the kitchen, which now contained a small table and mismatched chairs. She put her hands on her hips and looked around. "I thought our flat was tiny," she said.

"Two men don't need much," Rudi replied. He put the kettle on and spooned the coffee into two cups. He futzed around, trying to scrape something together for his great-grandmother. He couldn't guess why she was sitting here in Kreuzberg. He held his hundred questions.

"Men. Hmm." Oma smiled and sat at the table, took her cigarettes out of her purse, packed the box and lit up. Rudi slid the cups of hot coffee and a plate of cookies across the table. Oma seemed to be unusually short on words. She drank, smoked, ate a cookie with great deliberation and breathed huge, deep breaths.

The keys jangled in the door. Rudi was relieved. His father would be able to mediate, to explain Oma's being here, even if she wouldn't. Rudolf stepped in and stopped. He looked like the saucer-eyed dogs from *The Tinderbox*. He was obviously as surprised by her presence as Rudi was.

"Oma?" He peered down the hallway to make sure no one was watching.

"You didn't know she was coming?" asked Rudi.

"No, I didn't." Rudolf shut the door and put his valise down.

Oma met him at the door and he embraced her tiny form. "How did you . . . find us?"

Oma smiled. "You need a sofa," she said. "I'll go out and buy one tomorrow. And a better television, *meine Güte!*"

"Are you . . . staying?" Rudolf asked.

"Obviously, *Schatzi.*"

"How did you get here? Are you going to make me ask all these questions one at a time, or are you going to tell me what's going on?"

She sighed. "First you need to take me out and feed me a proper meal. I'll treat, *ja? Gut.*"

"That's all right, Oma," said Rudolf. "I'll take you out."

"Not on your life! I haven't been saving my pension and smoking bad tobacco all these years for nothing."

The three of them went to the lounge where Rudolf worked. It was empty in the late afternoon. Oma dug into a plate of schnitzel and chugged a tall pilsner. Once she'd eaten half the entrée and drunk a third of the beer, she was ready to tell her story.

"I've been planning to leave the East for a long time. I never wanted to live under that bunch"—she mimed Walter Ulbricht's famous goatee—"but when the Red Army came in, my flat happened to be in their zone. It was one of the only buildings in the neighborhood standing after the bombing—an accident of history. Some of my things were still intact—like my piano. And when you needed me, Rudolf, I was so pleased I could do *something* for you. And for my *babies.*" She squeezed Rudi's arm.

"I have been through two world wars, the Spanish flu, a depression, a king, four occupying armies and two dictators. And I'm sorry to say this—I know she's your mother, Rudi—I even survived all these years with Ilse. There's not much I haven't lived through. I'm resilient. I can figure out how to live in any circumstances. But I've been feeling the straitjacket tightening, and I had to get out."

"I'm sorry, Oma. That's terrible," said Rudolf.

"Is it? *You* left, didn't you?"

"Yes, and I feel awful about it."

She chuckled and sipped her beer. "You always do."

"I wish I could have found a way to bring all of us out together," said Rudolf, "but things broke down so badly with Ilse. . . ." He hesitated to say anything more in front of Rudi. "I had to make a choice, and I couldn't tell anyone."

"You're my *grandson.* You could have told me you were getting out. I would have helped you."

"Oma, you're seventy-nine years old. The Party leaves pensioners alone. Why would you leave your apartment?"

"Back in June I heard Ulbricht say something strange on television. *Niemand hat die Absicht, eine Mauer zu errichten!* No one has any intention of building a wall! And I thought, Wall? No. As soon as he said that, I made my plan. I always listen carefully to what that weasel says and then figure he's really saying the opposite. Anyway, I'm here. It was simple, really. I just took the train and walked."

"They weren't suspicious because of your bags?"

"What bags?" She lifted up her purse. She had left the *Deutsche Demokratische Republik* with nothing more than her pocketbook, stuffed with a few spare pairs of underwear and sixteen years' worth of cashed pension checks changed to D-marks. "You said it yourself, Rudolf. I'm an old lady. They think we just wander and dodder about. Nobody expects us to do anything more daring than adding black pepper to our scrambled eggs. And anyway, what are they going to do, put me in thumbscrews?"

"I have to know, though, Oma," said Rudolf, "how did you find us?"

"I went to see Charles."

"What? How does Charles know where we are?"

"Um . . . Vati, I told him," Rudi confessed.

"How could you—"

"Don't blame either of them," Oma interrupted. "Charles thought I should know. He gave me your address and told me about the bakery. And the lounge, Rudolf—good for you! Charles and I talk almost every day, didn't you know that? He calls to check up on me. Unlike my grandson." She smiled slowly, watching Rudolf fumble for words. "That was a joke. I know why you couldn't call. I hated to leave my little *Peterling*. If I didn't think he'd manage for himself, though, I wouldn't have gone."

"What do you mean, *manage for himself*?" Rudi asked.

"I asked him to come with me. He wanted to, but he has unfinished business at home. I left him everything he needs. He's going to come when he's ready. I didn't tell him I was coming to you. He still thinks you're living in Prenzlauer Berg."

"But you said he's managing for himself. Where's Ilse?"

"Ah. That's the other thing." She popped a bite in her mouth. "Rudolf, your wife is in an asylum. She had a breakdown. She's not getting out of there. It's all very sad."

Rudolf sat back in his seat and looked at his grandmother, unable to say a word.

Rudi, on the other hand, was wondering why no one was freaking out like he was. "We have to help her!"

"What would you suggest?" Rudolf fired back. "We go back across the border and hope no one notices?"

"She's my *mother*. How can you be so cold?"

"Don't you understand, Rudi? She's *safe*. People are looking after her," said Rudolf.

"It's true," said Oma. "Martin has taken charge of her care."

"Well, I'm going to go see her," said Rudi. "Omi, which hospital—"

"Oma, you can take the bedroom," Rudolf interrupted. "Rudi and I will sleep in the living room."

"*Schatz,* I'm a guest in your house. Let me buy a sofa for you, and I'll sleep there. I'll pull my weight. Oma Möser is no mooch."

"All right, you can buy the couch, but I'll sleep on it. I insist. And I'll take you down to Marienfelde tomorrow to get you registered. We can look into getting you a new pension."

Oma nodded and finished her meal. The three of them sat in awkward reunion. Rudi's mind scrambled. He wanted his mother, but he didn't know how to get to her.

It began to rain against the windows, and they hadn't brought an umbrella.

"Rain washes the city," said Oma, taking the last swig of her beer and sitting back in her seat, satisfied.

In the morning, Rudolf took his grandmother to Marienfelde to register as a refugee. Later on, Rudi and Charles got together at Der Spinner for Thursday "music school," trading records at the listening stations and introducing each other to the best—and most obscure—music from their two countries.

"Vati always says you can tell a lot about someone from the music in their piano bench," Rudi told Charles.

"That's true about a record collection, too," said Charles. "I always say beware of anyone who's only got radio hits on rotation without knowing what came before."

Der Spinner was full of kids, browsing, laughing and begging Tobias to put on *The Twist* so they could dance some more.

"Take a listen to this," Charles told Rudi. "I think you'll like it."

The Shirelles sang *Will You Still Love Me Tomorrow,* all teenage pleading and bop. But Rudi was distracted. He took off the head-phones.

"Omi showed up at our new place yesterday," he said.

"That's right, I gave her the address. Was it a good visit?"

"No, I mean she came as a defector. All she had was her purse."

"Damn." Charles whistled. "She didn't tell me she was doing *that*. Is she OK?"

"She seems . . . happy."

"So it's just your mother and Peter there now."

"Peter is there. But my mother is not. She is in the hospital."

"What happened?"

"She had a nervous breakdown, it sounds like."

"Lord, you all are carrying some heavy burdens," Charles mut-tered. He shook his head and rubbed his neck. "Listen, why don't I come by later? I want to get a Glenn Miller record for your Omi so I can give it to her as a housewarming. And I'll speak to your father. He may have some things he needs to talk about."

"Thanks," said Rudi. "Maybe he will listen to you."

Rudolf and Charles brought Oma into the bakery on Saturday morn-ing as soon as it opened. Rudi was working a morning shift, both for the money and to get out of the crowded apartment.

"Ein Kaffee mit Sahne," Oma instructed her great-grandson as Rudolf got them a table and Charles took out two newspapers, En-glish and German.

"What would you like to eat, Omi?" Rudi asked.

"Surprise me," she said, easing into her seat. "You have quite the variety on offer."

Oma had always been independent back in East Berlin, but Rudi had never known her to *buy* coffee, let alone fresh pastries not pre-served in polythene. She bought her clothes secondhand, smoked the cheapest cigarettes and let Rudolf and Ilse pay the rest of the bills. Meanwhile, she'd been stashing her pension in anticipation of leaving the Workers' and Peasants' State behind for good.

Charles and Oma sat together, and he handed her the English paper while he took the German, for language practice. Rudolf had already finished his pastry and was nursing his coffee while he read a copy of Rilke's poems. Rudi came by, freshened Oma's coffee and brought her a plate of springerle cookies, and Oma's face lit up. She ate one off the plate before Rudi even put it down.

"Oh, I missed these," she said. "Haven't had them in years. The bakeries in East Berlin are too austere."

"Why didn't you just come here once in a while and get some?" asked Charles.

"I tried not to get too comfortable," Oma replied. "I didn't want to pine for them too much."

"Well, you've earned it, Oma," said Charles.

"That's right, Charles. I didn't leave with only the clothes on my back for nothing! Speaking of, what do you think of my new outfit?" She stood up and showed off her new light blue slacks and printed blouse, a sheer scarf around her neck. She'd never worn anything like that before. Rudi suspected she hadn't bought new clothes in a decade.

"Glamorous! Very bourgeois," Charles joked.

Oma laughed her raspy laugh. "It's funny you ask." She leaned over and tried to whisper, but it wasn't quite low enough. "My father was an aristocrat."

Charles planted a kiss on her cheek. "Well, you look plenty fancy to me," he said.

"It's sad," said Oma. "That's why Rudolf couldn't continue with his music. They don't let the wrong class into conservatories. They had to take him down a notch and limit him to tuning pianos."

Rudi was annoyed. "Oma, why wouldn't you tell us?"

"Because they didn't have to worry about you, Rudi. You more than achieved class consciousness."

"Speaking of class consciousness"—Charles folded his paper as he rose—"I've got an appointment with Uncle Sam. Rudi, I'll take another cup of coffee to go and . . . um . . . a piece of this, in a box." He pointed to a cake in the display case, chocolate with cherries on top. "I don't know if they've considered this over there in your old neck of the woods"—Charles took a sip of coffee—"but maybe the workers and peasants just want to live their own lives, you know?"

"But they *can*," said Rudi. "No one is stopping them."

"Then why'd your grandma have to jump the border with her unmentionables rolled up in her purse?" Charles challenged.

"That's what it takes," said Oma. "These days, you have to fight for your own peace."

Rudi rolled his eyes.

"Be careful of thinking you're on the right side of history, kid," said Charles. "When you're only looking at your own navel, you may not see what's about to collide with you head-on."

The bells on the door jangled. *"Entschuldigung,"* said Charles, almost bumping into the customer at the door. "Well, hello there!" he blurted.

Rudi turned to see who was coming in—and dropped the handful of coins and bills he was carrying.

It was Peter.

Renate was with him, and she gasped when she saw Rudi. The brothers were both glued to where they stood, their faces morphing from shock to love to anger to confusion.

"What . . . the . . . *hell* are you all doing here?" they both said.

Oma covered her mouth and tried not to smile.

Charles patted the boys on their shoulders and left the family to their reunion.

Rudi and Peter grabbed each other in an embrace. Then Peter hugged his father and great-grandmother as Rudi bent to pick up the money he'd dropped.

Peter looked at his brother. "If you're working here . . . Do you mean—all along, you've been . . . in Kreuzberg?"

"Yes. Sort of. It's complicated." Rudi lowered his voice.

Renate sat next to Oma and introduced herself, asking if she was all right and complimenting her fabulous outfit.

The twins conferred. "I'm done with my shift," Rudi said. "Let's catch a matinee. I'll pay."

Peter was taken aback. "Is that all right, *Maus?*"

"Of course," she said, taking her leave of Oma with a handshake. "Looks like the two of you have some things to talk about. See you tonight, *Katze.*" Renate kissed Peter and headed in the opposite direction.

Peter and Rudi said goodbye to Oma and Rudolf, grabbed a couple of Berliners, and headed toward the Kino. When they walked past the big white sign announcing, in English, German, Russian and French, *You Are Now Leaving the American Sector,* Rudi almost halted, acutely aware of the international boundary beneath his feet. He put his hand in his bag and felt for the passport, hoping he wouldn't have to try to use it.

"Peter, I have to tell you something," said Rudi.

"OK. . . ."

"Aren't you wondering why I haven't called or given you my address? Didn't you wonder where Omi went?"

"She told me she was going to cross, but why are you here? You're supposed to be in an apartment in Prenzlauer Berg."

"Peter, you dummy, remember when those two guys told Vati he wasn't allowed to work in the West? He couldn't tell anyone. And you can't, either, Peter. Not even Mutti."

Peter's pace slowed almost to a halt. "She doesn't know, either?"

"Only Uncle Martin knows. I don't know how. But he came to see me. He got me a visa to cross whenever I want."

"Why do you need a visa? They hardly ever check. Look, we just walked right out of the American sector and no one even noticed. Besides, couldn't you just use your school ID? Pretend you still live there."

"Now that we crossed, like *really* crossed, and registered, we're technically fugitives. Uncle Martin said if they catch us, we could get *fifteen years*."

"Are you kidding me?"

"We're West German citizens now. But if I crossed without this"—he held up his visa—"that wouldn't matter."

They came to the Kino box office and Rudi bought their tickets and a box of lemon candies. They took their seats in the almost empty theater, lights still up, waiting for the movie to start.

"Well, now that you shared your news," said Peter, staring at the blank screen, "I have something to tell you, too. Mutti is in the hospital. It's a mental hospital."

The air hung heavy over them, and Rudi was quiet. "I know," he whispered. "Omi told us. Vati doesn't seem to care at all. What happened to her?"

"I don't know what it was, some kind of breakdown. It was probably a long time coming."

"Can we go see her?"

"You mean after the movie?"

"No, now."

"I don't think that's a good idea," said Peter. "It's not a pretty sight."

"I don't care if it's a pretty sight, Peter, she's our *mother.*"

"Tell you what—why don't you come to the cabaret tonight and stay over, and we can go see Mutti in the morning?"

"Is there some reason you don't want to see her?"

Peter hesitated as the lights began to lower. A fanfare played as the DEFA film studio logo faded onto the screen. "It's not that I don't want to see her. It's . . . I just need some time. You will, too. To prepare yourself. Besides, I'm trying a new act tonight. I have to focus." He took a lemon drop from the box.

"Fine," said Rudi. "We'll go see Mutti tomorrow."

"Meantime, come to the cabaret for some laughs. We're going to need them."

The movie was nothing special and ended like most DEFA movies: inspiringly *pro-Sozialismus.* They walked out into the August noon and took the tram toward Friedrichshain.

"Have you seen Angelika?" asked Rudi, looking blankly down Karl-Marx-Allee.

"You mean you still haven't called her?"

"No. Have you seen her with . . . you know . . . anyone else?"

"Not yet, but she'd have every right. She's wondering why you just disappeared on her. I was surprised you didn't at least try to get in touch with *her,* if not your actual *family.*"

"I thought about it, but it was too risky. I didn't know how to contact her without letting on where we were."

"*Ja,* that's one thing I can say about you, Rudi—you're not too good at playing games."

"What's that supposed to mean?" Rudi was irritated. He just wanted to know about Angelika. "Do you think she'll be there tonight? At the cabaret?"

"I guess so. She comes every week. Sings those beautiful songs. Hey, Rudi?" Peter asked as they got off the tram and walked to the apartment in Friedrichshain.

"Yes?"

"Don't mess this up. Girls like ours are once in a lifetime."

PETER

They were early getting to the cabaret. Without the neon light on, the cellar looked different, smaller, somehow, and stuffy, with an overhead light that flattened everything to gray.

"*Hallo*, Dad," Peter greeted Arno, who looked like a forty-year-old man—some of the kids called him Dad—but in truth was only twenty-four.

"You're here early!" said Arno, rolling out a small keg. His sleeves were pushed up, exposing his hairy arms, which were the same color as his hair.

"I just can't stay away," said Peter.

"Oh! *Abend*," said Arno, shaking Rudi's hand.

"I'm Rudi."

"Arno. I've seen you here before. Been a little while."

"Yes, I've . . . been busy. This is your place?"

"It's my building, yes. I was born right up there on the second floor. My grandfather and I live in that flat, and my sister and her

260

family in the one above us. It's getting harder to stay off the radar, but people have to have a place to be themselves, you know?"

"It's my home away from home," said Peter.

"Well! I'm glad. And now, since you two are here so early, why don't you light the candles to get some atmosphere in this place?" He pulled the string on the neon light, and the room instantly transformed. "Help me out here, will you, Peter? I've got to tap this thing." Arno and Peter hoisted the keg up onto the bar, and Arno held the brass tap to the bunghole as Peter hammered it in. Beer got everywhere, and Arno swore, but he patiently coached Peter through it.

"Sorry, Dad," said Peter.

"Don't mention it, son. Hey, you performing tonight?"

"*Ja,* I'm going to try something new I've been working on. Renate's bringing me some props."

"Oh, good. I'm glad you didn't let your last mishap end things. The only way out is through, you know."

Kids started filing in sporadically. Soon Sasha came down the stairs, and Angelika followed behind. Rudi didn't know what to do. It had been weeks since he'd seen her. He raised his hand in a guilty wave.

Angelika made straight for him like a twister. "Nice of you to show your face, Rudi. So. We finish the school year, and that's it? You've fulfilled your moral obligation, so you just drop me?"

"I didn't drop you, I—"

"I knew it. You're no better than the rest of them! Guess you don't want to be tainted before your last year as a student leader," she mocked him, poking him in the chest. She turned to walk away, but Rudi caught her and pulled her close. She tried to wriggle free, but he pulled her in all the way and embraced her.

261

"My father and I left the GDR," he whispered in her ear. "I'm not supposed to be here. You can't tell anyone. Only Peter knows."

Angelika softened and looked him in the eye. "Oh. Rudi. This is bad."

"It's not . . . I mean . . . it's . . . complicated. But I'm all right. I have papers."

"How'd you do that?"

"My uncle got them for me. So I could keep an eye on Peter." He nodded toward his brother, who was in the middle of kissing Renate.

Rudi and Angelika laughed.

"I'm sorry, Rudi. I just missed you. And it hurt that you didn't call."

"I know. I'm sorry, too."

"So what are you doing here, tonight of all nights?" asked Angelika as they got their drinks. "Is it a holiday I don't know about?"

"I'm going to visit my mother. She's in the hospital."

"*Mein Gott,* Rudi, is she all right?"

"I'll tell you more about it later. Let's just have some fun tonight."

"Rudi, you have to keep in touch with me, all right? Pick up the phone, send me a letter now and then."

"I'm sorry. I truly am," Rudi said, and properly kissed Angelika like it was the first time.

Arno called Peter's name off the list, and he marched up to the stage with a pillowcase stuffed with who knows what. "And now, *meine Damen und Herren,*" he announced, "come with me on a journey through the history of our glorious leaders . . . in three minutes or less!"

Out of his pillowcase, Peter pulled a big rope mophead and threw it over his hair, tugging the front over his chin like a beard, leaving only his eyes showing. "It's 1848! Karl Marx writes *The Communist Manifesto,* laying out the vision for our glorious future." He paused and looked intently at the crowd. "I must warn the sensitive ladies in the audience—you're about to see a series of bad men's grooming decisions. Doesn't anyone *tell* these guys? It's like, *Hey, Karl, you're turning into the Abominable Snowman, and Comrade Barber needs to feed his kids. It's time for a little snip-snip.*"

The audience laughed. He had them.

"But I digress. To 1917!" Peter dumped the mop hair, tacked on a paper goatee and tucked his hair into a white bathing cap as he talked. "Our vanguard, Vladimir Ilyich Lenin, leads the October Revolution, ushering in the first Socialist state! And, comrades, he is with us still, his body under glass in Moscow, like a freshly baked apricot torte. Mmm . . ." He licked his fingers. "Sticky and overripe. Just as a dictatorship should be. Now! 1928!" He continued without a pause, whipping off the goatee and cap and holding a big black comb against his upper lip like a mustache. "Comrade Joseph Stalin establishes the first Five-Year Plan, propelling Marxism-Leninism forward"—then he whispered—"much to the chagrin of the five million Ukrainian peasants who starve to death. But do not worry, comrades!" Peter shouted triumphantly, waving his finger in the air. "Stalin bravely—so bravely!—gorged on his endless supply of expendable young men and shat us out the other end, into the consoling arms of our beloved"—here, Peter put on a pair of glasses with bushy eyebrows, a mustache and a nose attached—"Groucho! Oh, wait, wrong Marx."

The people held their stomachs and howled. Peter took off the Groucho disguise and tacked on the paper goatee again. "I mean, our beloved Lenin, back from the— No, I mean our very own esteemed *Chairman! Walter! Ulbricht!*"

The audience went wild with applause for their puppet leader. Peter let all of the disguises fall to the floor as he drank in the cheers.

"That's it for me tonight! Stay safe out there. Because just remember, comrades, there are three kinds of people: those who tell jokes, those who collect jokes"—the audience joined in on the well-known punch line—"and those who collect people who tell jokes!"

Rudi had never heard Peter do jokes like this before. At home he was funny—hilarious, even—but he never skirted the line politically like he just did in the cabaret. Down here in this secret club, people loved Peter, but it wasn't because he was charming. It was because he was good. *At this.* And Rudi was proud of Peter. In awe of him. But in some dark corner of his gut, pressed down and stifled, he recalled the phantom feeling of his hands around his brother's throat.

After the set, Peter strode into a small room that served as the backstage, obviously high on the applause, wiping his face on a towel with one hand, unbuttoning his shirt with the other. The sweat spiked his hair, like he had a head full of nails. Rudi came up behind him with a clap on the back that squished the perspiration and made Rudi momentarily feel a bit sick.

Rudi wiped his hand on the front of his pants. "That bit with the mop and beards was . . . um . . . Anyway, I got some good photographs."

Peter patted his brother's arm. "Thanks!" he said. "I had the idea when we saw that billboard of Ulbricht and Lenin on the train to Munich. Remember that?"

"Oh, right," Rudi said. "That's what I thought."

"They've got to be the same person—you ever see them in a room together?" Peter laughed. "Hey, how about a milkshake?" He pulled off his sweaty button-down and undershirt and grabbed a fresh shirt from his knapsack. "There's that little Milchbar kiosk that stays open late. Renate has to work, but you should ask Angelika to come."

"Let's keep it to you and me," said Rudi. "We're going to see Mutti in the morning, so we shouldn't stay out too long."

"Let's go," Peter said. He put his arm around Rudi's shoulder, and the two of them walked up the basement stairs and made their way to the U-Bahn station, hoping they wouldn't have to wait too long for a subway.

Their train was halted in the tunnel for an inordinately long time. The other passengers griped back and forth about delays before agreeing that there must be some overnight construction going on. Rudi and Peter decided to get out at Alexanderplatz.

They nixed the plan for milkshakes. The night was awfully chilly for mid-August, especially after the hot compression of the train car. Their light jackets were barely enough, but Rudi figured the long, vigorous walk would warm them up. Rudi and Peter stuck to the shadows along Alexanderstrasse, walking quickly and quietly, their hands in their pockets.

"Let's go toward Heinrich-Heine-Strasse and split there," suggested Peter. "You can cross the bridge and I'll get a tram home. I think we should see Mutti another time."

There were more police and soldiers on the street tonight, but as long as the boys evaded notice, they didn't have to worry. No one wanted to be stopped and asked for papers this late, especially Rudi.

"Look at these Vopos," Peter scoffed. "These idiots take themselves so seriously. Most of them are barely older than us!"

"Still," said Rudi, "let's not get too close."

Rudi tensed his muscles to keep that warm feeling in his bones, to keep his thoughts of Angelika in and the cold night out. He was faintly aware of distant jackhammers, probably some crew fixing a road. The boys turned right.

Just then, every single streetlight went out, as though someone had thrown the switch for the whole city. But the boys realized it was only on this side, in the Soviet sector. The boxy Eastern skyline was silhouetted against the colored glow of Western nightlife. Instinctively, Rudi pulled his camera out of his bag and framed up a shot. Peter grabbed Rudi's arm and yanked him backward, hard. They ducked into a doorway, and Peter put his finger to his lips.

At the end of the street were gathered several police officers. Rudi realized how stupid he'd been. As nervous as the thought of showing his special papers made him, he'd been too cavalier, developing a sense of invincibility from having them. With this many Vopos on the street, they might decide to harass him just to get credit with their superiors. He couldn't depend on his Western citizenship, nor his visa. The game felt too big in this moment.

The boys turned around and made for another route, glad for the darkness that shrouded them but depending on the odd lit window and the faint light over the border to see where they were going. Something tinny and metallic was pinging the pavement, and as they got closer, they saw a work crew in the intersection ahead, guided by green-uniformed Vopos, unrolling a huge spool of barbed wire.

Rudi had to get back to the American sector, to his father and Oma. He hadn't told either of them he was staying out, let alone going back across the border to the East.

Rudi and Peter walked down to Bornholmerstrasse and into a new reality slicing across streets where they had walked freely that same day.

Sure enough, soldiers stood shoulder to shoulder, forming a human wall, while even more soldiers fastened wire to concrete pilasters. There were Trapos, transit police, at all the train stations, and the trams weren't running, either.

"We should go another way," said Peter. "This is weird. I don't like it."

"Let's split up. I can try Schilling Bridge."

"Maybe you should come home with me."

"It'll be fine. The quicker I go, the better."

But every border crossing they came to was blocked by spirals of barbed wire and soldiers posted a man apart, strapped with rifles.

Rudi and Peter looked at each other, scrambling for an alternative plan.

"Rudi," said Peter, "I think they're closing the border."

RUDI

The brothers walked all night, but Rudi and Peter could not find any route that did not culminate in a web of barbed wire. The sign announcing *You Are Now Leaving the Soviet Sector* was still there, useless and redundant. There truly was no going back now. Their previous life was bisected by razor wire and armed border guards. And as much as Rudi wanted to recover his life in the East, that life now lay somewhere in oblivion, every connection severed by soldiers, wire and concrete.

The sun was beginning to rise in the eastern sky. "Do you think they're lined up along the *whole* sector border?" asked Rudi. "Where did all these Vopos come from?"

"See that guard up there?" Peter pointed. "I'm going to ask him for information."

"Peter, don't—"

"Excuse me . . . what are these barricades for?" he asked the young guard, skinny as an iron post, with wide eyes and sunken cheeks.

"Anti-Fascist Protection Barrier," the guard answered, as though

his response had been prerecorded. Peter looked at Rudi and raised his eyebrows.

Rudi took a different tack. "I'm a . . . W-West German citizen," he told the guard. "How can I get back?"

"Well, the crossings are all closed, but I did hear that the one at Friedrichstrasse is open," said the guard. "Honestly, you should go now. They might close that one, too."

They thanked the guard and made their way toward Friedrich-strasse. "Maybe I can get through with you," Peter suggested. "*Twins against the world*, right?"

It was mayhem. Families were shouting to each other, crying, pleading with soldiers to let them cross just this once. The weird dual-country, split-city status quo they'd lived with for fifteen years—it was over. Overnight.

The guard had been right. Every possibility of escape was closed off. Peter and Rudi managed to make their way to the one open cross-ing. And who should be on duty at the Western side but Charles.

"Oh, thank goodness," said Rudi. "It's Charles. Maybe he can vouch for us."

They were halted at the East German checkpoint and stood in a long queue of people shaking their fists, demanding to be let into West Berlin. Their relatives—parents, children, grandparents—begged the *Ossi* guards, but they were all stone-faced, rifles at the ready. The desperate people in front of them might as well have been invisible.

"*The border is closed. . . . I repeat, the border is now closed. Only those with proper visas may exit. . . . All GDR citizens, please return to your homes. . . .*"

Rudi's heart pounded in his throat. All his crossings had worked until now, but what if this was the time his papers somehow wouldn't add up? What if his name was flagged on a list for *Republikflucht*—now, when the stakes couldn't be higher?

"Identification, please," said the guard at the booth. Rudi slid his West German visa through the booth window and put his sweaty palms in his pockets. He told himself not to speak unless spoken to.

The guard took forever, scrutinizing every millimeter of Rudi's visa, looking up at him, down at his picture, back and forth. Finally he snapped the passport closed and handed it back to Rudi.

"Next," the guard called.

Rudi almost burst out laughing with relief, but he held his smile until he reached the checkpoint where Charles was standing. He started to approach him—he wanted to talk to his friend, tell him what a close call he'd just had. But Charles's face was stony. He looked at Rudi and flicked his chin, motioning for him to move on.

Rudi heard a voice behind him.

"What about me?" shouted Peter, trying to shove past the guard. "Rudi, *what about me?*"

Rudi walked backward into the West, looking agape at his brother. Peter was flailing his arms in desperation, just like hundreds of others who were trying to rush the border. *What does he want me to do?* he thought. *I'm powerless. It's not my fault. He'll . . . figure it out. . . .*

"I'll . . . I'll see what I can do . . . ," he called to his brother. He shrugged, fumbled getting the passport back into his pocket, set his face toward Kreuzberg, and ran.

Rudi wasn't the only one. People ran or wandered or sat down suddenly on curbs or stood on sidewalk benches to try to get a better look. Rudi tried to weave through and lost his bearings completely. He found himself stuck in a crowd gathered around an apartment building on Zimmerstrasse. The building was flanked on either side by the now ubiquitous barbed wire, guards positioned right behind, but neither the wire nor the guards crossed in front of the building. It lay right on the border—the apartments in the East, the sidewalk in the West.

Everyone was staring up at the top floor, where a man held his little boy out of the window, dangling him over the crowd. Someone came running with a large bedsheet, and the people stretched the sheet out.

"Pull it taut!" they cried. "No slack, no slack! Oh my God, he'll die!"

The man let go of his son and he fell four stories, screaming, onto the waiting sheet. The boy bounced twice and was caught up into the arms of a woman, who held him as his father followed, through the empty air, into another country.

The same scene played out down the entire length of the street. One old woman jumped from a third-floor window. She did not move again.

By the time he found his way to his own apartment building, Rudi was exhausted. When he opened the door, Oma looked at him with instant fury and slammed the phone. Rudolf ran to him to hug him, Rudi hoped, to tell him how worried he'd been—but instead, Rudolf erupted.

"Where the hell have you been?" he cried. "I got back from work at four a.m. and you weren't here! It's total chaos in the streets. We've been up all night. Can you imagine what's been going through our heads?"

"I . . . I'm sorry, Vati, I . . ."

"Are they rounding people up? We don't know. Arresting them? *Shooting?*"

"Vati, I can explain. . . ."

"I told you so," Oma huffed. "I told you Ulbricht was going to build a wall. Sneaky bastard, doing it while everyone slept. . . ."

"Where were you, *Junge?*" his father demanded.

"I was . . ."

"Were you with someone? A girl?"

"What? Come on—"

"Oh, no—wait—could you have been so stupid? Were you in the East?"

Rudi refused to answer. He folded his arms across his chest, as though he could keep his heart from falling out and betraying him. He wished he could become one with the linoleum floor.

"Where's Peter?" Oma panicked. "*Mein Gott*—where's your brother?"

"Oma, please!" Rudolf halted her. He sat down at the table and sighed. "One thing at a time. Rudi, sit down. Do you remember what I've always said?" he asked, his tone finally calm. "There are family words, and there are outside words. That still applies here, and more than ever, since we can speak freely. I have to have absolute truth in my house. *Verstehst du?*"

"I understand."

"I want to know why you were in the East."

"Fine," Rudi sighed. He measured his words carefully. "Uncle Martin came to see me."

"Martin? Where? When?"

"At the bakery. He told me Mutti wasn't doing well, and that he could get me special papers to cross whenever I wanted to check on her."

"When did he see you?"

"A couple of weeks ago."

"You've been going there for a couple of *weeks?*" Rudolf charged.

Rudi dodged the question. "Peter and I were going to see her this morning, but we never made it."

Rudolf rubbed his face and leaned back in his chair with defeat. "Do you know how bad this could be? For you, for all three of us?"

"Yes. He told me we were criminals for crossing."

"Only a bankrupt country would call freedom a criminal act," said Oma.

"Oh, Ilse . . ." Rudolf almost broke down. "Peter . . . you said you were with him?"

"Yes. I . . . we . . . got separated at the checkpoint."

The three of them sat in silence. Their former country was officially off-limits, and the Möser-Fleischmann family found themselves on opposite sides of this terrible new barrier.

Oma rose and tried to call the old apartment, and the exasperated Western operator informed her that all telephone service to the East was suspended until further notice. Oma hung up and turned on the radio instead, scrolling through the dial. Not one station was playing music or soap operas or cultural commentary. Every station blared the voice of Willy Brandt, the mayor of West Berlin:

"A clique which calls itself a government has to try to fence in its own population. The concrete columns, the barbed wire, the death strips, the watch towers and the machine guns, those are the hallmarks of a concentration camp. It will not stand."

The newscaster took a sober moment and continued. *"In other news: the trial of infamous Nazi Adolf Eichmann will conclude tomorrow with closing arguments. . . ."*

"I should, um, get ready for work," Rudi faltered, walking toward the bathroom.

Oma flicked the radio dial off and lit her next cigarette.

PETER

In all the tumult, Peter had nothing to do but wait.

School was supposed to start again in a couple of weeks. His student summer was over, and anyway, with the closures on public transport, getting to the Potsdam farm on the S-Bahn would take hours. What he wouldn't give to see his dog—at least, he felt like Fox was his. Sitting on his bed in this flat, so utterly alone, he wished he had that dog by his side. He reached over into his laundry bag and pulled out his work shirt. It still smelled of sheep and hay. It made him want to cry like a little boy.

He tried calling the number Rudi gave him, again and again, but every time, a recorded message told him that phone lines to West Berlin were no longer operational.

How could he leave me like that? Peter wondered. *Just leave me at the checkpoint, like a stranger?*

It was maddening. This was a city. It wasn't an international border. It was a *city.* Only two days before, he'd casually strolled across the bridge. He'd seen his brother and his great-grandmother at the bakery and munched on a Berliner. Thousands of times he'd crossed the vapor-thin boundaries floating through the city. Now everyone felt the violence of the slice of razor wire dividing the heart of Berlin, from the stranded employee of a West Berlin business to the frustrated mother used to pushing her baby stroller to a nearby park. Disoriented people wandered the streets like automatons.

Peter flicked on the television for some answers. He'd had to rotate the antenna away from the West again after Glasses and Baby Face paid their last visit, and he didn't dare try under these circumstances to turn it back again. There was nothing on but vapid triumphalism from the East German news, about how the brave defenders of the working class had taken decisive action against the imperialist threat. But the radio—yes, he'd still be able to tune in to RIAS. So Peter sat on the sofa and tried to make sense of what was going on.

He was growing antsy, drumming his fingers on the arm of the couch, his legs bouncing restlessly. He got up, flipped off the radio and went to Rudolf's study to plink out the couple of songs he actually knew. He took a good, hard look at the apartment. How neglected it had become. Peter put on a record and began to clean the house.

He found a cardboard box and collected every stray item. Every piece of mail, opened or not. Pill bottles and ashtrays and bric-a-brac. Dirty dishes and cups his eyes had glanced over for weeks. He scrubbed the cabinets, dusted the windowsills, vacuumed the rug with the frustratingly powerless Omega vacuum cleaner.

But when he came to his mother's room, it was a different situation altogether.

It dawned on Peter than no one but Ilse had actually been in here since his father left. And even Rudolf had barely been occupying it at that point, Ilse having kicked him to the sofa. Peter pushed on the door, which was impeded by a mound of dirty clothes and bottles. He wasn't sure that he *didn't* see something scamper away into the shadows.

Peter stripped the bed. He pulled down the curtains. He piled up dresses and dirty underwear and satin robes and stockings and shoved everything into laundry bags, baskets, boxes—any free container he could find to take down to the coin laundry. There was too much here to wash in the bathtub, too much to hang on the clothesline over the courtyard.

He filled every rubbish bin in the apartment with discarded bottles of vodka and schnapps and beer. He stuffed all the bits of paper and receipts into bags. And when he turned over the mattress, he found a stash of both ostmarks and D-marks—not a hoard, but enough to break Peter's heart.

Finally he swept and dusted and vacuumed and rolled up the rug and put it in a corner. Sixteen years of his mother's life was—physically, at least—made sense of.

By now Peter was on a total cleaning bender. Everything in the house that could hold dust became repulsive to him. He wanted a completely sterile environment, free of all the clutter and complication.

And then, at last, the frantic machine of Peter's purge arrived at the door of his own bedroom.

He looked at the unmade bed, the posters on the wall—and his medals. The trophies and certificates that had been his pride were suddenly rendered meaningless. What did it matter that he'd won a rhetoric competition or placed second in the city track meet or gotten that acting award?

Peter was out of receptacles. He'd have to clear everything else before he could get rid of the trophies, so he crammed them all into Rudi's bureau drawers. What it all revealed was a layer of dust a millimeter thick, the ghostly outlines of useless props. He grabbed a rag, wiped everything down and set about the task of taking out the garbage.

"You'd be proud of me, Rudi," he said aloud into the air. "You were always the minimalist, but now it's me, the last one standing in an empty house."

RUDI

Rudi left the bakery on Tuesday at lunchtime and walked by the new barbed-wire border. Among the workers, he recognized a few kids from his old school—what a way to finish out *their* student summer. Already, work crews were retracting the barbed wire from a few days before, and in its place, stacking concrete blocks in squishy, imprecise rows, mortar oozing out through the cracks in a gray mass. It was brutal, decidedly unaesthetic, pure utilitarian harshness. People walked up to the Wall and stared at the concrete as though it might magically turn into glass.

No one spoke of anything else but the Wall. Radios blared analysis, from East and West.

"It had to be done," they said on the Eastern stations, *"because of wreckers who were draining the factories and farms of their laborers."*

People like Vati, thought Rudi.

"With the Wall containing the imperialist threat, we can pull together to share in the coming prosperity. From each according to his ability, to each according to his need, building the Socialist future."

Rudi understood, of course, why the Wall had to go up.

He just didn't know why it had to be so *ugly.*

And right now he couldn't help but feel that he was on the *wrong* side.

He felt the weight of his camera in his backpack. Uncle Martin would appreciate Rudi photographing all of this. He took the Leica out and began shooting.

He snapped a picture of the Wall, growing vertically from the cobblestones.

A man with a meterstick and surveyor's level, making sure the line of the Wall stayed precisely within the East German border to within a fraction of a centimeter.

A young American border guard, bewildered at the post he was being asked to stand.

Then, out of the corner of his eye, Rudi caught a quick movement. A Vopo had suddenly flicked his cigarette out of his mouth and was running toward him at full speed. Did the soldier recognize Rudi? Was he coming after him for *Republikflucht*? Terrified, Rudi did the most instinctual thing: he raised his camera and clicked the shutter just as the Vopo made a balletic leap over the wire and barely cleared it, flinging aside his rifle and running into a waiting US Army truck.

Rudi's mouth hung open.

"Did you see that?" someone asked. "That was incredible!"

He turned to see another photographer standing beside him; the man had also captured the moment and was laughing in amazement. Rudi didn't answer. He couldn't believe a soldier would want to deliberately risk that in broad daylight, and betray his country so openly. Rudi had been brought here without his consent or control. But this soldier had fled his post, given up everything, in a split second.

Why? How does he know life is so much better on this side? I wonder if he left his mother. His sisters and brothers. The people who needed him to stay.

Rudi came home and saw Rudolf at the table, reading a piano repair manual. Above the piano was the last thing Rudi would have expected: the photograph he'd taken of his parents at the Lenin party. What was it, exactly, that his father wanted? Did he think the photo would make him feel closer to Ilse, now that they were not only separated by mutual consent, but by a concrete barrier?

Oma was in the living room, sitting on the secondhand sofa and watching television, cigarette in hand as usual. Rudi put his camera on the table and sat by his father. There was one question rolling over in Rudi's mind. He thought of fifty ways to ask it, but none of them seemed right, so he opted for bluntness.

"Vati . . . why did we leave the GDR?"

Rudolf closed the manual, slid it to the side and folded his hands.

"Haven't I told you?"

"No. You never explained it to me."

"Or maybe you weren't listening," Oma quipped from the other room.

Rudolf sighed. "There's this thing your uncle Martin says all the time, and it bugs the hell out of me. You know what I'm talking about?"

"*Humans are very adaptable?*" Rudi snickered.

"Well, it would be comical if it weren't so true. You can get used to anything, Rudi. Let's say one day all the canned fish is missing. And you think, *Why canned fish, exactly?* The next week it's the sugar, or the mustard. And you just adapt and adapt—you make your own ersatz mustard, or you go without and let your food, like your life, get more and more bland. But you go on living. No one asks the big questions. No one thinks about the Soviets plundering our countryside, tearing up all the railroad tracks and sending the steel back to Russia for themselves—and maybe *that's* why your damn fish didn't make it to the shops for a month. Or a hundred thousand other mismanagements, while you read a newspaper report about the flourishing economy, even though your eyes tell you it's not true.

"And the movies? You're just happy enough to sit in a cinema and let the light flicker before your eyes, right? You're happy to be hypnotized and forget that you haven't had real milk in a year, or that your work quota's gone up and now you have to make double the bricks with half the straw, like the ancient Israelites building the pyramids. So you get used to every movie, every show having the same story line. You know there's only one, don't you? *A troubled youth is having a swell time on the outside, going to the parties, getting all the girls, but inwardly, he's tormented, and it leads him to his down-fall all because—are you ready?—he didn't join the Party, you see.*

"Again and again you dig another centimeter of dirt out from under your own feet, until you're in a hole so deep you can't crawl out. Well, Rudi, I didn't want to *adapt* anymore. I didn't want to live by lies anymore. I grew up in lies. I told myself I had to deny what was right in front of my eyes, because the *cause* was noble. It's always the *cause*. We were fighting a great evil, so what did it matter if life required a suppression of your gag reflex?"

Rudolf seemed far away, lost in another time.

"But what does it have to do with me? I don't even like canned fish."

Rudolf looked at his son with an intensity like he'd just seen some horror.

Oma rose from the sofa and came into the kitchen. "I heard you talking about movies," she said, shoving a handful of money into Rudi's hand. "Why don't you two go out and see one? I'm trying to watch my program."

"All right, Oma," Rudolf said, grabbing his wallet from the counter and putting the cash inside. "There's a whole world outside of Berlin, Rudi. Remember what I said—don't adapt. *Choose.*"

PETER

On the first Monday in September, Peter began his last year at Polytechnic Oberschule 5. It was the first time he'd ever gone to school without his twin brother, and whenever someone wasn't asking where Rudi was, Peter walked around in a state of unnerving quiet. It was as though an electric current ran between him and his classmates, a constant intrusive hum: To know? To be known? To speak? To remain silent?

His class schedule was packed, but he was glad for it. It was that much less time he'd have to spend in an empty house.

And it really was *empty.* He'd kept some of the bed linens from his mother's room, some of her essential clothes, but he'd sold everything else to a secondhand store. In his furious purge he'd sold the television, but he kept the enamel and brass telescope of his father's. He'd rid the place of clutter, things he knew weren't senti-mental but just thrift shop impulse buys. And books. He sold his comics to a used book shop, along with most of his play scripts, his copy of *Weltall Erde Mensch* and his mother's parenting book by the wretched Dr. Haarer.

He made up all the beds hotel-tightly, like he presided over a utilitarian domicile that belonged to no one. He put every dish away except one plate, cup and bowl for himself; he set up a study area with the turntable in the living room and made a rule that during study, only jazz and classical music were allowed. He ate at the table instead of on a tray; he kept his sneakers ready by the door for his morning run.

With so few distractions, his mind felt liberated and primed. Jokes came flowing out of his pen, and he practiced them in front of the mirror in his mother's bare room. He collected his props in a single suitcase slipped under his bed. When he wasn't tending to the basics of his schoolwork, he was focused on simply telling the truth through his comedy.

As Peter thought about the Wall, a plan began to emerge in his mind. He didn't even tell Renate about it. Much as he loved Kabarett Zusammen, his future prospects were limited to the cellar of a shell-pocked building in Prenzlauer Berg. Peter knew the time had come. He needed to get out.

Peter and Renate decided to take in a movie before her theater shift began. They walked through the Volkspark on the way to the Kino, her head on his shoulder as they listened to a back-and-forth song between a wren and a raven. Days were still warm, but the fading light ahead of autumn's chill beckoned couples closer together.

Peter and Renate stayed until the very end of the film *The Gleiwitz Case,* until the lights came up and they could hear the film strip flapping against the projector. He was riveted. How easy it was for ordinary Germans like him to be so captured by dogma that they would willingly fake an attack in order to start the war on Poland. The dizzying cinematography reinforced the alienation he felt whenever he was being asked to believe a lie. Peter couldn't look at his girlfriend, couldn't speak. The last scene still had his hands shaking. What he felt was more than an *emotion*, it was a knowing. A word flashed within him, as though there were a sign on his chest.

Longing.

That was it. It was so deep inside him, Peter suspected it might have been there before he even existed. He'd seen a hundred movies of all kinds, from different directors, countries, genres—but this was the first time it clicked into place for him. It was one thing to be onstage in a cellar or in a school. It was another thing entirely to put a story like this in larger-than-life motion.

They walked in silence through the corridor behind the other moviegoers. Peter put on his coat and shoved his hands into his pockets. As soon as they pushed the door open into the evening air, the man in front of them lit a cigarette so fast, he must have already had it between his fingers. The smoke and the vapor of Peter's and Renate's breath all mingled into the evening chill.

"That's it, *Maus*," said Peter, just above a whisper. The next words were out of his mouth a moment ahead of the terror. "That's what I want to do."

"Do what, now?" Renate bounced on her feet and hunched her shoulders to keep warm.

"Make films. I want to make films like that."

Renate made a sound in her throat, but Peter couldn't tell what it meant—*You'll never make it in the movies* or *Who do you think you are, DeMille?*

"Movies, huh?"

"Yes."

"You'd have to move to Hollywood," said Renate, taking lip gloss out of her purse and puckering.

Peter whipped a look at his girlfriend.

"What?" Renate said obliquely. "You would."

"It's just funny you say that, because that's what I wanted to tell you," he told her. "I'm making a plan. I'm going to cross over."

Renate was taken aback by his sudden declaration, but she was not surprised. "Oh."

"I'd ask you to come with me. But I know you can't leave your mother."

"No. I can't."

Peter wished he had more to say, more of an actual plan in motion. Instead they stood there, hoping the smoking man wasn't listening. Peter took Renate's arm and they began walking toward the Brecht theater.

"How will you do it?" Renate asked. "How will you get across the border?"

"I don't know yet. I could crawl in the shadows, I suppose." He made a creeping motion, like he was in a Hitchcock film.

"You could wear a disguise." Renate poked him. "You've got plenty."

"I've thought about that." He watched her laugh. "What? I have! Maybe I'll apply to emigrate. You know, the legal route."

"I hear that takes a long time."

"Something will occur to me when the time is right. But the one thing that scares me is . . . what does this mean for us, *Maus*?"

"You have to live your life, *Katze*. I won't make you feel bad for that. Maybe I'll make it out someday, too. Just not yet."

He pulled her tighter to his side. "Thank you."

"But what about your mother, Peter? You can't just leave her in some mental hospital."

"She's got my uncle Martin to look after her. I can't clean up any more of her mess."

Peter knew that was cold, but Renate didn't push back. It wasn't as though he could fix his mother. And he was right; Martin was in a better position to care for Ilse, anyway.

Peter got home at dusk and found the front door to the apartment slightly ajar. Right away his mind went to a break-in, but he took a deep breath. He knew he wasn't the only one with a key. He pushed his way in slowly and smelled cigarette smoke.

His uncle Martin was sitting on the sofa with the owl-shaped lighter in his hand, staring at the console where the television used to be.

"*Hallo,* Peter," he said, not breaking his gaze.

"*Hallo,* Uncle Martin," said Peter.

"I'm not sure how I feel about what you've done to the place. It's not as homey. But then, Germans do like things in order."

Peter sat in the armchair and put his book bag down beside him.

"It didn't make sense to keep so much around," said Peter. "Since everyone took off."

"Yes," said Martin. "You really are alone here, aren't you?"

"It's all right. It's easier to study, anyway."

"You cleared out your mother's room."

"I had to."

"I wish you'd called me. It wasn't right to get rid of her belongings."

"It was disgusting. There were things living in there."

Martin took a long pull on his cigarette. "I've come about your mother, actually."

"Why? Is she all right? Is she coming home?"

"She's gone, Peter."

"What happened? What do you mean?"

"Oh, I don't mean gone like *that.* I mean that she's . . . I don't know how else to say it . . . she's disappeared. Somehow she escaped the hospital."

"Do you have any idea where she went?"

"No, that's partly why I stopped by, to see if you'd heard from her. I had brought her a suitcase with some of her things, some clothes, that photograph of our parents. When I went back, it was all gone. She's vanished."

Peter collapsed back into the chair and rubbed his face. "What about that man she was with, you know, the night she . . ."

"That's a good question. Did you see him well enough to give a description?"

"I only heard him. I never saw his face or anything."

"Yes, well, he was one of many. I've followed up where I could. No luck."

"Does Rudi know?"

"I'm going to go tell him. Not yet."

"He never did get to see her in the hospital. He was going to, but the Wall . . . But it's probably better. I wonder if he could have handled it."

Martin finished his cigarette and snuffed it out in his teacup on the side table. "I don't know what to say, Peter. I'm sorry. My sister is . . ." His voice began to break, and he cleared his throat. "Well, she's Ilse, that's all. I'll let you know if I hear anything. Meanwhile, take care of yourself. I'll stop by to check in when I can."

"There's no need to do that, Uncle Martin. I can look after myself."

"Sure." He smiled. "Good luck, then."

Martin took his hat from the coat tree by the door, and Peter noticed the end of a wire sticking out of his valise, typical for a tinkerer like his uncle. Martin left, fastening the door behind him with the key.

Peter was stuck. *What* can *I do? Should I go look for Mutti? What would another kid in my position do?* He shook his head and slumped in the chair. This was all so consummately unfair.

RUDI

Rudi's first day at his new school was bewildering. Many times throughout the day, he had to suppress his scoffing at the benighted students and even the teachers. He was used to order and orthodoxy, not to mention a different approach toward everything from math to history. He was relieved when he arrived for his afternoon shift at Bäckerei Antoinette.

"The funniest thing happened this morning," Charles said as he paid Rudi for his coffee and pastry. "This man walks over to my checkpoint from the Eastern side—nice suit, hat, shined shoes, diplomat's visa. *You know Rudi Möser-Fleischmann, ja?* he says. I shouldn't have said anything, but it caught me so off guard. I said, *Yeah, I know him,* and he hands me an envelope, says *Danke* and heads back over past the Wall. So here it is, kid."

Rudi took the envelope with powdered-sugary hands. "It must have been my uncle Martin," he said.

"Now, how would he know that you know me?"

"I don't know."

Charles sipped his coffee. "That uncle of yours, Martin," said Charles, "do you trust him?"

"Of course. Why wouldn't I?"

"Didn't you say he was an optometrist?"

"Yes."

"Well, I'm scratching my head over it. It's really hard for *Ossis* to cross into West Berlin now. So if your uncle's an optometrist, why does he have a diplomat's visa?"

"He has a lot of friends who can do him favors, I guess."

"Mmm. You're a good kid, Rudi. Just . . . watch yourself."

Rudi shrugged and opened the envelope. Sure enough, it was from Uncle Martin.

> *Dear Rudi,*
>
> *How would you like to go for a walk together? I have some time off, and there are some things we should discuss. I'll meet you at the bakery at four o'clock. Make sure you take a break then.*
>
> > *Yours,*
> > *Uncle Martin*

"Everything all right?" asked Charles.

"Everything's fine." Rudi folded the note and put it in his pocket.

"News about your mother?"

"No, nothing. He just wants to take a walk when I take my break."

Charles sighed. "You know, I like this time of day," he said, leaning against the wall by the front door. "The city pretty much empties out, and I can catch my breath. The checkpoint's been busier than ever. We never needed a guard booth until they built that monstrosity over there, *die Mauer.*"

"It had to be built, of course."

"Of course?"

"To keep people safe."

"Safe from who?"

"Fascists . . . imperialists"—Rudi stumbled—"people here who want to take over and make it a Nazi state again."

"*Take over*? Interesting. Then why is it that very few West Germans want to go in . . . and so many East Germans can't get *out*?" Charles swirled his coffee cup. "You know, Rudi, all over the world, some things are closing and some things are opening. Take our two countries. Here, doors are closing, walls going up. In America, things are getting ready to open. Unjust laws are coming down, wait and see. Closing, opening. The question is which one you prefer."

"How do you mean?"

Charles looked down pensively. "When I was here sixteen years ago, in the war, I was in an all-Black battalion. I wasn't *allowed* to fight alongside a white man. I had to be willing to die for a country that didn't even treat me like its own son. When we entered Buchenwald, I saw men who didn't look like men. I didn't know *what* they were—walking skeletons. Robots—just mechanical, staring into space, like they were looking for their souls. We fed them by hand. We bathed them. We watched them come back into themselves.

"And then we went home, after fighting for freedom over here, only to go right back under the boot in our own homeland. Every Black man whose blood cries out from the ground of this continent is a testament against our wicked laws. And the war brought it into sharp focus. They desegregated the army, but they didn't dig out the root. Do you know how damn unusual it would be to do what we're doing right now where I come from? *You* serving *me* coffee, sitting down together, riding the train together, going in the same entrance to a music hall? Coming to your *house*?"

"I didn't realize—"

"When you've had a taste of freedom, you'd have to be out of your damn mind to go back behind a wall."

Four o'clock chimed on the small clock by the register.

"I have to go," said Rudi, clumsily hanging up his apron. "Until next time, Charles."

Charles nodded. "Think about what I said."

Sure enough, just as Rudi came out of the bakery, Martin turned the corner.

"Rudi!" he called, picking up his pace.

"*Hallo,* Uncle Martin," said Rudi, shaking his uncle's hand. "*Wie gehts?* Is everything all right? How's Mutti? What did you want to—"

"Slow down! I was going to be in the neighborhood, so I thought I'd look in on you. Nice of your, ah, friend to give you my note."

"How did you know he was my friend?"

"How?" Martin puffed his cheeks. "Oh—I saw you together once or twice, the music shop, here and there, you know."

"Oh."

"How are your photographs going? Have another batch to develop?"

"Yes! I've taken a lot of the Wall. You won't believe the one I got of a soldier jumping over—"

"The barbed wire?" They stopped at a newsstand. Martin pointed to each and every newspaper on the shelves. The picture Rudi had taken was all over the front page. He did a double take. Had someone gotten hold of his film? *Of course, that other photographer got the same shot!*

"Looks like someone beat me to it." Rudi shrugged, deflated.

"Don't let it discourage you," Martin said as he bought a copy of *Berliner Morgenpost* and tucked it under his arm. "At least you know you were on to something." They strode alongside the Wall, in progress along the road.

"It's kind of an eyesore," said Rudi, gesturing toward the growing gray barrier. "Wasn't there any other way they could've done it?"

"Resistance can't be dressed up in handsome stonework, Rudi. It's urgent. This is what they drove us to. Fascists hide behind imposing facades and carvings. It's part of their mythology. Tell the people those stories, and it lulls them into a dream."

"Still, there are a lot of beautiful buildings in Berlin. Maybe they could have—"

"I hear what you're saying, Rudi, but the true revolutionary can't be bought by beautiful trinkets or pretty architecture. You have to give it to the people, like lifesaving medicine. And sometimes, unfortunately, medicine is bitter."

They walked along, the September air still stifling, though the green was fading slightly on the trees.

"Listen, Rudi, I know you don't want to be here," Martin soothed. "You have a whole life on the other side, which you never asked to leave. Over there, you're a leader, Rudi. You're a force, with a future in the Party."

"Yes, but there's nothing I can do about it now. You said we were criminals. The border's *closed* now. I can't go back, not *really.* And . . . I can't leave Vati and Omi."

"But there *is* something you can do."

"What?"

"It's that wonderful machine in your book bag. Your camera, Rudi. You said it yourself: you've documented a lot of what's been happening with the Wall. Wouldn't it be nice if you could serve your country that way, and still go back to your father and great-grandmother, keep on baking your jammy Berliners and biscuits— and tear the beast from within? We don't want Germany to be divided. We want *unity.* Don't we?"

"Absolutely, Uncle Martin." Rudi's heart surged with a feeling of patriotism. He wanted to be this kind of good person. He wanted to be on the right side, the side that would save humanity, bring it back from the brink.

"You have a good heart. And I know you want to do the right thing. Are you interested?"

"What would I have to do?"

"Just be my eyes and ears. I'll make sure you have plenty of film," said Martin. "Then come visit me once a week and use my dark-room."

"That doesn't sound too hard."

"You know, the back-to-school dance is coming up at your old school. Why don't you start there? Tell your girlfriend to get dolled up, have some fun. That visa I gave you is still good, Wall or no Wall. Trust me, you're doing more than you know."

Rudi squinted at the lowering sun. Now that fall was coming, it was getting dark earlier, and he needed to get home. "How's everything else?"

"Well, to be honest, I'm worried about your brother. While you're at it, Rudi, when you come across to East Berlin, you might check in on him."

"You're worried about Peter? Why?"

"Only that he might . . . be getting into the wrong crowd. You know, he's growing out his hair, not really doing his acting. I haven't heard him talk about an audition since that one he bombed in June."

"Sure, I'll let you know what I find out."

"I know it's a new normal, Rudi. Things *are* different now, but there's no need to worry. Remember, Rudi. Humans are very adaptable. It's not the end of the world. It's just a wall."

Charles and Rudi rifled through the racks at the record shop on Thursday. Rudolf was over on the other side of the store, looking for new piano sheet music.

Rudi waved Charles over to his station. "This is from my youth club, the FDJ," Rudi explained. "It's so good, listen."

Charles put on the headphones and listened to a large ensemble singing in unison. The production quality was amateur, too much reverb and not-fantastic pitch. But Rudi hoped Charles would hear the heart of the message.

> *Unser Lied die Ländergrenzen überfliegt,*
> *Freundschaft siegt! Freundschaft siegt!*

> *Our song flies over national borders,*
> *Friendship wins! Friendship wins!*

"It's . . . lively," Charles said with a good deal of charity. "You really get down to this, huh? What are they singing about?"

"It's a song about friendship," said Rudi. "That if we work together, we will defeat war and hatred."

"That what the kids are singing about these days? All right, come take a listen to something." Charles brought Rudi to the other console. He slid a record out of its sleeve: Tony Sheridan and the Beat Brothers. "I'm excited they have this. I've seen these guys in Hamburg—they call themselves the Beatles now. Check it out." He put the headphones over Rudi's ears.

What Rudi heard almost knocked him backward. It was loud, so loud that he scrambled for the volume knob. The drums were as aggressive as a runaway train; the guitars were barely hanging on to their tune for all they were being twanged. And the singers! They hollered and screamed like kids running around at a playground. His senses were all excited, but his mind was vexed.

"What do you think of that?" asked Charles, grinning. "Blow your mind?"

Rudi took off the headphones and thought for a moment. "It's . . . ah . . . *enthusiastisch.* . . ."

"That, my young friend, is the sound of freedom," Charles said, smoothing his mustache. "Pure rock 'n' roll."

"Rock 'n' roll? It's not like Elvis. . . ."

"No, this isn't Elvis. This is the *future.*"

Rudi shrugged. "I think my record is also about the future."

"No offense, son, but *these* kids are going to take over the world."

Rudi put the headphones back on and listened again to his FDJ song. Quietly.

Rudi had a job to do. He had to keep his focus here in West Berlin, to make sure he didn't get lured in by people who didn't have the *proper* future in mind. A little piece of him closed off from Charles as they flipped the stacks of 45s.

Rudi changed the subject. "Charles, I never asked—do you have any children?"

"Me? Oh, no. I wanted kids, of course. But when my wife died, that was the end of that dream." He smiled sadly at Rudi and flipped to Bill Haley & His Comets. "So I reenlisted. Sometimes civilian life isn't a good fit for a soldier."

"Why did you come back to Germany?"

"It wasn't entirely my choice to make. There were other places I could have been deployed. They weren't going to send me into a combat zone—I was too old. But since I'd been here in the war, they figured I might know a thing or two about the place. Boy, were they wrong. This country never ceases to dish out a new conundrum every day."

At that moment, Rudolf sidled over.

"Found something good?" asked Charles, gesturing to the books under his arm. "You'll play those for us later, won't you?"

"Some after-dinner music," said Rudolf. "Oma is making Spätzle."

He winked at Rudi and held the books out to Charles. The one on top was vintage, protected in a plastic sleeve. It had Hebrew lettering on it.

"What's this say?" Charles asked.

"Jiddische Balladen," said Rudolf. *"Yiddish Ballads."*

"Interesting choice. I imagine it's hard to find things like this in Germany."

"Not if you know what to look for," said Rudolf. "This was something . . . sentimental. From my childhood." There was a slight waver in his voice.

"You must've had a complicated childhood."

"Why do you say that?"

"Well, it's not every day a German kid has a book of Yiddish piano music. But I'm only guessing. You know, I always wondered what happened to those folks, after the war. . . . Haven't met many since I got here."

"I know plenty of Jews," Rudi interjected.

"Do you, now?" Charles raised his eyebrows at Rudolf.

"Yes . . . plenty. . . ." The truth was, he didn't. He knew exactly three, and they all lived in a two-room flat with one solid chair between them.

"Uh . . . Charles, in Germany, we don't talk about this kind of thing in public." Rudolf shifted.

"Well, I'm not German," said Charles.

Rudi wished Charles would keep his voice down. He went back to shuffling through 45s, agitated and not wanting to talk anymore.

"How old did you say you were again?" he heard Charles ask his father. "In the war?"

"Oh, I've told you, I was just a kid. Ah . . . maybe we can talk about this later. Do you want to come for dinner?"

Rudi glanced up at his father. Other shoppers looked at Rudolf, too. A bead of sweat ran down Rudolf's temple. Rudi heard it land with a tiny pat on the plastic sleeve of the piano book.

Rudi turned away and walked to the used-records section, forcing his gaze back down to the record stacks. He pulled out a copy of Beethoven's Ninth Symphony, the Berlin Philharmonic, conducted by Fürtwangler, 1942.

The atmosphere at dinner was incredibly tense. Oma had absentmindedly added water to the Spätzle in spite of herself, and Rudi had burned the schnitzel. Rudolf seemed agitated and kept peppering Rudi with questions about school.

"Isn't there *something* you could do to connect with the other kids?" asked Rudolf, trying to get the rubbery noodles to stay on his fork.

Rudi wrangled his knife through the meat on his plate. "I have nothing in common with them at all. They don't *stand* for anything— no cause, no struggle. Just parties and dancing and—"

"You mean as though they're sixteen?" Oma threw in.

"Sixteen doesn't mean *childish*," Rudi said.

"I *want* you to go to dances and movies," said Rudolf, "and go out with girls and, oh, lose yourself sometimes, Rudi, just lose yourself."

"I have no intention of losing myself," Rudi scoffed.

"I mean in something meaningful. For me, it's music. For you, maybe it's your camera. Ah, wait! Isn't there anything you can do at school with photography?"

Rudi huffed. "Their darkroom's a mess." He finally took a bite of the tough schnitzel.

"What about a newspaper?" Charles suggested. "They must have a school paper."

"They do. It's terrible."

"Well, you could be part of making it better," said the soldier.

"Maybe you'd meet other people who aren't so frivolous as the dance-club types."

Rudi took a silent bite. "Maybe."

"See?" said Rudolf. "So you'll ask tomorrow?"

"I'll ask."

They finished their dinner with few words. "Rudi, do the dishes," his father ordered. He poured Charles a bottle of beer, and the two men went into the living room. Rudolf took out one of the piano books and began to play an American standard. Charles stood at the piano with his arm on the top, drinking his beer. He recognized the melody and hummed along. Rudi could barely make out their conversation over the running water and the music.

"Sorry about that bit at the record shop," he heard Charles whisper. "But some things don't add up. You said you were a kid . . . but you have two boys who are almost grown. What were you doing during the war, man?"

"I *was* just a kid," Rudolf repeated.

"Lying's a sin, brother."

"I don't believe in sin," Rudolf muttered. "Religion makes people kill each other. It starts wars and—"

"You know Hitler wasn't just talking about *religion*, Rudolf. He was talking about this." Charles pinched the dark skin of his arm and cheek.

"We know better now—we don't make those mistakes anymore."

"Are you sure about that? Germany's all healed now, is it? Then what's with the barbed wire and concrete cutting through the neighborhood?"

Rudolf stopped playing and closed the book. "I have an early-morning tuning," he said softly.

"Suit yourself," said Charles. "You know, Rudolf, I struggle with you. I like you and all, but I suggest you dig deep and start reckoning with the past instead of denying it."

Charles drank the rest of his beer in one swig and got his jacket. With a kiss, he thanked Oma for the delectable dinner, which she waved off as an obvious exaggeration, but she patted Charles's arm affectionately nonetheless.

"See you, Rudi. Good night, Rudolf."

The next day went better at the new school. Rudi only got lost once, trying to find his way from math to the lunchroom, but at least he couldn't be marked tardy for lunch. He took his tray to a half-empty table and tried to make himself invisible. Three boys and two girls slid down his way and introduced themselves. Rudi smiled and kept chewing.

The head of the *Schülerzeitung* was Frau Schäfer, who happened to be Rudi's history teacher. He assumed she was an unreformed fascist like the rest of them. Her view of history, after all, was the exact opposite of what he'd learned at POS 5. In fact, after Rudi failed his first quiz, she asked him to stay behind and told him just that.

"Whatever you learned in your old school, assume the answer is the opposite."

Exactly something a fascist would say, he thought. But Rudi tried it, and from then on, he was back on track to be a solid B student.

After class, he summoned the will to approach Frau Schäfer about the newspaper.

"Excuse me, Frau Schäfer, you're in charge of the school paper, right?"

"I am, Rudi," she said, more kindly than he expected.

"Well, I . . . I take pictures, and . . . my father said I should inquire . . . do you need a photographer?"

"It's funny you should ask, Rudi, because, in fact, we do. Our photographer graduated last year, and we haven't been able to find anyone to take over his position."

"What kinds of things would you need?"

"Oh, school events, mostly. But we have some very good writers who have fun ideas for city stories, human interest, that sort of thing."

"That sounds easy, I guess."

"We have our weekly meeting this afternoon, actually, in room 302. Come by and see if it suits you, all right?"

Rudi turned to leave but hesitated. "Frau Schäfer, there's just one thing. The darkroom—kids use it to fool around and stuff, and it's in bad shape. I'd need to be able to use it."

"If you come to the meeting," she said, "I'll see to it."

"Thank you," said Rudi. "I'll be there."

Rudi didn't want to expect much, but he began to daydream about the accolades he'd get from having his photos in the school paper. When he walked into the school newsroom at three o'clock, though, he was a little short of breath. Was his shirt always this tight and scratchy? Did everyone have to stare at him like this?

The last available chair happened to be—horribly—right next to Frau Schäfer, who beckoned him over. He had no choice. He knew she would ask him to stand and greet the others; he knew she would say he'd recently come from East Berlin and they should make him welcome; he knew she'd say he was there to replace their very talented recent graduate and that he had big shoes to fill. But he hadn't expected that they'd rise to their feet and *applaud* him.

What the hell are they doing?

He must have looked confused, because Frau Schäfer said, "There have been many brave escape attempts since the border was closed. It takes a lot of courage to leave the East."

Well, actually, I came just before it closed, and my father tricked me. I didn't want to come. . . .

But the kids looked at him, obviously moved, and he decided not to correct them. They wouldn't have understood.

"Let's move on to our agenda," said Frau Schäfer. "Monica, what are this week's features?"

"Right. Of course we want to focus on the situation at the border, the escapes and all. Rudi, could you shoot at the checkpoints? Maybe get some candids?"

Rudi thought of Charles and knew right away that they could do something interesting together. He nodded and wrote the assignment in his notebook.

"Bernt, how about you?"

"There's a football match tomorrow at ten, and on Sunday morning the American exchange students are going to do a basketball clinic."

"I'll be there," said Rudi, writing it down. His notebook filled with an itinerary of news stories for the rest of the month.

The meeting ended, and kids lined up to greet Rudi, shaking his hand and offering words of welcome and invitations to a party, another club, the local Milchbar. All he could think about was Angelika and whether she would let him take her to the back-to-school dance.

PETER

On gray days like this, the sun never truly set; it just got progressively darker. It would be night before Peter knew it. He sat on his bed, trying to write as quickly as the material came into his mind. It was possible that he'd throw out 80 percent of it, but one thought could lead to another so quickly, he might find his break-through any moment. He was glad he'd purged the place so he could concentrate like this.

Occasionally he heard the click of high heels on the courtyard pavement, and he imagined his mother walking through the front door carrying a bag of groceries, fresh and bright and in her right mind. Those little snacks he liked as a boy. A pack of chewing gum, just because. But he'd hear the person go up the other set of stairs and open the door to another flat, and the ache would make his heart fall. It wasn't Ilse and wouldn't ever be. There was no one there making sure he got himself to school, or filled the cupboards, or cleaned the toilet bowl. He kept the house in order in case she did show up, swallowed that lump in his throat and got back to work. It was all on Peter now.

Peter went through pocket notebooks like mad these days. He started buying them at the stationery store five at a time. He liked the spiral-bound kind because he could flip through them more quickly, and that counted when his hand could barely keep up with his mind. Sometimes he wrote actual jokes. Sometimes memories, observations about classmates, things he heard people say about the Party or the Wall, questions he had about his mother and father. If he needed to make sense of anything, it went in the notebook.

In class Friday, Peter nestled the little notebook into the binding of his astronomy textbook. It was a stupid error. His teacher thought he was writing in the textbook and came over to scold him for it. Herr Vogel snatched Peter's notebook and was about to read it out loud to the class, but he quietly asked him to stay behind instead.

"Peter," said Herr Vogel, closing the classroom door after the last student had left, "you've been distracted. Is everything all right?"

"It's fine."

"You know my policy: any non-class material, notes and such, I read aloud to the others."

"Yes, Herr Vogel."

"But I'm not heartless. Would you please read this to me and explain?"

Peter read aloud, his mouth suddenly dry. *"Mutti's nowhere to be found and I'm not going to leave her, even if I'm angry as hell at her."* He closed the book and looked at his teacher. "It means exactly what it says."

"Is your mother . . . truly . . . nowhere to be found?"

"No. She, uh, was in a hospital. She was committed. But she vanished. No one knows where."

"Who's looking after you at home?"

"No one, Herr Vogel. But I'm doing just fine. Better than ever, actually."

"I see. What did you mean, *not going to leave her*? If you can't find her, what does *leave her* mean?"

Peter had a sick feeling. He was learning a thing or two about trust these days, and he wasn't sure he trusted Herr Vogel. His teacher was a younger man, not a stodgy old Party loyalist. He softened the meaning of his next words, but only barely.

"I'm thinking of applying to go to the West after graduation."

"Oh." His teacher didn't look alarmed in the slightest. There was a long silence. Finally Herr Vogel rose and pulled the shade on the door. He spoke, barely above a whisper. "Do you need help filling out the application?"

Peter wasn't sure how to answer. "No, that's OK. I should try to find my mother first, make sure she's all right."

"If you need anything, let me know, will you? I'm here to help you. You shouldn't have to do all this alone."

"I appreciate that."

Herr Vogel looked intently at Peter. "Here's your notebook, then. Be careful who catches you with it."

Peter strayed from his usual route home from school, unconsciously tracing the way he and Rudi used to take into Kreuzberg. His mind parted in two: One side was completely autonomic, filling with moments of life and beauty, like the occasional tree with the first blush of autumn on its crown, and settling into the calm that comes from a long walk. The other hemisphere, however, was devising a code he could use in his notebooks, in case anything unacceptable happened again, like another teacher reading it—or worse, someone from State Security.

Around half past three, he approached the Oberbaum Bridge, as he always had. And that was when the heavy reality of his situation hit him.

When the Wall had gone up, as chaotic as it had been, it hadn't touched Peter's life. He'd started school, he'd written, he'd gone out with Renate, gone to the cabaret, written more. Especially when his mother disappeared, anxiety forced Peter to clamp down in order to cope. Things like a trip to Der Spinner or Bäckerei Antoinette didn't even cross his mind.

Until now, when what he needed most was to be able to wander through his own city and clear his mind.

The Oberbaum Bridge had been one of the busiest crossings in Berlin. Not only pedestrians and bicycles but cars and even trains went over it. Occasionally a persnickety guard would ask to see identification, but in an open Berlin papers had always been just a power game. Now the war-ravaged towers of the brick bridge peeked tantalizingly over the concrete blocks and sloppy mortar and barbed wire closing off any thought of crossing. Everything would forever be reckoned this way:

Before the Wall. After the Wall.

Before the Wall, the guards stationed here loved to break up their boredom by demanding papers from a teenage kid. But after the Wall, the once busy street was empty, patrolled by ghosts. Only one stranger stood there, chewing a hangnail, picking a thread, examining his hat.

Peter looked to the left.

Wall.

To the right.

More Wall, continuing all the way around the curve of the long boulevard. He could not see the river. The only clue to the river's existence mere feet away was the waterbirds flying above, looking for a place to land.

Peter walked home quickly, with panic fluttering in his chest, hyper-focused on his code language. He shut himself in, barely registering the quietude of the apartment. He gathered his notebooks and wrote. He wrote like he was meeting himself for the first time.

RUDI

That afternoon seemed like as good a time as any to try to visit his mother in the hospital. He wanted to go back to the old apartment and see if Peter would join him. If nothing else, he could borrow some clothes for the dance. But as he tried to cross the border, the guard looked at Rudi funny.

"Where did you get this visa?" he asked.

"What do you mean? It's my visa."

"This is a *diplomat's* visa."

"Yes," said Rudi. He hadn't known that. He couldn't let on how foolish he felt. Why would Martin give him a diplomat's visa? "What's the problem?"

"You look a little young to be a diplomat."

Rudi had to think fast. "Well, of *course* I'm not a diplomat." Rudi faked a haughty air. "My *uncle* is." How was he going to pull this off? His uncle was no diplomat—he was an optometrist. But he did seem to have an awful lot of "old school friends" who did him a lot of favors.

"And what's your uncle's name?" quizzed the guard.

"Martin Fleischmann."

The guard looked askance at him again and went to his booth, picked up the phone and emerged three minutes later.

"All right, *Junge,*" he said. "Go through."

The exchange went both as he had hoped—and as he couldn't believe. Rudi had taken a chance on someone recognizing Martin's name and doing him a favor. And it had worked.

Rudi walked to his old place and unlocked the apartment door. He was astonished at its emptiness. It had none of the hallmarks of their old family home. Peter didn't answer when Rudi called his name. It was just as well. He dialed Angelika and asked if she'd like to go to the dance with him. She was actually glad to hear from him, genuinely glad. She'd planned to stay home from the dance tomorrow otherwise.

The icebox was bare, but Rudi managed to make himself a snack of bread and cheese and a sliced apple. He sat on the sofa and took a deep breath. He had a real photography gig. Starting tomorrow, he was officially a photojournalist. Covering football matches and school rallies, sure, but also stories he wanted to tell, stories like his. Maybe he could start here, in the place he'd "escaped" from. He walked around the flat taking pictures, pulling back his familiarity to capture angles he hadn't noticed before. He'd never taken in the light that filtered through the smogged-up windows of his bedroom, with its louvered doors and his abandoned bed. Peter's cleaning the place out had revealed its atmosphere.

He went into his mother's stripped-down bedroom. The light in here was lovely, too; haunting, with particles floating along a beam of light like a painting by Vermeer. As Rudi snapped away, he flashed back to something he hadn't thought of since he was a kid. He wondered if it was still there. He opened the wardrobe drawer and, sure enough, found a pink silk bag of undeveloped film rolls that had to be years and years old. He shoved the whole thing in his book bag.

Rudi had an idea. He could develop some of these rolls for his mother and give them to her when he visited the hospital, so she could remember the good times. Maybe they were family pictures, of picnics and outings to the Baltic Sea, times before the war.

He remembered another stash of film, a box under his bed he hadn't been able to take with him. He was relieved that Peter hadn't gotten rid of that, either. He opened his bag and grabbed the rolls, a few of which were still in sealed packages. He realized, though, that a bag full of film would never make it through the checkpoint. Rudi went to the kitchen, got a pair of shears and cut a hole along the bottom of the lining of his bag, just big enough to pass the film canisters through. One at a time he slid them in, laying them methodically end to end so that instead of a jumble, they were stacked neat and flat. He placed his school books back in so they compressed the rolls inside their secret compartment.

Rudi left his plate and cup in the sink and made for the door.

As he opened it, he was greeted by the towering figures of Glasses and Baby Face. Rudi almost wet himself like he had in his kindergarten lederhosen.

"*Guten Tag,*" they addressed him. "Is your brother home?"

"I'm sorry, no. Is there something I can do for you?"

"I see," said Baby Face. "Young man, would you please see that he answers this letter right away?"

"Of course, *meine Herren.*"

"Thank you, comrade," the two men said in perfect unison.

Between being stopped at the border and having those guys show up at his door, he didn't dare risk a trip to see his mother in the hospital that afternoon. He'd give it some time, and come back for the dance the next day. Rudi waited twenty minutes, then made his way back to the West.

PETER

Saturday after school let out, Peter couldn't get home fast enough, exhausted for no good reason. He had been lying there longer than he realized when he heard a scuffle in the other room. Was that Rudi's voice?

"What are you doing?"

"Huh?" he groaned, still in a dreamy state.

"Peter," Rudi demanded, "what are you doing?"

Finally Peter stirred. "I guess I fell asleep."

"Well, go wash your face or something," said Rudi, rummaging through his brother's wardrobe. "We have to get ready for the dance. It's five o'clock already. I told Angelika I'd meet her at school at seven. Is Renate coming here or what?"

Peter sat up. "The dance?"

"The one you're supposed to be in charge of, remember? Do you have that extra sport coat, or did you get rid of it with everything else?"

"What are you doing here?" Peter asked his brother sleepily. "You should call before you come. Oh, wait, that's right. They cut the phone lines."

Rudi ignored him. "The back-to-school dance always happens this weekend. Don't forget, I helped plan them for the last three years. I wouldn't miss it."

"Did you tell Vati you were coming?"

"Um, sure . . . By the way, I'm going to stay here tonight." Rudi hopped in the shower before his brother could answer, but Peter found some sheets and a pillow and made up the bed.

When they were both getting dressed, Peter finally got the words out.

"Rudi, I'm serious, actually. What are you doing here? Do your papers still work? Since the Wall?"

"Uncle Martin wanted me to do something for him," he dodged. "Mainly, I came for the dance, to see Angelika. And I'm going to visit Mutti in the hospital tomorrow morning, if you want to come. I tried to go yesterday but I had a change of plans."

"Mutti? Didn't you know she was missing?"

"What are you talking about?" Rudi stopped buttoning his shirt and sat on his bed.

"Rudi, she ran away from the hospital. Uncle Martin didn't tell you? He came here Monday. He said he would tell you."

"I saw him Monday, too. He didn't say anything about it. . . ." Rudi was sober. He stared at the floor. His face began to draw tight with worry. "Peter, where could she be?"

Peter stood in front of the mirror and tied his tie. "Uncle Martin said he's working on it. I don't think there's anything we can do but wait."

Peter didn't know why he got fooled like this every year. As soon as summer neared its end and the new school year was about to start, he pictured himself showing up to school bundled in a hat and scarf. But, of course, September was just as hot as August, the air just as close and claustrophobic. And the same went for the youth room at school, where the students at POS 5 had their annual back-to-school dance—his last one. By this time next year, he'd be out of school and beginning the rest of his life.

The room was packed, and only the girls were dressed for the Saturday heat. Peter wondered why it was that boys had to wear long sleeves, a tie and a sport coat when girls could at least leave their arms bare. But he *did* love to dance. And Renate in that arsenic-green dress took his mind off the sweat. Or maybe it was Renate who was making him sweat in the first place.

It must have been she, because the music played by the tweed-blazered band was agitatingly boring, wimpy little cha-chas composed for grannies on river cruises, not for red-blooded teenagers with the need to put their hands on each other. The music was so tame, you could dance to it without even spilling your punch.

The next dance was called the Lipsi. Even the name was stupid. Everyone knew it was an invention of the State. The State! Inventing a dance! With the express purpose of pouring disinfectant all over the best years of their lives. Peter remembered when a dance instructor had come to their middle school Pioneers meeting to teach the Lipsi. Back then it was all you could do to get a boy and girl to touch each other, so it was perfect for the barely pubescent. But then it became compulsory to do the Lipsi at every social gathering. When the drummer would start that absurd Cubanesque beat, the teachers would suddenly light up as though they'd been plugged in,

and they'd give the kids a wink and a nod, as if to say, *There it is! This is what you kids like, isn't it?*

So with a faux-haughty smile and a ramrod-straight spine, Peter held out his hand to Renate and asked her to dance. He put a light palm on her waist, hers on his shoulder, and they connected with thumb and forefinger as though between them they were holding a dead mouse. They stood about five miles apart and began to shuffle their feet—without, of course, moving their dangerous hips.

That's when Renate started muttering something in time to the music. She was making something up, trying it out in her head, and once she knew she had it, she looked at Peter with a sly grin and said it louder:

> *Wir tanzen nicht die Lipsi oder zu Alo Koll*
> *Wir sind für Bill Haley und tanzen rock 'n' roll!*

> *We don't dance the Lipsi or dance to Alo Koll*
> *We are for Bill Haley and we dance to rock 'n' roll!*

Peter joined in, and pretty soon the entire room was chanting it to the beat. The musicians couldn't make out the words, but they detected, with pleasure, the heightened charge in the room—and the mention of Bill Haley—and gladly obliged to pick up the energy so the kids could break loose a bit.

The teachers, on the other hand, weren't happy. The *Schulleiter* sidled up to the bandleader and whispered some injunction, and the band instantly reverted to a more Socialist beat.

"I need something to drink," Renate huffed, and Peter followed her to the bank of long tables lining the side of the room.

Rudi and Angelika sat at one of the crowded tables, talking

softly. Peter watched his brother and smiled. Rudi couldn't take his eyes off of this girl. Her dress wasn't as fancy as the other girls', but she did transcend its simplicity.

As Peter and Renate made their way back to the table, one of their old classmates caught a glimpse of Rudi and made a beeline for him.

"Rudi!" he called. "I heard a rumor about you!"

"What rumor?"

"That you defected to the West!"

"That's ridiculous," Rudi said, signaling him to lower his voice. "How could I be here? I'm just at a different school, that's all."

"What's it like?" the classmate badgered. "Is it really different? Did you have to start in the FDJ ranks from scratch? Anyway, when you didn't show up to the summer meetings, we wondered! Well, glad it's not true! Good to see you! Peter's got some great things planned for fall, don't you, Peter?"

"It's not the same without my brother," said Peter. "Everyone misses you, Rudi. Don't they, Angelika?"

"It's true," she replied.

"Listen, let me catch up with my brother," said Rudi, pulling Peter away from the table. "We'll be back in a minute."

"Great, great. Well, see you around!" The classmate slipped off to annoy someone else, and Rudi ushered Peter out into the hall.

"What's the problem?" Peter asked his brother.

"I'm just confused because you seem far more concerned about cutting a rug with your girlfriend than figuring out how to find Mutti."

"Have you lost your mind? You're here at the dance, too."

"I know, but I didn't think you were going to let your hair down this much. What's the *plan*, Peter?"

"The plan is, Uncle Martin is in charge of this, not me."

"But we're her kids, Peter! We need his help to look for Mutti," Rudi said. "I need to tell Vati—damn, the telephones are blocked. I'll go home after the dance, but I'll come right back, and then we can search for her."

"Well, I'm happy for you, Rudi," said Peter. "I mean, I'm really happy you can cross back and forth, just like that."

"What's the problem?"

"You don't get it. It's different now, don't you understand? They're watching everyone. *I can't leave.* Not for an audition, not for a date, not for a ride on the carousel in Tiergarten, not for a Berliner at Antoinette's. The rules are different for me than for you. Those Stasi goons show up every other day, practically. One time I even came home and they were *in* the apartment. Said they were checking on a complaint by a neighbor. It's like they're punishing me for all of you leaving. Like I had anything to do with that. Like I wouldn't trade places with you in a heartbeat!"

"It looks like we're even," Rudi responded. "You know I'd rather be here."

"We could switch," Peter suggested. "Like *The Prince and the Pauper.*"

"You know I can't do that."

"Why not?"

"Come on, Peter. What do you want to do, swap the photographs on our passports?"

"Maybe."

"No way. Besides, you have a devoted audience waiting for you at the cabaret," Rudi scoffed.

"I thought maybe when you left me at the checkpoint, you'd try to help me out. You know, *twins against the world?*"

"It's a different world, I guess."

"Come on, Rudi."

"I'm sure you'll find a way to get what you want, Peter. It seems to rain gold on you every now and then."

Now Peter was lucid. He looked up and down the corridor at these safe walls he'd been surrounded by for ten years, he and his brother, as one. His skin prickled; his restless fingers tapped the wall.

"So that's how it is," he said plainly. Renate came out and halted between the twins. She took Peter's arm and led him out into the September night.

RUDI

"**H**ow did we come from the same parents?" Rudi wondered aloud, once he was alone in the hall. The door swung open again. It was Angelika. They stood face to face, trying to read each other.

"I was just coming back in," Rudi said at last, pushing past her.

Angelika grabbed his arm. "Hey, what's wrong?" she whispered. "You've been running hot and cold all evening."

"You know me," said Rudi, "life of the party."

Rudi went back into the dance with Angelika following after. He hung around her, milling aimlessly and eating crackers and cheese, saying nothing. He was fixed on Peter's coldness concerning their mother, like he was glad she had disappeared. Wasn't he worried about her at all?

The *Schulleiter* told the cleanup crew to be ready, came onstage and announced the last song of the evening. The band played a slow ballad, and Angelika grabbed Rudi's arm so suddenly that he almost dropped his plate. She pulled him onto the dance floor, and they began to sway. The intensity of her stare made Rudi's skin prickle.

"What is it?" Rudi snapped.

"Rudi, what's going on with you? We were having a good time."

How could he explain what he himself couldn't understand? He was so agitated, it felt like ants were crawling underneath his clothes.

"It's just some dumb nothing with my brother."

"I don't know what's between the two of you, but you have to remember he's your brother. You can't turn your back on family."

"You sound like my mother."

"Usually that's not a compliment."

"She used to say things like that to us all the time. Most of the time it was because Peter did something amazing and she didn't want me to be in his shadow."

"That was nice of her."

"I guess she wanted things to be completely fair. But that can't last, can it?"

Angelika didn't say anything. The song kept playing, and she put her head on Rudi's chest. He breathed in the fragrance of her hair. He rested his head on hers, but his mind wasn't still.

"Angelika," he asked softly, "why are you with me and not someone like Peter?"

She lifted her head and looked at him as they swayed. "Are you asking why I like you?"

He twirled a lock of her long hair around his finger. "You could be with anyone."

"Have you seen my social life? No one's banging down my door lately."

"Oh, so I'm your only option?" He was teasing, but it might have been true. "You know what I mean. Why me and not him?"

"Why do I like Rudi . . . ?" She pondered. "You're . . . sincere. You want to do the right thing. I might not agree with your cause, but I respect your commitment. And you were my friend when everyone else walked away. Besides, I can't resist those dimples."

Rudi smiled. He'd always hated his dimples. He thought they made him look like a baby, but maybe they did have a certain dignity. *It feels like a long time since I smiled,* he thought. *It kind of . . . hurts.*

Angelika put her head back down, and Rudi's heart unfurled with the last chord of the song.

Sunday morning, Rudi went straight to the bakery, late for the morning shift he was supposed to work. It was unusually busy, and he'd been too tired to even shower. Worse, he'd double-booked, forgetting about the basketball clinic that he was supposed to shoot, so the newspaper would have to publish the story without photographs. He felt bad about it, but after all, no one could keep *all* their commitments.

Besides, he'd been with Angelika. She *liked* him, even with the distance between them, even with the Wall making things so complicated. He had so much he wanted to share with her. At last, his shift ended and he made his way back to the little flat. He planned to spend the evening writing Angelika a long letter, telling her everything he felt for her.

Empty, Rudi thought when he came home. *Omi must be playing cards downstairs with Willi.*

The bedroom door was ajar, and Rudi could see his father's bed littered with the contents of a cardboard box. Rudi quietly inched his way inside.

He sat on an available spot on the bed among what looked like a bunch of vintage junk. Sticking out from under the box was a rolled-up piece of red fabric, which he unrolled to reveal a red armband emblazoned with a symbol Rudi rarely saw except in thrift shops or history textbooks: a black swastika on a field of white. He dropped it back on the bed as though it were the bandage of a leper.

Rudi surveyed the bits of metal and cloth and shell casings and folded paper. He picked up the box and rifled through it: these were war medals. He picked one up. It was heavy for its size, cast iron, with eagles and oak leaves and bent crosses. A chill came through the open window. Rudi held the medal up closer and examined it. It was tarnished, with a coating of greasy dust, and a smell came off of it, of metal and decay.

Rudi stuffed a handful of the medals in his pocket and closed the window against the chilly night. He went into the living room, away from that awful musty smell. A music book was open on the piano. On the cover he saw the words *Jiddische Balladen*—it was the one Rudolf had bought at Der Spinner. Rudi flipped through it and thought of Angelika and her songs, of her father and his books. He wondered if they knew any of these Yiddish ballads.

Just then Rudi heard a sound from the bathroom, a soft scuffle.

Rudi opened the bathroom door and clenched his jaw. He was not prepared for what he saw.

His father was sitting on the floor, slouched over against the bathtub. His hair hung in stringy pieces, peeling from its usual pomaded shell; his sallow face was encrusted with shame. His piano tuning tools were strewn about. His father held an awl in his fist. His hands were running with scarlet.

Rudi heard himself shout his father's name, like he was in another body. Rudolf didn't move.

Before he knew it, Rudi was in the stairwell shouting for Oma, for Willi, for anyone who could hear him. Willi opened his apartment door and ran upstairs in his bathrobe and pants.

"What's wrong, Rudi? Is someone hurt?"

"It's my father. Omi! *Omi!*"

Oma emerged from Willi's apartment with a cigarette in her mouth, a deck of playing cards in her hands. She climbed the stairs like someone twenty years younger without a bad knee and a weak heart. The playing cards fluttered in the hallway. Willi came out from the bathroom, looking green, and got on the phone right away. Oma and Rudi went into the bathroom. The linoleum, Rudi thought, looked like a painting.

"Rudi, go get me a pot of water," said Oma. She was as calm as though she had told him to make her a cup of tea. When he came back with the water, she had ripped down a towel into bandages and was wrapping them around Rudolf's wrists, cigarette ash falling into the blood in tiny sizzles.

Rudi, feeling useless, went and got his camera.

Oma, Charles and Rudi sat in the hospital hallway waiting for word on Rudolf. He lay sedated as doctors poured blood into his depleted body.

"You need to go to school in the morning," Oma told Rudi. "No sense in you staying here."

"No, Omi, I'm going to stay."

"Rudi, the doctors have him," said Charles. "Best thing both of you can do is rest. He'll need you most when he comes home."

The walk to school the next day was the longest Rudi had ever taken. He felt like all the blood had been drained from him instead. He'd gotten the day off from the bakery, and he couldn't help falling asleep in every one of his classes. Finally, after school, Frau Schäfer helped Rudi clean up the darkroom and posted a sign on the door:

NO ADMITTANCE WITHOUT PRIOR PERMISSION

Frau Schäfer looked at Rudi like she knew he wasn't himself. "The school building gets locked at six, Rudi, so keep an eye on your time," she said. "But if you need any help—"

"Thank you," said Rudi wearily. "I don't."

He got started right away, developing one roll of negatives after another, stuff for the newspaper, random rolls from his stash, and one of his mother's. The process flowed, flooding Rudi with renewed energy. As each roll emerged from the developer tank, he squeegeed and hung it, until he had seventeen strips of black-and-white film ready to print. Hopefully, no one else would come in and get dust everywhere.

Between visiting his father in the hospital and his afternoon bakery shift, Rudi wasn't able to come back for two more days. He strongly considered switching to the early mornings just so he could spend the afternoons in the darkroom, but he knew he'd never get his homework done. Or sleep.

When he did return, Rudi was pleasantly surprised to see that no one had been in the darkroom. Everything was pristine. He cut the negatives into strips and slid them into sleeves, printed contact sheets and got ready to see what there was to discover.

The first roll was from summer camp—Rudi must've been ten years old. Most of the pictures were of Peter doing acrobatics and antics on a trampoline. The next roll was only half-good; black squares meant that maybe Rudi had opened the camera and exposed the film before he knew what he was doing.

The third was from the night his father cut his wrists. The medals strewn on the bed. The piano book—black and white notes, black and white keys. The bathroom, tiles and tools covered in blood.

At last he came to one of his mother's rolls. As he'd hoped, there were lovely, charming photos of her family in the garden of a big house. She and Martin were dressed up in quaint children's clothes of the 1930s, flanking their smiling parents. Little Ilse had a mop of a hair bow perched on her head. Rudi laughed out loud—his mother and Uncle Martin were so adorable.

He was, however, somewhat troubled by the opulence of their surroundings—so bourgeois—but this had to be someone else's vacation rental, hadn't it? He knew his mother had come from the very city center of Leipzig.

The next contact sheet was from a ceremony of some kind. Ilse was a bit older. Her hair was in two braids, and she looked very smart in her white blouse, light cropped jacket, neckerchief and beret. Maybe this was her *Jugendweihe.* He scanned across. She was receiving a pin on her lapel. A couple of family shots, and then a close-up of her lapel pin.

A pin with a very distinct, spidery symbol.

A swastika.

Rudi stood up and turned around so quickly, he knocked the loupe across the table. His heart beat faster. He tasted bile.

More images emerged, of Ilse at camp under the banner of the Bund Deutscher Mädel. Ilse doing gymnastics. Ilse and her wealthy Leipzig family, posing with a group of obviously high-ranking SS officers.

His father's medals had proven him to be a Nazi. His father he could understand, because his flight to West Berlin had shown his capitalist sympathies, and, by extension, Rudi presumed, his persistent Nazism. But his *mother*?

Ilse was in the Socialist singing group at the telephone company; she attended every function. And the beautiful stories, the tales of the woods and rivers—could a Nazi care about those things? But these photos didn't lie. Rudi's head swam. Had his mother really been a Nazi? He refused to believe it. Maybe there had been a scratch on the negative. This had to be a mistake. He'd have to make an enlargement to know for sure. But he didn't want to develop one here. If any of the kids saw . . . Of course, he'd never admit these were photos of *his* family. He could say he bought the rolls out of curiosity at a flea market. He could say he was doing a project on exposing Nazis here in the West.

Rudi took down the remaining strips, cleaned up the trays of solution and shoved the contact sheets in his bag. *I have things to do,* he thought on his way home. *I have homework. I have a shift tomorrow. I'll deal with these another time.*

For now, the photographs of his mother went in the cutout compartment of his book bag.

Rudolf was in the hospital for three days. When he was finally discharged and sent home, he slept for another three. A nurse came by to change his bandages, but he couldn't be left alone. Willi took a shift, Charles took a shift. Oma tried to get some nourishment into him, but he was barely conscious. Every now and then, he shouted things in his sleep. None of it was intelligible except one name.

Gerta.

On the fourth day home, Rudolf sat up and asked for water.

Rudi was catching up on missed homework. Oma was passed out on the couch. The television was on, but the sound was off. Rudi immediately heeded his father's call, went into the bedroom and helped his father drink.

Rudi studied his father's ashen face, his smallness. A surge ran through Rudi's chest. He had one question.

"Who's Gerta?" he asked.

Rudolf looked stunned. He leaned his head back against the wall. "Someone I knew in another life. And loved. And probably killed."

Rudi rummaged through the hamper and found the pants he'd been wearing the night his father tried to kill himself. The blood hadn't been washed out. He reached into the pocket and took out the handful of medals. He dropped the medals on his father's bed.

"Iron Cross." Rudolf pointed to them one by one. "Those two crosses with the swords are War Merit, First and Second Class. Close Combat Clasp. Honor Roll Clasp. That round bronze one, that was my first medal."

A bitter taste filled Rudi's mouth, and he wanted to spit. "These are yours?"

Rudolf looked up, directly into Rudi's eyes. He answered plainly: "Yes."

"You were a Nazi?" Rudi whispered, the word curdling on his tongue. Bile rose in his throat.

"Yes."

"Were you . . . a soldier?"

Rudolf paused. "Eventually."

Rudi's lip curled. "Does Mutti know?"

"Of course Mutti knows."

Rudi got his bag and took the contact sheets out of the lining. He laid them down in a grid on the bed. Every photograph of Ilse as a young girl, beaming proudly in Nazi attire.

Rudolf was silent.

"You told me you had to have absolute truth in your house, Vati. But what about you? Why didn't you have to follow the same rules?"

"It's hard for me."

"They're just words, Vati. Just put them together and tell me the whole story."

His father stared at him for a moment, then leaned back on his pillow.

"Vati, we've been watching the Eichmann trial on television for months. How could you sit there, knowing you were the same as him . . . and say nothing?"

"Nobody talks about it, Rudi. Who would we have unburdened our souls to? The thought is absurd. Let Eichmann's story be enough. It's the witnesses who have to be heard. As for us, everyone just moved on."

Rudi's voice was dripping with bitterness. "You *moved on*?"

"The war ended. We cleared up the rubble, we lined up for relief, we rebuilt the city. We got married. We had children."

Rudi bolted up from the bed, running his hands through his hair, grabbing the back of his neck. He paced the tiny bedroom, the generic, worn carpet undulating beneath his stocking feet.

"You have to understand, Rudi, everyone played a part, said yes in their own way. The little grandmother on a farm, making her cheese and butter while the cattle cars rolled by. No one's hands are clean. We had a country to rebuild, and for better or worse, some ex-Nazis happened to be good at laying down roads."

"They hung those men after Nuremberg. Women, too."

"Would you like me to oblige, Rudi?" He held up his wrists. "Give it another try?"

"Forget it."

Rudi left the room, paced the living room and got his jacket. He had to get out of there, away from his father's deception, his dripping guilt. Every second breathing the same air made him complicit. Rudi opened the front door and stood there for a minute, then went back into the bedroom, wanting answers his father could not give.

How many other bedrooms are there in this country? thought Rudi. *How many fathers and sons have been having this same conversation every day since 1945?*

"I've been hovering here like a ghost, Rudi," said Rudolf, not lifting his eyes. "For years, just floating in this kind of . . . purgatory, followed around by millions of screams. I wanted it to stop."

"You should go straight to hell," Rudi observed flatly.

"I probably will," said Rudolf. "But if I'm damned, I'm in a very long line."

Oma woke up and got on the phone. She was laughing with whoever it was, her voice from the other room getting louder, until the whole atmosphere felt like a sick circus, with the laughing great-grandmother and this clown of a father. Apparitions of Eichmann's accusers filled the room, testifying instead to the horrors Rudi's own father had perpetrated.

Rudi didn't speak anymore. Neither did his father. They stared at the walls.

In the other room, Oma hung up the phone and flicked on the electric kettle. Rudi felt tainted, infected, holding the sins of his father in his own body.

I should have just left him there to bleed.

OCTOBER

PETER

Peter didn't resign as FDJ *Gruppenleiter* after all. Over the summer, he'd been sure he would hand it over to Rudi and walk away, but he wised up. This was a game that needed to be played properly if he wanted to get the right outcome: to leave this place with minimal drama.

At the October FDJ meeting, Herr Vogel supervised Peter's breakout group as they planned a field trip. Angelika's former friends huddled together in the circle of chairs, whispering. Peter proposed going to a harvest festival near Spandau, but one of the girls quickly reminded him that the neighborhood in question was now behind the Wall.

"Are you sure?" Peter asked. "I thought that was Soviet Sector."

"No, Peter, it's always been British Sector. It only juts out into Brandenburg. How did you not know that?"

"We've always gone to that one, though," said Peter. "Could we try to get a day pass, Herr Vogel?"

Peter read volumes in his teacher's expression. He knew Herr Vogel wanted to help, that he was just as frustrated by the new restrictions as anyone else. But his hands were tied.

"I . . . I don't think it works that way anymore—" the teacher stammered.

"There are other festivals to choose from," another girl interrupted.

Peter tried to control his frustration. "I'm sorry, but if the one you want is forbidden to you, is it really a choice?"

"They're trying to keep us safe," said the first. "Plus, that festival wasn't Socialist." The girls launched into a full-throated defense of the Wall and the lengths the Party was willing to go for the sake of their future.

Something in Peter felt fit to burst. He muttered something under his breath, catching Herr Vogel's eye. How quickly these people had invented a bright side to all of this, had adapted to their fetters, like painting flowers on prison bars.

After the meeting was over, Peter couldn't get out of school fast enough. He didn't want to go home. He had to breathe, even if the air around him was full of the first coal smoke of the year, furnaces firing up ahead of the October chill. He walked down to what was, until two months ago, the riverfront. The Wall was already beginning to tarnish, taking on the same patina as the rest of Friedrichshain, like the inside of a dormant stove. Peter took out his notebook and began to write.

They'd forgotten to replant the trees that had been obliterated at the end of the war, so the leaves that swirled around Peter's feet must have been imported. As he bent down to pick one up, the lot of them were swept up into a current and flew over the Wall.

If only it were that easy, Peter wrote as he walked. *Someone's going to figure this out. Whether over this Wall or under it, some people know it's better to be free than safe.*

RUDI

One Thursday morning late in the month, Rudi found a shopping bag on the table, and an envelope attached with his name on it. He reached into the bag and pulled out a box with the word *Rollei-flex* on it in sharp type. He took off the top. Inside was a brand-new camera in a brown leather case. It was beautiful, far more of a machine than even Uncle Martin's Leica.

Rudi opened the envelope and read the letter.

> *Dear Rudi,*
>
> *When I started reading Rilke, I began to see, for the first time, that I am only myself, and that my life stands or falls by itself. One line in* Letters to a Young Poet *showed me this:*
>
> *"For him who becomes solitary, all distances, all measures change."*
>
> *Solitude dispels the illusion that we are part of anything except humanity itself, not part of a movement or a country or a party. Not the Nazi Party, not the Communist Party. Simply ourselves, as our neighbors are themselves.*
>
> *All these years, I have been tortured by what I did to innocents. I deserve nothing but the pain I live in. Multiply this across millions, and you may understand our nation's contradictions. There are particular evils that belong to my generation. But they weren't the last. Evil did not die with Hitler.*
>
> *You could say that the Nazis did this to us, yes, but we*

all made our calculations. We came to believe that we were each simply a stick in a bundle of sticks, not people with distinct and different destinies, but a collection for someone else's use. And I see it happening again, under a new regime.

What I did, I did. No one did it to me. The need to belong, the pressure to conform, the constant externalized, displaced blame—these find a pinhole in your shame and wiggle you open, and the evil that already resides within you begins to seep outward. Do you understand? No one does it to us. It spills out from within.

As you become a man, you will see: you are on a path that only you can walk.

Vati

Rudi tucked the letter into his book bag. His father's poeticism only annoyed him. It was simple: the Nazis were monsters and he was one, too. All this talk meant nothing. Rudi wanted to hear his father condemn himself with clean minimalism. He wanted the world to be like a photograph, in black and white.

He worked his after-school shift at Bäckerei Antoinette, caught up in his duties. Oma sat with her coffee and newspaper. Rudolf came in and made straight for Rudi.

"*Hallo, Oma,*" he greeted his grandmother. "Rudi, can you take your break now?"

"I'm busy, Vati."

"There's only one other person in here besides Oma," he protested. "And that's your boss. He can take his break now, can't he?"

"No time like the present," said Herr Otto.

Rudi hesitated, the pot of coffee still in his hand. "Fine," he said.

He put the pot back behind the counter and hung up his apron. "I'll be back in twenty minutes, Herr Otto." Rudolf held the door for him, and they stepped out into the October afternoon.

"Where are we going?" asked Rudi.

"Let's walk along the canal," said his father. "Did you get the camera?"

"*Ja.* That's a really expensive one. Where did you get the money?"

"I sold the medals."

"Sold them? Who would buy things like that? They should've been burned."

"If I had burned them," said his father, "it would have bought me fifty more years of lies."

"I can't use that camera, Vati."

"Oh," Rudolf sighed, "I suppose that's your choice. Maybe you'll come back to it."

"I don't think so."

"Did you read my letter?"

"Yes."

"Do you have any thoughts about it?"

"Not really," he said, purposefully obtuse.

"Come on, Rudi."

"Bunch of excuses. Who cares? What does it matter to me?"

"Rudi, I understand you're angry."

Rudi stopped and got in his father's path. "No, you don't understand anything about me. Nothing. You were a fascist then, and you're a fascist now. Don't try to make yourself feel better about it by buying me presents."

"If only you could see through my lens," Rudolf blurted. "I can't choose another way of seeing—of *being*—than the endless replaying and rewinding of a film in my memory. I'm herding, harassing . . .

I'm shooting, feeling my hands—my musician's hands!—pushing a child against a brick wall, shoving an old woman across the pavement, her stockings shredding on the concrete.

"My memories don't come and go, like clouds floating by in the sky. They never stop. I can't *ever* forget what I've done. For sixteen years I've chosen silence. Denial. Suppression. And I'm done with it."

Rudi looked out over the Landwehr Canal, the willows slouching to touch the surface of the water. A few boats were out, bobbing along as the sun began to go behind the changing trees.

"You're going to keep hating me for a while," Rudolf said at last. "I accept that. But at some point you'll need to make peace with reality. It's not like you're going to find anyone with clean hands. Not in the entire world."

The autumn breeze broke the reflection of the trees in the canal into ripples. Rudolf and Rudi walked by families on their riverboats, girls biking along, a couple of British soldiers blowing off steam after a long shift. Rudi finally spoke.

"What I don't understand is—I mean, you knew we were learning about all of this in school. They told us they'd stamped it all out—fascism, antisemitism—that they'd purged all of it. Did it never occur to you and Mutti to sit us down and say, *Hey, boys, we did some things we weren't proud of when we were younger,* or anything?"

"I was so ashamed, Rudi. I couldn't put that burden on you. As for your mother, I'm sorry to say she didn't seem to feel shame about, well, anything. Let's just say she has a very strong survival instinct."

"Why didn't you help her?"

He hung his head. "Believe me—I tried to help her every day. It's been sixteen years of these cycles—frenetic energy and then collapse. Your mother was never mine, Rudi. She never felt a pang of regret for her past. But a person can't hold that forever.

"We became parents when we were your age," Rudolf continued. "It wasn't just that we were so young. We were *broken.* Our backs and our legs and our minds were broken. We saw things, Rudi. We did things. And when you know a thing is evil, and you *will* yourself to do it anyway, it awakens a beast within you, and there's no limit to what you're capable of. Not just me or Mutti. All of us."

Rudi looked at his watch. It would be ten minutes back to the bakery from here. They began walking back the way they came.

"I want to know the real reason you brought me to the West instead of Peter."

"Why did I bring you?" Rudolf laughed, incredulous. "Because, Rudi, I was watching you become like me. So dutiful, so convinced you were doing humanity a favor. That's what they all believe, don't you know that? Dictators, totalitarians, they convince us they're *good,* that they're on the right side. It's always *those people over there* who are the problem, that they're the ones hurting, even *killing* us. And we take the bait. We can't wait to follow the program. Speak the slogans. Load the guns. I wanted to be a good person, Rudi, just like you. I thought I was on the right side. Even as I was publicly shaming people in the street and sending them to their deaths."

All of this only made Rudi more furious. "Are you equating me with dictators and Nazis?"

"Of course not. But I recognize in you the same seed that was in me then. I couldn't continue to watch it spread its roots in you, too."

"I'm nothing like you," Rudi seethed. "Nothing. You're all excuses."

"I wish you could see," said his father, "that it's the complete opposite."

●●●●●

335

The Friday-afternoon rush subsided, and Charles and Oma had the bakery to themselves. They sat at their usual table, reading an English newspaper together.

"What is this going on at the border?" Oma asked Charles, pointing to a headline. "They're not letting American diplomats through?"

The soldier nodded. "Sixteen years, folks from the West could all come and go as they wanted. All of a sudden, like that"—he snapped his fingers—"the East Germans are demanding papers. Can you believe it? To be asked for papers to see an opera? In your own city?"

"We never learn, do we?" Oma mused.

Charles shook his head. "Just keep repeating the same playbook."

"What else is in the news?"

"Let's see: Chubby Checker was on Ed Sullivan . . . Ah! A recap of the Eichmann trial." It had been over a month since testimony had wrapped up, and in another month or so, there would be a sentencing. Charles straightened the newspaper and read aloud:

> *"Did you never feel any conflict between your duty and your conscience?" the prosecutor asked Eichmann.*
>
> *"It would be better to call it a state of being split," said the criminal in the glass box. "A conscious split state where one could flee from one side to the other."*
>
> *"One had to renounce one's personal conscience?"*
>
> *"You could say that, yes. One could have simply said, 'I am not going to do this any longer,' but I do not know what would have happened then."*
>
> *"But you also did not try that, did you?"*

"A *state of being split*," said Oma. "That seems fitting."

"Between duty and conscience," said Charles.

"You would have to become two people," said Oma. "One person who knows what is right, and another who ignores that and does what he is told."

"Duty and conscience ought to be in harmony, like mind and heart," said Charles. "But this fool says he was *split*."

"*Ja*," said Oma.

"You know, every day I stand in the middle of no-man's-land at that checkpoint. Which side am *I* on? Well, I'm over here as a man of peace. Like the angel said to Joshua, *Neither your side, nor your enemy's. I'm on the Lord's side.* And as Abe Lincoln said, *A house divided against itself cannot stand.* I've had about all the splitting I can take."

Rudi couldn't abide all this heady talk. Herr Otto had to leave the shop in Rudi's hands while he went to an appointment, and was growing increasingly frustrated with the boy as he tried to give him instructions. Once the door closed behind him, though, Rudi burst.

"I'm sorry, but of course you have to pick a side. These people over here are warmongers. Didn't you just say you're on the side of peace? Peace is the Socialist vision. *Frieden.* It's right there on every banner and newspaper. Don't you think they *mean* it?"

"Oh, I'm *not* a man of peace, Rudi. I said I'm here *as* a man of peace. But no, I'm a man of war. I've *been* through war. I'm trained to *kill* for what's righteous, just as I'm willing to die for it. And yet, here we are, doing the same dance all over again. Don't you see? I don't care about this side or that side, because I know what's in my *own* heart. So I turn the war in on myself instead."

"Listen to him, Rudi," said Oma. She got up and folded her newspaper. "This is a man who has lived. And now I'm going home for a nap after that delicious Berliner. Charles, I will say good night early," she laughed.

Charles helped her to the door and kissed her on each cheek. "You sure you don't want me to walk you home, Oma? I have a few minutes before my shift."

"No, *Schatzi*, I need the exercise," she said, and shuffled out into the fading sunshine with a wave of her hand.

Charles folded up his paper and began to collect his things. "Rudi, I'm enjoying this coffee immensely, but I'm on call in a big way. There are about thirty Soviet tanks waiting for the Kremlin's orders over at the Brandenburg Gate."

"You mean East German tanks," Rudi corrected as he took the inventory of the display case.

"No, I definitely mean Soviet," said Charles. At that very moment his radio crackled out an alert and he took the call. Rudi couldn't understand half of what the commander said, but Charles's face told him it was serious. "I've got to go. Shenanigans at the border. You don't have plans tonight, do you?"

"I was going to see Peter. He doesn't know what happened with Vati."

"I'm afraid the checkpoint is closed, young man. Those Soviet tanks got their orders, all right, and we've got our guns pointed in each other's faces. And it's all going down at my checkpoint. If I were you, I'd stay home and lock the door."

"Can I come see?" Rudi asked Charles. "Herr Otto would probably want me to close the shop."

"Suit yourself. I guess I can't stop you. But if things get hot, you'd better leave yourself a way out."

Rudi flipped the sign on the bakery door from *Open* to *Closed*, grabbed his bag and followed Charles to his checkpoint. Charles put on his MP helmet and disappeared into the fray.

For twenty-four hours, the world held its breath as the two lines of tanks held each other in a standoff at the border. Just when the city was starting to make its peace with the existence of the Wall, Berlin was poised for yet another crisis, and this time it could be global . . . and total.

Rudi pulled out his Leica. This would make a great feature for the school paper. He snapped photo after photo. As he was rewinding the roll and putting in a new one, he thought of the new Rolleiflex his father had given him, and he wondered how it would perform in a shoot like this. Such a beautiful machine bought at such a bloody price.

Hours later, radios sounded and the Soviet tanks backed up a few feet. The American tanks followed their lead, and slowly but surely, each side retreated from the threat of destruction.

After the specter of annihilation had passed, Rudi decided to throw caution to the wind and cross into the GDR, hoping Angelika would be at Kabarett Zusammen. It was frustrating not to be able to pick up the phone and call her. But he was here to tell his brother the disturbing news about his parents' past and about their father's attempted suicide.

The cabaret was packed after the drama of the tank standoff. Everyone needed a way to shake it off. Peter was getting ready to go onstage, and Rudi didn't want to get into it until afterward. He took a seat at a table and watched his brother go to work.

"What's with Germans and our salutes, you know?" Peter began. "Like, why are we so obsessed with stiff arm gestures, if you know what I mean? For instance"—he raised his arm oh so slowly as the audience cringed—"Hitler Youth Day, Nuremberg Stadium, 1937."

Peter extended his arm straight out, palm down in the Nazi salute.

"Now jump in your time machine and fly forward with me,

boys and girls, to the year 1961"—he bent his arm ninety degrees and touched his thumb to the top of his head—"at the Stadion der Weltjugend, for the rally of the Free German Youth!"

The audience laughed and groaned, recalling their own childhoods in the Young Pioneers. The twentysomethings in the audience were likely *still* enrolled in the FDJ. Peter used the few seconds of chatter to throw on his bright blue uniform shirt and tie the familiar neckerchief around his bare neck, looking like some bohemian painter living in a garret, sans beret.

"All right, let me be fair. I don't mean to compare the HJ to the FDJ too closely. In the HJ, those bastards were cruel, killing animals with their bare hands and such. But in the FDJ, they just *pet* them to death.

"And now, dear, tenderhearted ladies and gentlemen, I ask you to come once again back in time with me to that same rally of the esteemed *Freie Deutsche*—no, I mean *Hitler Jugend*. Kids and politics, what a match made in heaven, right? What's this? Chairman Ulbricht is about to speak!" He tore off the blue shirt. "Wait, no, did I get that wrong? Chairman . . . who? I'm so confused . . . all this German idealism! So much utopia!"

He suddenly pulled himself together, put on a khaki shirt, left the neckerchief, rolled up his pants, raised his fist in the air and shouted, *"Immer bereit!"*

The audience roared, and Peter got off the stage immediately. He headed right to the back room and collapsed in an old armchair, breathing it all out.

Rudi came in, red in the face.

"Rudi," Peter sighed. "When did you get here? You might have called ahead."

"You've used that joke already, Peter. Aren't you going to greet your adoring fans?"

"Leave them laughing, as they say. Plus, I don't have to deal with the claps on the back, the compliments, the questions."

Rudi was livid. "You've crossed a line, Peter," he scolded. "Comparing the FDJ to the Hitler Youth? That's *sick*."

"You have to admit, it's funny."

"It's everything we stand against! We're not Nazis. We're *für Frieden und Sozialismus,* don't you remember?"

"No, I'm sorry, Rudi, that's what you *think* those words mean. But behind the words, the slogans, it's darker than you can imagine. They use kids to prop themselves up. They always do. And I'm not playing ball anymore."

"I'm worried about you. This could land you in jail for years, don't you understand?"

"Not unless someone turns me in." He glared at Rudi.

"Well, it's a matter of time. If they don't know your family connections, they will soon. It can't stay quiet forever." He pulled Peter in close and whispered, "Peter, I have to tell you something. I found photographs. War medals. Our parents were *Nazis.*"

"Oh, seriously, Rudi? Don't you assume they all were, in some way? That whole generation? Even the most die-hard Communist had to make some concessions to stay alive."

"What? How did you know?"

"I did the math. We were born in Berlin in 1945 to a couple of teenagers. You know they used child soldiers at the end, don't you?"

"We don't have to be like them." Rudi rubbed his eyes. "There's something else. Vati tried to . . . he tried to kill himself, Peter. I don't want to see you lose your soul like he did."

Peter sank back farther into the armchair, trying to fathom what his brother had just told him. "I don't think Vati's lost his soul," he said soberly. "I think he lives every minute of every *day* in his soul, trying to claw his way back into his human self. As for Mutti, I think she's still back there, living like it's 1942. And I think time seems to be going backward for her."

Renate appeared at the door with two bottles of lemonade. Peter rose wearily to join his girlfriend, but Rudi caught him by the arm.

"You should work with things, not against them, Peter. You have a social responsibility. There's no place for Nazis here in the East. So why would you make these ridiculous jokes?"

Peter turned and marched into the middle of the room just as Arno was about to close for the evening. "Listen to this!" Peter shouted to the crowd. "My brother here says all the Nazis are in the West. Who here believes that? Whose father was in the *Hitler Jugend? Ja*, I see that hand! Anyone else? Don't be shy. Come on!"

"Peter, shut *up!*" Rudi grabbed his brother's elbow hard and tried to pull him away from his audience.

Peter lowered his voice, but a small group had gathered around them to listen. "Are you this naive, Rudi?"

"The Communists were in the camps, too, Peter. Remember Sachsenhausen?"

"They were in the camps. Sure. So then they should have known better. They should be the *last* ones to put their boots on our necks. And yet here we are, and the only place we can talk freely for a moment is in a basement that reeks of sweat and beer."

"It's totally different," said Rudi. "The Party has a plan. A vision. If we all pull together in the same direction, it'll be peace and safety for everyone."

"Oh God, listen to yourself, you sound like a poster. Another Five-Year Plan? And then another? You *do* realize that Hitler said the same thing? What do you think, he preached to millions of people, Hey, I have a great idea, why don't we embark on a project of systematic slaughter of our friends and neighbors? Won't that

342

be fun? No, that's not how he duped everyone. It was all for the fatherland, for the next generation, for *social responsibility*," Peter hissed.

"I don't even recognize my own brother," said Rudi. "How can you say these horrible things? In front of people—on a stage?"

"Easy. Because it's *true*."

Rudi's tone shifted, suddenly blasé. "You're so cynical, Peter. Why are you so angry? I thought you were a comedian."

"I'm a comedian because I can't escape the darkness, Rudi. But you—you can't escape your utopian fantasy. Your magical thinking."

"You just say that because you want to leave."

"You're damn right I want to leave! In fact, why are *you* here, Rudi?"

"I don't know."

"Then get out. And don't think you're staying at my place."

Rudi stared at his brother and shook his head. Martin was right. His brother was in the wrong crowd, and in this stinking cellar, Rudi's skin crawled with their poison. He left the cabaret, not knowing quite where to go. He'd never been told he couldn't go back to his own home. Or former home, or whatever it was. He began to see everyone he passed with a blurry sheen, a hint of a scowl on their lips, protecting some kind of dark secret of the past. If his own twin brother was lost, Rudi didn't know who he could trust.

Angelika hadn't been at the cabaret, so he took the S-Bahn to her neighborhood and made the long trek to her building. The light was on, so he rang the bell. She peered out of the window, saw him and motioned that she was coming down.

"Rudi."

"I didn't see you tonight."

"My father needed me," she said. "Come on up."

Herr Rosen sat in his chair, reading a book. He looked tired, unreasonably so.

"Ah, Rudi," he greeted him. "I'm reading this book about Goya's etchings. Come, come. Do you know this one? It's my favorite. *The Sleep of Reason Produces Monsters.*" He handed Rudi the book, and Rudi looked at the black-and-white print tipped into one of the pages: a man asleep at his table and, rising from his dreams, a cloud of goblins, owls and creatures of the night.

"That's good," said Rudi. "The composition, the contrast."

"Yes. Rudi, I must apologize to you for the last time we met. And for hanging up on you. My pain was still very raw, and I was lashing out at everyone. My daughters gave me a talking-to, and I have tried to calm down, find more peace, look at more art."

"*Bitte,* Herr Rosen, please don't mention it."

"There is this Wall now, Rudi. It was inevitable, of course. The GDR would have collapsed without it. It's all such an experiment, you know."

"They have their reasons."

"*The Party is always right,* isn't it?"

Rudi didn't want to answer. He felt he was being set up again to be yelled at.

"Well, they must do what it takes to preserve themselves, as base instinct demands," Herr Rosen continued.

"Sure." Rudi nodded, though what he really wanted was to go somewhere with Angelika. Anywhere but here.

"It could have been worse, Rudi. At least they still let me have a roof over my head." Herr Rosen suddenly looked at his daughter. "Angelika, did I do all right? Was I calm?"

"Yes, Papa."

"Don't let me disturb the two of you. Make yourselves some tea.

I'll go in the bedroom. *Bitte,* please, Rudi, make yourself at home."
Angelika's father shuffled off with his book and closed the door of
the bedroom.

Angelika and Rudi went to the corner with the kitchen. Rudi
pulled her close and kissed her. "The lamplight's really nice on you
right now," he said. "Figures—the one time I didn't bring my camera."

She smiled and put the kettle on while Rudi got out the tea and
cups.

"Where's Sasha?" he asked.

"She started taking the night shift at the hospital," Angelika replied. "How was Peter tonight?"

"Awful."

"Really? Did he bomb again?"

"No, everyone loved it. He's become a superstar since I was last
there. But he went way over the line. He equated the Free German
Youth with the Hitler Youth."

"I don't know." Angelika shrugged. "I see how he could make the
comparison."

"You don't see *any* problem with that?"

"He's talking about how they try to control kids, don't you get
it? How they try to lure us with fun and games and promises that
we're going to be the generation that changes the world. He's doing
important work. You don't see it?"

"Angelika, I'm a student leader. Or I was. I would have noticed
if it was like that. I wouldn't give my life to something unless it was
going to make a difference. I still believe in this. More than ever. If
you want to reap the benefits, you have to fully commit."

"Listen, I'm sorry, Rudi. You're so sweet, and I know you want to
do good. But something's come over you . . . like you're not speaking
your own words. I'm worried about you."

Rudi pushed her away with a jolt. "Maybe you should worry about yourself," he said, his words suddenly acidic, "and your crazy father."

Angelika turned off the kettle and looked at the floor. "I think you should leave, Rudi. You have some things to think about, and I can't help you work them out."

Two minutes ago he was holding this girl in his arms, and now she was telling him to leave. He had at least enough discretion not to slam the door at this hour of night, but he got out of Angelika's place as quickly as he could, red in the face, wiping away a furious tear with his sleeve.

It was too late to try to cross tonight. There remained only one place in East Berlin where he could lay his head.

"Well, of course you can stay here tonight," said Martin, who was still awake, though a bit rumpled. "But wait just a moment in the hallway, will you? It's chaos in here—give me a second to clean up."

He finally opened the door and let Rudi into the apartment. Martin must have had quite a mess on his worktable, which was now covered with a sheet. He made up a mat on the floor for Rudi.

"Just do me a favor and don't disturb that sheet, all right? There are about a thousand tiny pieces under there, and one little nudge will send them flying. Can I get you anything to drink?" Martin offered. "Tea, or warm milk? I only have the powdered kind, but I can put some nutmeg in it."

"No thanks, Uncle Martin—maybe just a glass of water?"

"Sure thing."

Rudi drank a bit and tried to get comfortable on the floor mat. "Uncle Martin? Do you think they did the right thing? "

"What's that?"

"You know, closing off the city, not letting people out?"

Martin searched for words. "Rudi, the Wall is called the Anti-

Fascist Protection Barrier. Why do you think that is? It's because the fascists are on the *other* side. We're not trapped. We're containing *them*."

"I didn't think of that."

"The fight for peace is hard, and it takes sacrifice. And you're part of that, Rudi."

"I want to be, but it feels like everyone around me is going crazy."

He told his uncle about his fight with Angelika. He told him about Peter's comparison of the FDJ to the Hitler Youth. He told him about his father's Nazi medals, his mother's photographs, seeing his father at the point of death.

Martin listened quietly to all of it. And then he put Rudi's cup in the sink, got in bed and turned out the light.

"Thank you for trusting me with all of this, Rudi. Let's get some sleep. We'll talk about it in the morning."

After breakfast Martin suggested they work in the darkroom. Rudi hadn't brought his camera, but he did have some rolls of film in his bag. They developed three rolls of negatives. The school dance. The portraits of Herr Rosen. Kabarett Zusammen.

In the pitch-black, Martin and Rudi did not speak about what was coming out of the developer bath. But finally, Martin cleared his throat. "I have some uncomfortable news, Rudi. I didn't want to tell you last night. You seemed so upset when you showed up."

"What? What's wrong? Is it Mutti?"

"No, no word on your mother as yet. I've looked everywhere. The police even interrogated her nurse. No, I saw *her* . . . what's her name? You know, your girlfriend. The one you had the fight with last night."

"Angelika? Where?"

"In the Volkspark. With Peter." He flipped on the red safety light.

"That's ridiculous. Why would she be with Peter? She barely knows him."

"It didn't seem that way to me," said Martin, "since they were kissing."

"Kissing?" Rudi's heart slipped and became lodged in his stomach. His vision instantly started to fracture at the edges. He thought he understood how Peter must feel when a migraine was coming on. "Are you sure it was them?"

"I looked again and again, Rudi. I'm positive."

They finished developing and fixing the last roll. Martin flipped on the light, and Rudi's fragmenting sight righted itself. "I'm sorry. But I thought you should know."

"No, that's all right," said Rudi. "It's good that I know. It would explain some things."

"Like what?"

"Last night she asked about Peter. She said he was doing important work."

"What work?"

Before Rudi could stop himself, he said, "Underground comedy. Political stuff, at a cabaret." He knew he shouldn't have said anything, not even to his uncle. But Martin was family, and he had seemed concerned about Peter, about the change in him. Maybe Martin would be able to help Peter the way he'd helped Rudi. Maybe they could help Peter turn his ship around.

"Wow," said Martin. "That could get Peter in huge trouble."

"I know."

"These people are degenerates, Rudi." He looked pensively into the developer tray. "I had a feeling something was going on with him."

"Peter's changed. I don't recognize him. It's like he's not even my brother anymore."

"How long has this been going on?"

"Since . . . I don't know . . . June? There are some photos from the cabaret on that last roll."

"All right, it hasn't been that long. There's still a chance to help him. Listen: don't tell him we spoke. You want plausible deniability. Do you know what that means?"

"Not really. . . ."

"Just keep being my eyes and ears. Maybe he'll settle down with a little time. But if he crosses a line, you just tell me, Rudi. I'm here to help."

"I will. Thanks, Uncle Martin."

"I'm here for you, Rudi."

NOVEMBER

PETER

Snow began to fall on Berlin early on a mid-November afternoon. In a few hours, the neon lights and Christmas markets of West Berlin would have cast their festive glow across the border, if not for the Wall. But in the dim haze, the buildings shimmered like they were smeared with grease.

Peter walked up Kollwitzstrasse, his collar turned up against the wind. He liked getting to Arno's early these days, helping him set up for the cabaret and shooting the breeze. It calmed him to be there among people who understood him and neither conformed nor expected him to.

When the puppets in his FDJ chapter drove him batty, he could come here and let it all fall away. In that cramped basement was the grace to make mistakes, because they all knew that was what it took to think, to create, to make art.

As he turned onto the street, two blocks down from the cabaret, he saw a black Trabant with its doors open. Two gray men were hassling a third, a skinny man with blond hair peeking out from under his winter cap.

Peter locked eyes with Thomas, just as one of the men pushed his head down into the car and slammed it shut. For only a moment, Peter froze and watched the Trabi drive away with his friend inside. He knew he would not see Thomas again.

This was coming too close. He couldn't afford to be casual any longer. Peter turned and walked the other way, breaking up his usual route, and killed the afternoon in a café instead, writing in his notebook, watching the snow turn from dust to slush, to a slick of ice encasing each and every cobblestone.

RUDI

L ook at this filthy city, Rudi thought as he walked to school, his hands shoved in his pockets.

More often than not these days, he walked with his fists clenched. His imagination worked overtime, crafting a hundred scenarios of Angelika and Peter together. He imagined them kissing. He imagined his brother's hands in her hair, on her blouse. He imagined Peter's reflection in her dark eyes.

It doesn't matter what I do, Rudi thought. *My brother gets everything in the end.* "*Twins against the world,* right?" he said aloud. "*Schwachsinn.*"

Why couldn't they go back to the days of playing cards or talking about girls or fantasizing about outer space? They were brothers, after all, brothers growing up in that tiny apartment, sharing a closet of a room without even a proper door. They had shared a womb, for God's sake. But now even the best memories were tainted. It all felt like a lie, like something twins are told to believe.

To top it all off, Peter was a wrecker, trying to tear down everything Rudi stood for, everything that was *good* and *right.* Rudi didn't want to imagine how far down into his brother's soul that rot went. It was something that had to be purged. Something so visible and ugly shouldn't be allowed to exist. He didn't know what he would do about it. He simply had his raw disgust. Rudi didn't only resent Peter. He was beginning to despise him.

He wasn't sleeping at night; when he did, he had nightmares. Weeks passed, and Rudi drifted in his classes. His grades were slipping, and so was his work at the bakery. He messed up a big party order—two hundred dinner rolls instead of sweet buns—and almost got fired.

The sight of his father made him sick, as did the incessant pollution of Oma's chain smoking. He was even snippy with Charles.

They met up at Der Spinner for music school later that month. Rudi was flipping through the jazz albums so fast and hard, the people around him turned and stared.

"Rudi, Rudi!" Charles chastised him. "You're going to crack a disc, and then you'll have to pay for it. Go gentle!"

"I know how to handle records," he scoffed.

Charles came up beside him and lowered his voice. "Man, you need to snap out of it and get yourself together. What's eating you?"

"You really want to know?" said Rudi.

"Yes, I really want to know what's making my young friend so intolerable to be around."

"Fine," he said, leaning against the rack. "My girlfriend is cheating on me. With my brother."

Charles winced. "Ouch. Are you sure about that?"

"My uncle saw them together in the park. *Kissing.*" The word made him want to spit.

"Have you talked to *her*?"

"No. Not exactly. I'm looking for clues."

"You've got to move beyond clues in this case, Rudi," Charles chuckled. "Go *talk* to her."

"What's the point? She's a traitor. And so is he."

"Rudi, don't let it fester. Talk to her. You owe it to her."

"I don't owe her anything. And I don't owe Peter anything."

"Trust me on this. What I wouldn't give for one more conversation with my wife—even if it was about something hard." He shrugged and put on another record. "You've got to communicate, son. First rule of love."

"I've got homework," Rudi deflected, slinging his book bag back over his shoulder. "Are you coming for dinner tonight?"

"Wouldn't miss your Oma's terrible cooking for the world," said Charles. "But do us all a favor and blow off some steam first."

Rudi slogged through his homework and helped Oma get dinner together. He couldn't tell if his anger was hyping him up, but she seemed to be moving slower than usual.

"I got a call from your teacher today, Rudi," said Oma. "You're failing two classes. I'm too old to be dealing with things like this."

"Sorry, Omi."

"What's going on with you lately? You don't go out, there's a dark cloud over your head, and—"

"I've just got a lot to do, Omi," Rudi cut her off. "When I'm not at school, I'm at the bakery; when I'm not there, I'm shooting for the school paper. . . ."

"Don't give me that. I'm not easily fooled. You're no busier than any other kid."

"In this stupid school, they say all kinds of things about the East, how they spy on people and ban books and movies. But I've never seen any of that. And yet *this* is supposed to be where people escape to and their dreams all come true."

"I have a feeling this isn't about school or movies." Oma took a long drag and drummed her fingers on the counter. "You're dissatisfied. It reminds me of a joke. Let me see if I can remember it.

"A man dies and goes to hell. When he gets there, they tell him he has a choice: he can go to capitalist hell or Communist hell. There's a big wall between them, complete with a checkpoint. So he goes to the capitalist checkpoint. The border guard is the devil, who looks like John F. Kennedy. *What's it like over there?* the guy asks. *Well,* says Kennedy, *in capitalist hell, we skin you alive, then we boil you in oil and finally we cut you into tiny pieces with knives. Then we put you back together and do it all again.*

"*Mein Gott!* says the guy. *I'm going to defect to Communist hell instead!* So he turns around and goes to the checkpoint to Communist hell, and of course, there's a long line. At last, he gets to the checkpoint, and the guard turns out to be a little old demon who looks like Karl Marx. *Listen, Karl,* he says, *I still have a choice between the two hells. So tell me what it's like in there.*

"*Here in Communist hell,* says Marx triumphantly, *we skin you alive, then we boil you in oil and finally we cut you into tiny pieces with knives. Then we put you back together and do it all again.*

"*Hold on,* the man says, *that's the same as capitalist hell! Why's there such a long line to get in?*

"*Marx sighs. Well,* he says, *we've run out of oil, there's no more coal and the factory's short on knives!*"

Oma laughed. Rudi did not.

His great-grandmother worked herself into a cough from laughing so hard. When she finally calmed, she said, "Listen, Rudi. The Communists believed we were all going to rise up and overthrow

Hitler. But we didn't. Because we all had to live our lives. That's what we told ourselves. He wasn't quiet about what he wanted to do. Some idiots bought the propaganda, believed in it, like a religion. But most people had things to do, *verstehen?*

"And so when the Communists came back from exile, they were ashamed of us. They were Germans, too. Easy for them to judge their country from far away. So what did they do? They turned all that shame into a government. Said we *deserved* another dictatorship because we couldn't be trusted to purge Nazism on our own. And you know, maybe they were right. Maybe people really can't be trusted to think for themselves."

Rudi stood with his arms crossed, angry even with his Omi. "To not fight against fascism is to *be* a fascist."

Oma smoked her cigarette and narrowed her eyes at Rudi. "Like I thought. This isn't about school."

Rudi excused himself to finish his homework in the bedroom. But homework was the last thing on his mind. He had to see for himself if what Martin had told him was true.

Saturday evening was bitter and clear when Rudi crossed the border. The guards weren't in the mood to mess with him in this cold wind, and they barely looked at his visa. When he got to the cabaret, Rudi sat at a table alone. Peter glanced his way but didn't come over to say hello. Rudi watched Peter like a hawk. Angelika flitted through the room, talking to friends. He could tell she was avoiding him. Peter said hi to Angelika, but that was it—he was glued to Renate the whole time.

It must be a trick, Rudi thought. *They're avoiding each other because I'm here.*

Play it cool, he thought, getting dizzy watching the room. *Don't let on that you told Uncle Martin about the cabaret. You want . . . what did he call it? Plausible deniability.*

"Rudi! Peter!" Arno hollered, waving them over to the bar. Reluctantly, they joined him there. Arno pointed to a headline on the front page of *Neues Deutschland* and said, "Look at this." He tapped it twice and got up to pour a drink.

Speculation That Eichmann Will Receive Death Sentence

"You were really into that trial, weren't you?" Arno asked Rudi.

"*Ja,*" he said, working his jaw. "They should hang every single one of those Nazis. Every one they can find."

His insides churned; everything seemed to zoom away from him, and he felt like he might faint or throw up. He had to get away from all these people. He felt like a stranger in his own country, in his own family. He felt split down the middle, from head to toe.

Rudi went into the back room and sat on the old sofa with his hands at his sides, feeling the rough texture of the upholstery, looking through the doorway at the neon haze shrouding the main room. In the mirror on the wall, Rudi could just see his feet glowing red in the reflection.

DECEMBER

RUDI

"**H**appy birthday, man!" said Charles, waving to Rudi as he passed by the American checkpoint on the way to school. "What are you, twenty-four today?"

"Sixteen—finally," said Rudi, clapping Charles's hand in greeting. He wasn't excited, exactly, but he felt a little freer today. He'd gone to Martin's after the cabaret, and their conversation had been clarifying. As angry as he was about Peter and Angelika, he convinced himself that he was helping them by telling Martin the address of the cabaret and when they would meet next. He had some ground beneath his feet now.

"I was just at Der Spinner," Rudi said, changing the subject. "Tobias told me some good bands are coming to Hamburg."

"Well, my friend," said Charles, "it looks like our next trip up north is going to have to wait."

"Why?"

"A conductor ran his train through the border and escaped last night, him and twenty-four other people. By midnight, that track was sealed the hell off, and now everything's being rerouted. We'll have to take a rain check, I think."

Rudi was instantly irritated. "I don't know why people have to make such a big deal out of all of this. They should get used to it and move on. It's not like anyone can change it."

"You've seen it yourself—the Wall's made people pretty desperate. Dozens of escapes, shoot-to-kill orders . . . they're risking their lives, Rudi."

"But it's not about one person, or twenty-four people. They're making everyone else pay for what they want."

"It's natural to want to be free. That's not selfish."

"No one is saying they aren't free. All I'm saying is that it's not just about one person."

Charles shrugged and took a deep breath. "Suit yourself."

Rudi looked at the ground. "Anyway, I should get going. Are you coming to my birthday dinner?"

"I'll be there," Charles said. "I'm baking the cake."

"Great!" Rudi brightened. "Can you bring some music, too?"

"I will. Bye, Rudi. See you tonight."

"*Schatzi*, pass the potatoes?" Oma asked Rudolf. Dinner was takeout from the restaurant down the street: currywurst and fresh pickles and bottles of lemonade. The little apartment was packed tight—Willi from downstairs chatting with Charles, debating the merits of Coltrane versus Getz and Parker, Oma and Rudolf swapping stories about Rudolf's awkward childhood foibles.

But this wasn't like his mother's parties, with dancing and school friends and her genius for drawing people out of their shells. And it wasn't the same, because it was the first birthday without his twin.

"It's so strange not seeing Peter on your birthday," whispered Rudolf, as though reading his mind.

Rudi soured. "*Ja*, I'll bet you miss Peter," he accused.

"What's that supposed to mean?"

"Nothing."

"No, Rudi, there's something you want to say."

Oma crunched on a pickle and listened in. Rudi's chewing slowed. He was going to have to stand behind his words now.

"Oh, come on, Vati, don't pretend he's not your favorite. Always has been. Gets one award and it's dinner at a fancy restaurant. Did you ever do that for me?"

"Can't I celebrate my son's accomplishments?"

"Do you even know what your precious son is doing? He's a criminal."

"A criminal?"

Now all attention was on their argument.

"Forget it," Rudi huffed.

"No, what do you mean?" asked Rudolf. "Is Peter in trouble?"

"Probably not. He'll weasel his way out of it somehow. He even craps gold."

Oma finally burst. "How, I mean how, do you live with this level of bullshit, Rudi?" she shouted in German. "How can you lie to yourself so thoroughly?"

"What are you talking about, Omi?" Rudi sassed.

"You compare yourself to Peter?" Oma yelled. "What are you doing? You come home and stare at the television, you wander the streets, you go to the Kino, take the occasional photograph. You're a do-nothing at school, half your film canisters go undeveloped—and you think the world owes you something? Did your father risk his life to bring you here for nothing?"

"No one asked him to," Rudi retorted. "That was his idea."

"*Scheiss*," Oma seethed. "How did we raise someone with such a tolerance for mediocrity as you?"

Her rebuke shocked him. He was used to her little jabs, but an indictment like this from Oma? It was so rare, it felt apocalyptic. Rudi did the only thing he could do: he laughed, in that infuriating, reflexive way that you do upon seeing someone trip or hearing about some absurd catastrophe. You don't mean to do it, you hate yourself for it, but the brain can only handle so much discomfort, and it comes out as ridiculous laughter. And yet he couldn't escape himself. Couldn't shed his anger, that little boy with the plate of cubed cheese, knowing his brother was, in this mysterious but real way, better than him. Not just in quantity—of awards, of good grades, of girls who liked him—but in human quality.

And there isn't a damn thing I can do about it, either.

If there was a star out there in some lofty galaxy with his name on it, there was a chasm preventing him from reaching it, and that vast space was named Peter. He could cross it, but he knew he wouldn't; he didn't have the will. The best he could do was lay a thick layer of comfortable self-deceit around himself, and continue to mulch himself with it.

All of a sudden, the buzzer rang, pulsing in a frenetic stutter.

"*Oh Gott,*" said Oma, "what now?" She leaned back hard in her chair.

"We're not expecting anyone else," Rudolf said. He got up and pressed the intercom button. "Möser, can I help you?"

"Rudolf?" said the staticky voice.

It took him a moment. "Ilse?"

"Mutti?" Rudi sprang from his seat and ran down the stairs. He threw open the front door. Rudolf came down in his socks and almost slipped on the last step. On the threshold, between the light of the hall and the light from the street, stood Rudi's mother. She did not look the same.

"Sixth of December," she said to Rudi. "Happy birthday."

"Mutti, what are you doing here? We've been looking for you—why did you leave the hospital? Where have you been?"

"How did you find us?" asked Rudolf.

"Rudolf, I'm so tired. So cold. I've been walking forever. Can I . . . can I just sit down for a minute?" She walked into the foyer, grasped the banister and collapsed on the bottom stair.

"Ilse, come on. We live up there. Let us help you. Come on." Rudolf and Rudi supported Ilse on either side and got her upstairs. They brought her into the apartment and led her to the sofa.

Oma turned around in her seat and stared in disbelief. Ilse was a mess. She wore filthy slacks and an overcoat with no color. Her left tennis shoe had a broken lace and a hole in the side. She smelled unpleasant.

And she was quiet. So, so quiet.

"Ilse?" Rudolf tried to get her to speak, but she only stared at the piano across the room. "Rudi, get your mother some water."

Rudi brought her a glass of water and a damp rag for her dirty hands and face. Rudolf wiped his wife's face with such tenderness, it seemed to bring her back around.

"I was looking for you," she said. "I tried to go home, but there was this . . . this *wall* in the way. I walked the whole way and there were no doors in it, not even a window. . . ."

"You've been in West Berlin the whole time," Oma chimed in.

"She must have been," said Charles.

"I had to get out of that hospital," said Ilse. "They . . . they did things to me there." Tears glossed her deadened eyes, and Rudolf pulled her close. "They did things to me."

"I won't let them hurt you," he said. "Do you trust me?"

She dissolved into his arms, and he led her to the bathroom and helped her into the shower.

Willi excused himself, tears in his eyes, and went back down-stairs to his flat. A minute later they heard a soft saxophone ballad drifting through the floor.

Oma sat at the table and looked at Charles. He put his head in his hands.

"Been a while since you two last saw each other," said Oma.

"Quite a while," said Charles. "I think I'll take my leave now."

"Charles, will you stay a moment longer? Please."

"This is a woman who hates me, Oma. Who probably would pre-fer I didn't exist."

"Is this the same woman? Or is it a shell hollowed out by her sins?"

Charles fished for his handkerchief and rubbed his eyes while he searched for words.

"You stayed to see Rudolf through," Oma reminded him.

"Rudolf was willing to look at himself. Is the same true of her? Can she see her own dark side?"

"There are many such hollow shells, in my country and yours. These two were very nearly killed by their pasts. The question is, Can they receive back their souls?"

"That remains to be seen," Charles proffered.

Oma Möser reached for her lighter. "Hand me those West ciga-rettes, won't you, *Schatzi*?" Oma lit up and put the kettle on.

In fact, Charles stayed. He joined Rudi on the sofa, the two of them staring out the window at the lights shining through a newly falling snow.

Oma handed them each a cup of tea and sat with them in si-lence.

"Rudi," she said at last, "I know I was harsh before. But nothing I said has to be the end of your story. You have a choice, you know."

"It doesn't really matter, Omi. There are always going to be people like Peter who just have it easy. The rest of us—like me and Mutti—we never get a break."

"That may be," said Oma. "And yet, you don't get to write anyone's story but your own."

She got up, took another dish out of the cabinet and fixed a plate of food for Ilse.

Rudi's mother emerged, showered and dressed, and ate like the food was breath. Rudolf played her favorite, Chopin's *Valse de l'adieu*, much slower than the composer intended. No one spoke.

There was no warning that Oma was about to collapse. As Rudolf let the last chord ring out, she crumpled to the floor as though her bones had vanished, like one of those thumb puppets that reduces into a pile of beads.

PETER

Peter came home from school to the empty apartment. He dropped his bag and stared down the hall. There was nothing new about the emptiness since Oma had gone, but yesterday was his birthday, and the silence was immense. He shook it off, walked to the dining room and dumped the mail on the table. There was an envelope among the letters, with his name typewritten, and no return address. He opened it, and his heart dropped.

OMA PASSED
FUNERAL SATURDAY

He was stunned, but he might have known. When he'd last seen Oma at Bäckerei Antoinette, Peter had a feeling. She'd been thinner, slower, stubborn but not as fiery. Three times he'd had a dream of her walking away from him. He'd told himself not to believe his inklings, but he knew. Oma knew, too. She walked away from her home and left everything behind. Her furniture, the very walls, seemed suddenly absent of her. On the discolored wall where her broken cuckoo clock hung, the little bird whistled the hour, and gave up the ghost.

There was no way he could get to the funeral. He cursed the Wall.

In his purge, there was one thing Peter hadn't cleared out of the flat: Oma's cigarette drawer. He rifled through packs of all kinds, opened and new, from the East and West. Peeking out from the back of the drawer was a sky-blue pack of Gauloises, with its winged helmet drawn on the front. It had been opened, and from the pack exactly one cigarette had been smoked. Peter withdrew another, lit it with Oma's owl lighter and, out the open window in the December chill, had a smoke in Oma's memory.

He read the note again and saw that he'd somehow missed the last line:

YOUR MOTHER IS HOME IN KREUZBERG

So. They found Ilse, and she was in the West. Peter put the note down and sighed. *I'm the last one in the East now,* he thought. *Officially stranded.*

The telephone rang and his ears twanged.

"I'm coming, I'm coming," he said as he wound his way through the rooms toward the telephone. "Peter," he answered.

"It's Renate."

He ran his hand through his hair and rubbed the back of his neck. *"Hallo, Maus."*

"What are you up to?"

"Huh. That's a complicated question," he said. "Normally, I would be up to quite a lot. It's my . . . ah . . . it's my birthday. I mean, yesterday was." He looked at the cigarette between his fingers. He wondered what Oma's hands had looked like when she turned sixteen.

"Peter!" Renate chirruped. "Why didn't you tell me? Let's go out!"

"You know what, could we just . . . could you come over? We could eat something here. I have some instant noodles. . . ."

"Let me make you a birthday dinner, *Katze.* I'll bring everything."

"Really, *Maus?* You'd do that for me?"

"Natürlich! I'll be there at five, all right?"

"Ja. OK. I'll leave the door unlocked. *Tschüss."*

Peter finished the cigarette and stamped it out in the kitchen sink. He put the pack of Gauloises back in the drawer—and cried his ever-loving eyes out.

The resulting headache, thankfully, did not materialize into a migraine, though it easily could have, given the implications of the news. Peter lay on his bed and stared at the ceiling, taking stock of how thoroughly his great-grandmother had occupied this place. And for how long. It had been her pride and joy when she and her husband had moved in, among the first couples to move into the brand-new building just before the Great War. Rudolf's father had grown up here before moving to Würzburg. This was the only home Peter knew. He wondered if the Party would make him leave. After all, it was a bit luxurious for a single high school kid.

God, how he missed Oma. Missed her curmudgeonliness, the flick of the owl lighter, her soft swears, her nylon socks hanging over the tub. And now she was gone.

Peter sat up and hugged his knees. He looked over at the wardrobe. On the side facing his bed, he saw something he had never noticed before. It was a small hole, the size of his pinkie nail. The hole was perfectly round. He opened the wardrobe door to look at it from the other side.

"Hallo, Katze!" Renate called. "I'm here! Happy birthday! We're just going to pretend it's today, all right?"

He'd look at the hole more closely later. Renate hadn't put down her bags when he went to the door and wrapped his arms around her.

"My Omi's gone, *Maus*," he said. "My Omi's gone, and she died on my birthday, and I was all alone." The tears came, and he wept months of pent-up sorrow on her shoulder.

"Oh, Peter." Renate set her things down and embraced him back. *"Mein Peterling."*

Her caress was so soft, so comforting. Renate's body conformed to his so completely. There was nothing he had to hold back from her. He kissed her; her face was wet with his tears.

"I love you, Renate," he whispered.

"Peter, I love you, too."

They kissed until they were tired of standing. Renate led him by the hand to the sofa and curled up beside him, caressing his face. He looked at her, this magnificent girl who saw him as he was. She could look through his performance, his talent, and see in him someone who she loved simply because he was *Peter.* He kissed her mouth, and she returned to him his innocence.

The evening began to wane, and Renate and Peter at last went into the kitchen to make his belated birthday dinner. They ate at the table, a ray from the streetlight streaming through the window between them.

"I applied to emigrate to the West," Peter said quietly.

"Oh."

"I wish it didn't have to be this way."

"There aren't many options. This is the right thing."

"Can you stay?" Peter took her hand.

"I have work tonight, *Katze*," she said. "Besides, the walls have ears."

"What do you mean?"

"Your neighbors are nosy. I saw one peeking out at me when I came up. And didn't you say those two Stasi guys are always showing up at odd times?"

"That's true—I wouldn't want you to get in trouble."

"Me? I'm fine, *Junge*. It's you I worry about. Once they start snooping around, they don't ever stop. You know it's gotten worse since the Wall. Think about poor Thomas."

She got up and cleared their plates. The dirty baking dish was still on the stove. "I didn't realize how late it was getting," she said. "I'm sorry. I hate to make you clean up your own birthday supper—"

"It's nothing," said Peter. "It was the best birthday I've ever had."

"I really do love you, *Katze*." She kissed him so softly, Peter thought his heart would break.

"I really love you, *Maus*."

Renate left quietly, and Peter went to his room and lay back on the bed. He'd had a new emotion every five minutes.

The walls have ears, Renate had said.

He remembered the hole in his wardrobe and got up to examine it more closely. He stuck his head into the wardrobe and tried to understand what he was looking at. That was when he heard his brother's voice.

"Hi, Peter," said Rudi, suddenly standing in the bedroom doorway. "Happy birthday."

Peter startled and stumbled backward out of the wardrobe. "Rudi! Uh, happy birthday. . . . What are you doing here?"

"I couldn't stay away. It's too awful. Omi . . ."

"I know. I got the note."

"What note?"

"I assumed you left it."

"Wasn't me. But I assume you know there's something else," said Rudi. He sat on his old bed. "Mutti came back."

"It said that, too. When?"

"Last night. She's been in the West this whole time, wandering the streets, trying to find us. She looked terrible. She's at our place now. I think her coming back is what . . . why Omi . . ."

"Had a heart attack, right? It was her heart, it had to be."

"I don't know what we're going to do," Rudi fretted. "The apartment in Kreuzberg is too small for us. It already was with Omi. If we could only come back here—"

"You don't want to be here."

"Believe me, I do. Every *day* I wish I could come back."

"What's left, Rudi? It's not the same place. We're trapped. Like rats in a cage. I mean, except you, for some reason."

"Maybe Uncle Martin could help you. Don't worry. Things can only get better. It's bound to loosen up."

"Are they better now? Because I'm waiting for better and I don't see it."

"Why are you so bitter, Peter?"

"*Bitter?*"

"Ever since you started going to that cabaret, you're so . . . so political."

"*I'm* political? It's the complete opposite. Why do politics have to seep into every crack of every conversation or class or picnic in the park . . . or *funeral*, for God's sake?"

"Because . . . well . . ."

"Does the Party have to know when I take a shit in the morning? Is that important?"

"Oh, come on. What are you talking about?"

"Why is there a fucking camera in my closet, Rudi?"

"Why would there be a camera in the closet, Peter?"

Peter reached into his pocket and produced a tiny nodule on a long wire. He put the miniature camera up to his eye, like he was spying on Rudi.

"What the—" Rudi grabbed the camera and inspected it.

"They must know about the cabaret," said Peter. "They must."

"How could they know? You're so careful."

"Maybe I was followed."

"You must have done something to make them suspicious."

"Really, Rudi?"

"I don't know, Peter. You sound paranoid."

"Let me tell you something. If I sound paranoid, it's because I know what I've seen."

"Well, you took the camera out of the wardrobe, didn't you? So whatever that was, it's over now. Just be on the lookout, you know, and take a different route when you go to the cabaret this weekend." Rudi collapsed on the bed. "Listen, the funeral is Saturday. I came back to ask Uncle Martin to try to get you a pass. Can I borrow a blanket and pillow? It's been a crazy couple of days. I'm so tired."

Peter went to the hall closet and got Rudi some bedding. When he returned, Rudi was already asleep. Peter covered him and put the pillow next to his head. He put his hand on his brother's shoulder.

"Happy birthday, *Dummkopf*."

RUDI

Friday *had* been a crazy day. Rudi hadn't been able to get ahold of Uncle Martin to ask for Peter's pass, so he got to school late, had to stay in the darkroom for hours afterward to meet his photo deadline for the Christmas edition and then arrived so late for work at the bakery that it was almost not worth going. He couldn't wait to get home and collapse, but until then began closing: wiping down the shelves, turning off the coffee, bagging leftover pastries for charity. Charles was the only one in the place, at a table reading the newspaper. Every now and then, Rudi saw him brush his hand across his eyes.

"Rudi," Charles called, "you all right, kid?"

"*Ja*, I'm all right. How about you?"

"I miss her," said Charles. "She reminded me so much of my grandma. Tough as nails. Tender, though. She used to take in all manner of people down on their luck. Drove my grandpa crazy. Yes, your great-grandmother was special. I'm glad I got to know her." He dabbed at his eyes with his napkin.

Rudi began sweeping up in front of the counter. "I got some photographs of her from the old place. I thought I would make an album for the funeral tomorrow."

The bells on the door rang. Rudi didn't look up. "*Entschuldigung,* I'm closing," he said.

"I heard about your Omi," Martin announced in German as he came in, wiping his snowy feet on the doormat. He looked Charles over and gave a slight nod. "A heart attack, so sudden."

Rudi beckoned his uncle closer and spoke softly. "Uncle Martin,

I'm glad you came. I've been trying to find you—can you get Peter a visa for the funeral?"

"Come on, Rudi, you know what's going to happen if I try that."

"But he was closer to Omi than anyone. Couldn't you?"

"I'm sorry, it's not within my power."

"Just a little cog in the machine, are you?" Charles muttered, eavesdropping. Martin shot him a dismissive look.

"I'm so sorry I can't do it, Rudi. I really wish I could—it's so, so sad. You can bring him a program. I'll send a condolence card, put some money in it."

Rudi saw Charles look away from them quickly. That was it, then. There was nothing more to say. Rudi swept the dirt and crumbs and snowy footprints into the dustpan and dumped it all in the rubbish bin.

Martin cleared his throat. "Rudi, I have a letter for you, but I'm hesitant to give it to you. It's from your girlfriend, Angelika. I'm sorry, your ex-girlfriend? I never did ask you what happened with that." Martin handed Rudi a pale lavender envelope. "Do you want it?"

Rudi studied it for a moment. She'd taken the time to write to him . . . and somehow it had gotten to his uncle, of all people.

"Sure." Rudi put it in his back pocket and finished sweeping.

"Didn't you say she goes to that cabaret with Peter? Maybe she wants to mend things." Martin tipped his hat and walked back out into the cold night.

Charles lifted his head from the newspaper. "What was that about? I didn't understand all the German, but enough to know you've got some . . . situations going on."

Rudi took the letter out of his pocket and opened it. He sat down across from Charles and read it. "Angelika wants to see me. It's probably nothing. Anyway, Peter can't go to Omi's funeral."

"You don't believe that, do you? Wasn't that the uncle who made all those things happen for you?"

"*Ja*, I don't understand. But if Uncle Martin says he can't, it must really be impossible."

Saturday morning was unseasonably warm, but gray clouds pulled together in the sky over Oma's funeral. Ilse was even quieter than usual. The last sixteen years with her grandmother-in-law had been fueled by conflict, but now she seemed genuinely sad. It was a simple service, with a pine casket and a bouquet sent by Herr Otto. Charles was a pallbearer, along with Herr König and other men from the Good Shepherd Church in Friedenau. They buried her in the cemetery a few blocks north of the church, in a patch of ivy, as a gentle rain shower washed the city.

The warm day yielded to an evening chill, and the shower turned to snow. It was a beautiful winter night, close enough to Christmas to coax the charm out of Berlin. Snow fell from the branches, pulverizing into powder, floating away in miniature clouds. People still went out, bundled in coats and hand-knits, an excuse for guys and girls to huddle together. There were movies to get to, weekend coffee to have with friends, relatives to see to before hitting the Monday grind again. There were underground cabaret performances to sneak off to and pretty girlfriends with whom to make amends.

Rudi had the letter from Angelika in his coat pocket as he crossed the border. When he got to the cabaret, she was talking with Arno. She saw him and gave a quick wave, but she stayed by the stage, getting ready to go on and sing. She was third to perform, two of her beautiful ballads, with Sasha accompanying her on guitar. Rudi's heart swelled. This girl was such an inspiration. He was full of hope for their reunion. He couldn't wait to kiss those lips again.

After her performance, Angelika got a bottle of soda and came over to Rudi's table in the far corner.

"Thanks for coming," she said, playing with the bottle cap. "It's been a while."

"I got your letter," said Rudi. "I want to say—"

"Please, Rudi, let me go first."

"No, let me please say this. I forgive you for kissing Peter."

"What?"

"My uncle told me. He saw you. But it's all right. I know it could never work out between you. He's not—"

"Is that what you think happened?" Angelika said with disgust. "Is that what you think of me? *Really?*"

"Are you seriously going to sit there and deny it? My uncle saw you with his own eyes."

"Your uncle seems to be everywhere." Angelika stared at him askance, reading his face. Rudi couldn't bear her gaze. She kept staring at him, taking swigs of her drink.

"What happened to you, Rudi? You used to be a nice person."

"I didn't mean anything by it. It was a misunderstanding."

"A misunderstanding? When you accuse me of cheating on you with your *brother*? You must not think much of me at all. We were worried about you. Sure, I bump into him here or at school, and we've talked a couple of times to try to figure out how to *help* you. You're turning into someone neither of us recognizes, Rudi. I can't stand it."

"Angelika, do you think . . . maybe it's you who's changed?"

"What are you talking about?"

"Look, it's fun to hang out in this stupid basement and pretend you're doing something important, but—"

"Listen, Rudi, I really liked you. Maybe I even loved you. But I can't trust you. It's like—am I going to get Real Rudi or Comrade Rudi?"

"What do you mean? I'm just one person."

"I saw the way you looked at my father," she continued, "like you were blaming him for what happened to us. No compassion, no doubt in your mind that he simply got what he deserved."

"He was making really strong accusations about the Party, Angelika. . . . If he got caught doing something wrong, then—"

"Let me tell you something, Rudi." Angelika's face was deadly serious. "Hitler said the Jews were Bolshevik revolutionaries, and Marx said we were bourgeois capitalists. That's the thing: we're whatever they want us to be, and after the dust and ashes settle, they say we brought it on ourselves. My sister and I watched our father have his whole life destroyed by people he considered *family.* People who never cared about him or us. And you're ready to defend them. So how about you don't get a vote on what happened to my family?"

How could she talk to him like this? After he'd done everything to impress her father—baking him cookies, taking really good portrait shots of him. He did it for *her.*

"Your moods turn on a dime over things that are so pointless," she continued. "You sulk when you don't get your way."

"Is there anything else?" Rudi's words dripped with acid.

"No," said Angelika, rising from her seat. There was no more anger in her face—only something like pity. "There's nothing else. I have nothing more to say to you. Goodbye, Rudi."

At that moment, Arno announced the next act, and Peter took the stage.

Rudi was mortified when he called him out by name.

"My twin brother over there, he works at a bakery, so this joke's for you, Rudi!

"A man goes to the butcher and asks for some bread. The manager says, *Comrade, this is a butcher.*

"*But you have no meat,* the man says.

"*Of course not. If you're looking for the bakery, go across the street where they have no bread!*

"Oh, wait, here's another one! A boy asks his father, *Vati, what will it be like when we have perfect Communism?* His father answers, *Son, there will be nothing else you need. You'll be completely satisfied.* The boy says, *But, Vati, what if there is a shortage of bread? Well, then,* says his father, *the bakery will hang a sign in the window that says:* Comrades, the Party Has Decided That You Do Not Need Any Bread Today!"

The audience loved it, nodding to each other and mumbling their commiseration. But it immediately grew quiet when two older men came down the stairs and leaned against the wall, their gray suits glowing red in the neon light.

They were none other than Glasses and Baby Face.

Peter shot Rudi a look, and suddenly nothing was quite so funny anymore.

But Peter didn't change his tone. Instead, he went with it. "And now, in honor of our two comrades who have just joined us, I shall regale you with a collection of classic jokes about our venerable State Security agency, everyone's favorite thugs, the Stasi!"

No one dared to applaud now, for their own sakes. Peter, however, looked high on this opportunity to take it right to the source.

"How many Stasi officers does it take to milk a cow? Twenty-two. Two to hold the cow's teats, and five to hold each leg and lift the cow up and down!

"Hans, Paul and another guy are sitting in a cell in Stasi headquarters. Hans asks Paul what he's in for, and Paul says, *Because I criticized Stalin.* Hans says, *But I am here because I spoke out in favor of Stalin!* They turn to the third guy, who's sitting there saying nothing, and ask him what he's in for. He answers, *I'm Joseph Stalin!*

"Why do Stasi officers make good taxi drivers? You get in the car, and they already know your name and where you live!

"Why do the Stasi work together in groups of three? You need one who can read, one who can write and a third to keep an eye on the two intellectuals!"

Glasses and Baby Face hardly looked amused, but they let him keep going.

"In all seriousness, comrades, I would like to recite to you from our countryman Johann Wolfgang von Goethe—that is, if the aristocratic *von* is permissible to you, *mein Herren*—and his masterpiece concerning the German soul, *Faust*."

Peter could feel the moment coming. They had caught him at last, and with him, everyone at the cabaret. If these were his last few minutes at Kabarett Zusammen, he'd better make them count. He allowed himself a moment to prepare:

Count to ten.

Tap each finger on the leg.

Take two deep breaths.

And he began.

> *Then give me back that time of pleasures,*
> *While yet in joyous growth I sang,*
> *When, like a fount, the crowding measures*
> *Uninterrupted gushed and sprang!*
> *Then bright mist veiled the world before me,*
> *In opening buds a marvel woke,*
> *As I the thousand blossoms broke,*
> *Which every valley richly bore me!*
> *I nothing had, and yet enough for youth*
> *Joy in Illusion, ardent thirst for Truth.*

Give, unrestrained, the old emotion,
The bliss that touched the verge of pain,
The strength of Hate, Love's deep devotion,
O, give me back my youth again!

Even the two Stasi goons had to applaud Peter's recitation. Glasses reached under his lens and seemed to be wiping away a tear, just before he made his announcement.

"Well done, young man. I love Goethe. Don't you, Dieter? Yes. However! This establishment is now ceasing operations, due to seditious activities against the Party. Will everyone stand and line up in front of me, please? Kindly take out your identification papers. Quickly now."

The cellar exploded into panic. Chairs fell over and tables were pushed aside as people stupidly tried to hide under them. There was only one exit, up the stairs, and that was blocked by the two Stasi officers. In the mayhem, Peter and Angelika were nowhere to be seen.

"Where's Peter?" asked Renate.

"How should I know?" Rudi's annoyance belied his preoccupation with finding Angelika. "What am I, his babysitter?"

PETER

The thing about being arrested is what it brings into tack-sharp focus, and what other things—self-will, alibis, the names you swore you'd never give—turn into an overcooked mash. The survival instinct counts for a lot. You cajole, you plead, you try to please your captors so they will take pity on you as the helpless victim of circumstance you believe yourself to be. The body's systems go dormant. Attention becomes hyper-real.

The thing Peter noticed as he was led away was how much tighter the handcuff was on his right hand than on his left. He kept trying to shimmy his watchband under the cuff so it wouldn't chafe so badly. He became obsessively focused on the metal on his skin. Not the van they put him in, disguised as a bread delivery vehicle, arranged into tiny prison cells inside. Not the total darkness and the way the too-short cell forced him to twist his knees to the side. Not the shouting of the other kids in the other cells, the swearing or the sound of Renate—he was sure it was her—softly crying.

In fact, other than the handcuff debacle, Peter was strangely calm. *All right,* he thought. *You knew this was coming. And here you are. Isn't this why you did it, after all? You could have stayed reciting Goethe or doing Brecht in small productions, FDJ skits, student competitions, but only because they allowed you to, because they control every word you say. You decided not to go along. You made the decision not to lie. And you're not going to now.*

"Shut the hell up back there!" The officers in the front of the van rapped on the grate dividing it from the cells. The voices turned to whispers, and there was nothing left to shout at. The endless drive drained the fight out of the captives. The shouts and screams became mutters, with only the occasional outburst. Soon the hours of driving, the hum of the road, the shifting engine became hypnotic. Now Peter could distinguish the voices of the others in the truck. *Renate. Günter. Arno.*

There was one other voice. It was a girl's voice, speaking in a language he'd only heard on television, during the Eichmann trial. She spoke to the rhythm of the van's wheels on the pavement. It must have been a prayer.

Peter's heart sank. It was Angelika. She shouldn't have gotten caught up in all of this. He could bear it, and so could Renate. They'd talked about it openly, planned for this eventuality. But Angelika was there to sing her folk songs. To remember. Not to protest.

At Kabarett Zusammen, Peter may have been the force, the laughing fist, the catharsis and the sweat. But Angelika was the whisper, the birdsong, the wind and the conscience. Her songs were a reminder of what can be.

Soon hers was the only voice in the van. Even the thugs in the front left her alone. As she sang, Peter calmed his breathing, repeating the names of the others who were here: *Renate. Angelika. Günter. Arno.* He'd finally grown still enough to slip the watchband between the handcuff and his skin.

"*Maus,*" he whispered, "can you hear me?"

"Yes, *Katze.*"

"This is all my fault. I got caught up in the freedom of the moment. But it's over now, I know that. I pushed it too far. I exposed us all to this. And I'm so sorry."

"Don't you dare," she reproved. "I don't think you went far enough for those bastards! How else are we going to be free, unless we speak?"

"But they're going to give us hell. They're going to ask about your mother. Aren't you worried?"

"No, Peter, I'm fine. It was the waiting that was killing me. My mother didn't raise me to shrink back. You have to take care of yourself now. Get yourself to Hollywood somehow. My path is my own. This is just the beginning."

The shriek of a garage door rolling up woke Peter, then the opening and slamming of each cell door.

Renate. Slam.

Angelika. Slam.

Günter. Slam.

Arno. Slam.

Finally he saw a pinprick of light at the back of the van, and his door opened. He was hurled out by his cuffed wrists into a blinding light. He tried to shield his eyes, but the person holding his cuffs wouldn't let him lift his hands. Peter blinked again and again to acclimate to the light as he heard his name being given, details of the arrest, numbers and more numbers—but he couldn't concentrate. The light made his head pound. His knees ached so badly he could hardly stand. He was intolerably thirsty. The damn cuff had slipped back off his watchband.

"Head down!" Someone behind him pushed the back of Peter's head. He watched his shoes advance—left, right, left, right—on the colorless linoleum until he was turned abruptly to the left. He stood in front of a painted metal door. The gear turning the bar mechanism clanked into place, and he was shoved inside a cell.

He took notice, yes, of the thin mattress on the sagging metal cot, the floor space only half as wide as his body, and the seatless metal toilet in the corner. But all Peter cared about in this moment was the key fitting inside the handcuffs and the blessed relief of shedding them.

The prison guard returned with a box and demanded all of Peter's possessions. Wallet. Loose change. Wristwatch.

"Will I get these back? The watch was a gift from my Omi."

He was answered with a chilly silence and a tossed uniform, tied up into a packet with string.

"OK, thanks. I'll change later."

"You'll change now, and put the clothes in the box."

All right, here I am, he thought, *and this is happening, as I knew it would. The question is, What am I going to do about it?*

It was a bland office with a large particleboard desk, trim painted seafoam green, a vaguely mod wallpaper from floor to ceiling. An aluminum gooseneck lamp arched impotently on the bare desk. Peter sat in a chair made for a middle schooler, his legs hiked up to his chest. The adrenaline from the arrest had worn off. He bounced his foot to stay awake.

The crack of the door handle startled Peter, and a man and a woman entered the room. The woman was thin, her blouse crumpled, with yellow pit stains. She sat in the corner and set up a stenograph machine. The man sat at the desk in a mismatched suit, a crooked olive-and-navy-striped tie. He leaned over on the arm of his chair. Even his glasses were cockeyed. *I wonder if his bathroom mirror's at the same angle,* Peter thought with a chortle.

"Is something amusing, comrade?"

"No."

"I hear you like to make jokes, is this correct?"

Peter thought it might be better not to answer that question.

The man folded his hands on the desk and breathed out heavily. "Peter Möser-Fleischmann, I am Inspector Linden. I have here your application for emigration to the West." The man opened a folder and slid a paper across the desk to Peter. "Is this your handwriting?"

"Ja."

"Why do you want to go to the West, Peter?"

"My family is there."

"But you're an independent young man. Living on your own, almost through school. And all of your friends are here. Right in this building, as it happens." The woman handed Inspector Linden a stack of papers, and he shuffled them, looking at their headings one by one. "You're very popular at the cabaret. They were all speaking of you. What is family compared to such friends?"

"Family's more important."

"Is that what your family thinks of you?"

"Of course."

"They left you behind, didn't they—when they all defected?"

"We were going through a lot. And if you people hadn't built that Wall—"

"Every single one of them," he tut-tutted. "Your own mother. She could have stayed with you after the divorce, cared for you. But she had . . . shall we say . . . other preoccupations?"

Peter looked at the floor. "Don't you say a word about my mother."

"I see here that your mother was institutionalized for psychosis. Did you know she was a manic-depressive? That she had . . . delusions?"

Peter folded his arms and rocked back on the little stool.

"No, I see you didn't. But it's to be expected with a past like hers. Tell me, when did she explain to you that she was a committed Nazi?"

"She didn't."

"But you must have known. Your father, too. Didn't you?"

Peter raised his eyebrows at Inspector Linden. "Everyone here is touched by it somehow."

The inspector ignored him. "You want to go to the West to be near them. To be like them. I hear that Nazis run pretty free over there. You must want to return to your fascist roots."

"*Fascist*," said Peter. "It feels so good to say, doesn't it? So satisfying, the way it fills the mouth."

"Careful what you say, Peter."

"Words like that make shallow people feel sophisticated. But people like you only have a list of fifteen words or so to make up your whole vocabulary. I learned them all in grammar school. Just mix and match."

Inspector Linden opened a desk drawer and rifled around. "*Shallow*, as you say. No, I may not be sophisticated enough to recite Goethe. I am just a bureaucrat. I have no power. But I do have a stamp. And—oh, look—I have another stamp."

He put both stamps in front of Peter.

"If I use *this* stamp, you'll get your emigration. We don't need people like you here, anyway. You're tearing down what we are trying to build. You'll have a fully legal status in the Federal Republic, and you'll renounce your citizenship in the GDR. But you'll be robbing the state of its vital labor. So I'm afraid—oh my—that this stamp means we extradite your parents and bring them back here to take your place. Your father will serve prison time. Your brother will be fine. He's been serving his duty quite well, especially in giving us the address of the cabaret. But of course, your mother will be recommitted. She needs more treatment for her . . . condition.

"Or I could use this *other* stamp and deny your emigration. Underneath your application here is your confession, already filled out. All it needs is your signature, your consent. You would serve *your* time, for sedition and other things. But as for your family—we would turn a blind eye. Because family is, as you say, more important than anything."

There was a quick knock, and a young lackey in an ill-fitting shirt pushed the door open. In walked a familiar personage.

It was Uncle Martin, holding his hat in both hands.

"*Guten Morgen*, Comrade Fleischmann," said the inspector. "I'll leave you two alone to talk."

"Pfft, Uncle Martin," said Peter, rubbing his bleary eyes. "I should have known you were part of this."

"You can't think I had something to do with you being arrested, Peter? I'm here to help you!"

"Showing up at my apartment? Hidden cameras? Roping in Rudi to inform on me? Your help is probably why I'm in here."

"That's a terrible thing to say, Peter. But we'll put that aside for a minute. It's a shame about your Omi. I'm sorry you were not able to attend her funeral yesterday."

The bottom dropped out beneath Peter. "Don't talk about my Omi."

Martin ignored him. "Poor Frau Möser, her heart giving out like that. The chaos in that little apartment must have been too much for her."

Peter clenched his jaw, his fists, tensed every muscle in his body. He turned red, and hot tears filled his eyes. "I said, don't talk about Omi. Don't even think about her. She saw right through you."

"Well. That's a terrible thing to say about your family. And you haven't even asked about your own mother. Why is that?"

"What do you want with me, Uncle Martin? I'm just a kid."

"You don't believe that. You haven't been acting like one. Your girlfriend certainly doesn't think so. And the Party doesn't care, anyway. Kids are the future of the Party."

"I don't want to be the future of the Party. What if this whole time, I just wanted to think my own thoughts? Create something meaningful? What if all I wanted was to be left the hell alone to live my life?"

"But it's not only your life to live. We all have to recognize that we're part of something bigger and more important than just us."

"Well, what if I don't want bigger, Uncle Martin? What if I want smaller? What if I'm not interested in walls and marches and the *Freie Deutsche Jugend* or building real Socialism?"

"Oh, it's very simple, Peter. It's a question of being on the right side, and you have to choose a side. You're either a fascist or an anti-fascist. There is no middle ground. Your brother knows this. Your father, well . . . he might have to learn that in a prison cell. It's really up to you."

So here was the choice before him: Sign a false confession, go to prison and let his family live in peace. Or buy his own freedom at his family's expense. Either way, he was giving the Party what they wanted. He read the charges against him, all laughable.

Peter leaned into the light and looked into Martin's eyes. It wasn't only fear he saw there. It was fear mingled with delight at having won a game. *If you know you live in truth,* Vera Schenning had said, *they cannot affect you with their lies.*

"Give me the confession," said Peter. "I might even have some things to add."

Peter's trial on Monday morning lasted all of twenty minutes. His false confession was the only evidence provided, and he was not given the chance to speak. *Guilty.* That was that. Martin caught up with Peter in the parking lot as he was being escorted toward a paneled truck.

"I spoke to an old school friend," he said. "They were able to get your sentence reduced."

"Really? I guess that's good."

"You're lucky. You could've gotten years. Instead you'll serve three months and then be put into the Volkspolizei."

"Me? In the police? Is that a joke?"

"Hardly. They'll be able to keep an eye on you that way."

"Can't I stay in jail instead?" Peter gave a sardonic chuckle.

"Very funny," said Martin, clapping Peter on the shoulder. "See you in the spring."

JUNE 1962

RUDI

In a few days Rudi would either be graduating from the *Hauptschule* or repeating the year and cramming a lifetime of opposing pedagogy into finals week. As soon as exams were over, he walked to the bakery, breathing sigh after sigh of relief. At least it was over. For now. Rudi sprang on his toes at the thought that, if only by a hair, he might never have to set foot in a school again.

In his hands he held a box of end-of-day pastries from Bäckerei Antoinette. Almost a year had passed since he and his father had landed in their tiny flat, alone, eating stale pastries out of lack. Now they were comfortable, or at least catching up to where they had been. But Rudolf's quietude had deepened six months ago when Ilse had walked through the door and Oma had died. Rudi's mother was a phantom, and though Rudolf's devotion to her was evident, the color had gone out of him. He hardly touched the piano, and even Rudi hesitated to put a record on, the silence was so brittle.

Rudi fantasized about going back to the East, back to his old life, to the FDJ. He had no purpose here. Uncle Martin came to the apartment every now and then to check on his sister, but since Peter's arrest they had nothing much to say to each other now except awkward conversation about camera gear and photo technique. Rudi would cross over in a heartbeat but for two things: the danger of jail for *Republikflucht* and a sense that he couldn't leave his mother.

"Vati," he said in a softish voice as he came through the door, "I'm home. I think I passed, but I'm not sure about the history exam. . . ."

His father sat on the piano bench, facing away from the instrument, leaning over with his elbows on his knees.

Rudi's mouth went dry. "What's wrong? Something with Mutti?"

"Eichmann's been executed," said Rudolf. "They hanged him, cremated him, scattered his ashes in the sea. That's it." He cast his hands apart and fluttered his fingers. "Nothing more remains."

Rudi was indifferent. "He got what he deserved."

"Yes, at minimum. And yet there are tens of thousands more Eichmanns. Here, there . . . everywhere. Always, until my entire generation is gone. And then?"

"Here, Vati, let me make you some tea. Do you want a Berliner?"

Indeed, Rudi did pass his exams, and graduation day came. Rudi and his parents were up early, more active than he'd seen them in months, but the fuss felt pointless.

"Rudi, aren't you ready? Please, I need to shave," Rudolf called through the bathroom door. "At least let me get my razor, and I'll use the kitchen sink."

"It's no big deal, Vati," Rudi said, slapping a bit more aftershave on his neck. He emerged, toothbrush in hand. "It's just a *Hauptschule* diploma. It's not like the Abitur."

"Still, it's a big day."

Rudi brushed his teeth in the kitchen, and Ilse came in, fumbling with the back of her pink Bakelite earring. Her glamour was gone, but her thrifting prowess was not. Like everything about her now, the tones of her pale yellow cotton dress and flat shoes were quiet.

"You look nice, Mutti," said Rudi.

"Thank you, *Liebschen*." She smiled and stood by the window. "Marti is going to meet us for lunch after your ceremony. Isn't that nice?"

"Oh." Rudi put his arm around his mother's shoulder, and they watched the passersby on the street below.

Rudolf came out, drying his face, and gave his wife a kiss on the cheek. The corners of her mouth lifted just a little. "We should be at the school at half past nine," said Rudolf, looking at his watch. He unlatched the window and pushed the sashes open to either side. He and Ilse leaned out and looked onto the street as the breeze blew in.

She closed her eyes and let it ruffle her hair. "Summer's coming," Ilse said.

"I wish Peter were here," said Rudolf into the West Berlin sun. "And Oma."

Rudi interrupted the moment. "Well, let's get this over with," he said, slipping on his shoes—polished, like Ilse had taught him—and the three of them made their way toward the school.

Rudi slung his camera across his chest and carried his folded-up graduation gown under his arm. He wished he had worn a short-sleeved dress shirt instead—or at least had waited until he got to school to put on his tie. As it was, he was beginning to sweat under his arms and along his waistband. The gown slipped a little from his grasp and sailed away behind him in the wind.

Rudolf jogged after it and caught the gown before it found its way under the next tram. He folded it badly and handed it back to his son. Rudi balled it back under his elbow.

"This stupid thing. Why can't a shirt and tie be enough? All this for a meaningless diploma."

Rudolf stopped him, took his son by the shoulders and said, "Let today be special. If not for you, then for us."

Rudi didn't want to look in his father's eyes. The pain there was pain that Rudi had caused. This should have been another in a series of his mother's celebrations, a full apartment, he and Peter telling stories, arms around their girlfriends. A table full of wrapped presents and envelopes full of cash and his freshly baked lebkuchen. Maybe Peter would have been able to hide his involvement in the cabaret just long enough to take his Abitur. Now he wouldn't even graduate from POS 5. He would be spending this day manning the Anti-Fascist Protection Barrier from a watchtower somewhere. Maybe he was looking through a pair of binoculars right now at his sad father, his diminished mother and his treacherous brother on the way to a barely achieved graduation.

"*Es tut mir leid, Vati,*" he said. "I'm sorry. Let's go."

Rudi lined up with his class in the hallway outside the auditorium, casting his glance over these strangers. He knew he'd never talk to any of them again. The school newspaper had been fun, and he'd gotten to hone his skills some, but they were so unserious. Such . . . *kids.* Rudi was ready to move on.

Over the last six months, he had told himself he had no reason to regret turning Peter in, but his absence gnawed at Rudi, made him fidgety. Their whole life, every roll call, every assembly, every lineup in every hallway had seen the two of them together. *Twins against the world*—but *P* came before *R* in the alphabet, and all of Rudi's memories involved the back of his brother's blond head.

There had always been that nagging seed of resentment, wanting Peter to trip on something and fall flat on his face so that Rudi could rise. And now that had happened, and Rudi had caused it. A fissure ran through Rudi's mind, glee on one side, shame on the other; self-righteousness on one side, self-loathing on the other.

A state of being split.

The pianist began the processional, and Rudi shuffled in with the fifty other students. He took his place in the middle of the auditorium. Nothing distinguished him in the ceremony. He would give no speeches, make no mark. Rudi stared through the chorus as they sang a song about spreading their wings or some such. On that night a year ago in Hamburg, Mahalia Jackson had made him question the state of his soul. This music, like every moment of this ceremony, was blank.

Suddenly he heard his name being called on the microphone, then a burst of applause from the audience. "Rudolf Möser-Fleischmann," the Direktor called again. "Please, Rudi, would you come up to the podium?"

A bead of sweat rolled down the back of his neck. He panicked to think why he was being singled out. He climbed the stage stairs and stood next to the Direktor, in front of one hundred and fifty strangers.

"Parents, you can see how modest he is. He was not expecting this award."

Award?

"Rudi, you have endured much this year. What a brave young man, fleeing oppression in the East, starting in a new school—a new country!—narrowly avoiding being trapped behind the Wall, separation from your own . . . your twin brother, yes? And then going on to serve on the school newspaper and capture, for generations of future students, a photographic record of this extraordinary year. In recognition of your bravery as a refugee and your growth in the art of photography, we present to you this Exceptional Citizen Award. Congratulations, Rudi!"

The Direktor clapped him on the back and handed the stunned boy a wood and metal plaque. One of the teachers gave him a bouquet and put an enamel pin on the breast of his robe. They turned him by the shoulders toward a camera with a huge flashbulb, and for a second he was blinded. Rudi blinked and saw his parents on their feet, applauding him.

He thought he might throw up.

Rudi made his way back to his seat to the applause of the auditorium. The Direktor's microphone gave a shriek of piercing feedback that reverberated through Rudi's entire body. An award? His photographs were utilitarian at best, the work of a lucky dilettante who rarely knew what to point his camera at. He wasn't brave for living in the West. Like everything else in his life, it had simply *happened* to him. He'd adapted, all right—to the plans of others, while someone else had paid the price. This award was a joke.

He put the plaque and flowers under the seat in front of him, rose slowly and began to walk out of the auditorium as heads turned away from the class president giving her speech. Rudolf stood and followed him, and when Rudi got to the door of the school, he bolted. His father called after him, but Rudi was out of his sight in an instant.

He ran all the way to the checkpoint in his graduation gown, his cap long gone, camera bouncing against his side. He still had his visa in his pocket. Maybe the guards could help him find out where his brother was stationed. He'd go to him and unburden himself, confess everything he'd done. Maybe Peter would hate him. That was all right. At least Rudi would get this all off his chest and find closure. Maybe he really could trade places with his twin—switch out the photograph on the visa, let Peter go to the West, and recapture his old life in the East, where he had some significance.

Rudi was forming a pretty good plan when he saw his uncle Martin in the distance, coming through the zigzag of barricades on the Eastern side. He lifted his hand in greeting and tipped his hat to his nephew.

Charles came out of the guard booth and shook Rudi's hand.

"Well! Here's the graduate! Congrats, man! What's the hurry?"

"Oh . . . I had to get out of there . . . ," Rudi bumbled. "Too many speeches."

"True enough," said Charles. "Look, *hier kommt dein Oncle!* How's my German sounding?"

"*Gut.* But I— Charles, can I ask you a question?"

"Sure, kid."

"How do you know when you've gone too far?"

"Too far? In what way?"

"What if someone doesn't *mean* to—"

"I'm sorry, Rudi, would you excuse me a moment and step aside?" Charles interrupted. "I need a word with my colleague about our next guest here."

Rudi moved to the curb and greeted his uncle. "*Hallo,* Uncle Martin."

"*Guten Morgen,* Rudi! I'm surprised to see you—did you just come from school? You didn't have to meet me here. I was going to join you at the restaurant."

Charles emerged from the booth, and Martin displayed his visa. "I'm sorry, sir," said Charles, "something's not right with your papers."

"Now wait a moment, I have a visa," Martin protested.

"We have reason to believe you've been engaging in illegal activity in the American sector," said the other guard.

"My buddy here can get to the bottom of it for us," said Charles. "Isn't that right, Jim?"

"That's right, Captain," Jim responded.

"Good man," Charles commended him.

"Look here," said Martin. "I've been through this checkpoint a hundred times. I have a perfectly good visa. Can't you read it?"

"What do you mean, *can't I read it*?" Charles grimaced.

"I . . . I mean no offense. You're that friend of my brother-in-law's, aren't you? My nephew is right over there. Don't you recognize me?"

"I don't know, after a while you all start to look the same. But"— Charles got up close—"on closer examination, you do have a familiar face. Yes, as a matter of fact, I do recognize you."

"That's right, why don't you let me through? I have my nephew's graduation lunch to get to, after all."

"Yes, I was hoping to go myself. Shame I'm on duty. But, you see, I've been hard at work on an interesting project, so allow me to tell you a story. You know, seventeen years ago, I was here in Germany as a soldier. Berlin sure looked a lot different then. A lot can happen in seventeen years, isn't that right?"

"Yes, I imagine so," Martin said. He shifted his valise to the other hand and fiddled with his hat.

"Imagine this: You come back from a war, only to be treated as a second-class citizen by a country you almost died for. You protest that treatment by simply sitting at a segregated lunch counter. And then you watch your wife get beaten for it, and you sit at her bedside as she dies from her injuries . . . and you realize that none of those animals who killed her know the price you paid to keep them free."

"That's unfortunate, but we all lost a lot in the—"

"See, sometimes, at night, I get haunted by things I saw in the war. Vivid, it comes back to me, like it's still happening. My battalion stops at the gates of a strange place. I get out of my vehicle—we're delivering water-purification equipment, see—and I step into the deepest circle of hell.

"Someone tells me we're in a concentration camp. *Buchenwald,* they call it, *beech forest,* like a name out of a fairy tale. Only there are no trees. Instead I see bodies, everywhere, and this is six days *after* the camp was liberated. I can't imagine what it was like for those poor bastards who got there first.

"Well, out of the corner of my eye, I see this weasel of a man over behind a pile. He's sleek and filled out, not like the other living skeletons. And he's changing his clothes. Imagine that, changing clothes in the middle of an operation like this. And I sidle up and see that he's getting out of an old uniform, and it's an SS uniform, and he's putting on prisoner clothes and shoving things in his pocket.

"Do you know, that man had the nerve to come up and thank me? For *saving his people,* he says. And I say, *Who are your people?* And he says, *I'm a German Communist, part of the Buchenwald resistance.* So I send him to get some rations while I go and have a look at that uniform. I tear the name patch out of the lining. Ask some of the inmates if they knew of an SS man named M. Fleischmann."

Charles looked again at Martin's visa. "*M. Fleischmann.* They tell me he was one of the most brutal guards in the place. See, I knew you looked familiar!"

"That's ridiculous," Martin scoffed. "How many M. Fleischmanns do you think there are in Germany?"

"Well, now we come to the nature of my project," said Charles. "I've been observing you for a few months now, M.F. And I never do forget a face, especially when there's two of them on one neck. This whole time, you've been using your nephew to spy on his own family, convincing him he was serving a righteous cause. But you crossed over an international boundary here to do it, and suddenly the rules you're used to operating under no longer apply."

"You think you know," Martin protested. "But everything I did was for my family. They were going down the wrong path. I didn't want them to get hurt."

"You *snake*. Using a kid, making him think he's a good person for informing on his own brother. Not just a snake, but a chameleon—changing your colors to suit your environment. Well, now we'll see how you adapt to a prison cell. Jim, get this man out of my sight."

Charles thrust the visa into the hand of his partner and restrained Martin's wrists as a car drove up to collect him. His business finished, Charles turned to Rudi. "Now, Rudi, where were we?"

But Rudi was already walking away, fast. He ignored Charles calling after him. Without his uncle's backing, his own visa would be meaningless. He had precisely twenty seconds to cross the Eastern border before Martin was hauled off to a United States military prison. The Eastern guards were trying to understand what the tumult was all about at that American checkpoint, and, thus distracted, they let Rudi cross into East Berlin.

PETER

The water flowed between the banks of the River Spree, noiseless beneath the volume of people coursing along the border fence. There was no pushing, no coercion, just a desire to arrive, to open out onto the designated Platz. Rumor had it that a concert was about to take place in the West, one that could be seen and heard and reveled in from this side of the Wall.

Peter was dressed in his drab green border guard uniform, gun slung over his shoulder, walking to the tower to begin his shift. Kids gave him a wide berth, as if he were a leper.

As though you're not next, Peter thought. Someone spat on him. Peter spun around to see who it was—but everyone had turned their faces away from him.

He said, loud enough for the spitter to hear, "Hey, idiots, I'm with *you.* Don't do anything stupid."

He arrived at his watchtower and climbed the ladder. Up in the booth, he saluted his partner, Horst, and made all the usual niceties, then grabbed his binoculars and began his watch.

"What a crowd today, huh?" said Horst. "What do you think that's all about?"

"You haven't heard?" Peter said. "Supposed to be a concert on the roof of that building there."

"No shit? They're going to try to watch from here?"

"Yup."

Peter panned the crowd, remembering what civilian life had felt like, before the prison beatings, the cold of his cell, the hunger that almost took his mind. His jaw worked back and forth as he tried to shove away the memory of sitting on the bench in the interrogation room for hours, trying to claim control over his own thoughts while the Stasi played their psychological games. *Zersetzung.* The Undoing.

And then there had been the shock at looking up and seeing his own uncle, not pleading his case and making deals, as at his arrest, but behind the desk, part of the apparatus itself, dangling more threats to make him comply, to convince him that coercion was equal to choice. He clung desperately to good memories, to the feeling of deep laughter, the hum of a full theater, the dinner with Vati after he won the drama award. Sometimes the energy it took to retain what was real made shadows take on flesh. Once, after they didn't let him sleep for forty-eight hours, he swore that Oma was in his cell, making him herring on toast and offering him a drag of her Gauloise.

Peter continued to scan the river, the bridge. The crowd was growing louder. He knew what was next. Men in uniforms just like his would begin to corral the kids into inescapable corners, grabbing their hands behind their backs in restraints, pushing them into windowless vans disguised as bread trucks. The ones who shouted the loudest, who cared most about being free to enjoy an open-air concert with their friends, they were about to get it the worst.

"Selfish bastards," said his comrade, a sniveling middle-aged man who endlessly picked his face. "Don't they know what the rest of us are sacrificing? What makes them think they're better than us?"

Maybe if everyone minded their own business, Peter thought. He hardly spoke to Horst. He was positive he was an informant.

Horst drew his lunch out of a paper bag and began munching. "Bet we'll get some attempts with this crowd," he said, still chewing. A crumb of white cheese fell on his chest. "I'll call in a unit."

Peter nodded as Horst radioed the alert. Escape attempts were less frequent than they'd been in autumn, but now that the weather was warming, people would try the river again. Horst reached for his gun in the corner of the booth and figured he'd better inspect it. Someone might try to cross the border today.

RUDI

What next? Rudi wondered. He took the S-Bahn to his old neighborhood but decided not to get off there. He got off by the Oberbaum Bridge instead. *How do I find Peter?*

Jutting out impotently from the endless stretch of the Anti-Fascist Protection Barrier were the remains of a little staircase that had once been someone's front stoop. He peeked over the top, like a kid trying to see above the kitchen table, and could just see the river beyond. A chilly breeze reminded him of the night the Wall went up. Rudi pulled his graduation gown tighter without zippering it. Strange how his head never felt cold, but his neck—now that was something worth protecting.

He'd hidden the Rolleiflex from his father under the gown so he could take pictures after the ceremony. After all, it was too good a camera to let molder in its box. He lifted it to his eye and began to capture his surroundings.

Rudi hadn't calculated where he was actually going to stay tonight. The apartment was gone now. After Oma's death and Peter's imprisonment, it had been requisitioned by the Party and given to a suitable family. Martin had arranged for Ilse to come and get the last of their things out. Martin took all of Peter's notebooks and medals. He gave Rudi back his movie poster.

A ferry boat passed beneath the bridge, and Rudi thought of calling Angelika. He lowered the camera for a moment and stared into the distance.

Rudi could have switched the photographs in their passports, it was true. It was possible there was still some way to fudge their papers. But now he second-guessed his impulsive border crossing. *Maybe Peter doesn't want to leave. I mean, it's not like he's tried to contact* me *since he was arrested. He's probably changed his mind.*

And besides—is it my fault? My responsibility? Rudi questioned himself as he lifted the camera.

The flowing river. *People take their own risks. That's not on me.*

Click.

The clouds passing overhead. *It's time for me to think about what I need now.*

Click.

Two boats crossing each other as one went under the bridge. *Who's going to be in my corner?*

Click.

All this time I've been thinking about everyone else. How to help them. How to protect Peter, encourage him to think of his future, to stop messing with bad people. How to help Vati reckon with his past.

Click.

Well, I am tired of helping everyone else. No one seems to want my help anyway. So now it's my turn.

Click.

Rudi suddenly had the biggest craving for a Berliner, and he might never see the inside of his bakery again. All because of Peter.

PETER

In Vopo training—brief though it was—Peter turned out to have great aim. He could have been assigned some crummy street patrol, but they put him on border monitoring instead. At least up in the tower, the city wasn't closing in on him. He had a 360-degree view of East and West.

The last escape had been a week ago. Just as he'd predicted in his little notebook, people found the most creative ways to flee. Sometimes they were successful. Often they were stopped by a bullet, and stopping them was supposed to be his job. Being right by the river meant a lot of people tried his crossing point, either by jumping in the river or by leaving footprints across the pristine sand in the kill zone. Peter's partner was eager to stop them but at least knew he was a bad shot. Instead, Horst became something of a backseat driver.

"Get the imperialist bastard," Horst would shout. "Serves him right."

The orders were *shoot to kill.* Peter made sure to always miss.

Most of the people who tried to cross the Wall were still kids, twenty, twenty-four years old. College students, apprentices. People like Renate and Günter. One of the guys who'd been caught had even been to the cabaret a few times. Peter didn't hear about it in the news but through whispers—escape attempts didn't really make the newspaper. The Party could brook no bad press. When the victims *were* mentioned, it was as enemies of the State, people without concern for their fellow citizens. Reprobates who were so in love with fascism that they'd put their own desires ahead of their comrades', just like Horst said.

Peter stood and aimed his binoculars once more at the crowd, then turned to face the river. He saw the line of Vopos facing the crowd, hands poised on their truncheons.

Count to ten.

Tap each finger on the leg.

Take two deep breaths.

"I've got to relieve myself," he told his comrade.

"You can't just piss over the ledge? That's what I do."

How revolting, thought Peter. He turned around and began to descend the ladder. "I'll be right back."

RUDI

By the entrance to the bridge, Rudi could make out a mass of people approaching. There were hundreds, maybe even a thousand. It wasn't a holiday, as far as he knew; no reason for a parade; no signs or banners to mark a Party march. Still, they came, murmuring like a beehive. Rudi looked up the street the other way. A phalanx of Vopos came from the other direction. He wasn't sure, but it looked like they were holding billy clubs.

Would they try to storm the checkpoint and cross the bridge? No. They were calm, nothing like a mob. They passed the checkpoint and kept walking toward Treptower Park, opposite the tall office building on the Western side.

Then Rudi heard the sirens coming. A bank of police cars met the procession head-on. Rudi raised his camera, grabbing careful scenes of the fray. He perched himself on the banister to get as clear a shot as possible. The Volkspolizei emerged from their cars, batons in hand, and Rudi felt sick to his stomach. He didn't want violence. *I'm a man of peace,* he thought, *and my country protects peace.* Whatever that crowd was, the State would have a good reason to disperse it.

The crowd began to fold in on itself as it turned back, but another bank of cars headed people off from behind. Several vans—a dozen or more—parked behind the Vopo cars. The police surrounded the crowd completely.

And then the beatings started.

"No!" people cried out. "What are they doing? They're hitting them! No!"

A smattering of kids on the fringes managed to peel off and

scurry down the side streets. But as for the rest, it didn't matter how much they pushed against the police. The Vopos rained blows on those who resisted; they cuffed the others and herded them five at a time into the unmarked vans. The screaming was incessant. A gunshot warned the crowd to settle down. These weren't revolutionaries; they were only kids on their way to do kid stuff, but in this moment, they were enemies of the Socialist order.

Rudi kept shooting until he finished the roll of film. He reloaded the camera and began to shoot again, but in his periphery he saw an unusual movement.

A man, a border guard, was climbing down from a watchtower built right up against the Wall. Before he reached the bottom, he jumped over the Wall, ran along the bank and dove headfirst into the River Spree.

Rudi couldn't believe he was getting this on camera: a border guard defecting, using the melee on the other side of the Anti-Fascist Protection Barrier to cover his own escape.

The guard's hat came off and revealed a head of blond hair, cut high and tight. He looked familiar. Rudi pulled away from the lens—no, he could see closer through it. Was he seeing this right?

It was Peter. The escaping guard was his own twin brother.

Rudi kept shooting. A shrill whistle blew, shouts from a pair of Vopos, a siren from the watchtower. The people on the bridge ran to the edge and pressed up against Rudi so hard, he thought they'd push him right over the rail.

"*Halt!*" came a voice over a loudspeaker from the tower. Peter did not stop.

"*Halt! Stehenbleiben, oder ich schiesse!* Stop! Or I will shoot!"

Then a shot rang out.

PETER

Peter paddled faster. Bullets began to fall around him like jumping fish. The current was bringing him closer to the bridge, slowing his pace as he was pulled diagonally instead of straight across. The whole span of the River Spree was East German territory. But once he touched the other bank, Peter would be on Western ground, out of reach of GDR authority.

A crowd on the Western bank gathered, cheering for Peter, urging him on. A few people ran down to the bank, broke branches off riverside trees, and held them out to him as he desperately reached for one after another and missed. An East German police boat was speeding up the river against the stream. Peter was running out of strength.

RUDI

*I*f they catch him, thought Rudi, *it'll be his second offense. He'll be in prison for years.*

He wanted to help Peter, but what could he do? There was no way out of the crowd. So he kept taking pictures.

Suddenly, one shot. Two.

Three. *Four.*

And the sound of the bullet finding flesh was close enough to hear.

Rudi's mind was on fire. Blood encircled Peter, but Rudi couldn't see where his brother had been hit. The exhausted swimmer slowed and did not make another stroke. He drifted, closer and closer to the police boat.

And then a group on the Western bank put their branches together, catching Peter as the current spun him into their trap. Three men reached out for him and pulled him ashore.

Peter was in the West.

Peter's eyes were open.

And Rudi had captured it all on film.

AUTHOR'S NOTE

We learn from history that we do not learn from history.
—Georg Wilhelm Friedrich Hegel

Berliners emerged from questions I had while writing my first novel, *What the Night Sings.* I had learned what was next for Jewish survivors of the Holocaust, but what about the perpetrators? What happened to people like Rudolf Möser, a member of the Hitler Youth, who informed on his classmate Gerta Rausch? And then, what of the children of that generation? How are we to learn from a history we cannot change, and not, as Hegel warned, to miss its lessons?

After the Allies failed at their initial attempts to purge Nazism from the populace, East and West Germany took opposite approaches to reckoning with the past. The problem was complex, as every institution in the country was stained—from the smallest village mayoralty to art museums, schools and the national government—and it was logistically impossible to prosecute every citizen.

West Germany, where I was born, chose a policy of democratizing the institutions and reintegrating former Nazis, with the hope of rehabilitation over time. This had mixed success and posed many problems. East Germany, on the other hand, adopted a policy of denial of the mere existence of former Nazis in its population, and the imposition of a new, Communist dictatorship, both to shame the people for their past sins and to claim the moral high ground in opposition to the West. But ultimately, it was Western leader Willy Brandt, and not Eastern leader Walter Ulbricht, who knelt at the Warsaw Ghetto memorial and openly acknowledged Germany's complicity in the murder of millions.

The lessons of the Holocaust are many, and though there is always more to learn, we somehow understand the most important one: we must never get to that place again. Yes, the human race is a brotherhood. That's a charming thing to say, but one of the earliest stories we have about brotherhood, Cain and Abel, is also the story of the first murder. And it repeats throughout history: Cambodia. Rwanda. Burma. China. Ukraine. And we are no exception. No passive solution will suffice to overcome the kind of inhumanity we can enact on each other. So, where to begin?

First: we must refuse to live by lies, especially with our use of words.

In the front of this book, just below the copyright notice, you'll see a line that says "Random House Children's Books supports the First Amendment and celebrates the right to read." Why are the freedoms to speak and read so important? Because, messy as it often is, it is by *speaking* that we learn how to *think*. Often, we either change or confirm what we believe because we hear something coming out of our own mouths. It's by speaking and thinking that we understand the nature of reality itself.

And we need to speak and think, more than ever, precisely because we are in a crisis of reality.

As a follower of the philosopher Georg Hegel, Karl Marx believed in history as a moral force, moving purposefully and inevitably toward a utopian end. Hegel's predecessor, Immanuel Kant, had rejected the Greek-Jewish-Christian notion of a knowable reality (*logos*) for a belief that *nothing* is knowable, and that reality can only be criticized—and dismantled—to achieve a moral end. This is not just a philosophy about history, but a theory about the nature of reality itself. Marx knew that to actualize the goal of Communism would require a total reinvention of society from the top down and bottom up, or as he put it: "[the] ends can be attained only by the forcible overthrow of all existing social conditions." In 1917, the Bolsheviks in Russia took him up on the challenge, and many nations have followed suit, including, in 1949, the German Democratic Republic.

It wasn't possible for Marx to know the real-world outcomes of the theory he and Friedrich Engels had helped to codify. Nothing like the Communism they proposed had ever existed before, nor had the kind of total dictatorship it necessitated—the repression of individual rights, the confiscation of private property, and the silencing of all dissent by eliminating the right to free speech. In the end, the grand experiment cost the lives of at least 100 million people across several countries, including the starvation of four million Ukrainians in the state-instituted famine called the *Holodomor.*

Much is being said nowadays about the need to place limits on the freedom to speak openly, at risk of giving offense. It seems to me extremely cynical to assume that the main reason our fellow citizens might want to speak freely is to cause harm to others. The vast majority of those who wish to assert their right to speak are doing it for a variety of justifiable reasons, ranging from the basic right to live their daily lives and explore what it means to be human to the ever-present need to hold our governments and institutions to account. Millions have considered this a right worth dying for.

Over the last several years, the entire global population has been hit by wave after wave of crisis, which has been seized by opportunists with ready-made solutions to vastly complicated problems. We have seen what lives inside of our compatriots when fear is introduced into the mix. Notice how isolation has disoriented us, making us desperate with loneliness. Notice who is eager to control others' behavior or words or public image. Influencers provoke us into crafting Frankenstein monsters of half the nation; we simply stitch the latest evil trait onto the effigy and drag it into the public square to be burned. We must resist the subtle seduction to reduce our neighbors to low-resolution caricatures, rather than relearn the art of living together freely under a shared framework.

We are a communal species, dependent on each other more than we can fathom. We all desire to be "on the right side" of things, but even with that intention, we acquiesce to wrongdoings, small and large, out of self-preservation, the thread of lost opportunity or prestige, moral superiority, or simply a desire to be left alone. This causes us to be split down the middle of ourselves. And so, echoing the logic of Adolf Eichmann, the average person—a police officer, a schoolteacher, an artist—will excuse himself by stating that he was "just following orders," in hopes that the Machine will not grind him in its gears. He may even come to like the Machine. He may even come to operate it.

We mustn't deceive ourselves into a perverse form of American, or Western, exceptionalism, thinking ourselves incapable of this irresistible aspect of human nature—the desire to suppress the "other." We mustn't excuse our own pet atrocities just because we believe the outcome is morally justified. A free society is messy, always poised on the edge of decay. Like a house, it must be maintained by constantly revisiting and renewing our commitment to each other's freedoms, especially the freedom to speak, to create—yes, even to fail.

Why did Cain killed his brother Abel? Because Cain bitterly resented his brother for possessing what he lacked. Instead of bending the knee and searching out how he could make a better offering to existence—namely, offering himself—Cain could only see his brother standing in the way of what he thought he deserved. That kind of deep resentment is woefully natural for human beings, as many mass movements can attest. That is why, in addition to refusing to live by lies, resentment and offense must be actively resisted. In myself first. And last. And at every point in between.

Maybe you feel it, too: a kind of dim light settling on the world, a slight tremor beneath all things. You suspect that you are in the midst of an era of enormous change. And you didn't ask for any of it. It's overwhelming at times. Words take on different meanings, like "Wordplay," that episode of *The Twilight Zone* where everyone is suddenly speaking in garbled English. You're disoriented, and you feel like you've read this story before, but all around are voices telling you not to believe what you think, see, feel, somehow know to be true.

But you also suspect that you were born at this time for a reason, and that you might even have a part to play. I feel it, too. It's because we are living in one of history's rhymes. But if history rhymes, then it must have poets. Artists can be our guides through the murky woods.

Dissident artists like Czech playwright Václav Havel, Russian author Aleksandr Solzhenitsyn, Chinese artist Ai Weiwei and Cuban performance artist Luis Manuel Otero Alcántara, all of whom survived repressive regimes, political imprisonment and torture, give us a place to begin: First, do not go along with what you know to be false. Second, commit to living in the truth. This doesn't always require a soapbox or a public statement. Sometimes the best resistance is to live a life in which you know that your words, like your thoughts, belong only to you.

GLOSSARY

Abitur: university placement exam

Apfelsaft: apple juice

Banhof: train station

Berliner: literally, a person from Berlin; also, another name for *Pfannkuchen,* a jam-filled doughnut specific to Berlin

Bitte: please; you're welcome

Brauhaus: brewery restaurant

Comrade: in German, *Genosse/Genossen,* a way of addressing a fellow Socialist

Da: yes (Russian да)

Danke/Vielen dank: thank you; thank you very much

Deti: children (Russian дети)

Die deutsche Mutter und ihr erstes Kind: *The German Mother and Her First Child* by Dr. Johanna Haarer. A parenting book that advocated strict detachment from one's children in order to raise committed and dutiful Nazis. After the fall of the Third Reich, the book was reissued without its overt Nazi references. The last edition was published in 1987.

Die Mörder Sind Unter Uns: *The Murderers Are Among Us* (film)

Die Partei hat immer recht: the Party is always right

D-mark, or simply "Mark": the currency of West Germany

Dummkopf: blockhead

Freie Deutsche Jugend (FDJ): Free German Youth, the only approved youth organization in the GDR

Freundschaft: friendship, the official greeting among members of the FDJ and Young Pioneers

Freut mich: nice to meet you

Für Frieden und Freiheit: for peace and freedom, a common slogan in the GDR

Für Frieden und Sozialismus seid bereit! Immer bereit!: For peace and Socialism be ready! Always ready! Official salute of the FDJ

GDR: German Democratic Republic (*Deutsche Demokratische Republik,* or DDR), known colloquially as East Germany

Gruppenleiter: student leader in the FDJ

Hauptschule: standard high school (West Germany)

Hurensohn: son of a bitch

Ich verstehe: I understand

Ich will meine Mutti!: I want my mommy!

Jugendweihe: Socialist coming-of-age ceremony designed to replace Christian confirmation and initiate youth from the Young Pioneers into the FDJ

Kino: movie theater

Konsum: a state-operated grocery-store chain in the GDR

Krimi: television crime drama

Lebkuchen: a soft ginger cookie

Liebchen: little love (term of endearment)

Märchenbrunnen: a fountain in the East Berlin Volkspark, featuring fairy-tale characters

Marzipanstollen: a cake-like pastry made with almonds

Meine Damen und Herren: ladies and gentlemen

Milchbar: café serving frozen treats, like ice cream and milkshakes

Mutti: mommy

Nazirein: literally, free of Nazis. An allusion to the Nazi policy of making Europe *judenrein,* or free of Jews.

Nie wieder Krieg! Nie wieder Faschismus!: Never again war! Never again fascism! Slogans of the Socialist Unity Party (SED)

Oma/Omi: grandma; great-grandma

Ostmark: East German currency, worthless outside of the GDR

Pfennig/Mark: German currency (100 pfennigs = 1 mark)

POS: *Polytechnische Oberschule,* vocational high school

Raus: get out
RIAS: *Rundfunk im amerikanischen Sektor,* a radio and television station
broadcasting across Germany from West Berlin

Sahne: cream
Sandmann: a popular children's television propaganda series in the GDR
Schatz/Schatzi: treasure; little treasure (terms of endearment)
Schülerzeitung: school newspaper
Schwachsinn: bullshit
Settler colonialism: in Socialist theory, a term denoting the takeover of a
region/country by a group that is not indigenous
Setz dich zu mir: sit here by me
Sotto voce: (Italian) in a soft voice
Spätzle: a cross between a noodle and a dumpling

Trümmerfrau: literally, "rubble woman." Women tasked with salvaging and
cleaning the rubble of German cities destroyed in the war

Und Sie: and you

Vati: daddy; dad
Volkskammer: East German parliament

Was stimmt nicht: what's wrong
Weltall Erde Mensch: "Universe, Earth, Man," a book given to every East
German teenager at their coming-of-age ceremony
Weltjugendlied: a song of the FDJ
Wilkommen: welcome
Witze: jokes

Zuckerwürfel: sugar cube
Zusammen: together

In this book, several terms are used that have loaded political connotations
today. Following is a simple framework for understanding these terms without
bias.

Marxism is the philosophy behind Communism*
Communism is the end goal of Marxist philosophy

Socialism is the political system implemented to achieve Communism

Fascism is the practical method of ensuring compliance**

Authoritarian—policies dictated by leadership without input from the people

Totalitarian—the reconstruction of the entire system toward the political goal

A simple way to think of Communism is the government's ownership of all production, in order to ensure equal distribution and eliminate differences in outcome—"from each according to his ability, to each according to his need"* (Karl Marx and Friedrich Engels, *The Communist Manifesto*). Because Communism needs the whole society to work properly, this type of system must be totalizing.

**Fascism, in its broad meaning, does not necessarily connote either left- or right-wing ideology, but strategies of control. The "philosopher of fascism," Giovanni Gentile, illustrated the concept with the image of a bundle of sticks—all sticks must be tied into the bundle, a complete assimilation of the individual into the collective.

RESOURCES

BOOKS

Arendt, Hannah. *Eichmann in Jerusalem*. New York: Viking Press, 1963.

Arendt, Hannah. *The Origins of Totalitarianism*. New York: Schocken, 1951.

The Book of Genesis: Chapter 4.

Funder, Anna. *Stasiland: Stories from Behind the Berlin Wall*. New York: Harper Perennial, 2002.

Havel, Václav. *The Power of the Powerless*. Armonk, NY: M.E. Sharpe, 1985.

Herf, Jeffrey. *Divided Memory: The Nazi Past in the Two Germanys*. Cambridge: Harvard University Press, 1997.

Lewis, Ben. *Hammer and Tickle*. New York: Pegasus Books, 2009.

Lipstadt, Deborah E. *The Eichmann Trial*. New York: Schocken, 2011.

Morehouse, Maggi M. *Fighting in the Jim Crow Army: Black Men and Women Remember World War II*. Lanham, MD: Rowman & Littlefield, 2000.

Riley, Kerry Kathleen. *Everyday Subversion: From Joking to Revolting in the German Democratic Republic*. East Lansing: Michigan State University Press, 2007.

Solzhenitsyn, Aleksandr. *The Gulag Archipelago*. Paris: Éditions du Seuil, 1973.

Solzhenitsyn, Aleksandr. "Live Not by Lies" (essay).

Sowell, Thomas. *Marxism: Philosophy and Economics*. New York: William Morrow, 1985.

Taylor, Frederick. *The Berlin Wall: A World Divided, 1961-1989*. London: Bloomsbury, 2006.

Taylor, Frederick. *Exorcising Hitler: The Occupation and Denazification of Germany.* London: Bloomsbury, 2011.

Yad Vashem. "Antisemitism: From Its Origins to the Present" (online course).

Yelchin, Eugene. *Breaking Stalin's Nose.* New York: Henry Holt, 2011.

PODCASTS

Cold War Conversations

Radio GDR

MOVIES

Berlin: Schönhauser Corner, directed by Gerhard Klein, 1957.

Born in '45, directed by Jürgen Böttcher, 1966.

The Devil's Confession: The Lost Eichmann Tapes, directed by Yariv Mozer, 2022

Downfall, directed by Oliver Hirschbiegel, 2004.

The Eichmann Show, directed by Paul Andrew Williams, 2015.

Eyes on the Prize, PBS series, 1987–1990.

Hannah Arendt, directed by Margarethe von Trotta, 2012.

Immer Bereit: Junge Pioniere in der DDR (documentary), directed by Lutz Pehnert, 2016.

The Lives of Others, directed by Florian Henckel von Donnersmarck, 2006.

The Tunnel, directed by Roland Suso Richter, 2001.

The Twilight Zone, "Wordplay," Season 1, Episode 2, directed by Wes Craven (1985).

For more movies made in the GDR, explore the DEFA catalog on kanopy.com, which is a free movie lending service connected to your local library.

ACKNOWLEDGMENTS

As I write this, my grandmother, Marge Young—the inspiration for Oma and the most generous person I have ever known—is getting ready to walk into the sunset. She held me as a newborn, who slept in a dresser drawer in a German apartment, and I read her this book about Germany by her bedside, as it's my turn to care for her. Thank you, Grandma. Everything has been from you and for you.

A book of this scope, with its high demand for precision, could not have been written alone. Thanks to my editors, Karen Smith and Melanie Nolan, designers Alison Impey and Cathy Bobak, and everyone at Knopf whose collaboration I value more than you can know.

My agent and friend, Lori Kilkelly, seems never to tire of encouraging and advocating for me. You hold my arms up when I can't.

Ladies, find you a husband who loves you like Ben Stamper loves me, and who also doesn't take your crap like Ben Stamper doesn't take mine (which are often the same thing).

Alban and Arden, in everything I do I try to make a slice of the world better for you and your own children in some small way. I love you to the moon and stars and am so proud of you.

Thanks to my mother, Eileen Mezzo—our journey together is ours alone, and I love you.

Incalculable help was rendered to me by Jonny Renger, who endured my endless and granular questions not only about German syntax but also about German mindset and culture. Thank you for your kindness and encouragement.

Eugene Yelchin's and Andrey Tamarchenko's upbringings in the USSR were front of mind. The responsibility I feel as an author to tell the truth is exponentially heightened by knowing you both.

Joshua Ramey patiently helped me understand Communism and the relevant literature from an inside perspective. Thank you for your clarity and erudition.

Will Ford III and Matt Lockett show by example how the story of Cain and Abel can be reversed. Thank you for your friendship, brothers.

To Pastor Brandon Whitfield, thank you for going deep, especially in our conversations about race and brotherhood. There's nothing like eternal family.

Ruta Sepetys, Felicita Sala, simply: thank you.

Andrew Thompson, Bart Stamper and Alban Stamper, thank you for guiding me to pertinent military information and helping me understand this story through the eyes of a soldier.

Sheila Gaisin, through her experience as a Jewish expat student in 1960s Berlin, opened my perspective even wider. Shlomo Gaisin and the band Zusha, your music made its way into Angelika's songs. I hope you hear your influence in Kabarett Zusammen.

Martin, Josef, Katie, Yvonne, Renate, Michel, Maria and Sam, thank you for allowing me into your experiences of a divided Germany and Berlin.

Margo and Morgan Ganon, Karen Smith, Abigail Liu and Jessica Smith, thank you for generously giving me deeper insight into your lives as twins.

My readers—Michelle Minto, Dr. Mary H. Patterson, Max Uzoamaka Medina, Noelle Rhodes and Cassie Saquing—thank you for believing in this work.

And to all of you who read my books and allow them to become part of your own story, thank you. Keep writing to me. I'm listening.